Armageddon's Song

Volume Five

'Crossing the Rubicon'

ANDY FARMAN

Copyright © 2014 Andy Farman

ISBN: 1499627785
ISBN-13: 978-1499627787

ANDY FARMAN

DEDICATION

To my wife and son, Jessica and Edward Eric, with all my love.

Templar Platoon, Z Company, IJLB, Oswestry.
Guards Company, IJLB, Oswestry.
The Guards Depot, Pirbright.
2nd Battalion Coldstream Guards.
C (Royal Berkshires) Company, 2nd Battalion Wessex Regiment.
253 Provost Company, Royal Military Police.
'B' Relief, South Norwood Police Station.
Z District Crime Squad, Croydon.
Thornton Heath Robbery Squad (Temp)
4 Unit, Special Patrol Group.
4 Area Specialist Counter-Terrorist IED Search Team.
'D' Relief, Norbury.
A Team (North) Walworth.
The East Street Market 'Dip' Squad.
Peter O'Rourke, Steve Littel, John & Wendy Allen, the best CAD Operators in the business.

To everyone out there who gets up in the morning, and does good things for others!

'Crossing the Rubicon'

Chapter 1   1

Chapter 2   36

Chapter 3   93

Chapter 4   126

Chapter 5   167

Chapter 6   206

Trivia   223

Cast   231

Terminology & Acronyms   238

Contents

MAP ILLUSTRATIONS

Macquarie Pass 1   28

Moruya 1   44

Moruya 2   49

Macquarie Pass 2   78

Macquarie Pass 3   80

Monte Bello Islands   100

Cebu & Mactan   105

Cebu Strait Minefield   106

Operation 'Vespers'   155

'The Depot'

I visited the Guards Depot the other day,
only it's the 'The Depot' no longer, all the Guards gone away.

A place once alive with martial noise,
for the creation of men from that of mere boys;
the British Army's best, and no idle boast,
now 'The Depot' is silent but for the wind and the ghosts.

'Cat Company', which sat beside the square,
had borne a board of memorable dates there,
remembering battles, fought on foot, horse and tank
by those who had skirmished, and of men stood in rank
It honoured their courage on many a foreign field
but the board is now empty and the paintwork has peeled.

No Guardsmen, no Troopers, no Corporals-of-Horse,
no men from the battalions returned for some course.
The ranges are silent, Sand Hill overgrown
'The Queen Mary' is mildewed, forlorn and alone.

I visited The Depot the other day
but the Guardsmen have gone, up Catterick way.

(Andy Farman. Pirbright, 1996.)

ACKNOWLEDGMENTS

Where to start? There have been so many who have helped and encouraged with the writing of this series. Time and advice given freely, but here we go, and in no particular order, and with added thanks to the several hundred of you out there who comment and contribute to the blog and online page regularly.

My Mother and Father, Audrey and Ted Farman, who taught me to enjoy books more than the goggle box (I hasten to add that it did not include any affection for text books, however.)

My Uncle Richard and Cousin David, (From the Farman's colony in the Americas) for technical advice on matters maritime, nautical and the Chinook.

Jessica of course for putting up with it all, and an apology to little Edward for only playing with him before his bedtime because I was writing all day.

Bill Rowlinson and Ray Tester for inspiring two of the characters, and Bill's bountiful knowledge of firearms and police tactics.

Friend, actor and author Craig Henderson has qualities recognizable in young Nikoli, the Russian paratrooper. It is inevitable that people we meet will rub off on characters who appear in our stories.

Jason Ferguson of the US Army and National Guard PSI for his sound advice on all things US Military, translating my Brit mortar fire controller orders into the US variety, and test reading.

The lovely and witty Irina Voronina for her advice on low byte sources for graphic tools (one of several of her current post-Playboy careers.) Another former glamour model, now turned TV Producer (when not partying) Tracey Elvik, for adding some wisdom to Janet Probert's character, I almost made Janet a Mancunian too.

Nick Gill and Andy Croy for their invaluable help with the editing and waking me up to how bad my writing had become since leaving school. Adrian Robinson for invaluable help with the file size reduction problem for map insertions.

Paul Beaumont knowledge of radio communications and military 'Sigs'.

Paul Teare for test reading, Brendan McWilliams for helpful suggestions which were predictably along the lines of 'more paras.'

Chris Cullen, Paolo Ruoppolo, Tobi Shear Smith and Steve Enever, test readers extraordinaire.

Lyynard for HTML indexing the book.

CHAPTER 1

Australia

(3 minutes: 10 seconds after the Chinese ICBM launch)

Ian McLennan Park, Kembla, Woolongong: New South Wales. 40 miles south of Sydney.

Friday 19th October. 2353hrs.

All was quiet; the sky was as of diamonds strewn on black velvet. Certainly no one still living in Port Kembla could remember there ever *not* being light pollution before the enforced blackouts. On the odd previous occasion that a brown-out occurred, Sydney was only a mere 40 miles away and the glow from the city that never quite slept, would eclipse the stars to the north. Now of course, nature's great free light show was available to all, weather permitting.

Master Sergeant Bart Kopak of the 11th Armored 'Black Horse' Cavalry Regiment had once more 'dropped by' on the excuse of seeing how things were with the Brit unit he had, for a time, acted as liaison to. His tank company's fighting positions were sited to cover the beaches at Kilalea State Park and Minnamurra, ten miles away. His company location was now no longer at the racetrack with divisional headquarters, but on a field beside the Shellharbour Club, closer to where it was expected to fight. Bart seemed to manage to find plenty of reasons to visit the divisions HQ though.

Vehicles that were not on emergency business were not permitted to approach the man-made hill occupied by the 'The Queen Elizabeth's Combat Team' during the hours of darkness and so Bart left his Humvee at the bottom of the hill with his load bearing equipment in the back. It was a beautiful night and he hoped that would play in his favour when he saw Rebecca. Taking just his M-16 he walked the rest of the way, first looking in on the small unit's commander. Captain Hector Sinclair Obediah Wantage-Ferdoux, RTR, otherwise known as 'Obi Wan' to his troops and simply 'Heck' to everyone else, had just returned from Darwin with the main tank gun rounds and the two 120mm rifled barrels that had been

1

gathering dust. The practice of not keeping all of ones eggs in one basket was well under way at the ordnance depot. It had been a hive of activity, dispersing its stored munitions to a multitude of smaller, scattered magazines along the coast. As a consequence it had taken six hours before anyone had been available to begin loading up their trucks with the boxes of rounds. The needs of the small British contingent were pretty low on the depots list of priorities. Heck was tired and hungry so Bart did not stay long and left the British tanker to it.

Sgt Rebecca Hemmings was not at the REME LAD area but was instead taking her turn on the watch keepers stag roster in the CP. Bart's arrival was an excuse to step outside for a breath of air. The sentries and those manning the CP were in CBRN Dress State 3, they all wore clumsy NBC overshoes, smock and trousers. Gloves (Cotton: Inner: Small) already inserted in the rubber outer protective gloves in the respirator case with the mask ready for instant use. Her hair was dusty, sweaty and needed its daily wash. Hardly glamorous attire, but to Bart's eyes Rebecca could just as well have been in crystal slippers, ball gown and wearing a diamond tiara.

They lay on the grass bank looking at the stars and talking about anything but the reason for his constant visits. Bart had been steeling himself all day for what he wanted to now say. He had run through in his head every word of a prepared speech but just as he was about to broach the subject Rebecca sat up, suddenly alert.

"What is it?" he asked.

"Sssh!" She hushed him. "Listen."

Her ears were better than his but then he picked up the faint sound of a distant siren.

The fire stations, police stations and town halls all had installed air raid sirens upon the roof of the buildings and they had been sounded for the well-publicised air raid drills and civil defence exercises. The drills had become progressively more numerous to the point where they were in danger of becoming self-defeating, and road traffic accidents had quadrupled with the onset of the mandatory blackout. Australians were increasingly inclined to stay indoors when the air raid sirens sounded.

The distant siren was joined by another, and then another, with more joining in until every siren along the coast was sounding that mournful wail.

"I didn't hear this advertised on the radio." Rebecca said standing and looking out across the town.

"STAND TO!" Tony McMarn's voice bellowed from the direction of the CP and someone began bashing mess tins together, the audible warning for troops in the field to suit up and mask up.

Rebecca immediately stopped breathing and pulled her respirator from its case.

"Shit." Bart cursed. The perfect moment ruined by an unscheduled drill.

The light came then, and both his and Rebecca's shadows appeared briefly before disappearing in the harsh whiteout glare of a nuclear explosion.

Somewhere someone screamed, someone who had been looking north at that moment.

They both dropped to the ground and gradually the light lost some of its awful intensity. Rebecca pulled on her gloves, and now fully suited she squeezed his arm, shouting at him to get to his NBC kit also. Then she nodded a quick farewell and left, sprinting back to the CP as fast as her overshoes allowed.

There were a series of explosions somewhere, the biggest emergency maroons he had ever heard, and they were all in the sky above.

"It has started." he said to himself and risked a look to the northern horizon where a massive fireball sat above what must be Sydney. Bart picked up his M-16 and ran back across the hilltop in the direction of his Humvee.

In the CP there had been shock, but training had taken over and they were moving out to the combat teams FV-432 armoured command vehicle.

The infantrymen of the Royal Green Jackets were pulling closed the troop doors of the Warrior IFVs, and the four Challenger IIs were starting up.

Everything in the CP's 9 X 9 tent, attached to its rear, from maps, to Watchkeeper's Logs was transferred. The tentage was just for practicality anyway, room to breathe.

Transfer complete and Rebecca ran back to her CRARRV, the armoured repair and recovery vehicle version of the Challenger I. She slowed as she came across a fallen figure but she did not stop. NAIAD had activated after the overhead explosions and was still sounding its alarm.

On reaching the vehicle she clambered up its armoured glacis to the hatch, removing her webbing and passing it down inside before following it through and sealing the way behind her.

Tears coursed down her face behind the eye pieces of her respirator as she plugged in the radio jack.

Heck's voiced sounded immediately, asking each callsign for a sitrep. They answered in turn; the individual tanks, the infantry fighting vehicles, the QM and the combat teams attached personnel. Heck would have his 'Higher' demanding a sitrep of him so they answered clearly and concisely. The combat team had one wounded; an infantryman with severe eye injuries from the nuclear flash, and one of the QM's storemen was missing, as yet unaccounted for.

"Hello Sunray Eight Eight this is Sunray Tango, send sitrep, over?"

She took a deep breath before answering.

"Eight Eight, negative Casrep this callsign but one times Kilo India Alpha from our friends, over."

Indian Ocean.
0003hrs.

A pitch black night on an ocean running ten foot swells. Only the unbroken cloud covers internal electrical activity, offered any respite, or any visual clue as to the position of the horizon. It was a place without life, too deep, too far from shore or reef to support fish, and too hostile for non-aquatic life to survive. Just briefly, for a moment, the wind carried the sound of helicopter rotor blades fading to nothingness. Once they had departed only the sound of the wind and waves remained, although a stench of diesel increased by the moment.

Flotsam burst to the surface, freshly rendered wooden fittings, the splintered grain almost white against more weathered areas. Paperwork appeared to percolate up from the depths, single sheets, an old copy of *The West Australian* and a waterlogged paperback book, Neville Shute's *'On the Beach'*. To this detritus of tragedy were added fearful cries, spluttering, and a flailing of limbs.

Two young women and five men, hundreds of miles from the nearest land, coughing and spluttering, with sinuses flooded with salt water and in shock. The only survivors of the Royal Australian Navy diesel electric submarine, HMAS *Hooper.*

Several minutes passed before the relief of still being alive took hold, but there then followed the full weight of their situation, their deaths were merely postponed.

Commander Reg Hollis struggled to make sense of what had happened. He had been beside a junior ratings mess, speaking to Petty Officer Penman, and the boat was at sixty feet, snorkelling to charge their depleted batteries. A violent explosion somewhere forward had plunged the vessel into darkness, and the sea burst in as the boat turned vertical, facing the bottom of the Indian Ocean, five miles down.

The greatest cause of death to submariners in both peace and war is not drowning but onboard fire and explosion. An emergency oxygen generator producing hydrogen and coming into contact with seawater, which will cause a fire, or volatile torpedo fuel igniting explosively, those are the main culprits.

He had heard nothing prior to the explosion, no alert, no closing screw noises, just nothing.

A second explosion split open the vessel a moment later while she was still near the surface, venting air in a giant gout of an oxygen bubble which propelled wreckage and crew members, the dead and the living, towards the nearby surface and that was how he and several members of the crew were here, floundering in the waves.

Something bumped against him, startling him; he put out a hand to fend it off and touched a mattress in its waterproof plastic cover. He clung to it gratefully for a moment before calling out, telling anyone who could hear to swim towards the sound of his voice.

The first to reach him was male, and that was all he could discern. It was too dark to see anything but another's head above water.

"Grab a hold of this." Reg helped him get a grip on the mattress. "Commander Hollis here, who's that?"

"AB Daly sir." Able Seaman Philip Daly, a career sailor who could probably have made PO by now but for an over fondness of beer and fighting during runs ashore.

"What happened, sir?"

"No idea, absolutely no clue, sorry…who else got out?"

"I heard PO Penman shouting, and there are a couple of others, a few bodies too."

They could hear others and together they kicked, steering the mattress in the direction of the sounds of splashing and choking.

Leading Seaman Craig Devonshire and AB Stephanie Priestly were together towing PO Penman. A few minutes later Honorary

Acting Sub Lieutenant Chloe Ennis emerged from out of the darkness. Chloe was the baby of the wardroom and in reality still a Midshipman, temporarily promoted at a local level because she was a hell of a more pleasant visage than Tommo, the Engineering Officer.

Last to arrive was LS Paul Brown, vomiting up diesel fuel he had swallowed inadvertently.

They were all about done in, and the Petty Officer clung to the mattress as his rescuers panted and gasped. There was very little room around the mattress for seven of them, and only room for one, the injured petty office to get a grip with both hands.

LS Devonshire had a waterproof pen light which he awkwardly lit, and they then got to take stock of their situation.

"Is there anyone else, did you hear anyone else out there?"

They had not but Reg had them all call out together as they and the mattress reached the apex of a swell.

Only the lonely wind replied.

Taking the torch Reg shone the light at each of them in turn. He wondered if he looked as shocked and scared as they did. Young Stephanie's eyes were as large as saucers, but it was the Petty Officer he was most concerned about.

Derek Penman was deathly pale, and a deep cut in his scalp was leaking blood down the side of his head into the water.

"The way I see it." said Reg. "We have six hours until dawn, we just have to hang on and stay awake until then."

He shared a little hope with them.

"There is a yank nuke in the area out of Pearl, she was to relieve us and she had our course and speed." He said earnestly.

"They'll find us in the morning."

Reg shone the light again at the injured man, noting his out of focus stare.

"Petty Officer…Derek, can you hold on for six hours?"

PO Penman paused and then nodded.

The cold was invasive, eating into the tissues of the body and Reg knew that if they were going to see the light of day they had to do something positive to stay awake.

"Okay, we'll play a little game of general knowledge, and I'll start with an easy one." He could hear at least one person's teeth chattering already.

"In 1858 the first recognised Aussie Rules match was played, between Melbourne Grammar and Scotch College." He paused a moment before asking the question, knowing they were all trying to remember their sports trivia, such as what the score had been and who had scored what.

"Who umpired?"

"Tom Willis!" said Stephanie instantly, and felt rather than saw the men staring at her. "I've got six brothers guys, whaddya expect?"

"Correct...you choose the next question Steph."

"Thank you sir, and in payment for that 'Boy' question, answer this...how many tampons are in a pale pink box of Lil-Lets?"

There was laughter from Chloe but silence from the men.

"It's going to be a long night." Someone grumbled.

Lightning flashed, and just for a split second Reg saw a dorsal fin.

Mao carrier group, Indian Ocean, West of Australia: 0005hrs, same day:

Vice Admiral Putchev watched the clouds flashing with internal electrical activity overhead and listened to the lonely wind. The fleet was running blacked-out as usual, and each vessel an undefined dark mass against the ocean. He could almost imagine he was the only human left, but he knew there were probably other solitary figures on the other ships doing exactly the same as he was.

The beat of helicopter rotors sounded for the second time in the last half hour. Was it the same two aircraft returning or had the earlier machines merely relieved these two?

He sensed he was no longer alone, and another came to stand beside him at the rail.

"It is going to be a stormy night Admiral, and not just with the weather." Captain Hong said after a minute or two.

"How so?"

"The American stealth bombers have attacked our ICBM silos, and my country has launched in reprisal." The captain explained. "It has prompted our planned attacks upon New Zealand and Australia to begin earlier than I would have desired, if it had been up to me. But I am just the bus driver around here."

This venture, the invasion, was a Chinese effort with support from Russia; as such the PLAN Admiral and the commander of the Third Army's 1st Corps paid only lip service to the Russian contingent. Putchev was the advisor on carrier operations but the more the Chinese sailors mastered its intricacies the less important the Russians had become to them and their hosts became more and more distant.

It was always going to be a difficult marriage. The Cold War between East and West had seen more Russian and Chinese dead in border skirmishes at each other's hands, than by NATO. As such, the Russian surface vessels all had large armed 'Liaison Staffs' from the People's Liberation Army Navy on board so the Chinese Admiral could sleep soundly without fear of his allies turning on him.

Trust was not easily fostered after decades of enmity.

Only Captain Hong, the *Mao's* skipper, had made any effort to form a friendship. But as he had said, his role was merely the daily running and the functions of the aircraft carrier.

Karl Putchev felt the deck shift beneath his feet and the throb of the engines increase. The long, slow, almost leisurely cruise due south was at an end.

"You've launched ICBMs?"

"We must go below Admiral; the fleet will shortly begin to prepare for NATOs response." He moved towards the nearest hatch. "And there is also a bothersome noise in the engine room I would like your advice on."

The engine room was the only place on board that they could really be sure that no listening device could be effectively employed.

Making their way down through the lower decks they maintained a professional chatter until standing beside a piece of machinery tucked away in a corner.

"My understanding is that the strike only found success here, in Australia, and that the city of Sydney has been destroyed...moreover, chemical weapon are to be deployed against targets on land, and this may have already begun."

Vice Admiral Putchev felt a dread coldness at the news.

"What word of your own armies in Europe, my friend?"

A cynical smile appeared on Karl Putchev's face.

"We have forced some river or other and NATO is in full flight."

"What, again?" Captain Hong said, in mock surprise. "That's every day this month, isn't it?"

RAAF Pearce, nr Perth: Western Australia: 0007hrs.

It was warm and sunny, far too nice to be in school on a day like today. The heavy old wall clock ticked away hypnotically as Nikki and the rest of Miss Goldmeyer's second grade class cast longing looks out of the window.

After a long and bitter winter the spring was here at last.

Chalk scratched upon the slate blackboard as Miss Goldmeyer hurried to write out their assignment before the lunchtime bell sounded its gentle chimes.

"NBC RED ONE!...STATION SCRAMBLE!...NBC RED ONE!...STATION SCRAMBLE!"

Miss Goldmeyer placed down her chalk and turned to face the room full of six year olds.

"Girls, quickly and quietly now, open your desks, put away your books and man your aircraft!"

With a jolt Nikki came awake, the klaxon screaming in between the tannoy's order for a general scramble, to get all serviceable aircraft off the ground and warning of a suspected incoming nuclear, biological or chemical weapon attack.

"NBC RED ONE!...STATION SCRAMBLE!...NBC RED ONE!...STATION SCRAMBLE!"

Candice was fighting with the zipper on her sleeping bag as Nikki rolled free of hers, tugging hard she released her RIO and grabbed her helmet before sprinted for the door.

In the corridor she was shocked to see two armed personnel, 'Adgies', Air Defence Guards in full nuclear biological and chemical warfare suits with respirators and helmets, looking like bipedal insects with torches gesturing at them to go left, not right, down the central corridor of the accommodation block. Panting she burst through the doors at the far end to see an open back four ton truck, its canvas removed and with its tailgate down just starting to pull away, it was almost full. Aircrew from a half dozen different nationalities were stood holding on to the tubular frame meant to support the missing canvas roof and sides.

1 Squadron RAAFs flight of F/A 18Fs attached to Pearce tore down the runway in pairs, a perfect minimum interval take-off, and Nikki found the need to scream at the top of her voice in order to be heard over the Super Hornets.

"WAIT!"

The truck did not stop but the driver was keeping the speed right down as he watched them in his wing mirror, and the two USN aviators sprinted after it.

Hands reached down, Nikki tossed her helmet into one helpful pair of hands and grasped another, being hauled physically aboard where Candice joined her a moment later.

Someone pounded on the truck cabs roof and the driver floored the accelerator.

Several of the other passengers were pulling on NBC suits one handed, hanging onto the trucks roof frame with the other; others were in various stages of donning theirs. Neither Nikki nor Candice had been issued that item. Theirs was in the stores aboard the Nimitz awaiting their collection, and their signature for them of course.

An already suited RAAF squadron leader had a mobile pressed to one ear and his other arm looped around the roof frame with the palm pressed hard against the other ear, trying to listen.

"Is this a drill?" Candice asked.

"Hell no." a voice answered. "The bastards nuked Sydney."

"But our ship is there!" She blurted.

"Not anymore it's not, darlin'."

"DAMN!" exploded Nikki angrily. "That's the second time."

Someone shone a penlight at the name-tag on her flight suit.

"Oh, you're that Pelham!" another faceless voice said, with a little bit of awe.

"No such thing as too many veterans in the ranks, welcome aboard Lieutenant Commander." said another.

The truck held Australians, New Zealanders, Taiwanese, Singaporeans, Filipinos, Japanese and Americans. Nikki was unique in being the only American present to have seen air combat in World War Three, but the Asiatic crews on the truck had all lost that particular cherry.

The Anzacs still had that bitter-sweet, and terrifying experience to come.

The truck went onto two wheels as it made the turn towards the dispersal, the driver working the gears but barely coming off the gas as he applied the clutch. The tailgate rose and fell with a crash, bouncing open and closed, dangerously unrestrained, the locking pins and chains whipping against the paintwork. No one was going to risk broken fingers and other bodily harm by capturing the tailgate, so a clear space existed where the whipping chains held sway, the crewmen and women pressing together defensively back towards the cab.

"Brace! Brace!"

The driver made no attempt to slow for the speed ramp but steered so that the front wheels took it square together. First the front wheels left the tarmac and then the rear axle, Candice screamed as the truck became briefly airborne before slamming down hard on the front axle and bouncing wildly.

"God, but it'll be a relief to get off this truck and back into combat!" Nikki said with feeling and the laughter erupted, a nervous release for some of the other passengers.

They were not the only vehicle delivering pilots to the flight lines and Nikki could even see crew on push bikes pedalling furiously.

Shouted conversations were taking place around Nikki during the breakneck ride, but these were drowned out by Pratt & Whitney turbofans and General Electric turbojets.

The first aircraft to release their parking brakes were Australia's last pair of F111Cs, leaving their camouflage net 'hangars' and taxiing at high speed, anti-shipping ordnance in the shape of four AGM-84 Harpoons each carried on under-wing pylons. Right behind the F111s were a trio of Republic of Singapore F5 Tigers with a mixed AA and anti-radiation load-out.

As soon as he could be heard the Australian squadron leader shouted for attention, putting away the mobile phone he had been pressing to his ear.

"Listen up, we're doing this one on the hoof so I'll keep it simple. RV for everyone is 100 miles due West at Angels fifteen. 'Magpie Zero Seven' is the call-sign for AWACS on this and they are working on an anti-shipping strike so keep your ears to your radio but no speaking unless first spoken to. Radio silence people, let's not give the bastards advance warning we are on the way!"

No writing was required and no questions were asked.

"Any Navy here?"

Only Nikki and Candice qualified there.

"Can you Elephant Walk?"

"Yessir, I flew Tornados on attachment with the RAF in Germany." Nikki replied, but Candice looked blank.

The squadron leader nodded, satisfied and address everyone present.

"Once again, observe radio silence until you are called by Magpie Zero Seven." He paused for emphasis. "Watch the Marshals', keep it tight and we'll all get off the ground and get a shot at payback!"

As the truck reached the dispersed aircraft it slowed but did not stop and aircrew dropped over its sides, rolling as they hit the ground only to rise and sprint to their charges.

Nikki leaped out, landing and rolling before running the remaining distance. She couldn't find the damn entrance under the camouflage netting at first and was cursing as it was hauled up by rope from inside.

However long she had been asleep had been enough time for the ground crew to fuel and arm their Tomcat. Two AIM-7 Sparrows, four AIM-9 Sidewinders and a pair of AIM-54 Phoenix sat on the pylons, a drop tank added to the loadout.

"What's an Elephant Walk, sir?" shouted Candice to the Australian squadron leader as they both landed on the grass and arose.

"About fifty miles a day, lieutenant."

The ground crew, suited up already in the charcoal impregnated trousers and smocks but without gas-masks on, had already started up their F14 and the crew chief held up for her the weapons safety pins that had been removed. The aircraft was hers and ready for combat. Nikki was lowering herself into her seat as Candice climbed the ladder.

Candice fumbled with straps.

"Relax Ma'am." A technician shouted and deftly connected radio jacks, oxygen and her flight-suits air bladders.

"First time?" he asked, meaning her first for real mission with war shots.

She nodded.

"You'll do just fine ma'am!" he yelled over the engine noise.

A ground marshal's illuminated wands signalled them forwards urgently and a moment later Nikki got the thumbs up that all personnel and equipment were now clear.

She released the parking brake.

The marshals were linked together on a stand-alone radio channel, working in unison.

"What's an Elephant Walk, Nikki?" asked Candice.

"This." Nikki replied simply.

The marshal waved them forward with both wands before pointing one wand angled down to their right wheel and the other moving up and back over his shoulder.

The Tomcat left the 'hangar' behind and turned right onto the taxiway.

Candice twisted around, looking at aircraft of all types that had appeared in front and behind.

"You've seen pictures of herds of elephants walking one behind the other, holding the tail of the elephant in front with their trunks?"

"Sure?"

"That's how this procedure got its name. It's the fastest way to get everyone off the ground but it's kinda tricky." Just as if to highlight the point the jet blast from the F16 ahead of them caused the Tomcat to rock violently.

"I guess we don't do this that much in the navy?"

"Not until they build a carrier the size of an airbase, no."

It was like a conveyor belt; the line of aircraft moved steadily on and as they reached the end of the taxiway the aircraft immediately turned onto the runway where scant seconds later, when the preceding aircraft were only a couple of hundred yards down the tarmac they received clearance to take off.

Every airworthy aircraft on the base was on the taxiways or hurtling down the runway.

The marshals' job now was to keep an eye on the interval between each aircraft to avoid collisions or aircraft being flipped over by jet blast. The marshals had their respirators still in pouches around their waists and ear defenders on their heads instead.

Nikki and Candice had their oxygen masks unsecured.

Eventually they were near the end of the taxiway in third place, a marshal signalling the two F-16s ahead of them to turn onto the runway and run up their engines

A flash overhead made them look up sharply through the canopy but there was nothing to see and it was not repeated.

The marshal pointed the illuminated wands sharply down the runway and hunkered down in a squat, clear of wings and the ordnance hung off the F16's hardpoints.

The Falcon's pilots opened the throttles and the two aircraft powered down the runway.

"Our turn now." Nikki said, looking at the crouching marshal.

He did not rise and the glow of the F16's engines got further and further away. As they lifted skywards Nikki frowned.

"What's the delay?" Candice asked, puzzled.

A cold shiver ran down Nikki's spine.

"Put your mask on Candy!" she hurriedly clipped hers in place and ensured the oxygen was flowing.

"What?"

"Mask on, do it now!" she ordered.

The marshal remained squatting on the edge of the runway, his back to them.

Had an aircraft been making an emergency landing he would have signalled them to hold, but he had not moved a muscle.

Nikki came off the brakes and the Tomcat turned left onto the runway, but Nikki did not wait for the marshal, she immediately pushed the throttles forward to full military power, the afterburner kicking in.

"What about the marshal?" an alarmed Candice exclaimed.

"He's dead, Candice."

The wheels retracted just moments after the runway dropped away below them. With no idea as to whether the attack was over Lt Cmdr. Nikki Pelham kept low and the throttles through the gates to put distance between their aircraft and the field they had just departed.

Candice was twisted around in her seat staring back with a kind of disbelief at the blacked out airbase. The dead body beside the runway was no longer invisible, only the marshal's lit wands could be seen but even they were soon swallowed up by the night. She had never in her life seen a for-real dead person before and yet things seemed so normal down there, no shooting, no exploding bombs like in the movies. How could people have simply ceased to live, just like that?

"Is anyone else taking off?" Nikki asked her.

There was no reply.

"Candy!"

"Sorry...yes, yes they are still taking off."

The radar intercept officer turned back to her instruments.

"There is a chemical attack going on, maybe even a biological weapon attack, but don't freeze up." Nikki said. "I know its scary shit that is happening, but you need to focus."

Nikki took them out to sea at wave top height until the coastline of Western Australia was far behind before pulling back on the stick, taking them up to join the stacked aircraft.

They orbited for some time before all the Pearce Wing had assembled.

Various flights were addressed by their callsigns and were then ordered to new frequencies where they received mission specific briefings. They could see the stack getting shorter as these began their sorties.

Eventually it was their turn.

"Smackdown, Smackdown?" an Australian voice sounded in their headsets. *"Smackdown flight receiving Magpie Zero Seven?"*

"Smackdown Zero One." responded Nikki.

"Two"

"Three"

"Four"

Her flight of F-14s from USS Nimitz's air wing answered in turn. She had not yet met any of them, only having arrived in Australia a few hours before.

"Smackdown aircraft, Magpie Zero Seven... take a heading of Two One Eight, regroup at Angels One Eight and rendezvous with Belly Dancer, a flight of two, Foxtrot triple One Charlie's, Bar Fight, flight of three Foxtrot-5s and Texaco." instructed their controller aboard the AEW&C, a Boeing E-7A Wedgetail of 2 Squadron, Royal Australian Air Force.

"You are CAP for Belly Dancer's anti-shipping strike."

Nikki rolled them right, coming onto the new heading and bringing the stick gently back until the artificial horizon on the HUD showed them wings level in a gentle climb. The rest of the flight formed up on her.

"Smackdown aircraft, Magpie Zero Seven, intel update...there are multiple ongoing attacks on air, sea and land bases with both conventional and chemical weapons all along the coastline of Western Australian. Belly Dancer's target is a trio of surface warships with a six handed Sierra Uniform Two Seven CAP overhead."

"'Magpie Zero Seven, Zero One?"

"Go."

"Are these the Pearce shooters?"

"Negative, that was a submarine launched weapon. Belly Dancer's sortie is against an outer picket of the main fleet."

"Zero One, rog'"

"We aren't going straight for the carriers and troop ships?" Candice asked on the intercom.

"Been-there-done-that-got-the-life-raft." Nikki said. "A fleet is like an onion, especially this one, lots of missiles...we have to unpeel it first, at least some of it." she switched back and called up the RAAF bombers and KC-30A Airbus tanker.

Gerry Rich was all business, the Outback charm on hold as they put together a quick plan. Flt Lt Teo Koh and his pilots were veterans of Operation Enduring Freedom. 'Wild Weasel' sorties were their bread and butter and they would precede the F111Cs by twenty seconds to suppress the warships air defences in attacking their radars.

It would not be complicated but it did rely upon the Tomcats making themselves the centre of attention.

After tanking, the Tomcats switched to the drop tanks and turned directly toward the Sino Russian invasion fleet three hundred miles south.

Climbing to 34,000ft they split into two pairs in close trail, with 01 and her wingman, 02 in the lead and 03 and 04 tucked in tightly behind.

The SU-27Ks saw them coming at 160 miles out. Their 'Slot Back' radar was not the best as the aircraft were designed for fleet defence where extended radar coverage by Kamov KA-31 AWAC helicopters would be dominant.

By lucky coincidence another strike by other members of the dispersed Nimitz air wing operating out of Esperance Airport had taken the Kamov out of play with a long range Phoenix shot, taken while flying a similar ant-shipping strike as their own. The Kamov had been destroyed and its replacement was only on the *Admiral Kuznetsov's* elevator on its way up to the flight deck, not on its way up to operating altitude.

The Flankers flew a racetrack course, five miles between each flight and one of the flights of three SU-27Ks turned north to confront what their radars told them were a pair contacts. They closed rapidly to 30 nautical miles where Nikki and the Tomcats ejected their belly tanks. Nikki launched two AIM-54 Phoenix missiles and her wingman one, following quickly with three Aim-9 Sidewinders. The AIM-54s sped harmlessly past the first Flanker flight at mach 2.5, apparently wasted shots, and to their eyes AIM-9 missiles due to their speed.

The Tomcats continued in without deviation, and on detecting the second launch of missiles the SU-27K Flankers chose to fight, not flee, and bore in.

The second flight now turned in also, going to burner in order to gang up on the two detected intruders.

Vertical jinking proved only 66.6% successful for the first Flankers and one parachute floated down. Now only at 16 miles out did *Smackdown* 03 and 04 go to burner and head for the second flight of Flankers. Nikki and her wingman closed with the first pair and launched short range AIM-7 Sparrows.

The surprise of finding four aircraft to contend with was matched by a realisation that the three missiles that had 'missed' were not falling out of the air at 22 miles but had now accelerated towards the second flight at mach 5.

Flankers Three, Four and Five killed their own burners in order better manoeuvre, twisting and turning to escape, allowing the second pair of Nikki's Tomcats to get to knife fighting range.

With the Tomcats holding the Chinese CAP's full and undivided attention the three Republic of Singapore Air Force F-5 Tigers came in at wavetop height on the trio of Russian surface combatants, closing from different directions.

Their targets were the *Syktyvkar,* a large ASW warfare Udaloy class destroyer, and two multi role Krivak-I frigates, the *Yoshkar-Ola* and her slightly older sister ship, the *Samara.*

Without the early warning coverage of the Kamov the warships only detected them at fifteen miles out. The Krivak-Is launched SA-N-4 Gecko SAMs, and the Tigers emptied their rails of AGM-88 HARMs, the high speed anti-radiation missiles, and turned away.

Samara had two missiles targeting her and *Yoshkar-Ola* had four.

Turning to face the threats and reduce the frigates radar profiles their mortars threw out chaff and shut down their radars, trusting the Geckos to switch to their terminal guidance radars in the absence of command guidance from the warships.

An AGM-88 remembers where its target's last position is and as it was approaching at 1400mph the frigates positions were not greatly altered by the time the big missiles reached them. Fire broke out on *Samara's* forward deck as a HARM detonated close in, severely damaging her boxy four tube Silex anti-shipping launcher on the foredeck. Ironically it was the AGM-88s proximity fuse that had saved the warship a potentially fatal blow. The HARMs proximity fuse fired short of the superstructure owing to passing beneath a chaff cloud.

Three AGM-88s were dummied by chaff from *Yoshkar-Ola* but the fourth struck the bridge and 146lbs of TNT blew the upper works apart and started a raging inferno.

Damage control went into top gear, high pressure hoses being run out aboard the *Samara*. The night was as dark as pitch but astern of them the *Yoshkar-Ola's* position was discernable by the angry glow reflecting off the cloud base. The damage control parties worked on with chaff still being ejected, the loud reports of the mortars made even shouted commands difficult to hear. The mortars bundles burst apart, the tin foil strips carried off by the wind as a short-lived dummy radar target, the light of the flames reflecting off the shiny aluminium lengths as they drifted astern.

Yoshkar-Ola was injured but not defeated. As horrendous as the damage appeared it would take a month at the most to repair in a shipyard, but the explosion had robbed critical areas of electrical power. The main breakers had popped and needed to be reset by hand, the work of but a moment, but the mortars firing circuits were not battery powered. No chaff was being launched until that item was put right.

Samara's firefighters on the foredeck ducked as two Harpoon anti-shipping missiles screamed overhead. The big missiles ignored her in favour of a larger target, a chaff cloud, but that fell to the waves and dissipating before they reached it. Beyond though, was an even bigger target, just six miles away.

Syktyvkar had reacted to the air defence picket ships initial warning of approaching anti-radiation missiles by putting her own radar to standby.

Two great fireballs, one to starboard and one astern of *Samara* were roiling skywards. A Harpoon had dived down to skewer the frigate, penetrating to below the waterline and detonate in its magazine. *Yoshkar-Ola* blew apart and once the smoke had been carried a little distance away by the wind there was only burning fuel oil remaining upon the surface and wreckage falling from the sky. The Krivak was gone.

Belly Dancer 1 and 2 had met with complete success but they had ordnance left, so what to do now, run with the winning streak or play it as briefed? The *Bar Fighters* had expended all their anti-radiation ordnance and were heading home at wavetop level, so there would be no interference with other ships air defences and sensors other than that produced by the F111C's own jamming pods. High above the clouds the Tomcats were mixing it with the Flankers, keeping them off the Australian bombers backs so they could make their planned attack and egress.

Discretion won over.

This was just Round 1 and they had succeeded because it had been a team effort. The F111Cs cleared the area on burner.

For the Nimitz Tomcats it was not quite as simple as for one thing they were heavily engaged, and for another they wanted some payback for the destruction of their carrier.

Nikki's Sparrow had missed, her opponent rolling inverted and banking hard to get in behind 03 and 04 for missile shots. She followed, but instead of banking as the Chinese pilot had done she extended slightly, dropping beneath the Flanker before pulling back on the stick. They were high above the cloud and by the light of a half-moon she saw her enemy's outline above her when she craned her neck.

A touch of rudder and she selected 'Guns' for a difficult deflection shot to take the Flanker as it accelerated ahead. Just a caress of her thumb and the Tomcat shuddered, vibrating as the M61 Vulcan cannon barrels rotated. 20mm shells nailed the underside of the Flanker's nose, shredding the radar assembly and tearing up the cockpit floor. The instrument panel and canopy exploded before the pilot's eyes, and fragments of exploding shells wounded him in both legs.

The damaged Flanker broke right, the pilot choosing to stay with the machine and attempt a recovery aboard the *Mao*. His radar was out and he had a hurricane blowing through the cockpit at 32,000ft. If he had not been on oxygen he would have lost consciousness.

He was a good pilot and if his opponent was feeling chivalrous he would probably make it.

Lt Cmdr. Pelham's family, her friend Chubby, and both of her ships were gone forever. Screw chivalry, she sent a burst of cannon fire into the side of the cockpit and the Flanker continued its right banking turn, rolling into a dive, a dead hand on the stick.

The second Flanker was attempting to get behind her wingman for a short range missile shot, so both Tomcats broke hard left before he could establish a lock. The Chinese pilot should have broken left also, to pass to the rear of the Tomcats and got the hell out of there, diving for the cloud but he didn't, he kept that left turn hard on, trying for the missile shot they had denied him. His airspeed bled off rapidly, the stick got soggy in his hands and the aircraft departed from controlled flight. Before he could find the airspeed to recover, one of Nikki's AIM-7 Sparrows found him, exploding the aircraft.

Two SU-27Ks were diving for the cloud and the flight reformed, less Smackdown 03 who had taken an AA-8 Aphid up a tailpipe, but two good chutes had been seen.

Four for one, and three of those scalps went to Lt Cmdr. Pelham.

Two fresh flights of bandits were coming up to do battle so Nikki took them home, turning east and calling for a tanker as they called it a night.

The Udaloy destroyer *Syktyvkar* was left behind by the fleet, as was *Samara*. But *Samara* had lost her mast and had no communications but she rendered aid to the other stricken ship's company before putting about and making for the closest repair yards, those at the forward logistical supply and support base for the Australian invasion force, China's 3rd Army, at Cebu in the Philippines.

Syktyvkar burned all through the rest of the night until the fire at last reach the magazine and she too blew up.

The Pearce Wing had recovered to various regional airports and the *Smackdown* flight was given a steer to Perth Airport but this was a risky move. The wing's aircraft were short on offensive and defensive ordnance, and vulnerable on the ground.

RAAF Hawks, flown by instructors, were the CAP for that part of Western Australia, tanking from a Japanese Air Self-Defence Force KC-135 and remaining on station until the approach of fatigue.

Nikki led her flight of three remaining F-14 Tomcats along the taxiways, the last to arrive. They followed a yellow airport services vehicle driven by a member of the airport fire brigade, and he wore a hazardous substances protection suit with its own oxygen supply. On the sun baked earth beside the north perimeter road she and Candice shut down and waited until fire hoses washed down their aircraft, every crevices was blasted with both water and chemical neutralizers. Then of course it was their turn but chemical foam showers spared their blushes.

Now at last they had proper NBC protection issued them, and fresh G-suits, their own not in need of laundering. The still wet name tapes and squadron flashed were transferred to the bare Velcro patches on the new items.

They learned from the decontamination team that VX, Sarin and Mustard/Lewisite had been used along with Blister Agents in thirty two separate locations in Australia and eight in New Zealand. So far it seemed that they had all been delivered by submarine launched missiles, each vessel launching on multiple targets. Forty four had died at RAAF Pearce during the attack there. Six were service personnel whilst the remainder were civilians, all of whom had died in their sleep in houses beyond the perimeter, on the downwind side of the field.

The chemical agent used on RAAF Pearce had not been typed in its raw form due to the speed with which it had broken down into a harmless form, presumably by design, and thereby allowing troops to occupy the target area if need be. It was not one of the persistent VX family of agents, and it had killed even quicker than that wickedly deadly compound. The agent, even its name a secret, had been tentatively matched via WHO records with a weapon that had seen limited use in the 1980s in Afghanistan. A post mortem of the victims would confirm that later.

RAAF Pearce would be reopening for business after dawn as WHO reported that sunlight was believed to cause complete evaporation in harmless form. No one was taking chances. A small, former naval barracks, now a privately run retirement home on the coast of New Zealand's South Island, had been targeted with Anthrax-R, delivered by another submarine launched missile. They had all died, not easily and not pleasantly either.

The Chinese opening offensive actions against Australia and New Zealand had been devastating in regard to Sydney, and highly effective in disrupting military operations. The Pearce Wing, for example, was now separated, albeit temporarily, from its base and its ordnance to launch further strikes. As far as the effects on the largely unprotected civilian population were concerned, they were both angry at the enemy and scared. An early figure for the dead was 200, but as VX had been used at Woolongong and its Port Kembla suburb, that town alone would likely see that figure exceeded.

With a clean bill of health from the decontamination team the Tomcats taxied to the International Terminal, parking between a

Virgin Australia A330 Airbus and a 747 in Qantas livery. There were few civilian aircraft there though, at that terminal, the domestic side of the airport was far busier by comparison.

When the sun came up the crews sat under the wings, awaiting a fuelling truck if they were instructed to relocate any great distance to one of the RAAF reserve fields.

Lt j.g Candice LaRue was hyper at first, talking at fifty thousand miles an hour, replaying her first combat, over and over until the adrenaline wore off and she crashed, exhausted and depressed.

At last she looked at her pilot with normal eyes.

"Who is 'Chubby'?"

Nikki stared at her.

"Why do you ask?"

"During the combat, you called me 'Chubby' a bunch of times over the intercom."

Unwilling to explain, Nikki merely apologised.

Coffee and sandwiches arrived but before they finished them the exodus of military aircraft began, returning back to Pearce to rearm, and disperse again while they prepare for further sorties.

RAAF Pearce in the daylight looked almost tranquil but they were glad to be fuelled, rearmed and relocating before the day was done.

The post-strike assessment had been grim. Their own sortie had been far more successful than any other of the Pearce Wing missions. Six aircraft had been lost from their wing alone, nineteen in total from the aircraft available for the defence of Australia and New Zealand.

Invasion was imminent, that much was certain, and from the enemy fleets position it could land south of Perth, but why would it give itself a thousand miles of the Great Victoria Desert to cross to reach New South Wales, the obvious target for invasion? Quite what it would do once it reached New South Wales was a conundrum. Would it land in the west and roll up the major cities, Melbourne and Canberra?

At lunchtime came the news that the Battle of Europe had ended in defeat for the New Soviet Union and the Red Army had ceased hostilities. A reconnaissance flight was despatched to confirm or deny that the fleet was fragmenting, but it returned shot up, and reporting that the fleet was intact and 'a bit lively'. It could not differentiate between Russian missiles and Chinese missiles, or if the CAP that had pursued it was off the *Mao* or *Admiral Kuznetsov*. However, the pilot of the 3 Squadron RAAF F/A-18 was quite happy for anyone else to have a looksee using his Hornet, once the brown adrenaline was sponged off the seat of course. The pilot's droll humour was typical of the Australian air force but the next news to reach them was sobering.

Sydney, so much the icon of Australia in the eyes of the rest of the world was gone and fires on the outskirts were being allowed to burn out of control. Initial tests indicated a high presence of an isotope that had no part in the highly complex chain reaction required to cause a nuclear explosion. The element, Cobalt-60, had only one purpose for its inclusion in the weapon. By adding cobalt to the casing of the device the Chinese had produced a very 'dirty bomb' as the element is a source of exceptionally intense gamma rays.

The so called 'nuclear footprint', the area where the highly irradiated dust was falling back to earth, was currently out to sea. It was being carried west on a wind off the arid desert, blowing through the Blue Mountains and taking the fall-out ocean ward. The normal prevailing wind for the time of year was north easterly though, and as far north along the coast as Corindi Beach people were taking to the Pacific Highway and evacuating. If the wind changed in the next two days, and was more northerly than usual, the scientists warned that three hundred miles of coast would be rendered uninhabitable.

Vast tracts of the subcontinent are arid desert where water is scarce so it is not surprising that major inland cities are a bit few and far between. The majority of Australians lived within a few hundred miles of the sea. Where to relocate the displaced population was a major problem.

The crews, especially the Australians, were itching for another chance to hit back but a proper strike was being planned and the limited air and sea power was being preserved.

The best place to defeat an amphibious invasion is whilst it is still at sea and the second best is on the beaches themselves. The invading army cannot all land at once, it has to do so a piece at a time. If those pieces can be defeated on the shore and prevented from forming a beachhead, the invasion will fail.

To defeat those units though, you have to be at the right beach and with enough force to do so.

The Kiwis were in Australia; because that was the best chance they had of defeating the People's Liberation Army. No invasion fleet was threatening New Zealand, and would not do so until Australia was subdued. The small New Zealand Defence Force, 11000 strong, including Reserves, were almost all of them in Queensland, involved in the defence of Brisbane.

The Australian Army, the US 5th Mechanised Division and the infantry brigades worth of troops from Japan, Taiwan and Singapore were in New South Wales.

They needed help, sooner rather than later, but the NATO armies in Europe had taken a hammering, and victory had been a close run thing. Everyone in Australia and New Zealand expected Britain to come to its aid, just as the Anzacs had done for them in two world wars.

Indian Ocean: 0952hrs.

They had been at the mercy of the wind and currents, drifting ever further towards that wild ocean with no restraining shoreline worth mentioning.

Figures clinging to the mattress on a wave tossed sea, far from land. Each was wondering who would be lost next and to what, the sharks or hyperthermia.

There had been plenty of bodies, floating face down in the water, dead submariners from the diesel electric vessel HMAS Hooper, but the sharks dragged those off and still returned for more.

They were oceanic White Tips and the largely lifeless deep water oceans were their highway from one coast to the next.

Blood leaking from Derek Penman's head wound had probably attracted them in the first place but the petty officer had not been their first victim.

Four hours after Commander Hollis had spotted the first shark, Midshipman Chloe Ennis let out an involuntary squeal when something brushed her leg and a second later Leading Seaman Brown was snatched away. Derek Penman died from hyperthermia two hours later, his body drifting away before sharks found it. The dead are at least silent when sharks consume them.

Dawn had arisen but the day brought no respite, just more horrors. They had seen a fin circling them. As it grew bolder it closed in and the survivors collective splashing had scared it away, but it did not leave. More fins appeared and five more times they splashed and shouted but with each occasion the survivors were a little more tired, the splashing less frightening, and LS Craig Devonshire had died when the sharks were just not frightened anymore.

The captain of the PLAN hospital ship, *Shén ēn*, the Divine Mercy, had witnessed the predator's boldness for himself. The *Shén ēn* came across the figures in the water as it was looking for survivors from its own ships, lost in the air attacks on the fleet earlier that day. It hove-to and its launch collected the survivors from the water, but even after they were in the ships boat the predators had nudged its sides, unwilling to let the remaining sailors escape.

Commander Hollis, Stephanie Priestly and Phil Daly were led below in a state of shock, the screams of Chloe Ennis still fresh, coming just minutes before the ship had reached them.

They were now prisoners of war but the captain would not report their presence immediately, not until they had at least had a chance to recover from the shock of their ordeal. He had two sons in uniform and he hoped that if they were in danger then an enemy would act mercifully towards them also.

Port Kembla.
1100hrs.

Within ten minutes of the VX chemical attack, following so closely on the heels of the Sydney blast, the combat team had been on the move, off the hill and westwards to the wooded lower slopes of Mt Kembla.

5th US Mech's decontamination unit set up in a field well clear of the population and the Brits were the first through, driving on to just below the escarpment, in the aptly named Windy Gully.

The team's personnel carried out personal decontamination in pairs, the buddy-buddy system ensuring no square inch missed the puffer bottles of Fullers Earth or the bang-and-rub of the DKP1 pads.

Vehicle by vehicle, and then the vehicle interiors were also subject to the neutralising powder.

It was an hour before dawn before they were done, but there were no complaints. The American master sergeant had been well liked and popular, even winning over the very protective technicians and mechanics of Rebecca's light aid detachment.

The entire division had upped sticks and moved location, even those units unaffected by the attacks.

Heck's combat team slept in their vehicles, with a crew member on radio watch, and at two in the afternoon Captain Danny King came to collect Heck for an O Group at the 902nd Infantry CP, informing him that he had been attached to this unit for two days but word had somehow failed to reach the Brits. Still an oddity and despite the addition of the leftover ammunition from the main gun evaluation tests the combat team had found itself shunted off once more like an unwanted child to stay with distant relatives.

The O Group was not a happy event as the 902nd's CO was bigger on rhetoric than he was on contingency planning.

"After due consultation with the local mayor, and after careful consideration of the input of all parties involved, I have assured him that this unit will meet the enemy on the beach and pin him there, regardless."

Heck was pretty sure that the Chinese 3rd Army fitted the category of the 'all parties involved' but they had not been consulted.

The 902nd had wonderfully prepared forward positions. On the walk through that it's CO, Lt Colonel Taylor had conducted, and Heck was half expecting to see hot and cold running water in individual soldier's holes.

"He's not very flexible is he?" Heck had remarked to Danny and Briant Foulness, OC of the 902nd's attached tank company.

Fall-back positions existed as marks on a map, not holes in the ground, ready for occupation. There were no forward fighting positions for his team's tanks and IFVs and Heck was about done with being no more than a potential 'spent johnnie'.

The news that the war in Europe had ended was welcome but as there was no physical sign that the Russians were calling it a day in the Southern Hemisphere, they, the defenders, were no better off. The Russian ships remained with the approaching invasion fleet.

On the conclusion of O Group, Heck and the American tankers had their own meeting before Heck returned to Windy Gully with a plan of his own. He called in at a local plant hire depot on the way.

The Macquarie Pass

The combat team's available manpower was sent down onto the plain behind the town where JCBs from the plant hire depot joined them in creating fighting positions there. Heck and Tony McMarn then travelled west along the Illawarra Highway to the Macquarie Pass. The Pass led the way through the escarpment and on to Canberra a hundred miles beyond, an obvious target for any invader. One other road led through the same gap, the Jamberoo Mountain Road, looping around from the south to join the Highway at the top of the Macquarie. Heck found a good piece of ground to defend, one that dominated both the pass and the mountain road. This was the men's and the JCB digger's next task.

Mao carrier group, south west of Adelaide, South Australia: 1200hrs, same day:

The attacks on the fleet had clearly been an uncoordinated, knee-jerk reaction by the defenders; coming in the wake of the nuclear strike and chemical weapons attacks. The losses in surface ships had been far lighter than Vice Admiral Putchev had expected they would be. However it seemed that the Australian and allied units had launched their own operations, a piecemeal effort instead of a solid counterpunch. Only in the air had their enemy found any real success. The Chinese pilots were still inferior in training and experience, but that was only to be expected. One cannot win the Le Mans twenty four hour race after just one driving lesson.

He retired to his small cabin at 2am for a few hours' sleep before returning to the bridge.

There was, he sensed, a distinct coolness displayed towards him by the PLAN sailors he encountered on the way and he stopped by the compartment that his small liaison team worked out of. They too had picked up on an almost hostile vibe from their hosts.

"Is there any news from the fighting in Europe that could account for that?" he asked the petty officer.

"No sir, we have no contact with Moscow as the satellite link is down, apparently."

The fleet had three dedicated communications satellites serving it, a triple redundancy to ensure uninterrupted contact.

"Get the *Kuznetsov* on the radio, this should not be happening."

They had their own communications setup, It allowed them to

contact their own ships as well as their fleet headquarters, without interfering with this ships own essential business.

Heavy jamming was evident, so heavy in fact that it seemed the Australians had a very powerful dish pointed at the fleet, or the source was very close by indeed.

Karl left immediately for the bridge, seeking Captain Hong, who he knew was scheduled to have the watch but armed sentries barred his way. Vice Admiral Putchev waited patiently until the Mao's Exec, a man who Karl Putchev had never really taken to, came on to the bridge wing.

"The Captain will see you now, Admiral."

Karl strode towards the Captain's chair, stopping short in surprise. A complete stranger sat there.

Bond Springs Airport, Northern Territories, Australia. 1323hrs.

The No. 47 Squadron Hercules started its let-down earlier than planned, landing on a different airstrip to the intended one too. Squadron Leader Stewart Dunn did not have hands on control of the aircraft, he was the captain but Flt Lt Michelle Braithwaite was more than capable of handling the landing, even on three engines. The port inner had lost oil pressure and so they had feathered it and put down at a small airstrip twenty two miles northwest of Alice Springs Airport.

The three Allison Turboprops kicked up a red dust storm on the dirt runway which increased significantly as the blade angle of the propellers altered to shorten the aircraft's landing distance.

The airport manager/ ground controller / fuel truck guy was eyeing them curiously from his seat in the shade as it shut down near the largest of the field's buildings.

The flight engineer explained their problem and sat down to wait for a mechanic and a clutch of customs inspectors from Alice Springs.

Thirteen in all, the five aircrew and the eight troops laid out their Bergans and equipment, which brought a few grins from excise men and bush pilots alike, the latter having wandered over to watch.

"You're not from around here, are you?"

The snow skis and arctic whites were inspected along with their other kit.

"Is this all of you?" an inspector asked the last man. "Big aeroplane for just a handful of you, it'll take forever to fill in that eco footprint."

"We set out with more." said a tired voice, by way of explanation.

"Is this your bag and did you pack it yourself?" he said to the last man."

"No, it is not mine and I did not pack it" said the man presenting it for inspection. "Sorry."

"Who is the bags owner and where is he?"

"Corporal Rory Alladay. He won't be needing it anymore."

It was a bergan like any other, showing signs of hard use and its padded carrying side stained dark with its owners sweat from many locales, from Dartmoor to Gansu Province, ultimately. Rory's blood also left its mark on the arctic white cover, the specks and splashes now turned dark. The customs man opened a side pouch, which happened to be the one holding ID discs from those who had died during Operation Equaliser, those that they had managed to recover the tags from. The customs officer went rather quiet and zipped the pouch back up.

"Sorry mate, I thought you'd just come along to get into the war."

"That's okay officer."

The M&AWC had been 'in' since the beginning, although Major Dewar could not recall any official declaration of war by the New Soviet Union or by the People's Republic of China.

On their eventual extraction and recovery to India they had all learned that the European aspect of the war had ended with a defeat for the Soviets and that several European governments had largely been ousted by the military, beginning with the UK. SACEUR had arrived in newly liberated Berlin two days later and had been arrested by German Federal Police, only to be released within the hour by German Panzer Grenadiers after a short exchange of gunfire. The German government's action had been the deciding factor for its military and by midnight the same day it too had been replaced.

India had seen new orders for Garfield Brooks and his Green Berets, ones that took them to the Philippines. They had shared a beer once the parting of the ways had come, as the SAS Mountain Troops specialists and the remains of the M&AWC were bound for the Blue Mountains of New South Wales.

"You realise that once this is all over the USA is going to move heaven and earth to get back to the old way of doing business with Europe?"

"As I hear it, this is just a temporary thing, a cleaning of house with a couple of years' worth of work for the Serious Fraud Office going through MP's finances, and an end to the nanny state."
"Big Brotherism." Gareth corrected.
"Absolutely...a repealing of a big bunch of laws."
There was a lot of military activity in India, Malaysia and Indonesia as those countries geared up now that the nuclear threat had been removed. China had a big military, but it was already stretched. The Philippines refused to be pacified, and guerrilla warfare had broken out in Japan and Taiwan, tying down forces it could otherwise have used as a threat to the rest of Asia. Its one big remaining field army, 3rd Army, was not as yet committed to holding ground. It had to take Canberra and the Australian cities, and then take the north and south islands of New Zealand in order to be freed-up to put Asian states back in their place.

Richard thought that Australia was a sub-continent too far for the PLAN and they had not learned from the mistakes of the Philippines. 3rd Army had been reorganised so as to employ fewer MBTs, but it was still too mechanised for New South Wales. He had more 'mountain leaders' enroute to Australia to replace the M&AWC's losses and he fully intended to show the 3rd Army how small units on foot ate big units in vehicles for breakfast when they got into forests and mountains.

Arbuckle Mountains, Oklahoma.
Tuesday 23rd October, 0313hrs

The President had not expected too much change in the way the war was being conducted, now that the fighting in Europe had ended, and the next move of his command post evidenced that.

General Randolph Carmine began with a briefing on events in Europe, in particular with the units that were being reorganised and readied to send to the Pacific.

The British had acted swiftly, setting the pace for their neighbours and the newly formed 1st Guards Mechanised Division were just awaiting shipping and escorts to form their convoy. 2CG, 2nd Battalion Coldstream Guards with Lt Col Pat Reed now commanding it, 1WG, 1st Battalion Welsh Guards and 1IG, the 2nd Battalion Irish Guards, were the Warrior equipped infantry, The Scots Guards and Grenadier Guards had older but upgraded FV-432s.

The Life Guards were the armoured reconnaissance element from the Household Cavalry, and the Kings Royal Hussars were the heavy armour. 32 Regiment RA's MLRS and 40 Field Regiment's AS90 155mm SP were the divisions artillery, along with engineers, signals and all the logistical units that made a fighting unit work. Three of the Foot Guards battalions though were going to be without their IFVs for a month, Australia needed troops immediately and so they would go ahead by air in the light role.

A Highland Brigade consisting of 1st Battalion London Scottish, 1st Battalion Argyll & Sutherland Highlanders (having absorbed the 7th/8th Battalion of territorials) and the 1st Battalion Cameron Highlanders was also forming. The Royal Scots Dragoon Guards were the Highland Brigades armour. Artillery for the Scots was yet to be included until amalgamations or temporary attachments from various units could take place.

8 Infantry Brigade, consisting of the 3rd Battalion Royal Green Jackets, the 1st Battalion Light Infantry, which had absorbed two rifle companies from the regiment's second battalion to bring it up to strength, and finally The Wessex Regiment, a combined battalion made up of the survivors of 1 and 2 Wessex. 8 Infantry Brigade would also arrive in Australia by air to be employed as light infantry.

"The sending of a leg infantry by the Brits is a good move." General Carmine explained. "It is boots on the ground in the mountains, not tyres or tracks, which they need right now if the landings do proceed. And we have 10th Mountain Division emplaning also, for that very purpose."

Having dealt with the initial reinforcements, the general moved on to the enemy, and their intentions.

"Assuming the Chinese 3rd Army's 1st Corps can get ashore, the key, as both we and the Anzacs see it, is to keep the Chinese on the coastal plain until we can muster the muscle to kick them back into the sea." General Carmine stated. "Of course there is their 2nd Corps to contend with, although that is a long way off yet, and its 3rd Corps, which is mainly reservists and second rate equipment, but a lot of them. 3rd Corps is awaiting 1st Corps ships to return and collect them, so that is a pressing need for a redeployment of SSN and SSKs."

"Still no sign of the Russian element of the fleet detaching?" The President asked, but he also knew what the reply would be. He had had a frank discussion with Premier Torneski and she was insistent that her ships had been ordered home, but were not responding. The President was inclined to believe her, especially as that part of

Europe was turbulent right now, and having troops on hand would be a bonus.

A briefing for the small, select group known as 'The Choir' was the next order of the day and for once grizzled military or intelligence men had not given it.

A brunette who looked somehow familiar was the NSA briefer. Owing to the high security surrounding 'Church' the members tended to be senior staffers and middle aged in the main. This NSA representative was short of thirty.

"I know you, don't I?" the President said.

"Yes Mr President, you made me the systems security chief for the NSA. I debugged the RORSATs." Sally Peters replied.

The President swung around to look at Paul Stanley, the current chief of the NSA. Jack Graham, his predecessor, had been one of the casualties of the Washington DC bomb.

Next to Paul Stanley was sat another woman young enough to be a daughter to most of the rest of the room's occupants. The green eyed redhead found herself the centre of attention as everyone else followed the Presidents gaze.

"And who may you be, young lady?"

"Alicia O'Connor, sir. I was contracted to work for Sally."

"On?" the President enquired.

"Digital manipulation."

The President grinned and clicked his fingers, pleased with himself. He remembered Ms O'Connor's name appearing in a report by Scott Tafler, and that was another good man gone, to an assassination squad, in Scott's case..

"You've worked out how the Chinese did what they did to our satellites and you can now do it to them, too?" he said to Paul Stanley.

"It is not quite that simple unfortunately." Paul Stanley said apologetically.

The plasma screen monitors came to life and the President watched in silence as first Sally Peters, and then Alicia O'Connor took to the floor to explain the complexities of their proposal as well as the very real and obvious risks.

The President stared at the screens.

"Son of a bitch." he breathed, his eyes going from one screen to the other.

Southern Pacific Ocean. 838 miles west of Guam. 1054hrs.

At a depth 600ft, the Sea Wolf class Hunter/Killer USS *Twin Towers* made ten knots as it made its way west, passing the older scenes of conflict, the tiny islands of Peleliu and Angaur, to the north of them.

Captains Pitt's original orders had been to relieve the Australian diesel boat but that was no longer deemed necessary since the invasion fleet had altered course for the sub-continent. His new orders were to disrupt the supply line from Cebu, the logistical base for the PLAN 3rd Army. He was to join up with a British boat, HMS *Hood*, and together they were to find and sink tankers and merchantmen.

The NATO navies did not have that many hulls in these waters at the moment, and diesels were at a premium. The shallower waters with their thousands of islands, big and small, were not an ideal area of operation for SSNs, and SSKs were even thinner on the ground.

There was something about the orders that puzzled him; it was in the wording, or lack of it.

'Find and sink enemy cargo vessels and tankers'. Did the admiral who issued the orders just assume that his captains would take the sinking of troopships and RO-ROs as a given? He was used to all the 'Tees' being crossed and the 'Is' dotted to prevent any ambiguity. He had nothing solid, just a nagging suspicion that someone knew more than they were telling. The intelligence bulletin regarding the PLAN 3rd Army's 1st, 2nd and 3rd Corps was also in an almost précis form. 1st Corps would try to bulldoze its way to Canberra but if it failed then it would hold the ground it had taken, and await the other two corps arrival. Okay, that was sensible, but when were the other two corps expected, and by which route, the Indian Ocean or the Pacific?

The only solid information was that of the number of units expected to be guarding the supply line from the Philippine Islands, but that figure was a little on the low side and there was no explanation given for this. Where were the rest of the SSK fleet, and the dedicated surface warfare ships? He was probably going to have to wait until peace broke out before discovering those answers.

The *Hood* was rearmed and running fast and deep to join with them in as short a time as possible. In the meantime he would take the *Twin Towers* into the deep Philippines Sea until the Brits arrived.

He reckoned that his crew were ready to start hunting for real, instead of the constant drills and problems he had given them since clearing Newport News.

Rick had a very different crew now to the one he had started out this war with. Only Ensign Hannigan remained from the first crew of the USS *Twin Towers.* Promoted to Lieutenant j.g as a reward for being the only officer still capable of standing watch, he was now boss of the sonar shop.

The Seawolf Class submarine had been towed in to Portsmouth, Virginia, too badly damaged to make headway on her own during that 2nd Battle of the Atlantic, as it was now being called. But for a torpedo proximity fuse mistaking her still deployed sonar array for the *Twin Tower's* hull; they would not be here now.

'The Tee Tee' had put to sea again following repairs in dry dock, and her skipper and Lt Hannigan had left hospital in time to be assigned to her.

The current crew had a small core of professional submariners and the rest were reservists or draftees in the less technical roles.

Young Mister Hannigan had a natural ear for sonar and even though it was not required of him he could still be found donning a headset and listening for hours at a time.

USS *Twin Towers* slipped through the depths with her new array streamed and listening intently as she headed for her captains chosen area on their first hunt.

CHAPTER 2

Canberra International Airport, Australia.
Friday 26th October

Looking some 100% more presentable than he had during his previous outing on the media, Lt Col Pat Reed led the way into 'Arrivals' at Canberra International Airport. The media were there covering the arrival of 'The soldiers of The Queen, come to Australia's aid from the Mother country' as some of the older Australian's thought, or 'The Mutineers' according to others.

Back in the UK he and Annabelle had not been left alone with their grief. The media, and certain factions of the community, sought them out wherever they went, and so when Brigadier General Salisbury-Jones, who commanded 1st Guards Mechanised Brigade, had asked him to command 2CG he had discussed it with her before agreeing. Their own personal grief could not be addressed fully until this war was finished.

1st Guards Brigade arrived in Canberra as light infantry, their vehicles making the journey by sea and not expected to arrive for a month. 1WG and 1IG were veterans of 1(UK) Mechanised Brigade on the Saale; 2CG was largely untested in this war, although veterans of Bosnia and Iraq were in the ranks. 1 Company was pure veteran from the current conflict, made up of 1CG men, as were the mortar and recce platoons in 2 (Support) Company. 1CG's Anti-Tank Platoon had been destroyed at The Wesernitz and the 82nd Airborne men had provided the hybrid battalions anti-armour needs in Germany. It was strange not having those men around now and the 'Odd Couple' had been a fearsome fighting team.

Jim Popham and Pat had spoken briefly by telephone since the civilian government had been ousted in the UK. No doubt the US Intelligence had been eavesdropping the whole time but he had been pretty thoroughly grilled by US Army Intelligence due to his and his men's association with 1CG. They were now training for some airborne operation or other, but Pat would have been happy to have them with this battalion right now.

His own personal grief could not be addressed fully until this war was finished There were others missing, the Tim Gilchrists who he would never see again, and the Colin Probert's of the regiment, those who were still recovering from their wounds. Colin had been particularly badly treated as Simon Manson had painted that courageous soldier as being a craven coward in order to justify his own serious shortcomings on the Wesernitz.

1CG's reputation, smeared by Danyella Foxten-Billings with the former PM's blessing, and the assistance of the gutter press, was now cleared. Their portrayal as unworthy rebels in battle had only been corrected by becoming the ultimate of rebels in many eyes, and that was the final irony.

A small core of Vormundberg veterans and their rescued wounded from prison cells were now working under RSM Probert to rebuild the regiments First Battalion back in the UK. Colin had declined the commission as he lacked the financial means to be a Guards Officer in peacetime and would have had to transfer out of the brigade.

Pat ignored the press, the outreaching arms and the microphones they held. He had briefed his men to do likewise and some fairly inflammatory questions were shouted at the men in order to illicit a reaction. Despite his orders one of his senior NCOs was now having a squaring up to a well-known reporter who had, in frustration, grabbed the arm of a passing soldier.

"I have a right to an answer, the people of Australia have a right to an answer and I am their voice!"

"You have the right do you?"

"Yes, I believe I do."

"Were you at on the Wesernitz?"

"No."

"Were you on the Elbe?"

"No."

"Were you with the International Division at The Vormundberg?"

"No."

"Then you haven't earned the right to Jack-All, have you Hinney?" said CSM Osgood. "What's yer name by the way?"

The internationally famous reporter told him the name that politicians and celebrities alike courted or stepped softly around.

"Never heard of you."

The battalion, and the rest of the Foot Guards, collected their equipment and moved off in Australian Army Unimogs along the Federal Highway to reinforce Woolongong and Port Kembla.

Two hours later the 8th Infantry Brigade arrived at Canberra and headed off in a different direction, along Kings Highway towards a little coastal town. They would relieve the Australians there so that Bateman's Bay defences could be beefed up.

Sergeant 'Baz' Cotter was no longer an Acting Company Commander, he was getting the hang of the Platoon Sergeant's role with No. 12 Platoon, D Company, of the amalgamated Wessex battalions. All the men, the rankers, were veterans but there were a few teething problems. Former 1 and 2 Wessex men still considered themselves members of their original companies. One example was in 2 Section where they were all ex-C (Royal Berkshire) Company men of 2 Wessex and still wore the Brandywine flash behind the Wyvern cap badge. The Platoon Commander had taken their reluctance to unpick the stitching of the red flashes, and their permanent removal, as something of a personal challenge to his authority. Mr Pottinger was not a veteran; he was the product of advanced officer training. Baz had been very respectful when he had suggested that Mr P use the situation to the platoon's advantage, as in a means to foster healthy competition between the sections. This would of course have to be properly handled by the right leader, but the result could be the best fighting platoon in the battalion. The platoon commander had not responded well to the suggestion though, and at a platoon leadership meeting he had publically ordered Corporal 'Dopey' Hemp to remove the Brandywine from his beret before the meeting commenced. If Mr P had thought that he was earning support from the other two section commanders he was very much mistaken. Mr P had pointed at his epaulet, at the very low profile embroidered 'pip' that marked him as a commissioned officer, before telling them their fortunes as he saw them. The section commanders all had day jobs to go back to, even after serving sentences in 'Colly' if it came to that, and all were combat veterans who had been recommended for gallantry awards. As Corporal Dave Whyte of 2 Section succinctly put it, he had 'done his bit' and Mrs Whyte would be quite happy for him to sit out the next bit of Global unpleasantness in a nice safe prison cell, but who was going to run Mr P's rifle sections for him, hmm?

As a direct consequence of that meeting there was now an 'Us and Him' atmosphere within 12 Platoon which the CSM had quickly picked up on, and had directed the brand new Sergeant Cotter to deal with ASAP. Mr P however, would merely glare at his platoon sergeant and point at his epaulet whenever that subject came up, which was thrice daily, on good days.

Baz Cotter secretly wished that the Australians would leave wonderfully prepared positions requiring zero work by themselves, and the PLAN to continue to take its time before attempting a landing. After all the blood and snot, the snow and ice, followed by the rain and mud in Germany, perhaps some fun in the sun on the beaches was in order? Perhaps all that was needed was some fun-bonding to put things straight, a little surfing and a barbeque or two in quiet little Moruya?

The Tasman Sea, east of Moruya, New South Wales. 2100hrs Friday 26th October

The captain of the Improved Kilo class diesel electric submarine *Zheng He* spared a quick glance around the control room to check all was in order before taking his seat. He groaned when he sat down, he was deathly tired and indicated to his steward that he required yet another coffee.

Captain Aiguo Li had been in command of the *Zheng He* for less than a day, replacing the former commanding officer who had suffered a major stroke and cardiac arrest at sea. Prior to that, he had been in Cuba, in another ocean entirely.

Following the failed attack upon the European Space Agency launch facility in French Guiana, Li had faced the fact that without logistical support his Juliett class diesel *'Dai'* was not going to make it home on her remaining fuel. He had managed to stay one step ahead of the French Atlantique and the anti-submarine corvette, but things had become more complicated with the arrival of a British vessel, HMS *Westminster*, to make the hunt more interesting for the hunters. His orders were to 'scuttle and evade', but he had instead limped into Havana harbor in Cuba where they had been received as heroes.

Anti-American and anti-all-things-Western feelings were running high. Food shortages, particularly fish, were having a bad effect on the civilian populations in the region. America had set of nuclear depth charges that had saved the convoys but had a dreadful effect on fish stocks, the weather and the harvests.

The surprise arrival of the Chinese submarine, so far from home, had become a propaganda coup for the Cuban government. A French ASW corvette, the *Commandant Blaison* and the British ASW frigate HMS *Westminster* sat off the coast, demanding the surrender of the vessel and its crew. If the newspapers were to be believed, the entire US Navy was sat just over the horizon. Somehow the media in those parts had chosen to forget the two nations and two fleets that the PRC had used its nuclear weapons on without hesitation.

Captain Li was feted as the David who had taken on the American Goliath, and when the Ambassador to Cuba from the People's Republic of China showed Li into his office in the Embassy he did not leave a revolver and a single round upon the table and discretely withdraw. No mention was made of the mission's failure to prevent further launches; instead it had somehow become a highly successful and daring commando raid to sink the 'armed merchant freighter' *Fliterland* at her moorings, thereby preventing her cargo from being used against the peoples of China.

Li was tempted to explain to the Ambassador that the vessel had been unarmed, empty, and as good as abandoned but for a security guard in a gatehouse, but that would have been pointless.

His family back home was safe, and he was still drawing breath, which was always a plus.

Aiguo Li was now promoted to Da Xiao, Senior Captain, and put on a special flight home. His crew remained with the *Dai*, and the sunshine, and the extremely friendly Cuban girls. The Exec was now the Juliett's skipper and Li had not the faintest clue as to what was in store for himself when they shook hands and said farewell.

Li's orders were for him to return to Beijing but instead his flight had been diverted, delivering him to Mactan in the Philippines, and a fresh set of orders.

He read his these new orders as he descended the airstair of his comfortable Air China Boeing 747, with its moorishly luxurious 1st Class seating, and he was rereading them as he continued across the tarmac and into a very functional Antonov that fetched and carried for the *Mao*.

The journey had been a nightmare with violent storms along the way before he had his first, and hopefully last, carrier landing.

Only torrential rain had been there to greet the 'Hero of Kourou' as he crossed the flight deck and into a Z-8KH helicopter for a rendevous with his current command. The winching down onto its deck with a sea running was also an experience he had no great enthusiasm for repeating.

There had been considerable changes in his county's, and fleets, fortunes. For the time being the PRC was no longer the possessor of a nuclear arsenal, and furthermore she stood alone now against the West.

"So we had better win this one then." He thought in reflection, considering China's current circumstances.

He was once more conducting an inshore covert operation but this time with none of the training and preparation that had preceded the previous mission.

He had special forces aboard once more, and a submersible riding piggy back. All he needed now was for Captain Jie Huaiqing to arrive at his side equipped with some of the most random and bizarre details imaginable to make the experience complete.

Alas the mercurial Jie Huaiqing had not made it back. Dead, captured or evading, he had no idea what had become of Jie or any of the special forces who had swum ashore off Devil's Island.

Aiguo Li had been picked because he was the Chinese navy's most experienced captain in the business of inshore raiding and covert ops, but as Li was aware of no other living captains in that line of work it had kind of put that written compliment into perspective. Li's job now was to carry out the plans that were supposed to guarantee a swift landing by the invasion fleet, and a back door to the Australian capital, Canberra.

New South Wales offered some fairly impressive natural barriers to an invader trying to reach Canberra. Dense forests, rivers and mountains that barred the way to the capital, and the few routes through the mountains were all defended by the small Australian army, navy and air force, with assistance from other countries.

The good news was that those defences were on the coastal plain waiting for the Chinese to roll up along the few roads that were available in an attempt to use the even scarcer passes through the mountains.

The enemy was of course aware that the invaders were a long way from home and had relatively few helicopters, at least until such time as suitable airfields could be captured.

The Chinese 3rd Army's 1st Corps would land before dawn at several beaches, not just the one. It was logical to assume an invader needed a central beachhead and it was also logical that the beachhead would be where the defenders were barring the way to a Pass.

Someone on the Chinese planning staff would beg to differ with that assumption.

"Conn, Sonar...new contact bearing zero eight seven degrees, range ten thousand meters, speed twelve knots. Classify as civilian coastal traffic, Captain." She was an old and noisy coastal freighter trying to go about her business under the cover of darkness. Their previous contact had been doing likewise, and that had been a small tanker.

At some point in this war, thought Li ruefully, I may actually get to do what submariners are supposed to do, sink stuff.

To his mind the empty and docked *Fliterland* did not count.

Another half hour brought to the control room the state employed cut throat who commanded the special forces unit. He lacked the charm, wit and quiet wisdom of Jie Huaiqing; in fact he seemed devoid of humour completely. Li shook his hand and wished him luck. There would be no pick-up by this vessel, no need indeed for any further participation. The men would link up with the army once the landing had succeeded.

The submersible would tow his men inshore at the northern end of the target beach, dropping them off as the teams targets drew close.

The shoreline here was defended, but not to the same extent to which Port Kembla and Batemans Bay was. Kembla had the port facilities required as a base for future operations, as well as access to one of the few passes through the mountains to the west. Batemans Bay was linked to Canberra via the Kings Highway, Route 52, and it was just half the distance in comparison to taking the steeply winding road that zig-zagged up the escarpment of Mt Kembla to the Macquarie Pass.

Zheng He put about and moved quietly away, back out into the deep waters that offered greater safety than the inshore shallows.

Behind them, two pairs of swimmers who had already detached from the submersible and would next abandon their rebreathers in six feet of water. They crept ashore at Moruya

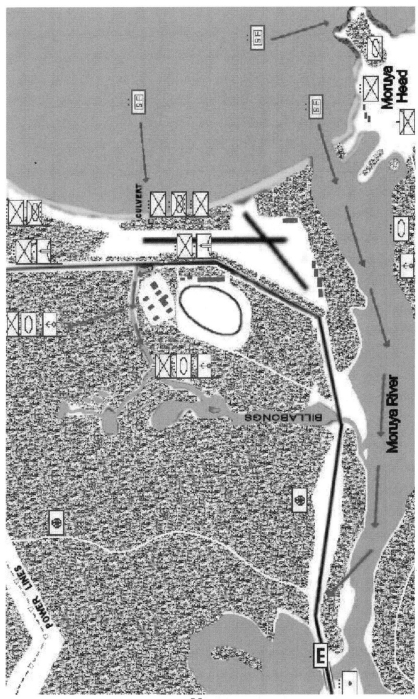

Moruya

North Beach, crawling slowly up out of the surf using the noisy runoff from a drainage culvert as cover.

Soldiers of the 1st/19th Battalion of the Royal New South Wales Regiment were dug in inside the trees bordering the sandy beach. The citizen soldiers were well trained and alert, but unaware that the weakness in their defence had been spotted on a digital movie taken by a Chinese family on holiday two years before.

Behind these defenders lay a small airports runway and behind that lay more alert Australians with guns, but the special forces troopers bypassed them all, crawling 439m through the culvert, beneath the runway to the saltwater stream that fed it. From there the troopers split up, heading for command posts.

At the mouth of the Moruya River the next four kicked away from the submersible and swam for the cliffs at Moruya Head. The night climb was not the most difficult any of them had previously undertaken, and they too sought out the company CP for the defenders of Shelly Beach.

The submersible would enter the river and secure two bridges, killing the waiting Australian sappers before they could blow them, and directing precision shellfire onto a gun battery nearby.

C Troop, D Squadron, 1st (AU) Armoured Regiment attached to B Company, 1st/19th Battalion, Royal New South Wales Regiment: Moruya North Beach, NSW. 0412hrs Saturday 27th October.

The shelling of the beach, and the Burrawang Forest behind it, came as something of an unpleasant surprise for the citizen/reservists and regulars alike for two reasons. Firstly, this was a heavily forested area that stretch twenty six miles inland. Only an idiot or a Chinaman who'd been sat in the sun too long would chose this spot to invade Australia, which at least had been the opinion of the soldiers up until an hour before. Secondly of course, they had been expecting to be relieved by a Pom infantry brigade.

'Tango Four Three Charlie', a German built Leopard 1 that was older than even the old man of the crew, Trooper 'Bingo' McCoy, the twenty eight year old driver, rocked on its tracks as a shell exploded in the trees nearby. The vicious splinters were little threat to the tank, but a deadly danger to the infantry who shared this ordeal by fire.

The Australians had decided on replacing the old main battle tanks with American M1A1 Abrams, but the war had occurred before that process had begun.

"This is just a diversion." opined the tanks gunner, Che Tan, and not for the first time. "The real effort will be up the coast. I'm tellin' yer, that's how they'll play it."

They were in a hull down position well to the rear of their fighting positions, beyond the boundary of Moruya Jockey Club, the race track north of the river of the same name. Che was Australian born and bred; his parents though had arrived as refugees from Vietnam. There was nothing inscrutably oriental about Trooper Tan; he said it as he saw it.

"They'll get bored and bugger off in a minute."

A near miss shook the vehicle, red hot steel splinters striking its armour.

The rest of the crew in the turret stared accusingly at the gunner for tempting fate.

"A minute?" asked the driver. "I've got five dollars if someone's got a stopwatch and better odds."

They were suited and masked for NBC, three quarters of a mile from the beach, back from their forward fighting positions amongst two platoons worth of the Royal New South Wales Regiment, along with a pair of ASLAV armoured recce vehicles of the $2^{nd}/14^{th}$ Light Horse. The racetrack, a coastal road, a copse and an airfield runway lay between their current position and where they would fight.

Either side of C Troop's current location, were the company headquarters of the infantry, occupying a dug-in CP, mortar pits and trenches. The infantrymen had no armoured fighting vehicles; just canvas topped Mercedes Unimogs in a harbour area further to the rear. The clerks and storemen huddled in the shelter bays praying that no direct hit would end them instantly, and no near-miss would collapse the trench upon them and end them slowly.

"Seriously though," Che said. "What are we doing here? It's not tank country; there are rivers and billabongs all over the shop, and enough trees per acre to make a billion matchsticks."

"Colour, dash and daring, boy," Chuck Waldek, the loader said. "Colour, dash and daring, 'cod without us this would just be another mindless shitfight between their moron grunts and our cut-lunch-commandos" as he referred to volunteer reservists.

The tanks crews had made good use of the aforementioned trees, cutting branches and foliage to strap to the turret and flanks with D10 telephone cable. By doing so they spared their cam nets and also took their cover with them whenever they moved.

The barrage lifted, shifting to possible reinforcement routes, sealing off the Australians from help.

"Hello all Tango callsigns, this is Tango Four Nine, 'Wicked Lady', over."

A and B Troops responded, and then it was their turn.

"Tango Four Three Alpha, 'Wicked Lady', over!"

"Tango Four Three Bravo, 'Wicked Lady', over!"

"Tango Four Three Charlie, 'Wicked Lady' over!" Gary Burley, the tanks commander replied.

"Tango Four Nine, 'Wicked Lady', out."

Sergeant Burley switched to intercom.

"Okay Bingo, let's go, get us to the first firing position, the landing craft have been spotted heading in!"

A hundred metres spacing between the vehicles, they moved slowly forwards like articulated garden features, leafy branches seemingly growing out of the steel plate. They manoeuvred around trees until reaching the chain link fence surrounding the race track and accelerated. Four Three Charlie's driver ignored an open gate in order the trash a long length of the fence which they carried with them, entangled over the front of the Leopard.

"Well that was smart, wasn't it?" Gary said to the driver in censure.

"Bollocks, the amount of money I've lost in this place I reckon I must have paid for it twice over." Bingo grumbled back. He had picked up his nickname because he was so addicted to giving away his cash to bookies after each Army Appreciation Day (payday, in Anzac parlance), he had even been spotted sat amongst blue rinsed old ladies in Bingo Halls trying to win it back before his wife found out.

The Leopards were illuminated by the blazing spectator's stands and stables. The horses, and much of the local population, had moved away over the previous week when it became evident that invasion was inevitable.

"Bloody hell, if you spent enough here to qualify as an owner then I reckon yer about bankrupt now, mate!"

The racecourse had received the attention of naval gunfire, as had the small provincial airport, where flames were leaping high from the hangars and buildings, clearly visible above the trees to their right.

The damage wrought to the fence seemed rather trivial in the face of what the invaders were doing. When Banjo repeated it at the other side it became snarled up with the first one they had crashed through, leaving the fence raising sparks as it trailed behind them across George Bass Drive, the coastal road.

Bingo slowed as they entered a copse of trees just before the airport runway, as this was the infantry's in-depth position. Running over someone in the dark here was a distinct possibility.

On the far side of the runway lay the final thin strip of trees before the beach, and as the tanks reached midway across the runways tarmac something emerged from behind the extreme left of those trees.

Gary was staring through his night sight at the mass of green hues and saw the thing appear.

A Ming Tz combat hovercraft was rounding the fighting positions, outflanking the Royal New South Wales Regiment defenders before disgorging its infantry. The 7.62mm machineguns in its turret firing into the first positions, but the 23mm automatic cannon mounting engaged the trio of Leopard tanks.

The Australian Leopards had the far reaching Royal Ordnance L7A3 105mm rifled tank gun, but its long rang was not required. Four Three Charlie fired on the move, the HESH round doing wicked damage to the armoured hovercraft just four hundred metres away.

Four Three Alpha also fired; the troop commander's Leopard hit the Ming's fuel tank. Three hundred gallons of high octane aviation fuel went up in a fireball, engulfing the hovercraft and the naval infantry.

"HESH UP!" Chuck shouted, closing the breech and informing both Che and Gary that the main armament was reloaded, and what it was loaded with.

There were still Chinese infantry from the Ming who were active, those not caught in the burning Avgas, and two were knelt and aiming RPG-26s at the Alpha tank.

"Infantry action, half left!" Gary shouted to the driver who abruptly steered their Leopard in that direction in order that the coaxial 7.62 machine gun could be brought to bear.

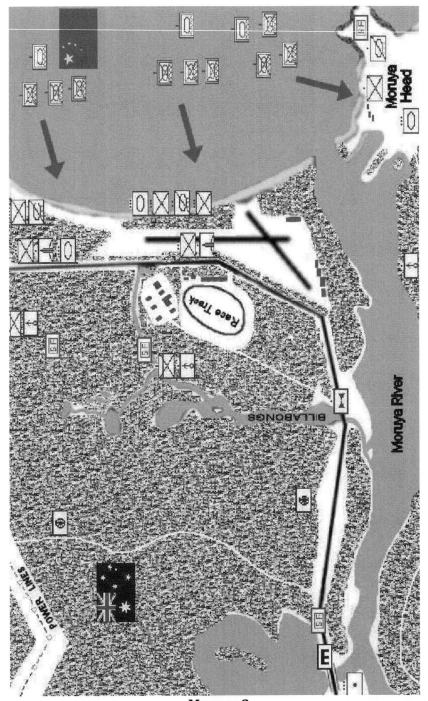

Moruya 2

Even without the night sights the enemy were clearly visible in the light of the burning combat hovercraft. Gary missed with the first burst but succeeded in putting them off their stroke, a rocket launched by a rattled operator sailed above the troop commander's tank, missing by a good ten feet. The second burst dropped them and they lay unmoving, just inside the trees. None of the enemy was wearing NBC clothing, Gary noted, and reported the fact to the troop commander.

Chuck steered Four Three Charlie back on line, looking for the access point to their first firing position.

A tree leaned drunkenly across the path of Four Three Charlie; its fall arrested by its neighbour, but as they approached it resumed its journey downwards, slowly at first as the branches supporting it gave way. Its final plunge left it supine on the edge of the copse.

"We can climb over that, no bother!" Che said as Bingo swung them hard right, away from it and towards an alternate position.

"Yeah, but could we reverse back over it, though?"

The possible alternative route out of their original choice of fighting hole was forwards, onto the soft sand of the beach where getting bogged down in full view of the enemy was a distinct possibility.

"Three Four Charlie, this is Sunray, grab a position and get busy f'Christ sake!"

The troop commander and the Bravo tank were already engaged.

"A thank you and a please wouldn't go amiss at this point." Che remarked to no one in particular.

Although they had been at the location a week it was now difficult to recognise where the prepared firing positions were due to the shelling.

"STOP...back up!" Gary had spotted the position just as they were passing it. Banjo steered them in, and swore when he saw what was awaiting them.

"Bugger me, but there are a lot of the bastards!"

A half dozen more of the big Ming Tz hovercraft were heading in, with amphibious Type 63 tanks, a PT-76 variant, and IFVs bringing up the rear. Behind the amphibious infantry fighting vehicles and light tanks came the infantry and tank landing craft of a more conventional nature

Far over to the right, on the far side of the mouth of the Moruya River at Shelly Beach, two more of the infantry carrying Ming Tz hovercraft were already moving up the beach, a third sat half submerged and burning in the surf. Gary reckoned the one they had already destroyed on the edge of the airfield had somehow mistaken this beach of Shelly, but either way, the enemy were already moving ashore either side of them.

To their left, there sat one of the Light Horse ASLAVs in a hull-down-hole and firing its 25mm Bushmaster auto cannon at the nearest hovercraft, but with little effect upon the Ming's armoured hull. The high explosive rounds made a pretty sight as they exploded, but that was about all.

Che fired, aiming for the cockpit and it swerved right, clearly damaged but still a threat. The Bushmasters HE rounds had more success on its more lightly armoured sides.

"UP!"

Che ignored the damaged Ming; the Light Horsemen were directing fire into the now exposed compressors at the hovercrafts rear. Its skirt was deflating and it was settling in the water a thousand metres offshore, with its hull already perforated at the sides it would sink.

Gary put his eye to his sight to see where the gunner was aiming.

"No, forget the skirt; you'd need to make a hundred holes to have any effect."

The tank round scored a direct hit on its cockpit and it too veered right, a slave to the engines torque now its pilots were also dead.

There was no artillery or mortar fire landing, only their own direct fire to take on the oncoming waves of landing craft.

Gary was happy that Che and Chuck had everything in hand and he quickly switched to the infantry company net. No one was answering the requests for fire missions. He flicked up to the battalion net for the 1st/19th, Royal New South Wales Regiment and they seemed to be having the same problem. Only D Company's CP seemed to be on the air and they had fought off an attack which killed a signaller and the CSM before the attackers departed.

Gary switched back and called the troop commander but Lt Jenkins had already discovered the problem for himself. The troop commander had also tried to call in close air support to compensate for the lack of artillery, but there was a major effort on to attack the fleet itself, now that it was at its most vulnerable. The navy and the air force were fully engaged he had, been told. Obviously the good news with that was the lack of enemy air strikes on the beaches, but it was a mixed blessing.

The Alpha and Bravo tanks both fired on the closest hovercraft as it reached the surf and its bow doors opened but the enemy who emerged flung themselves into the water to douse themselves. The HESH rounds had set the troop compartment alight.

The remaining hovercraft pulled up the beach and disgorged their loads before immediately reversing, heading back down the beach. The Infantry hammered the Chinese troops with grenades, rifle and machine gun fire. The three tanks destroyed both of the hovercraft before they could escape to collect further loads of troops.

All supporting enemy fire had switched to the A and C Company depth positions, but once they were suppressed the fire would renew on their own positions.

Pinned down on the beach the Chinese troops took cover as best they could as they no longer had the weight of numbers required, thanks to the Royal Ordnance L7 105mm rifled tank guns.

The Leopards now engaged the amphibious tanks, and IFVs but these were turning away, heading for the beaches north of them.

The enemy were ashore either side of them and the landing on their beach had been diverted as the Chinese reinforced those successes.

"There's a marked absence of artillery and mortars, have you noticed?" Che said.

"We know." Gary replied. "Something got screwed up good and proper... we're picking up the grunts and moving out before we get cut off." The troop commander was passing on the orders of the 1st/19th's battalion commander to the B Company platoons.

Che's jaw dropped and he looked back in his sights at the dead hovercraft.

"Well that's not bloody fair!"

The infantrymen were appearing now, carrying their wounded, and abandoning the dead. Their comrades, the fallen, had been stripped of weapons, ammunition and specialist equipment. The I.D tags went to the platoon commanders of which one was now a corporal, the platoon commanders and platoon sergeants shared trench having received a direct hit.

To their north and south the amphibious IFVs and tanks were approaching the shore.

Someone rapped on the turret with a bayonet and Bingo backed up.

"There's not that many grunts on board, are you sure we got the lot?"

They headed back across the runway, but at a tangent this time. The hovercraft behind the trees was burning fiercely still, onboard ammunition cooking off in the heat.

Gary could see the depth platoon on the infantry falling back towards their company headquarters location. According to their contingencies they were to withdraw through it and back to where their transport was cammed up and waiting.

Naval gunfire resumed, falling on the positions they had just vacated. Trees fell or exploded when struck directly by the warships shells.

The troop now headed parallel with the runway, the infantrymen clinging to the strapped on natural camouflage. Ahead of them the airport buildings were a raging inferno, but there were no shell craters on the tarmac of the runways that Gary could see. Obviously they wanted serviceable runways for immediate use. He switched to the battalion net where their troop commander was requesting an RV with a Casevac. Whoever was the 'Hawkeye Rep' for the Army Air Corps on the other end was not being helpful, requesting an NBC Chemrep be prepared and sent before deciding whether to agree to a dust-off or not.

"Tango Four Three Alpha...listen up!" said their boss, losing his patience. "As *already* reported, the enemy were *not* suited and booted, and the fact that we have *wounded* IS a Chemrep. They'd be dead otherwise!"

A voice cut in, having obviously been listening to the exchange.

"Gremlin Zero Two inbound along the river." The New Zealander accented pilot said. "Where do you want us?"

"Tango Four Three Alpha, on the highway west of the airfield."

"Gremlin, roger that... ETA four minutes."

'Hawkeye' remained silent throughout the brief exchange between Aussie tanker and Kiwi Huey pilot but could not have been happy at being bypassed in such a brusk fashion.

Gary went back to trying to get a handle on what had occurred during the last twenty minutes. The company sized combat teams to the north and south had been defeated, as in destroyed or sent packing. The 105mm howitzers of A Battery had certainly not fired on the craft approaching their beach, and neither had each infantry company's 81mm mortar section.

There had been no obvious air support but no enemy aircraft either, so perhaps somewhere something had worked as desired.

Shattered light aircraft lay wrecked, the Cessna 172s and Piper

Cherokees, the pride and joy of the holders of PPLs the world over were smashed or burning.

"Tango callsign, Gremlin...?" the RNZAF helicopter pilot shouted. "We took ground fire from Princes Highway Bridge as we overflew it."

"Tango Four Three Alpha, nervous Foxhounds or enemy forces, over?"

"Gremlin, not known, and we will egress southeast to avoid."

The troop of Leopards and ASLAVs were drawn up in a hurried all-round-defence and the casualties were being carried by their mates when the distinctive heavy *'thwopp, thwopp'* of the Huey's wide blades drew close. It swung in from the river, which it had followed from its own holding area.

The PNG equipped door gunners leaned out, not trusting mere 'grunts' with the safety of their aircraft as they looked for telegraph poles, cables and other obstructions.

The machine settled on the highway without shutting down and the door gunners waved over the casualties. The wounded were loaded up, including the two who had died on the short journey between the beach and the Huey.

Once full, the aircraft immediately took to the air again, heading across the river as there was little chance the sentries air recognition skills had improved in the last few minutes, if indeed so called 'friendly fire' by nervous sentries was the case, and not the enemy, Gary thought.

He was in the hatch of the Charlie tank with the GPMG on its pintle mounting, ready to provide covering fire, and as the infantrymen of the two platoons remounted he was shocked to see how few remained. Half their number was missing. He looked back towards the beach, where the bombardment was now tailing off. He realised that less than half an hour had passed since the order had been received to move into that position. Only their own infantry's dead were occupying it now.

The Alpha tank moved off, taking them along the road beside the Moruya River to where the infantry's Unimogs were harboured up and they again took up all-round-defence as they debussed and remounted the Unimogs.

The depth platoon arrived, carrying the extra burden of the 81mm mortars and news of what they had found at the CP location. The mortar crews were dead, grenaded in their holes, as too had been those in the CP and its defence trenches on either side.

The enemy, probably special forces, had no doubt been disconcerted to find the troops Leopards with the CP but once C Troop had moved out the enemy had moved in. It was an unsettling feeling to know the killers had been so close.

The ASLAVs led the way now, taking them to an RV to reorganise with whatever remained of the battle group.

After a few hundred yards they came to the small North Head Drive Bridge which was wired for demolition and guarded by a section of sappers. The combat engineers were all dead and their bodies dumped in the water. The wiring from the demolition charges had been cut and the cables removed. Also missing was the engineers Unimog. The 105mm Howitzer battery lay beyond the bridge but it had been destroyed by naval gunfire before firing a shot.

Gunfire from further upriver turned out to be their own tanks of A Troop, less Four One Bravo, and the depth platoon of A Company 1st/19th Royal New South Wales Regiment. They had caught the special forces in the process of doing to the Princes Highway Bridge what they had already accomplished at the North Head Drive Bridge.

An ASLAV reconnaissance vehicle was burning on the southern bridge approach, having been destroyed by a shoulder launched weapon.

The sound of the gunfire being exchanged between the Australians and the Chinese masked the sound of their own approach, taking the Chinese troopers by surprise. Two escaped by diving from the bridge and into the Moruya River but the remaining six fell to the Leopards coaxial and pintle mounted machine guns.

The senior surviving infantry officer and the troop commander dismounted to inspect the demolition charges as A Troop and the surviving A Company men crossed the river. A Chinese trooper hung suspended beneath the bridge by a safety harness. He looked to be dead but neither man was feeling particularly charitable or particularly willing to approach in case he was only playing dead. These men had caused a level of death and disruption seemingly out of proportion to their small numbers. Mr Edwards gave the signal to his loader, who was now manning the Alpha tanks pintle mount and the trooper received a short burst.

"If he wasn't dead before, he is now."

Approximately a quarter of the charges had been removed and all the wires cut, however the cables had not been removed as they had been at the previous bridge and stripping insulation in order to reconnect the wires by twisting them together did the trick for a forty metre section of bridge. Not enough to permanently deny them the use of the bridge but enough to require the service of a bridging unit.

"Sir!"

The infantrymen had searched the dead and come up trumps with a map.

Very disquietingly, all of their positions were marked upon the Chinese map, but so too was a chinagraph circle, the significance of which was immediately apparent.

"Sneaky buggers... but why didn't we think of that, too?"

The Chinese planners had spotted the flaw in the Australian defences centred on the few roads through the forests.

Two things linked all the communities in New South Wales, no matter how far from the coast or how high up a mountain, the all-weather tarmac roads, and power lines. 125m wide swathes had been cut through the forests to accommodate the tall steel pylons. Like Roman roads they tended to take the shortest route between two points and the inclines these pylons marched up could be pretty fierce, but it had not rained for some time, the ground was baked hard in the sun and the hills were negotiable by the Chinese Type 98 and 96 as well as the older Type 88 MBTs. The circled area was on one such cleared avenue that led all the along the coast to the Kings Highway, the Canberra road, behind Bateman's Bay where the bulk of the brigade was.

They remounted without further delay and headed north, the small force of five Leopard 1 MBTs, two ASLAV recce vehicles and three platoons of infantry. Mr Edwards reported his findings and a suggestion that was accepted after just a few minutes.

Bateman's Bay was under heavy bombardment, the supposed precursor to an attempted landing upon Long Beach on the north of the bay and Corrigan's Beach opposite it on the south side. But Bateman's Bay was now just a diversion apparently, much to the chagrin of the commander of the Australian 1st Brigade. It is one thing to be outnumbered and out fought, but it is another thing entirely to be outsmarted by an enemy, especially when you have the home advantage.

Port Kembla was receiving comparatively light bombardment around the port area when compared to the weight of fire on the town itself, and the beaches of course.

D Company of 1st/19th Royal New South Wales Regiment joined them with forty men and its mortar section but in all, half a squadron of Leopard 1 MBTs, two thirds of an infantry battalion and a battery of 105 Howitzers had been lost. The enemy were ashore and moving for their next objective.

At Moruya they had accounted for more of the enemy than they had lost themselves but the figures did not add up. Australia's armed forces had been run down until they were only capable of short term international interventions.

The Tasman Sea.
0425hrs.

The invasion fleet had split into two divisions and turned east, in towards land once night had fallen. The Australian and allied navies and air force had launched a major strike at the northern group containing the carriers. HMAS *Sydney* and HMAS *Darwin* had been sunk, along with RSS *Vengeance,* ROCS *Tzu I* and the USS *Stethem*. Nine other allied surface warships were damaged, three seriously, in the Battle of the Tasman Sea, with the newly recommissioned *Spruance* class destroyer USS *Conolly* being beached at Cape Howe.

The sheer weight of surface to surface anti-ship missiles and laser guided naval gunfire had overwhelmed the far smaller allied force.

In the invasion fleets core only the aviation support vessel *G'doa* had been destroyed, hit twice by air launched AGM-84 Harpoon missiles intended for the carrier *Mao*. Two LSTs had been damaged, one seriously. The Russian assault ship *Lubyanka* had been hit by one of USS *Stethem's* BGM-109 Tomahawks but the missile had passed through the hangar without detonating. Four of the outer screen had been lost and a further four damaged.

In the air battle, eleven of the *Mao's* air wing and twelve of *Admiral Kuznetsov's* had been lost in the air battle but replacements stationed at the former Benito Ebuen Air Base on the Philippine island of Mactan were already enroute.

The Pearce Wing had sortied out of RAAF Williamtown and three small provincial airports north of Newcastle, NSW, in a coordinated attack upon the invasion fleet. Their wing attacked from the south and the combined RAAF Williamstown, Amberley and Richmond squadrons came in from the north.

The theory had been to divide the enemy air defences, drawing off the carrier wings so they could not interfere with the naval engagement, and penetrate the warship screen to get at the carriers, troop transports and LSTs from the seaward side. The unfortunate matter of the enemy having more than enough surface to air ordnance to go around meant that only the second aim met with any real success.

The carrier aircraft waited for the air defence warships to put the allied aircraft in a defensive stance before attacking, but superior training and experience won over. Most of the allied losses in the air came as the air battle drifted into the engagement range of no fewer than seven enemy warships. Despite their own aircraft being endangered someone had ordered the warships to resume launching air defence missiles, and two enemy aircrew had died at the hands of their comrades, but twelve allied aircraft were destroyed also. The aircraft from RAAF Pearce no longer qualified numerically for the term 'Wing'.

"Are you okay back there, Candy?"

They had lost a further aircraft from the flight, so the odds were not in their favour with regard to surviving a further two missions.

"That was pretty scary, like a hundred times more than the last time." her RIO replied, but she had done a damn good job in Nikki's opinion.

They had battle damage; a bite had been taken out of their port vertical stabiliser by debris. Lt Cmdr. Pelham's ninth victim had almost taken the Tomcat with it when a burst from the Vulcan cannon had exploded the SU-27 that had itself destroyed *Smackdown* Zero Three. With depleted defence stores and multiple surface to air missiles tracking them they had disengaged and evaded. Once well clear, 01 and 04 used landing lights to look each other over for any other damage. 04 was okay visually but 01 also had damage from cannon fire in the trailing edge of the starboard wing.

Smackdown flight were supposed to land at Illawarra Regional Airport to refuel and rearm but the area was under attack so *Magpie* gave them a steer to HMAS Albatross, nine miles inland, south of the town of Nowra.

After thirty minutes a contact appeared on radar at their three o-clock and *Magpie* identified the aircraft as *Belly Dancer* Zero One, now the last of the famed Australian F-111C 'Pigs', and it was not only damaged but it had declared wounded on board.

Belly Dancer Zero Two was gone, and that aircraft had last been seen heading toward the carriers and their screen at wavetop height. Zero One had attacked the *Mao* at the same time but her Harpoons had either been destroyed by flank defences or had struck the Chinese carriers auxiliary, the *G'doa*. There had been no transmissions, no warning, and no clue as to the second F-111C's fate. Whatever had happened, it had been sudden.

Nikki called up the F-111C, with a knot of dread in her stomach. Despite her best intentions she had developed feelings for the Australian pilot. The Pearce Wing aircrews, particularly the former Nimitz aviators and the crews of the two F-111Cs socialised together, but Nikki stuck to soft drinks, not trusting herself around him if the tequila was flowing. Lt (jg) LaRue, on the other hand had no such inhibitions where the opposite sex was concerned, especially as she had decided that any day could well be her last. The crew of 'Belly Dancer Zero Two' Pilot Officer Jack Smith and Flight Lieutenant Russell Doe had both pursued young Candice.

"*Belly Dancer* this is *Smackdown*, how is it going over there?"

"*G'mornin…it's been better.*" The Mick Dundee persona without any attempt at VP was not a good sign. They were in trouble.

"*Smackdown* is joining from your nine o-clock."

"*Rog'*"

"Put some light on the subject and we'll do a visual inspection."

They closed in until the F-111C's landing lights came on.

"Jesus Christ…!" Candy uttered over the intercom. Even the landing lights were intermittently flickering on and off due to the damage. The electronics were shorting out somewhere in the battered and holed airframe.

The F-111C was in bad shape with numerous hits by cannon fire, and it was flying on just the port engine, and that engine was trailing smoke. A vapour trail was also evident in the lights. The aircraft was losing fuel and height, and from the handling of the aircraft the avionics were damaged, the pilot wounded, or both.

"How are you and Macca doing?"

"Macca is drifting in and out. Its blood loss and shock but I've managed to trick his G-suit, so that should help." The main purpose of aircrew G-suits is to squeeze the legs tightly via inflatable air bladders during high speed manoeuvres. Gravitational forces will force blood down to the wearer's feet otherwise, therefore the suits help keep a supply of blood to the brain and prevent blackouts. By inflating the suit's legs for wounded crew, it keeps blood near the core organs where it is needed and not in the legs where it is not as vital to survival.

In order to check the starboard side Nikki passed over and ahead so as not to risk igniting the leaking fuel. There had been a fire in the damaged starboard engine and part of the fuselage was missing, exposing the shutdown Pratt & Whitney turbofan. From experience, Nikki guessed that the fuel leak was as result of a second attack; otherwise the aircraft would be in charred little pieces at the bottom of the sea.

"'*Dancer*, we won't cross your six as you are losing fuel and it appears to be coming from your starboard side..." she went on to catalogue all the damage she could see.

"Thirty four miles to Albatross, *Dancer*, at your current rate of decent you'll be about in the weeds by then. I recommend you eject the capsule once we are feet-dry."

"Negative on that as Macca needs medical assistance, and there is an intermittent red light on the ejection system." The F-111 cockpit was in effect a survival capsule that in theory would parachute the crew down safely and remain sealed for water landings. Before she could respond, the AWAC cut in.

"*Belly Dancer, Magpie Zero Two?*"

"*Go, Magpie.*"

"*Albatross is closed due to damaged aircraft and trapped crew on both runways, copy?*" Had the aircrew not still been in the aircraft in question, the wrecks would have been bulldozed clear to re-open the runways.

"*Dancer, copies.*"

"*Jervis Bay is your only alternative, and it is a designated emergency field with arrester gear on 'Two Six'. I recommend a straight in approach from the east.*" The controller aboard the AWAC continued. "*They are alerted and setting up for you.*"

It was further to fly but there was nothing more to say, and they carried out a course correction that put the civilian aerodrome on the nose at twenty miles out.

"*The good news is that Jervis Bay's got a bar in its flying club and its open all hours, unofficially of course.*" The controller added. "*I hope you can have a drink on me, Dancer.*"

Despite his best efforts, Gerry couldn't maintain height and they were at just five hundred feet now. They had to cross the high cliffs of Cape St George and then the nature reserve's woodland which extended to within a half mile of the threshold.

Nikki directed 04 away to recover at Canberra whilst she and Candy remained in company with the crippled aircraft.

Gerry contacted the aerodromes tower but kept the gear up, even when the breakers at the cliffs base came into view out of the darkness.

Nikki kept the Tomcat on his wing even though the treetops seemed close enough to touch. The F-14 was nose high, its variable geometry wings fully forward at 20° and flaps at 35° to keep pace with the Australian aircraft.

Jervis Bay aerodrome was barely discernable ahead of them. The flare path was lit but at low power, giving the minimum assistance required for the pilot to land. An ambulance and fire truck's stood ready; although no emergency lights flashed they sat with engines idling and only the vehicle sidelights on.

The aircraft cleared the trees a half mile from the perimeter where the land gave way to low gorse and scrub. There was now nothing between them and the tarmac except a ragged hedge running across the end of the aerodrome. Gerry dropped the gear, struggling to keep a stall at bay and the wings level.

Nikki applied power, drawing away as the F-111C crossed the threshold.

Candy was twisted around and peering back, she saw the aircraft bounce before racing along the tarmac for a few yards, and then the gear collapsed. Australia's last F-111C slammed onto runway, skidding along on its belly and raising sparks that ignited the leaking fuel.

"NO!"

The cry came not from Candy but from Nikki when the night cloaked aerodrome and surrounding area were suddenly revealed to her as 'Belly Dancer 01's' fuel tanks behind the crew capsule exploded, and the stricken aircraft disintegrated in a ball of fire on the runway.

The Tomcat banked left with its pilot informing the tower she was entering the pattern for Three Three, the second runway. Lt (jg) LaRue half expected them to be diverted to Canberra but they got their clearance.

Barely had the aircraft rolled to a halt and shut down when Nikki left the aircraft without assistance, removing her helmet and unbuckling, dropping to the ground and sprinting away towards the crash site.

The aircraft had been completely destroyed, the scattered wreckage burning furiously. Beyond the crash, in the light of the flames, she saw a stretcher being hurriedly loaded aboard the ambulance and she shouted for it to wait but it drove away rapidly, leaving her beside the runway, panting for breath. Helplessly she watched it depart and then turned back to the burning wreckage, the firelight revealing to her for the first time the collapsed parachutes and ejection capsule sat on the grass on the far side of the tarmac with Flt Lt Gerry Rich beside it being examined by a medic.

She forced herself to walk across to him.

"That was quite a run." he said. "And anyone but me might think you cared."

Nikki did not respond to the remark but instead looked towards the flying club, just barely visible beside the hangars.

"Did someone say something about there being a bar here?" she nodded apologetically to the medic because he had not finished and she was just getting started.

"Are all his bits and pieces still intact? I know he doesn't have much use for his head but it's not going to fall off and roll away somewhere is it?"

"No Ma'am, but the aches and pains of ejection will start to tell in the next few hours."

"Thank you."

Taking Flt Lt Rich by the arm fairly forcefully she marched across the field to the clubhouse where sure enough there were a bunch rubbernecking regulars at the doorway, drinks in hand watching the action on the runway.

"Gangway...make a hole...officer coming through." Nikki arrived at the bar with a hundred dollar note.

"Four fingers of Tequila, twice, and ten dollars in change...and where is the Ladies Room?"

As the drinks were poured Gerry watched in a kind of bemused wonder as the American aviator palmed the change and disappeared briefly into the women's washroom before reappearing, muttering about Aussies not knowing what century this was.

Nikki's next stop, the men's room, was marked by a hurried exit by a regular, still doing his pants up. When she reappeared Gerry was still stood staring in wonder.

In one go, Nikki downed the glass of spirits and glared accusingly at Gerry until he did the same.

"Now, come with me."

He did not really have an option as she again proceeded with purpose, holding onto his arm and led him out of the club house and around the back of the hangar. Once there she pressed something into the palm of his hand.

"There was only one left, so make it count." She began to hurriedly unzip her G-suit as she leant against the hangar wall.

There was enough light left from the fire for him to see the print on the packaging beneath the cellophane.

'Ribbed for her pleasure.'

It only took a moment to sink in before Gerry Rich was also hurriedly unzipping.

Port Kembla.
Dawn.

With the air and naval attacks defeated the invasion fleet divided, the southern group splitting to sail directly to Bateman's Bay and Moruya. The bombarding of the beaches and defences went on in earnest before the landings began at Moruya. The general opinion was that the Moruya landings were a diversion, and one easily contained on the two highways that cut through the forest and hills between Bateman's Bay and the beaches at Moruya.

At Port Kembla though it was a major effort to seize the port and the town, and the defences were being pounded by rocket and naval gunfire.

Heck and the small combat team had left the harbour area below the escarpment once the invasions fleet's course change and formation had been detected. This had been expected for several days, and the only mystery was why it had taken the Sino-Russian fleet so long to act. The Challengers and Warriors then occupied the positions they had prepared at the rear of 902nd Infantry, and waited.

Despite the Allied victory in Europe, the defenders in Australia were not that much better off. The NATO forces in Europe had suffered near defeat and a frightful attrition, but there were two British, two French and one German Brigade afloat and an airlift was bringing infantry in the light role to Australia's shores. However, no combat aircraft had arrived from either the USA or Europe and the media in Australia had just begun to ask why.

Fortunately, for the moment, the enemy air forces were absent, but from the combat teams location they could see the 902nd receiving a hellish bombardment.

Heck would not have occupied those forward positions until landing craft were sighted, had he been the American CO of course. There was plenty of other better cover, and close enough to the beach for rapid movement between the two.

Heck had listened incredulously on the battalion net as the 902's CO reacted to the losses of two of his company CPs, by ordering Captain Briant Foulness to bring his Black Horse Cavalry M1A1's into the forward fighting positions to *"Take the heat off the naval bombardment"*. Two hours later and the PLAN were moving ashore in the face of uncoordinated and greatly weakened defending forces.

Lack of a flexible plan and fall-back options had resulted in crippling losses, during which the CO had suddenly become unresponsive. A fighting withdrawal had begun, and with no orders from Lt Col Taylor all morning Heck had coordinated with Briant, covering the Americans with the Challengers extra-long reaching L30A1 120mm rifled gun.

Six of the Abrams MBTs were still serviceable, one had been destroyed by a direct hit from a naval shell, and two had been recovered under fire by the tank company's own M88A2 Hercules and Sgt Rebecca Hemmings CRARRV, towing the vehicles to the rear. A further Abrams was seriously damaged by a hit to the engine deck that immobilised the tank, although the crew fought on until ordered to abandon the vehicle and destroy it.

Heck peered through the sights at the top of the grassy bank before Minnamurra beach where it bordered Kilalea State Park. A Chinese Type 63 amphibious tank had been sat there burning until a few minutes before, blocking the exit off the beach at that point. Heck's tank had killed it with a HESH round, its armour too thin to require a sabot round. The hatches had blown off and the Warrior fighting vehicles had killed or wounded the crew as they had bailed out, the Rarden cannons accounting for them all. That had been their first round fired in anger during this war, although the crew had all seen service during the invasion of Iraq and its aftermath.

Minnamurra Beach was hedged in by water as it was a long tapering tail with the Minnamurra River at its rear. The far bank of the river was lined by a sea wall for much of its length. The quickest way inland was via Kilalea, into the right flank of the 902nd Infantry Regiment, but the Royal Tank Regiment Challengers 2s were covering the 902's withdrawal with highly accurate long distance fire. After the first amphibious tank had been knocked out a second had tried to bulldoze it out of the way, exposing its thin belly armour as it rose up out of the dead ground beyond the bank. That effort had seen a predictable ending, a HESH hit on the belly had set off the onboard munitions and it had blown up, the turret flying off as if it were made of cardboard, not steel. The enemy's next attempt to clear the exit had been to attach tow cable and drag the hulks away one at a time. As Heck watched there was a rush of infantry up over the bank and towards the tanks firing position. The Royal Green Jacket's snipers killed the leaders and the Warriors engaged the remainder with their 30mm cannons.

"Sunray Tango One One, this is Yankee Four Six...everyone that could get off the headland and Shellharbour beach have done so."

"Sunray Tango One One roger, roger out to you...hello Sunray India Three One, move now over!"

The Royal Green Jackets reversed out of their positions, heading away to join the Bradleys, SPs, M125s and a clutch of support vehicles that had been to the rear.

The Black Horse tank company had covered the left flank as the two infantry companies withdrew off the Bass Point headland in their Bradley fighting vehicles, those that were still able of course. More of the Bradley's fighting positions contained burning vehicles than those that did not. The enemy had walked their gunfire back and forth over the headland for over an hour before beginning their landings. There was a lot to be said for playing the shell game as a defender, by preparing several sets of alternative fighting positions including dummy ones, but Lt Colonel Taylor had at best used one cup instead of three, and a glass bottom one at that.

The Abrams, Challengers, Warriors and eleven Bradley AFVs, six M125 and the 902's battery of 155mm SP Paladin guns seemed to be the only survivors, but there had to be others, surely?

The Type 98 that next roared up the exit ramp had been delivered to the beach by landing craft. It was a main battle tank with ERA plates like scaly armour covering it but it fared no better. Tango One One Charlie and Delta had been waiting patiently with sabots loaded and fingers on the trigger for anything heavier than a Type 63 to stick its head over the parapet. Both Challengers fired in the same instant and the Chinese stopped dead in its tracks at the top of the ramp and began to burn, no one got out.

The Challenger troop withdrew in pairs, covering one another and joined up with a waiting platoon of M1A1s.

They were hard pressed by Type 63 light tanks that had come ashore nearer Shellharbour where the beach had been defended by only the dead. Although the Chinese tanks 85mm guns lacked the single shot kill ability when engaging the American and British tanks, the same was not true for the guns effect on IFVs such as Warriors and Bradleys. The seven MBT's fought as a rearguard in terrain that for now did not favour their main tank guns greater killing range.

They fell back from Kilalea into the affluent suburb of Shell Cove. The residents had departed but their homes lay in ruins, shattered by rocket artillery and naval gunfire, whole streets were ablaze.

The tanks leapfrogged back, using fire and manoeuvre to cover each other and the lighter armed IFV's as they withdrew to the combat team's next position.

Thick smoke from the burning residences meant that the thermal sights had to be engaged, but that did not prevent the Challenger from colliding with a parked car. Abandoned by their owners in favour of something more practical, the his and hers vanity rides, a yellow Porsche 911 for her and a silver one for him were parked bumper to bumper in the street where they had been damaged by shrapnel, and the paintwork was blistered in places. An expensive repair job, but doable. Tango One One's left rear track raised only a little as it met the front end of the silver sports car. First one and then the other were crushed beneath the left hand track of the reversing MBT. About the only thing salvageable were the car alarms that continued an almost outraged blaring as the armour disappeared into the smoke.

"This is Yankee Four Six, step on it guys, the streets either side of you have armor trying to get ahead of you and take you from the rear!" Braint Foulness had been re-joining with the remaining forces with the majority of his company. They now stopped as the flanking movement became apparent in their thermal sights.

"Tango One One, not being an old Etonian I can't say that sounds pleasant."

The Abrams destroyed the lead tanks in either street, forcing the Chinese armour to use the wrecks as cover, or to attempt to cut between streets over the gardens where at least one found a swimming pool made an effective tank trap.

A HESH round struck Heck's Challenger a sold blow, blistering the armour plate and thoroughly rattling the crew about but it was an ineffective hit, and a lucky one at that as the Type 63 had no thermal or even night sights. Tango One One fired on the move, destroying the light tank

The end of the residential block fell away downhill to where a man-made obstacle in the shape of the Shellharbour Road cut through the side of the hill. The cutting on the uphill side varied between fourteen and ten feet down onto the dual carriageway, and the JCBs had dug a ramp, albeit a steep one, wide enough for a single Challenger to negotiate should they require it. The once neat lawn between two houses on James Cook Parkway had already been chewed up by IFVs, and the tanks completed its ruination as in single file they followed the fighting vehicles to negotiate the hillside and ramp.

Heck's troop crossed the carriageways but did not immediately continue downhill. They used the incline as a hull-down firing position and waited for the Type 63s to discover the tracks over the lawn and follow them. Quite sensibly a light tank took an over-watch position as the first troop of the light amphibious tanks descended, once the leading vehicle was on the ramp the four Challengers fired almost as one, destroying the covering Type 63 and leaving the ramp and its approach blocked for the time being.

They had bought a little time, or so they thought, and used it to best effect by catching up with the infantry fighting vehicles which were now in company with the SPs and support vehicles.

The night was ending with the dawn of what would otherwise have been a glorious day weather-wise. A suited and helmeted but unmasked Sergeant Rebecca Hemmingway stood in the commander's hatch. She held the pistol grip of the GPMG on a swivel mounting beside the hatch. Aside from the crews own personal weapons this was the vehicles only means of protection. The CRARRV's Perkins engine drowned out all but the explosions back in the town they had recently left. Now they were heading for the Macquarie Pass, a twisting and winding Illawarra Highway would take them there, to where her LAD's 4-Tonner was already setting up a field workshop.

A flash of light caught her eye, the low morning sun reflecting off something ahead of them on the road. Raising her binoculars she saw several vehicles coming down the highway from the top of the escarpment but the trees made identification difficult. If they did not have a 60 ton Abrams in tow the business of getting off the road and into cover would have been easier but the CRARRV and the Hercules with their tows crunched through a wooden fence and into a stand of trees just large enough to accommodate them all. Far from invisible they were at least difficult to spot until closer to. They shut down and waited, calling up the command tank and Tony McMarn's Warrior with a sitrep.

This was cattle country, dairy cows in the main, and the wide ranging fields lay on rolling countryside with rises and dips, speckled with clumps of trees. To the west the farming land ended with a forest that stretched to the foot of the escarpment and lined the sides of the pass.

Rebecca had her headset on as she was speaking with Heck, and she had the binoculars to her eyes, stood up on top of the CRARRV in order to observe the road in the direction of the vehicles she had seen. It was the driver of the Hercules who heard the sound of helicopter rotors, several of them, but whoever they were they were using the folds in the ground and the trees as cover.

Their own air assets numbered just two Blackhawk aerial command posts, all the rest of the division's aircraft having been destroyed on the ground at the makeshift heliport on Tunks Park in Sydney. They were therefore unlikely to be friendly.

Rebecca saw movement, just for a brief instant, in the field to the left of the road. Two helmeted soldiers running towards the highway, all that had been visible of them as they were now in dead ground behind a fold. So brief had been the sighting she could not identify whether they were friend or foe.

After a minute at the most, two US Humvees appeared on the road but before the watchers could react an ambush was sprung with RPG-26s and automatic weapons.

"Hello Sunray India Three One, this is Eight Eight, contact, at grid 5673 2558, on the south side of the Illawarra Highway, two friendly vehicles bumped by enemy infantry with light anti-tank weapons, numbers not known, over?"

"Sunray India Three One, we are still thirty minutes...." Whatever Lt McMarn was about to say was lost in complete silence. Rebecca changed frequencies several times before removing the antennae. Only with the aerial removed did the distinctive 'Hash' sound resume. They were being subject to 'silent jamming' and the radios were now of no use whatsoever until a runner arrived with a new DFC RANTS, (Diagram (of the radio net), Frequencies, Collective

calls, Radiation, Address groups, Nicknames, Timings and Security.) that incorporated fresh channels to work on.

The firing paused, announcing that the ambush was over; both Humvees had been hit and stopped, and when the gunfire resumed it was with single shots as the coup de grace was administered to the occupants.

This was not some random vehicle ambush, she realised, but the securing of a landing zone. The Illawarra Highway between Australia's capital and the New South Wales coast had been cut, boxing in the defending forces to prevent their escape. This was probably just the 'point' she had witnessed at work, and other loads would be on the way. This seemed to be born out as she heard the sound of more helicopters approaching.

They flew in assault formation, a dozen Z-8s, the copied Aérospatiale SA 321 Super Frelon, with a pair of Harbin Z-9s riding shotgun until nearing the LZ where the Z-8 troop carriers moved into two columns of six. They lost altitude rapidly, descending toward a large field that was now secured by a platoon of marines. Four more loads awaited the medium lift helicopters, a battalion sized cork to bottle up the retreating US forces before they could reach another defence line.

Rebecca felt completely helpless, unable to influence events at all as the cut-off force approached.

The Harbin Z-9s reacted first as their electronic warfare suites warned that they had been locked up and the smoke trails rose rapidly from the forest.

One gunship and four of the troop carriers fell to the eight stingers that had been launched, and although the second gunship had avoided the Stinger aimed its way by radical manoeuvring whilst dispensing flares, it turned toward the forest and received surprisingly accurate small arms fire that although harmless to the crew or the aircraft's vital parts, armoured as they were, it was nonetheless disconcerting.

Eight more Stingers were launched by expert operators who had all reloaded in record time. The last Z-9 was struck by four of the missiles and three more of the larger Z-8s were destroyed in flight. The remainder broke off the assault landings, diving away and seeking distance and cover as they departed the area.

Dairy cattle scattered in distress as burning helicopters fell in fields and woods to the south of the highway. A sound akin to scattered fire-fights began as the small-arms ammunition, grenades, anti-vehicle bar mines, light anti-tank and surface-to-air missiles cooked off in the different fires. Every man had carried backbreaking loads in order to spring an effective trap on the US units in Port Kembla. A good plan and one that would have worked if properly supported with naval gunfire and close air support, but at the end of the day even a force the size of the Sino-Russian fleet has finite resources and a limit on the number of simultaneous operations it can effectively support.

The land war that had raged for months in Europe and South East Asia was less than twelve hours old on the coastal plain of New South Wales, and yet some thirty members of China's 1st Marine Division who were securing the LZ, combat veterans all, and fresh from the jungle fighting in the Philippines, were expertly and confidently engaged by a company of infantry emerging from the forest who moved like it was their bread and butter. The sound of small arms fire and detonating grenades was out of sync with her view of the action through her binoculars, caused by the time delay involved in the sound of the company attack reaching her position. It was a continuous movement, fire was poured on whilst troops moved, sometimes under cover of smoke, moving quickly but with an economy of effort that exposed themselves to incoming fire for bare seconds, and then they were laying down fire whilst others moved.

One by one the marines positions were taken until a group of less than a dozen banded together, lying behind a fold of ground at one corner of the landing zone.

Smoke from a crashed and burning Harbin Z-9 helicopter gunship wafted across the surviving marine's position at the fickle whim of the breeze. Their radio operator was dead, one of the first to fall under the gun of a sniper pair attached to these newcomers, but they must have felt some degree of hope when the flowing fire and manoeuvre from the attackers from the forest ceased. The infantry company were seemingly reluctant to close with them, but the weight of fire levied against the marines increased as if they were compensating for this reluctance to engage at close quarters.

Flung objects appeared in the air from the proximity of the crashed helicopter on the flank of the Chinese marines, thrown long and hard but with an accuracy born of practice, and after the grenades detonated their throwers appeared from out of the smoke in a rush, taking the survivors at the point of sharpened steel. Their faint war cries carried to her, arriving only after the bayonet work was done.

The sound of battle from the edge of the forest ended but to her alarm she found that four of the Chinese marines had escaped notice elsewhere on the landing ground and were heading her way, appearing out of a thick clump of uncleared bush, the biddy bushes and mimosa left by a farmer as cover from the elements for his cattle. They were employing fire and manoeuvre as they fell back towards the coast and unless they changed direction they would soon see the armoured recovery vehicles in the stand of trees beside the road. She gestured to the commander of the M88A2 Hercules to take the left hand pair with their 50 calibre and she disengaged the safety on the GPMG, pointing a weapon at flesh and blood for the first time in her life instead of paper Figure 11 targets. Rebecca had never been able to fathom how some people were so quickly able to forgive the killers of their loved ones, and as she certainly had no such merciful urge or inhibition she closed one eye and took up the first pressure on the trigger. The American tanker had never been more than a friend, even though he may have wished otherwise, but she killed the first marine in the name of her dead husband and the second one for Bart Kopak.

Hardly had the last spent case and metal link bounced off the CRARRV's glacis with a metallic ring when she heard a whistle off to her right. She had not even seen the flanking movement until she was whistled at to gain her attention, and then hailed from cover, very close-in by an infantryman wearing a US issue paratroopers helmet and Yank jump boots. He was wearing DPM and holding an SLR, not an SA80, and when he spoke he was unmistakeably British. She wasn't aware of any other British army units in Australia but he was definitely not one of Tony McMarn's Green Jackets from the Home Counties.

"Howay darlin'...gan canny wi yer gimpy, bonnie lass!" she had indeed been careful with the GPMG, applying the safety catch and identifying herself and the American heavy recovery crew.

Another figure appeared from the far side of the road, rather more conservatively dressed and with the blue-red-blue divisional flash of the Guards Division on the arm of his combat smock.

"Stott, what have you got here?" he asked after dashing across the road and rolling into cover on reaching the other side.

"A good looking lumpy jumper of a rough engineer, sir."

As mixed metaphors went, she had been called worse in her time.

The top of the pass was a hive of activity as Heck's Challenger reached level ground again. The newcomers were the 1st Guards Infantry Brigade and had arrived on the sub-continent only a few hours before. They had no maps to speak of, only basic equipment in general, but they had picks, shovels and a wealth of combat experience so they chose their ground and had already begun to dig in and to build stone sangers. Communications was currently being carried the old fashioned way, by runner, given that the limited numbers of radios available were still subject to local jamming. However the Signals Platoons were all laying D10 field telephone lines and stringing them between trees. A discomforting task employing the groin strain inducing climbing spikes, with their horizontal teeth strapped to the inside of the wearers boot soles.

No sooner had his tanks gained the top of the pass when a runner sought him out, and he, Briant Foulness and Tony McMarn were guided to a hurriedly put together O Group. Having introduced themselves they sat back and listened to the Coldstream Guards battalion CO begin with a brief, concise and no frills introduction

The brigade command element had been in the two 5th Mech Humvees that had been ambushed, Brigadier General John Salisbury-Jones was dead along with the rest of his staff and so as the senior battalion commander, Pat Reed was assuming acting command of the brigade.

"One thing we are short on is about everything we realistically need to fight a battle, but we are the British Army so we are used to that."

Elements of 902nd Infantry Regiment and the 11th Armored Regiment, two platoons in Bradleys, a platoon of Abrams and a pair of M125s had also made it out. They had 'gone firm' at the top of the other road up the escarpment, the Jamberoo Mountain Road, eight miles to the south and the Irish Guards were already enroute to join them under the command of their 2 i/c until their CO could rejoin them after the O Group.

"I can tell you what I know from before comms' were disrupted by jamming, and that is that the US 5th Mechanised Division and the Australian Army units in New South Wales are falling back from the coast. We, as allies, are hugely outnumbered and defending this coastline would basically require twelve divisions, not two. Giving ground and using the escarpment and mountains as a natural defensive barrier, is the only sensible move."

The senior surviving officer from the 902nd arrived, looking ashen. Unless other members of the regiment had made it out then a full three quarters of the unit were now dead, wounded or prisoners of the People's Republic of China.

"Lieutenant?" Pat said to the American.

"Sir?"

"My last battalion was pretty much shot to pieces in its first action of the war, too." he said kindly. "With the help of some bloody good soldiers from across the Atlantic we were back in the fight with a vengeance, so the very least I can do is return the favour, young man."

Pat placed the lieutenant's 902nd element with the Welsh Guards in-depth to give them a chance to reorganise, and then he brought the O Group to an end.

"Gents, about now the Chinese are securing the port in readiness for bringing all their forces ashore, which will take time. But I am guessing that in just an hour or so they will come at us with what they already have in order to catch us still off balance, so get off back to your men and prepare for a ruck."

Half a mile west of Mogo, NSW.
0800hrs.

Tango Four Three Alpha was burning. It had been struck in the rear by multiple RPG-26 rockets and disabled, the heavy engine covers blown off as if they weighed nothing at all. The crew were able to bail out and take cover but the driver had gone in the opposite direction to the remainder, and had then been shot in the legs and captured.

The remaining Leopards were upslope, further along the trail towards the rear of Bateman's Bay, but unable to assist in a rescue without robust support from numerically more infantry than they had in order to clear the trees, which seemed to be infested with RPG armed Chinese. The Chinese infantry were also accompanied by at least one good sniper, and the Australian infantry were now short by an officer and two NCOs as a result. The Aussie infantry were too few in number and the small force of tanks and infantry had given ground quicker than it would have liked.

Lieutenant Edwards, his gunner and loader were four hundred metres from the rest of the unit and had a grandstand seat in their place of concealment as enemy infantrymen approached their driver. He was lying on the ground some twenty feet from the Leopard, in a lot of pain but holding his hands up in surrender. The Australian infantry and tankers could see the enemy and the driver clearly, but could not open fire without endangering him too. If the Australians expected him to be treated in accordance with the Geneva Convention they were in for a terrible surprise. Flames were licking out of the engine bay now and the wounded man was dragged by the arms over to the tank whereupon those arms were broken with rifle butts and the helpless man heaved up and tossed screaming into the flames. The Bravo and Charlie tanks opened fire with their machine guns but the enemy used the tanks bulk for cover as they slipped back into the forest.

Seven enemy tanks, IFVs and APCs had been destroyed by the Leopards as they withdrew along the power line avenue, buying time for the forces in Bateman's Bay to pull back beyond the Clyde River. Once all were across the delaying action could be curtailed with a dash for the Clyde River Bridge, which would be blown behind them. It wasn't working out that way though. The mortars had already departed, ordered back to join other sections beyond the river. It had seemed sensible at the time but that was before the two companies of enemy infantry had appeared.

Those same infantry were waiting now, the two Type 98s the Leopards had destroyed would need replacement but once the Chinese brought up more armour, the advance would continue.

"Hello Address Group Golf Echo, this is Address Group Kilo Victor, fetch your Sunray, over."

"Screw me." Che exclaimed. "There's a bleedin' Pom on the radio!"

Corporal Dopey Hemp paused, yet again, to allow the line to straighten before he continued, much to the ire of his platoon commander. Mr Pottinger managed to annoy Dopey also, by noisily moving forwards to berate the section command in a loud whisper, ordering him to speed up. Instead of which Dopey halted in cover and sank down onto one knee. Accordingly, his section, and then the platoon did the same. They were in thick woodland west of the power lines and had flanked the Chinese infantry by using a rambler's footpath. They had now left that path, turning east, and they were now advancing to contact, counter attacking the Chinese. At the first shot the mortars would lay it on, isolating the Chinese point company so that they could be destroyed by the men of the

Wessex Regiment. Getting in close, whilst still retaining command and control before the firing started, was the hard part though.

"With all due respect, sir, you made me and my section point and that's what I am doing." Dopey replied as levelly as he could. "Close quarters work in a wood is pretty much the same as close quarters work at night, which is two things I've done, and everyone in the platoon have done for real a few times, but you've only read about in manuals." He then stood, turning his back on Mr P and gestured for his section to stand and move on again.

If looks could kill, as they say...

Baz Cotter had seen the exchange and knew now that the platoon had a serious problem if the boss was allowing his personal feelings to over-ride sound judgement. The platoon commander was livid and could not see he was in the wrong. Not a good note for the platoon to start this battle on. He moved across to speak to the officer to apply some oil to the stormy waters but Mr Pottinger was having none of it. In their whispered exchange the platoon commander made it clear he wanted Corporal Hemp's stripes. In order to deny snipers a target no one openly wore rank badges anymore but Baz opened his mouth to add a voice of reason and was silenced by the officer pointing to his epaulet, yet again. Baz found that response by the boss to any issue he felt he should have the last word on to be intensely immature and irritating. It was a mannerism that had quickly been seized on by the platoon comics who would mimic 2nd Lt Pottinger whenever he was not around.

Like it or not, the CSM was going to have to speak to the OC about having a serious word with the platoon commander of 12 Platoon.

Looking at his watch Gary Burley was wondering if the English troops had got themselves lost in the woods. It had been quiet since the murder of the Alpha tanks driver, but far away along the line of power lines there were three dots that got bigger by the moment, three more of the Type 98 tanks, zig-zagging erratically as they came on, making a long range shot with the 105mm rifled guns a difficult proposition, and they did not have the ammunition to spare.

There was a single rifle shot, an old SLR if memory served, away on the right somewhere, and after a paused there was the sound of AK fire. More rifles joined in and this was followed by short bursts from GPMGs. Mortar rounds landed on the left of the cleared area and further downhill on the west side, preventing enemy troops on that side from reinforcing their comrades. By accident or design, WP rounds landed in the second belt of mortar rounds. The firing on the right had built up to a crescendo when the first of the Chinese infantry broke cover. They had been advancing all morning with their companies on either side of the trail, professional troops outnumbering the Australian's part-timers and pushing them back, ever backwards, and their confidence had grown accordingly. Now they had been flanked by a force of greater size, and a force that was not made up of reservists on their first day of war. To stand and engage them in a firefight was to court a flanking movement.. These infantry did not stop, they knew the importance of momentum in a close quarters fight and the Chinese were now on the back foot.

Driven from the trees they now came under fire from the Australian tanks and infantry up the trail, and they could not even risk a dash across the open area beneath the power lines as the forest at the other side was now a raging inferno. Those who went back the way they had come did not reappear, and those who braved the open ground received the same level of mercy as had been meted out to the Alpha tanks driver.

Lieutenant Edwards called out before standing and identifying himself to a soldier in European pattern camouflage clothing, the man was carrying an SLR with a very bloody bayonet attached to the business end. He had to shout to be heard as the flames across the way had taken hold. Lt Edwards was a native of New South Wales and no stranger to forest fires, they had to move, and fast.

Within five minutes the Wessex went from tactical mode to VBQ, run very bloody quickly mode. Issues such as a world war took second place in a forest fire if you happened to be in that particular forest at that time. The wind was blowing south easterly and the dry weather which the Chinese planners had seen as a positive factor in bypassing the roads was now working against them.

3 RGJ was digging in behind the Buckenbowra River with the River Clyde as its left flank. 1LI was on the other side of the Clyde and after the Clyde River Bridge was blown up behind them, 1 Wessex moved to the Light Infantry's left and began to dig in also. The Royal New South Wales Regiment, Light Horse and 1st Armoured Regiment needed to reorganise and they moved to begin in-depth positions behind the British units. There was initially very little to-ing and fro-ing between the depth positions and those of the British units. But that first afternoon and evening were a no-show for the Chinese who were coping badly with a major forest fire sweeping

towards units and supplies that were already ashore. As the digging was completed the work routine ended. Brews were put on and foot traffic commenced between the trenches of the Brits and Aussies. The British knew none of the tricks unique to soldiering in the field in Australia, and the Australians knew little detail of what had transpired in Germany. Bush craft and combat lore were exchanged, tips and tricks to surviving were explained, and as ever, the bullshit artists of both armies told some whoppers.

Macquarie Pass
Same time.

Pat's estimate was on the generous side as no more than ten minutes had passed before he was informed of movement down on the plain between the forest and the coast. The sides of the pass are flanking by protrusions in the escarpment walls, like great buttresses they extend toward the plain. The most obvious of these is to the north.

Pat made his way to a rock sangar O.P at its tip where Lance Sergeant Stephanski and another familiar face were located. Bill squirrelled backwards out of the sangar to make room for the CO.

"Okay, what am I looking at?"

"Either friendly forces who escaped, or captured Bradleys and assorted US vehicles, including a mobile command post, sir."

The spotting telescope was pointing a section of the North Macquarie Road some four miles distant. It was a minor road that joined the Illawarra Highway with the northern outskirts of Port Kembla. Eleven Bradley's and four M113 APCs with Humvees and canvas covered trucks were negotiating the narrow road.

Sgt Stephanski tapped Pat on the shoulder and pointed to the right slightly and there was the anticipated Chinese force advancing and using the Illawarra Highway as its axis of advance.

Trees and the rolling landscape were keeping the two forces hidden from one another but that would not be the case when the US Army vehicles reached the highway.

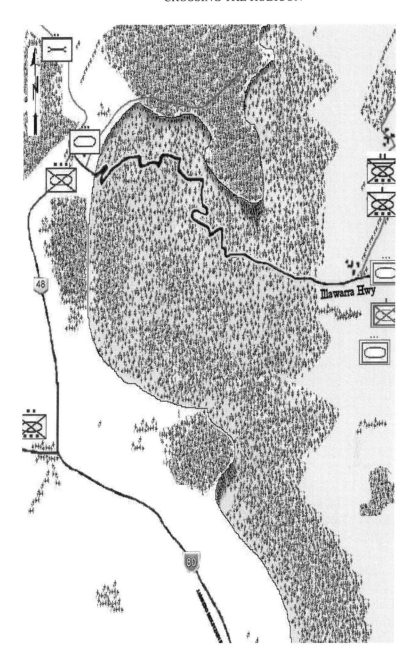

MACQUARIE PASS 2

Pat had to admit that he had not really given any thought to the possibility of captured equipment being used against them, and with no radio communications he could not ascertain if they were under new ownership.

Pat had no such quandary with the Chinese armour though and on picking up the O.Ps telephone handset he gave it to Big Stef to do the necessary via the Paladin's fire control centre. Both formations were well beyond the range of his 81mm mortars, but the 155mm battery was another thing.

Before the Paladins could open fire however, the leading Chinese tanks sighted the US Army vehicles and solved that question of ownership. They immediately opened fire.

It was fortunate that the arrival of the 155mm shells went some way towards spoiling the game for the Chinese, but they could not save the US formation from severe casualties. The boxy, high sided M577 Command vehicle was easily recognisable for what it was and targeted, it narrowly missed immediate destruction.

Three Bradleys deployed their infantry loads in an attempt to cover the withdrawal of the remainder of the convoy. With nothing to fight back with it became a dash along the highway to reach the top of the pass. The Chinese however were not going to simply permit that to happen. Harassed by the artillery they overwhelmed and destroyed the rear-guard, but lost an APC and a Type 63 tank in the process to FGM-148 Javelins.

With three burning Bradley IFVs in their wake they set off in pursuit.

The scene of the earlier ambush marked the extreme limit of the 81mm mortars range and those US vehicles which reached that point all survived to ascend to the top of the Pass. Three more Bradley's, an M125 Mortar carrier and Lt Col Taylor in his command vehicle were not amongst them.

Heck was sat on top of his Challengers turret watching the enemy armour and waiting for them to enter the engagement areas for his troop which he had worked out days before. Pat Reed, at a very brisk jog, past by and shouted to him a warning.

"I wouldn't sit there if I were you young Captain." and pointed up at the heavens as he made his way towards where the battalion CP was being dug. "For what we are about to receive, etc, etc!" he called over his shoulder.

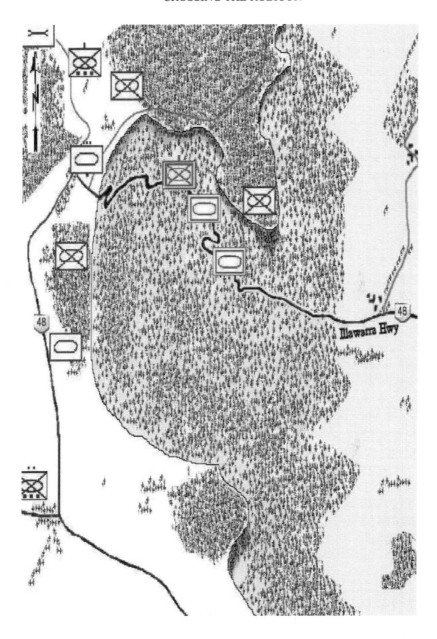

MACQUARIE PASS 3

Heck slipped inside and pulled closed the hatch. Four minutes later the first shell landed.

They did not possess anywhere near enough D10 wire to connect the Irish Guards and 902nd unit along the Jamberoo mountain road with the Macquarie Pass. As far as communications between both sites were concerned a 19th century despatch rider on a horse would have been more use than the field radios, at that point at least. The signals platoon therefore found unaffected frequencies and formulated a local DFC RANTS that got the brigade back on the air, but they still relied on the field telephone network wherever possible. Communications between 1IG and the brigade was thenceforth by radio to a vehicle at each site and these moved between transmissions. The Chinese signals intelligence section was very good at DF'ing their radio communications and their artillery cooperation was fairly impressive, making matchsticks of ten minute old transmission sites.

Artillery brought ashore by landing craft expended all of their current stock of ammunition in an attempt to provide a creeping barrage to 'shoot-in' the armoured assault as well as disrupt communications, but that single, steep and twisting, highway was their undoing. Heck had sited the firing positions well and his troop was able to destroy the slow moving vehicles at long range on that morning.

The elderly Type 63 tanks had served their purpose in making the landings a success, but their reward that of a reconnaissance by fire. The 3rd army were able to learn something of the defender's abilities and positions, but the road was littered with a battalions worth of dead vehicles and men.

Port Kembla, New South Wales.
1343hrs, Tuesday 30th October.

Shén ēn moved slowly past the breakwater and into the main harbour of the port. Smoke still rose from the ruins of the fire gutted steelworks and tank farm beyond, destroyed by the retreating Americans. The hospital ship crept forwards, staying in the channel cleared by the naval mine disposal divers. Just inside the entrance to the main harbour the mast, funnel and the top of the superstructure of the destroyer Gémìng protruded from the water. She had been the first vessel to enter and mines had blown out her bottom.

It took a further hour to safely dock and a waiting squad of marines on the quayside came aboard and took custody of the survivors of HMAS *Hooper.*

Commander Reg Hollis and Able Seamen Stephanie Priestly and Phil Daly were placed in a captured Australian Army Unimog and driven through the largely empty town until they eventually arrived at a very large barbed wire enclosure. It was pretty much like the prisoner-of-war camps they had seen in the movies, complete with watch towers. Instead of huts however, there stood row upon row of steel cargo containers. Silent, curious faces stood at the wire watching the new arrivals.

Reg Hollis did not bother to try and estimate their numbers, because there were an awful lot of them.

In a hut that served as the administration block, outside the wire, the details from their identity discs were recorded before each was photographed and fingerprinted. It was a fairly nerve wracking time but at least they had not been simply taken off the ship and executed on the dock. Stephanie was particularly nervous owing to leers and comments from their captors. Commander Hollis and AB Daly placed themselves protectively either side of her.

After an hour they were led into the camp to the first row of containers nearest the gate and shoved non-too gently inside by their escort. It was Spartan, to say the least, with a single desk and chair upon which sat a Caucasian male in Russian naval uniform. The shoulder boards looked impressive but Reg was no expert on the enemy's rank titles.

The Russian officer was busy writing in a ledger and did not immediately look up, but when he did so they looked on a face that was intelligent and wore a kindly expression.

In remarkably good English the officer explained where they were and also what their current circumstances were with regard to the Geneva Convention. He then asked them for their names, numbers and what vessel they were off.

Commander Hollis answered first.

"I am sorry sir, but we can give you only our name, rank and serial numbers. As the Camp Commandant I hope you can understand our position?"

There was a pause followed by the appearance of a slightly wry smile by the Russian.

"I am not the Camp Commandant, I am merely the senior ranking prisoner." explained Vice Admiral Karl Putchev.

Arbuckle Mountains, Oklahoma.
Tuesday 30th October, 0900hrs

The previous week had been very much one of successes followed by reversals. Having found that the NATO membership in Europe was continuing the fight under its various military leaderships it had then become apparent that the previous, democratically elected governments, had been prepared to make their excuses and depart the stage, abandoning the USA now that their borders were again safe. If the President had ever allowed himself to believe that genuine trust and friendship existed between national leaders, then this had been a rude shock. Theodore Kirkland, as it happened, was disappointed on a personal level but as a politician he had harboured no such illusions. The military men had their own code of loyalty but he was saddened and staving off the self-loathing for another time because he knew what would occur shortly after this war was eventually won. The politician's code would eventually be triumphant and bring about a return of the old status quo.

The first briefing of the day was very much Russia related.

The President was the last to arrive having learned of the death of Jacqueline Shaw and required some privacy and a telephone. Henry Shaw was at the family home with his youngest son, Ryan, who was back from Parris Island on compassionate leave. It had to be a very empty, very lonely house now with three of the Shaw family suddenly gone forever. The President had kept the telephone to his ear for fifty rings, he counted each one of them, but Henry wasn't picking up.

"My apologies for a tardy start to the day." the President said as he took his seat and produced a pair of spectacles from a case. "Bear with me please; I have been living underground so long that I've turned into a damned mole."

He knew everyone in the room except the civilian stood patiently before them, and from the notes he held in his hand the President felt safe to assume this was the criminal psychologist or behavioural whatever, who worked for Terry Jones.

"Dr Ben-got, is that how you pronounce your name?"

"Ben-go, Mr President, but I answer to any number of pronunciations when the audience is senior to me, which is often."

"My apology once more Doctor, please start in your own time."

The likeness of Premier Elena Torneski appeared on the plasma screen behind him.

The President had expected a lot of psychologist's long words and references to syndrome this, or that, with a mention of bed wetting here and there but Austin Bengot had been with the agency as a consultant for a while. He presented a report with mumbo-jumbo at a level that a non-tabloid newspaper reader could understand, balanced with that of an intelligence analyst. If he was by nature a self-opinionated expert, he wisely left that facet at home when he had come to work that day.

Someone somewhere had managed to find information in a very short time in order for Austin Bengot to present to the President. Elena Torneski was a very dangerous individual in situations of conflict. She was a control freak and sociopath with abandonment issues, a sadist with no discernable conscience who was in denial of her own masochistic traits. There were two eye witness accounts of her apparent nervous disposition and fear of firearms and violence, whilst three others described completely the opposite. She would manipulate the opinions of others with apparent ease in order to put them off their guard. Finally, of course, Dr Bengot came to what the President and Terry Jones already knew of the woman they now had to deal with as leader of the Russian Federation. The human character springs from the most basic source and like it or lump it, a person's sexuality shapes their psyche.

"It always seems to come down to this common denominator doesn't it, Doctor?"

"Depending on whom you read, Carl Jung or Erica Jong." The psychoanalyst said with a wry smile. "Nature, the psyche and individuality...a gene's way of taking ground, holding it, and wearing a cool tee shirt no other gene has as it does so.

Up on the screen there appeared a surveillance photo, quite possibly one ordered by Torneski's predecessors, either KGB or in the office of Premier. Walking away from the camera was apparently Torneski on the beach at a Black Sea resort and behind her, a noticeably subservient one pace behind, were two young ladies in G-strings with identical hair and the tattoo on the right side.

"You will have read or heard previously that her companions all have an identical tattoo, the dog's paws, on the right buttock."

This was certainly the case with Svetlana, and two former associates they knew of who, unlike Svetlana, had not managed to avoid the beatings and gang rape when they had abandoned Torneski. The copies of hospital records and photographs of their injuries had been acquired and added to the Torneski file.

"The tattoo is Premier Torneski's marking of these girls as being her personal property for life."

"I thought it was just some fashionable kink?" the President questioned.

"No sir, she is branding them." Dr Bengot explained. "Premier Torneski sees herself as the Alpha Male."

The President stared at the psychologist, wondering if he was joking, or even screwing with him as head doctors are wont to do, to see how a person reacts. He looked next at the image of Torneski on the screen and concluded that Dr Bengot had been entirely serious. He shuddered at the thought of what 'earning' that tattoo may have entailed but preferred to think on it as coincidental. At the end of the day some things were just best left unknown.

"Let's move on, Doctor." he instructed. "You will have noticed I presume that these partners she chooses share certain physical traits?"

"I am afraid that you are not entirely correct in that assumption, sir." Dr Bengot brought up several photographs of young women who were all attractive but their looks were of a variance.

"The green eyes and chestnut hair, the sculpture of the chin and cheek bones, the shape of the mouth...?" the doctor asked, turning to look over at the President with a questioning expression.

"Precisely, Doctor."

"That is a fairly recent occurrence, within the last few years in fact, and it points to an obsession, so I would assume that someone, somewhere is 'The one that got away', of course."

Terry Jones looked over at the President, habitually, and effortlessly, doing so in a way that Dr Bengot failed to notice.

The President noted the expression in the CIA chiefs eyes, even if his face gave nothing away.

"You mentioned ownership for life, I believe?"

"Indeed, they are her toys, she does not share and neither is Premier Torneski the forgiving and forgetting type. Mr President."

"She gets mad *and* she gets even too?"

"It is not such an unusual trait." Austin Bengot stated. "I have been divorced four times, so I speak from experience."

"Really?" the President exclaimed, and then added with a mischievous smile. "Is there a technical term, probably in Latin, for multiple marriages, Doctor?"

"Libido."

The President laughed aloud.

"Well you are working for entirely the wrong people if you intend to make those maintenance payments and also eat for the entire month too."

The President next asked as to the best method of manipulating a personality such as the new Premiers.

"With extreme caution sir, because should Premier Torneski discover, or even suspect that is being played, the response is likely to be violent."

Dr Bengot concluded his briefing and made to leave when the President stopped him with a final question.

"We have an operative who was once close to the new Premier." the President said. "Would she be more or less at risk now that Torneski is in a very powerful position?"

"Did your operative require reconstructive facial surgery at some point after their relationship?"

"No, definitely not." stated the President, removing a photograph from Svetlana's file and sliding it across.

"Ah" remarked the doctor after a moment studying the picture, before glancing at the rear of the print to read the words, and in particular the date that her lover of the moment had written with a flourish in biro.

"The one that got away..." Dr Bengot said with absolute certainty. "...and the first appearance of the tattoo, it would seem."

Austin Bengot handed back the photograph.

"In answer to your question as to the risk this young woman now faces, well Premier Torneski no longer has anyone who could offer censure, she answers to no one Mr President, and therefore it follows that this lovely young creature, your operative, is now in more danger than ever."

The President again looked across at Terry Jones.

The CIA chief left the room, needing to telephone Sir Richard Tennant in private.

"Mr President?" Austin asked. "By any chance is this operative aware that she is the object of this obsession?"

"I have no idea, doctor."

The President meant to ask Terry Jones that question but it slipped by, buried under the weight of other pressing matters.

Dr Bengot departed but the face of Elena remained on the screen as Terry Jones returned to deliver his agencies findings with regard to the delay in bringing the Red Army in Germany to heel.

"Mr President, the best thing about having someone in power who is disliked by their own people as much as they are by the opposition parties, is the wealth of dirt that is freely offered up on them." Terry stated.

"At the time of the former Premiers death the Red Army in Germany was expected to succeed without any requirement of battlefield nuclear weapons being deployed. It was Torneski herself who introduced to him the notion that the weapons were needed, obviously in order to effect a quick exit from the Premiers side and alert us to his whereabouts. Torneski was well aware that had nuclear weapons been used against us then France would certainly have launched an immediate nuclear counter strike even if we and Britain had not."

The President nodded agreement.

"However, Torneski immediately seized power from the Deputy Premier and had the General Staff and Front Commanders replaced with her own people, and applied the spurs, not the brakes."

On the screen there now appeared messages to the new Front Commander from Torneski ordering full chemical weapon use of all stocks available.

"Where did these documents originate and how satisfied are you with their authenticity?"

Terry handed across a binder. Just because everyone in the room was cleared to be there, did not mean that they had to know every detail that he knew.

The President read for a minute before returning the binder.

"So she took our money and still tried to stiff us." he grumbled. "Well that is politics, I suppose."

"There is something else too sir."

The President noted the tone and braced himself for bad news. "Go on?"

"The information that Anatolly Peridenko ordered the murder of our people in Scotland, it seems certain that it originated from Elena Torneski."

"And?"

"False, Mr President." Terry stated. "One of the team now in custody in Britain just blew the whistle on it. The aim of the mission was the abduction of Svetlana Vorsoff and her delivery to the person who ordered the operation."

"Elena Torneski?"

"Correct Mr President, but she had already departed for Russia. They did not know that of course so they wanted Major Bedonavich alive in order to learn her whereabouts, by means of extreme persuasion of course."

"Is that the current euphemism for torture, these days?" the question was rhetorical and he went on. "So do we know what happened at the house, that morning?"

"We do indeed sir; this guy was one of the snatch team. Major Bedonavich made a fight of it after everyone else was dead, but he knew what was in store for him when they had him cornered on the bridge; he jumped in front of that train rather than talk."

A long silence ensued as the President considered all this fresh information.

"Maybe not today, perhaps not tomorrow, but that bitch is going down."

General Randolph Carmine had already briefed the President on the Russian warships that remained with the Chinese fleet. Satellite surveillance had discovered a large Prisoner-of-War compound outside Port Kembla where the majority of those behind the wire wore Russian naval uniforms. It must have come as something of a shock to the Chinese when against all odds Russia had lost the war for Europe and ceased hostilities. Their remaining enemy had however rolled with the blow, cut the Russians off from any communications with their own command and then seized the Russian Pacific Fleet ships that accompanied the invasion force. Several days had followed with flights from China delivering naval personnel to Mactan and their onward transfer to the fleet.

It highlighted just how adaptable the People's Republic of China was but they were all of them, the President included; now kicking themselves over the lost opportunity. The disastrous and costly attack on the invasion fleet by the allied air and naval forces could have had a very different outcome if the allies had known the warships were basically running on half strength crews for several days. An attack when the fleet was in turmoil could have made all their current plans unnecessary. Always providing that they won the war there were going to be armchair tacticians and mediocre historians milking this one for decades to come.

Terry Jones, Joe Levi and Sally Peters were the only ones remaining seated an hour later as *'Choir Practice'* took place behind sealed doors.

"General Carmine, I am about ready for some good news for once, so I am hoping that you can oblige."

The General nodded affirmation.

"Mr President, in Australia the Chinese 3rd Army's 1st Corps landed successfully, as expected, unfortunately, but they also almost pulled off a flanking movement that would have been impossible to counter had it not been for a determined rearguard action by the Australians."

The Moruya landings had almost worked in opening a fast road to the capital, and they spent a little while going over future possible moves by the Chinese before getting down to the business of *'Church'.*

Operation *Evensong* was a huge gamble and its failure, and also its success, would end the intelligence windfall contained within the CD found in the combat smock of the dead paratrooper, Colonel General Serge Alontov.

"The Chinese 1st Corps did as expected, landing in the face of sparse defences and making a dash for the capital. Australia's unique topography worked in our favour, and will continue to do so as allied troops carry the fight to the enemy with patrol actions until the arrival of the real convoys from Europe, *Matins.*"

"Patrol actions, against four mechanised divisions?"

"It has already begun Mr President, for example, a pair of snipers with the Coldstream Guards are making the very necessary function of taking a dump, one of deadly hazard now for the soldiers of the PLAN's 1st Marines. Ten dead in three days, so the Chinese grunts are taking a dump in their trenches instead." General stated. "It is hot weather, it's unsanitary, it's a drain on both morale and resources, as you can see." A translation of a daily sitrep by that unit showed a fairly heavy level of ammunition expenditure in response to the snipers single shots.

"It is only a matter of time before self-inflicted wounds start showing up on the medical reports." General Carmine explained. "And when that happens to a unit, then its combat effectiveness is on a downward curve."

Satellite images, courtesy of the 'Church' software showed each units position and status. The 1st Corps of China's People's Liberation Army had gone defensive.

Much of the coastal plain of New South Wales was now in the hands of the Chinese but even their 3rd Army's First Corps lacked the bulk to force the mountain passes, as they had seen.

For four days the fleet sat just off the coast as the troop ships, Ro-Ro ferries and tank landing ships unloaded at Port Kembla, but on the fifth morning the sun had risen on a very different seascape, the fleet had departed in the night. 1st Corps of China's 3rd Army was on its own with just a single carrier air wing's worth of support operating off airstrips on land.

"They are waiting for the other two corps to arrive, for 2 Corps to resume the attack, possibly from fresh landings that bypass the mountains, but it's a hell of a long drive from Melbourne to Canberra for an armoured army." he said, indicating the coast to the west of that city. "Their 3rd Corp is the least able, combat wise, and would be required to hold the ground the other two corps had taken, and of course protect the logistics chain."

"Which is where Sally and her people come in." the President smiled. "I just hope it works as hoped or all this good stuff..." He waved towards the feeds from China's own satellites. "...is lost to us for good and ever."

Sally kept a straight face as she moved the satellite view further north.

"Mr President, these radar images you can see are the convoy's carrying their 3rd Army's 2nd Corps westwards to defend Singapore from of own convoy from Europe, approaching Asia via the Suez Canal."

The view changed again to that of the Atlantic, where nothing remarkable at all was happening.

"And now our own satellites take on things..."

Activity wise, it was a complete reversal.

Randolph Carmine explained what was occurring.

"They know that coming via the Panama Canal can take a whole week longer than the Suez route, depending on the weather." he said. "And of course any convoy would be entering a shooting gallery once it cleared the Suez canal and entered the Indian Ocean. Three quarters of China's submarine fleet are heading that way with the intention of sinking that convoy and the ones now following it. Many of the Chinese boats are operating out of Singapore, which is a good base to command trade routes and the sea lanes just as Britain did when it was a colony of theirs."

"How do we deal with the time differential, those submarines and also their eyeballs on the ground in Panama?"

General Carmines solution for dealing with China's agents who report all shipping movements in the Panama Canal was a simple one, and met with the president's approval before moving on to the question of timing.

"As regards the time differential, well the lead convoy slows for the remainder to catch up well before the Suez Canal, which is a sensible move, tactically sound as it increases the number of escorts so that will not raise any suspicions." The General tapped a finger on the screen, right above the Indian coast. "India and Pakistan are, as you know, about to begin hostilities with China. India has a sizeable fleet and it has good ASW capabilities, plus of course they have something we need desperately, diesel electric boats and they are already moving into the waters we want them in, prior to their countries openly declaring for NATO. In return for their active participation they of course get a greatly weakened bully of a neighbour for a time, at least that is the plan. If nothing else, Tibet may get its sovereignty back. India and Pakistan will for once be fighting someone other than each other, so that could be a benefit in the future."

"And *Dumb Blondes*." put in Joseph Levi, the Chief Scientific Advisor to the President. "Pakistan has a couple of those." It was an old and tricky solution to the problem of otherwise quiet, diesel/electric submarines requiring air to run the noisy diesels periodically in order to recharge the batteries. By making their own supply whilst submerged, the submarine remained constantly silent instead of periodically noisy. Instead of snorkelling near the surface, or even running the diesels on the surface, a 'dumb blonde' remained deep and extracted oxygen from concentrated hydrogen peroxide using steam turbines and a potassium permanganate catalyst. Britain had for a while led the way into the development of the system after WW2 with HMS *Excalibur* and HMS *Explorer,* which the crews soon nicknamed HMS *Excruciator* and HMS *Exploder* due to the high risk of fire and explosion. The official name for such systems was the harmless sounding 'Air Independent Propulsion' however.

The General and Sally waited silently now as the President mulled over the situation in his head, looking for brickbats.

"What is your best estimate for the life expectancy of *'Evensong'*?"

"Seven hundred and sixteen hours, twenty three minutes, Mr President." answered Sally Peters, glancing at the wall clock. "The remaining time until 'Vespers' begins, but in the meantime we are currently doing to them what they did to us, only better."

Once 'Operation Vespers' began and the first parachute appeared then 'Church', their ace in the hole, would be redundant. China would know that they had been compromised.

"Zoom in on that first convoy again." requested the president.

To him it looked exactly like a view from a photo reconnaissance feed, even down to a squad performing PT on the upper deck. There was not repetitive action at all; no wave was exactly like any other.

"And this is O'Connor's work?"

"Yes Mr President."

"The young lady has talent." The vivacious redhead had read the Peridenko file and had deduced what the late Russian KGB chief had in store for her at his dacha, had she accepted his amorous offer. It only added fire to her determination to get even for the way she had been manipulated over her seemingly purely commercial work Peridenko and Alontov. The file had recently been updated with an account by an air stewardess of Peridenko's death. The air stewardess had also been close to ending up in a shallow grave in the woods but for the arrival of Alontov.

"As her handiwork for Peridenko helped persuade China to enter a war against us, she was eager and willing to assist with the payback."

"Okay, let us move on to Vespers as we are committed now, and it beats the hell out of reading their mail but not being able to act on any of it."

The satellite view moved again, centring over the Philippine Islands.

"Reconstitution by the European airborne forces has been a problem as they were scattered all over the Red Army's rear areas in Germany. They took a real beating but they did an outstanding job there. However, units like Britain's '2 Para' and Belgium's 3rd Lanciers-Parachutists were all but wiped out. An 85% casualty rate, in their case."

The view zoomed in over the Southern Bisayas.

"Their 3 Para fought as infantry in Germany and were excluded from the airborne operation at the end, so they are itching to jump into action again, and if nothing else 1 and 2 Para will never let them live it down if they finish the war without jumping out of some perfectly serviceable aeroplanes even if there is no one waiting to take a shot at them when they land."

A list of units that were taking part in the airborne element of *Vespers* now appeared upon the screen. Two entire brigades from the US 82nd Airborne Division would take the airfield and two bridges that connected the small island of Mactan with the main island, Cebu. It was a task best performed by a division, but the 82nd had been a significant contributor to SACEUR's airborne gambit in Germany and the brigade that had taken part needed to rebuild significantly. The reserve brigade for *Vespers* was instead an Anglo/French unit comprising the French Foreign Legion's 2 REP, Britain's 3 Para and their supporting artillery and combat engineers.

The naval side of the operation was primarily the US Navy delivering the 3rd US Marine Expeditionary Force once the airborne units had seized the targets airport.

"The operation is a simple concept Mr President. Cut off the Chinese 3rd Army from resupply by taking its forward logistics base from the air, and then reinforcing by sea via the nearby port before the Chinese 6th Army comes and takes it back."

"How long will the paratroopers have to wait before they are relieved?"

"Twenty four hours at the very outside, Mr President."

Some plans don't even survive until first contact.

CHAPTER 3

PNS Karchi, Cebu Strait, 2 miles south west of Mactan.

*"Conn, sonar...*stationary object, range zero six nine, bearing zero two two...classify as anchored sea mine."

The ultra-low frequency sonar, similar to a Chinese *'Mouse Roar'*, in the bow of Pakistan's very quietest of her submarines, identified yet another mine in a comprehensive series of mine fields protecting the vital Chinese base in the southern end of the Philippines archipelago. The *Karachi* had begun the dangerous task of identifying minefields and safe channels a two full weeks before Pakistan declared war on the People's Republic of China. Captain Muhammad Khan was proud of both his vessel and his crew, with just cause. The majority of his country's navy joked about his vessel and would resign in order to avoid being assigned to its crew. They nicknamed the *Karachi* the *Bipatā*, 'The Calamity' owing to its air independent propulsion system. In truth there was no such thing as a 'minor' accident as even a slight leak in the system could result in a catastrophic fire whilst submerged, merely by the volatile fuel making contact with low grade steel or aluminium. The benefits though were an ultra-quiet boat that did not need to snorkel or surface in order to recharge its batteries; they made their own air and discharged the exhaust into the ocean. Her hull was lined with triple layered rubber panels to complete the acoustic vanishing act once submerged.

"Both engines back... slow together."

"I think that is about it Captain." His First Lieutenant said as he marked the mines position on the chart.

It had been a long and perilous two weeks mapping the minefields in preparation for an upcoming operation of some kind. The PLAN had mined the area extensively to guard against incursions by both submarines and surface vessels. To the north of Mactan the minefields extended from the treacherous Calituban Reef, off the island of Bohol, across the Cebu Straits to encompass the single beach north of Cebu City that was suitable for amphibious landings. The only break in the dense field of anchored sea mines and acoustic mines was a temptingly inviting channel that was in fact a trap. The only safe channel was a deceptive dog-leg affair at the southern end of the straits, which led first into a safe fishing zone before angling sharply northwest. From the town of Carcar to Talisay City the coast was a rock garden. The Americans had previous experience with the Talisay beaches from WW2 where they had come ashore to take back the island from the Japanese, but the waters off Talisay were now also heavily mined. This left only the inner safe channel from the safe fishing zone to the Mactan Channel, and *Karachi* had yet to map that as a possible route for assault ships.

"Will we transmit the results now, Captain?"

It was possible that there were remote controlled, command activated, acoustic mines in the inner channel. A flick of a switch at the first sighting of an invasion force could turn that channel into a death trap.

"Yes, we will carefully retire and send our results to date, but before I can announce that we are done here I want to follow a freighter all the way in, and use the low frequency sonar to check for any surprises." No other submarine in the Pakistani, or Indian Navy for that matter, could have achieved what his vessel and crew had done. "There is no way I am going to have our work here criticised as being incomplete, not after all the hard work everyone has put in to it."

Several hours after transmission they returned to the end of the inner channel and sat on the bottom of the safe fishing zone, waiting. A large Chinese fleet supply vessel eventually approached, and following the usual procedure that *Karachi* had listened to on many occasions in the last two weeks, it stopped outside the entrance to the inner channel and awaited a pilot to guide them safely through. What they could not of course see was the securely locked metal case that was handcuffed to the Pilot's wrist as he transferred from the pilot boat to the ship.

With the fleet auxiliary back underway the *Karachi* moved carefully and quietly beneath her wake with the mine-seeking sonar active.

Just inside the channel proper the deckhands on the auxiliary flinched as a large explosion a hundred yards off their stern caused the sea to heave up a huge geyser of water and debris, laced with rubber acoustic panels.

Talisay City, Cebu.

It was proving to be a busy week for Sergeant 'Bat' Ramos of the Philippine National Police. His was the responsibility for all incidents, criminal and accidental, along the coastline that lay within the bounds of Talisay City. First of all had been the appearance of bodies washing up on the beaches, all of them Pakistani Navy personnel. The local commander from the occupying PLA 6th Army had come along in person, and had even posed for a photograph beside the corpse of a Pakistani submarine captain.

The photograph would probably be used to help support the fiction that the garrison was in 100% control of the island. It was questionable as to whether the adoption of Mactan as a major military base would have occurred so quickly if China's high command knew what the real situation on the two islands was, even before the arrival of special forces.

Bat would have expected that the Chinese would have been more concerned about the defences being compromised, but at least as far as sea defences were concerned they now acted like householders whose expensive burglar alarm had worked as advertised. They were smug rather than worried.

Since the second, successful, invasion of Cebu the police force had been disarmed, relieved of such equipment as radios, and put back to work as usual but with some supervision by Chinese Military Police. Bat did not have anyone looking over his shoulder two days later when he attended the second incident of the week on the beach, the PLAN navy were already there when the call arrived so an MP dogging his steps was thought unnecessary. A small ferry, the *Henrietta*, had been beached, its hull damaged by an explosion of some kind, and it had settled in the shallows before the tide had gone out, leaving it looking rather forlorn.

PLAN marines stood guard and looked him over as he approached but assumed his MP watcher must be nearby. They did not stop him climbing aboard or even from approaching the bridge where raised voices could be heard.

The ferries Master was standing shamefaced beside a Chinese pilot who looked even more wretched. The Chinese naval officer in charge of harbour traffic was beside himself with fury, pointing frequently at a portable TV set beside the ships wheel and a metal case with a handcuff dangling free from its carrying handle.

Bat was pretty much ignored as he stood on the fringe of the little drama, listening carefully whilst managing to look harmless and ignorant of any foreign language skills.

China was rapidly expanding Mactan International Airport and the attached, former Philippines Air Force base. The work force, all forced labour, had initially come from those residing on Mactan. However, after the existing runway was repaired after the disastrous initial invasion attempt, it was widened and lengthened. Two further runways were added and all this expansion displaced many of the small islands inhabitants. Eventually there was no Filipino left living on the island of Mactan as it became a high security zone. Workers and labourers were still required however; vast storage depots and warehouses do not build or maintain themselves. The two long road bridges across the causeway between Cebu and Mactan proved inadequate for the increased traffic and therefore ferries were required to ease the strain and tailbacks. *Henrietta* was one of a limited number of non-Chinese-military vessels that were permitted to move workers to and fro, but under guard of course. The ferries had some kind of device attached to the hull which kept them safe from a new type of sea mine, but the device only worked if connected to another device which the pilots carried with them in the metal cases. Bat would have loved to have just gone over and had a look at what the fuss was all about but that would have been most unwise. He stayed where he was, looking like a dumbass flat foot copper as he heard how the pilot had boarded the ferry and connected his device to the ferry's electrical supply before giving in to his weakness for alcohol. With the pilot below in the captain's cabin sharing a bottle of scotch, and the Chinese bridge sentry asleep on a chair on the wing, the helmsman had decided to watch his favourite TV show as he went about his duties. There was only one plug socket on the bridge though. A plug from the case dangled on a cable next to the electrical socket, a socket that was still occupied by the TV sets plug.

Bat quietly departed, stepping over the body of the bridge sentry and being careful not to get any of the blood and brain matter on his shoes. He was safely clear when he heard the sound of two gunshots coming from the ferry, and he listened carefully in case anyone had noticed him on the bridge and thought that four bodies were required instead of three to maintain security over the issue. No hue and cry followed and he made his way to a street food vendor near his police precinct house where he ate lunch and paid for it with a fifty pesos note folded around a piece of paper. Within six hours Colonel Joseph Villiarin, commander of the guerrilla forces on Cebu, had received the information and summoned Major Garfield Brooks. A micro second burst of energy transmitted the warning that told the members of the 'Choir' that the naval side of *Vespers* had a very serious flaw.

140 miles west of the Monte Bello Islands, Western Australia.

It was very hushed in the control room, not quite so silent that a pin could be heard falling, it was however rather close.

The sonar operators sat the most quietly of all, and those with eyes open were not actually looking at anything, their heads were in the same place as those with their eyes shut.

USS *Twin Towers* edged ahead, barely making headway, at a depth of 500 feet.

"There he is again." muttered Lt Hannigan, the head of the sonar shop and a natural 'ear'. Somewhere ahead of them was a very quiet diesel electric boat, probably an Improved Kilo, the *Zǒng Shènglì*, and almost certainly the vessel that had almost put a torpedo into their hunting partner, HMS *Hood.*

For the past two weeks the hunter killers had done a roaring trade in the waters off the coast of Western Australia, racking up tonnage of both merchant vessels and warships, although the majority were carrying fuel and supplies to the PLA 3rd Army in New South Wales.

COMSUBPAC, the headquarters of the US submarine fleet in the Pacific, had noted a distinct absence in enemy submarine traffic in the waters between Cebu and Australia. Many of the vessels that had carried out the chemical attacks were now operating out of Singapore, waiting for the reinforcing convoys from Europe to enter the Indian Ocean. Not all had left Australian waters though, and those vessels didn't run on plankton either, there had to be a support vessels somewhere.

USS *Twin Towers* and HMS *Hood* had been diverted from interdicting the sea lanes to that of hunting down the Chinese submarines supply vessel.

The stalk lasted all the way to a small group of islands off the coast of Western Australia.

"Raise ECM"

It was a stormy night up top, a typhoon was blowing and making the helmsmen work hard and earn their rations. Rain was deluging the island and the runoff was having an effect upon buoyancy. Fresh water does not allow for the same level of buoyancy as salt water, and there was something of a tidal race created by the cluster of small islands and islets of the Montebello group to be contended with also.

The *Twin Towers* captain let his helmsmen get the measure of the seas before proceeding. His helmsmen were both reservists, one was a skipper in his own right although he described himself as a delivery driver of pretty things, taking billionaires yachts from the builders yards to the customers, wherever they may be on the planet. The other was a bass guitarist with a rock and roll band, internationally famous but now unrecognisable with cropped hair and an absence of earrings and eye shadow.

The thin wand of the ECM mast and both the attack and search periscopes were made of the same stealthy material as the F-117A and B2 bombers were constructed from. The ECM detected powerful search radar emissions from the supply vessel that would possibly have 'seen' the previous ECM mast and periscopes that the TT had carried. They had been replaced at the time of the boats extensive repairs.

"Raise 'Search'." Captain Pitt ordered and danced the 360° waltz a time or four as he visually checked for surface and air threats both near and far.

Satisfied for the moment, he swung the periscope on to the Kilo's bearing.

"Lo-lite...magnify." He muttered to himself, adjusting the controls set into the periscopes handles. "And record."

There in a lagoon was indeed a support vessel; a converted North Korean flagged whaling factory ship, *Jeonseung,* in civilian livery, although Green Peace would have been pleased to learn of her conversion to a role other than its original one.

"Well I don't know if she is a genuine NK or not, but we will send all this footage off, just in case those people are going to pile in now."

"Captain?"

Rick turned to look at the speaker, sat at the ECM board.

"It isn't much, but I am detecting a higher than normal radiation count, sir."

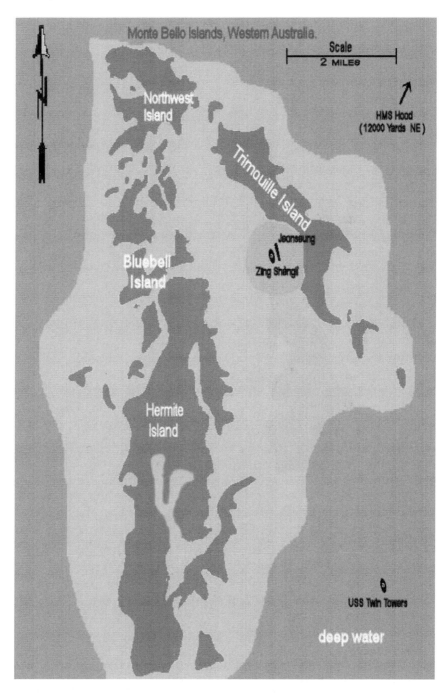

"Well it isn't coming from Sydney as the wind has been easterly, as near as dammit, and it is not a Russian boat with paper thin reactor shielding." Rick said, but to his crewman's puzzlement he did not expand upon that answer.

His Exec was looking at the lo-lite monitor screen and checking with Mr Hannigan as to the Kilo's precise position.

The Chinese diesel boat was on the surface and riding high with her ballast tanks completely filled with air, but even so with the tide as it was the lagoon should still have been far too shallow for it, indeed the 'whaling factory ship' should have been almost scraping the bottom, and she drew less than the submarines she serviced.

As hiding places went, it was an ideal location; the island was shielding vessels in the small lagoon from radar surveillance, even from the air. Ground radar clutter showed what any operator would expect to be there, rock and sand

"How are they doing that?" he asked.

"Add another twenty five feet to what is written on the chart and you will see that there is sufficient water under their keels."

The Exec frowned.

"Can I ask where you are getting your information from Captain?"

"History books, young man. Those and additional navigation notes for mariners" Rick smiled. "Up until 1952, the 3rd of October to be precise, the depth of the Trimouille island lagoon was forty feet. And then of course Great Britain anchored the frigate HMS *Plym* in the very spot the Kilo is now occupying and set off a 25kt nuclear weapon in the ships magazine. It created a bowl in the rock floor of the lagoon that left the anchorage twenty five feet deeper than it had previously been." He pointed at the chart. "Look at the curving shape of the shoreline there on the chart, a half century ago or so, it was a pretty straight line. And now check the navigation notes and you will see that the date of the last depth finder recording was the day before the blast, on the 2nd October 1952. The test results were classified top secret, including the crater dimensions, and the area is still 'hot', as the ESM has confirmed. Only a few 'Rads' higher these days, but enough to discourage most visitors, and all ocean survey vessels."

Rick noticed the looks on the faces of crewmen who were trying work out if their captain was a genius or an ace bullshitter.

"And that, Gentlemen, is the reason why the information is out of date around the Monte Bello Islands group, even on the most recent charts."

The Exec checked and looked up in surprise.

"Well I'll be!"

"Always check all available information on navigation. That way you won't have the embarrassment of hitting a shoal that was lifted during a recent sea quake, or a wreck from a previous storm."

The fuelling and replenishment at sea procedures had begun under the cover of darkness and the typhoon.

"Signal our friends with the GPS coordinates, and inform them that they can exact revenge for the brown trousers that the Kilo gave them last Thursday. We will provide the necessary damage assessment."

HMS *Hood* had remained seaward, beyond the horizon, during the USS *Twin Towers* stalk to cover the American vessel against the possibility of another enemy boat sneaking into her blind side, her baffles.

The Royal Navy submarine launched a single UGM-84 Harpoon anti-ship missile in the direction of the lagoon. As it neared the target the missile popped up to 2000 feet where its IR seeker located the two vessels. Switching to terminal attack mode the Harpoon dived into the North Korean vessel, detonating the sixty three torpedoes and submarine launch missile re-loads it still carried, along with its almost full fuel tanks.

Once satisfied that the Kilo had also been destroyed in the massive explosion the USS *Twin Towers* put about and returned to the deep waters to continue the interdiction of the supply lines.

Arbuckle Mountains, Oklahoma.
Wednesday 31st October, 0210hrs

The President entered the secure briefing room behind General Carmine. He was nursing a cup of coffee and looking tired, but he still kept a weather-eye open for any sign of the doctor, Admiral Glenn. The physician knew damn well that the President was being supplied with coffee against his direct instructions, but he had not yet discovered the source. It was a little like a hackneyed scene in an old 70s cop show, with the President disappearing to meet his 'dealer' once a day and palming a small bag in some shadowy corridor. The difference was that no cash changed hands and no drugs were involved, just enough ground coffee to provide the President with an illicit mug of Java once a day after the admiral had turned in for the night. Henry Shaw had caught a brief look at the supplier one time and he had confided in General Carmine. It was a little anticlimactic to learn the mystery man's secret identity, but looking at it logically it was unlikely to be anyone else given the circumstances they were all currently living under. 'Huggy Bear' was the man with the key to the catering supply store, the Presidents chef.

"Good morning Mr President, I am sorry to disturb you at this late hour but there have been developments that required an unscheduled, though limited *choir practice.*"

The President looked around the room and saw that it was just three of them; Terry Jones was also present but not Joseph, Sally Peters or Alicia O'Connor from the NSA.

"A Soldier and a Spy." The President observed. "So does that make me the Tinker or the Tailor?"

"I thought we were a choir, sir." General Carmine said with a smile.

"Choirs don't have cool titles General, in fact I never heard of a solo tenor having anything like a street credible nickname."

Terry Jones sat quietly without joining in; he had seen the President in jovial banter mode before, and it usually meant that he knew bad news and difficult decisions were on the way. It was the presidents way of dealing with it, of staving off the grey moods that always followed meetings such as the one they were about to have now.

"Street gangs used to get the best nicknames, but when they started to call nicknames 'tags' they got predictable. Too many zees and letter eez, they may as well throw away the rest of the alphabet." he seated himself and took a sip of coffee. "The old time gangsters had the best nicknames. You'd be 'Carbine' Carmine, Terry would be 'Slippery' Jones, whereas Joseph would be 'Brains' and the ladies would be 'Slinky Sal' and 'Red', naturally."

"And you, Mr President?"

"Just call me 'The Boss', Carbine."

Terry Jones tapped a keyboard and the mood evaporated as a map appeared upon the screen.

"Mr President, this is *Vespers* objective, the island of Mactan, and we have added all the data collected by some very brave men from the Pakistan navy."

"How wide are the Cebu Straits?"

"Nineteen miles wide, at that point."

"That is one awful lot of mines that they have laid."

"In the region of four thousand, at our best estimate anyway, Mr President."

"What is the revised estimate to clear a channel to the beaches General, I assume it is longer now than the previously promised twenty four hours?"

"Ten to fourteen days, sir."

The President went quiet.

They had expected that there would be some minefields laid, both at sea and on the beaches, but this was an extraordinary operation that the Chinese had undertaken.

"What about this channel here, the one the Chinese vessels use. Surely we can fight our way along that?"

"Unfortunately not, as it would seem that the Chinese have developed a sea mine that recognises friend from foe, Mr President. It can detect the stealthiest vessels without those vessels being aware of the mines presence."

"How do we know this?"

"The submarine that mapped the minefields reported that they intended to follow the inner safe channel to check on any additional defences." Terry explained. "She was lost with all hands, sir."

Terry Jones went on to report the discovery of a device by a policeman working for the Philippines underground on Cebu.

"The Chinese call it Língjiǎo, the Caltrop mine, obviously named after the spikes on a rope that can be quickly deployed to prevent access, and as quickly retrieved."

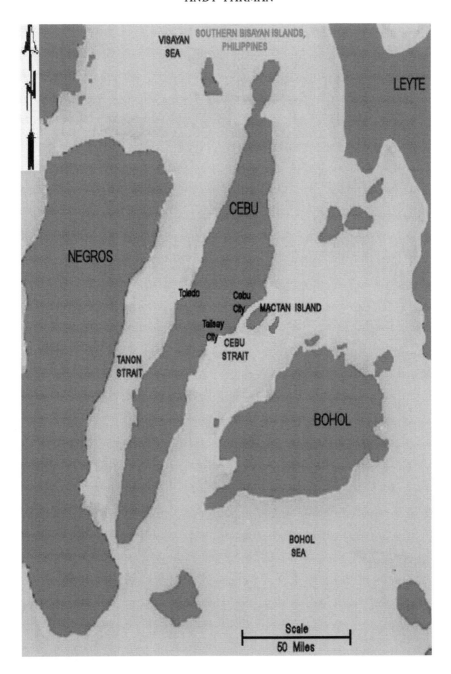

CEBU AND MACTAN

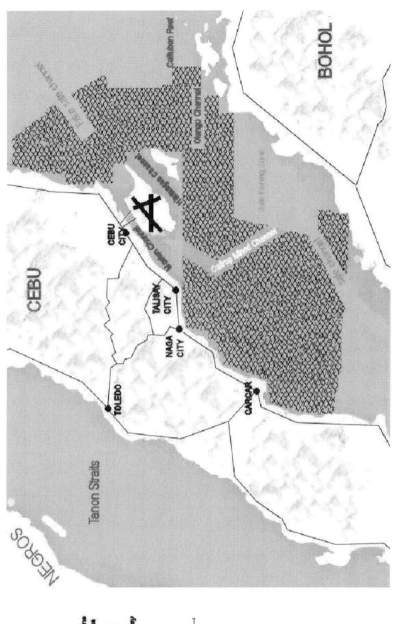

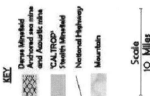

CEBU STRAIT MINE FIELDS

"We aren't going to be able to relieve those paratroopers on the same day they jump in, are we General?"

"No sir, but we are working on a revised plan, and we may have to do it the British way."

"Please enlighten me General; it has been a long day."

"The Falklands War sir, the Argentinians fortified the capital, Port Stanley, and dug in facing the sea, with sufficient forces to defeat a landing and mining the shoreline heavily."

The President nodded, now aware where the General was heading.

"They did the unexpected; they landed on the far side of the island and fought their way across."

"So where is our San Carlos Water, General?"

"The Tañon Straits sir, to the north of Cebu, and they land at a small ferry port called Toledo. From there they cross the mountain spine of the island and take them from the rear, as it were."

"Is it feasible?"

"Sir, the Japanese Imperial Army took Cebu the same way back in world war two."

"I'm betting that the defenders didn't have a mechanised brigade and close air support in 1942."

The Presidents face took on a very grim visage as he looked at the terrain that the 3rd Marine Expeditionary Force would have to cross.

"Is this the only road?"

"It is the only direct road, but there are two others, sir."

"Do they have sheer drops at the side too?"

Neither the general nor the spymaster answered that one.

"Okay, time estimate?"

"It is just thirty miles, so it is possible the marines will cross the island the same day."

"I think gentlemen that the airborne force needs to be increased by another brigade."

"That is not possible sir, we are staging out of Phanrang and Vũng Tàu air bases in Vietnam and the use of those bases is strictly time limited. The aircraft would need to make a second drop and the Vietnamese want us gone after the transports have refuelled."

"Really?" the President was surprised. "When was this time limit tagged on, and what reason did they give?" The President had of course been briefed on the original offer.

Leaving his chair he stood before the screen, arms crossed and wearing a thoughtful expression.

"Who else did you speak with, after the Vietnamese of course?" he asked Randolph Carmine.

"I have spoken with no one in regard to bases for *Vespers*, sir."

"But?"

General Carmine had met with the commander of the small Royal Brunei Navy the day before over access to fuel and victualling for the region. The admiral had confided his disquiet at the members of the government who were allowing the business community to influence their decisions over disputed territory. The general was not exactly a stranger to that kind of pressure and had sympathised.

"Now it becomes clear." said the President, wearily. "I think that Vietnam and Brunei... and Malaysia too, bet your life on that one... are also about to enter the war, although not necessarily for the greater good, most certainly for their own."

"The oil under the Spratly Islands, Mr President?" asked Terry Jones, who had just worked it out.

"Yes indeed, although Brunei doesn't have a snowballs chance in hell with her tiny armed forces the Vietnamese intelligence services will have learned of General Carmine's meeting and jumped to the wrong conclusion." reasoned the president. "The Philippines and Taiwan are also claimants to the islands but they are under PRC occupation. The PLAN seized the Spratlys with elements of their 1st Marine Division the day after nuking the Taiwanese back to the stone age."

Terry brought up the region on the screen

"Those marines are now in Australia?" queried the President, having exhausted his general knowledge of military events during that period. "So what do they have holding those islands now?"

"A parachute battalion, a quartet of fast attack boats, and a nuclear threat that the PRC no longer possesses." Randolph replied.

"They haven't reinforced?"

"No sir and those three countries you just mentioned will have all noticed though, you can bet on that."

"There will never be another more opportune moment for Malaysia, Vietnam and Brunei to try an end run against China for possession of the islands." Terry mused.

It would be welcome indeed to have someone else in the region provide a headache for the Chinese, but without doubt that headache would be passed on to the USA at the conclusion of this war, trying to restore peace in the region.

"Do you have any idea when the attempt to snatch the islands is likely to begin?"

"If I were the Vietnamese I would move the second we land troops on Mactan, Mr President."

"At least we now know why they are being so helpful and cooperative in allowing us to stage out of their air bases. We will be running interference for them, even if we didn't know it, and the time limit they attached after noting your meeting with Brunei means they slam the door on our presence in-country, and any possibility of our attempting to influence the issue in any of the other countries favour." The President shook his head in exasperation at having been played.

"We could have used those vessels, troops and aircraft in the invasion of Cebu." he grumbled.

Terry Jones made no comment but he was willing to bet that in attempting to capitalise on the fighting between the allies and the Chinese, that Vietnam, Malaysia and Brunei had outsmarted themselves and unwittingly their combined forces were about to quadruple in potential value to the allies.

"Okay, back to the problems at hand, and if we can't send a few more battalions can we at least send something to give the *Vespers* airborne element an edge?"

It took an hour of discussion before contacting the countries concerned after concluding that a British unit which had just arrived by air in New Zealand, for onward transport to Australia, did have something that could assist. It would mean moving the unit to Australia's Northern Territory where the Royal Air Force C-17s of 99 Squadron would make a 3,600 miles round journey to deliver them to Mactan, supported by the elderly but trusty Boeing 707 tankers of 33 Squadron Royal Australian Air Force.

Eurostar terminal, St Pancras station, London.

It was hardly the most glamorous means of arrival but the specialist was satisfied that it was low profile, hoisting a battered backpack onto one shoulder and joining the queue for passport control and customs.

Old jeans and a cheap overcoat, a little stained and very threadbare, fitted perfectly with the hair that needed a wash and comb.

The process took an hour, and a tube ride to a seedy bedsit in Brixton followed. The room above the hair stylists shop had been kept securely locked and there was no sign that anyone had entered since the current lock had been fitted.

Several new changes of clothes in a suitcase placed above a cheap wardrobe were all in the specialist's size.

After a few hours' sleep the specialist began work.

The target had been injured and sent to a clinic in the Thames Valley for treatment. It was an exclusive establishment, treating injured police officers who remained there as residents as they recovered. The information had cost the specialist a thousand pounds but access was impossible under the circumstances. A visual surveillance from across the valley by way of a sniper scope had however confirmed the target being in residence.

Goring-upon-Thames, the nearest town, had several pubs frequented by the patients from the clinic but in three days the target had not appeared in the town. On the fourth day the target disappeared, departing unexpectedly.

Dr Austin Bengot would have been both flattered and alarmed if he had learned that he was known to the specialist, but the specialist could not know that the doctor's report had been the reason for the targets vanishing in the night.

More money, twice as much this time, got the specialist a name, a new lead to the new location. It was a very clever hiding place really, as instead of the target hiding on a lonely mountain on the other side of the planet they had been kept where a searcher would not necessarily look.

The targets language skills were being sought by the same people arranging the concealment, and the accommodation would turn out not to be a cave, far from it.

Sir Richard Tennant boarded a southbound underground train on the Northern Line, departing the carriage once it arrived at Stockwell. The service was much improved now that the war was far away and the fuel was again arriving in quantity.

Rather than leave the station he instead sat and read his newspaper, glancing up on occasion in a seemingly innocent way to check on who else was nearby. It was a sound counter surveillance tactic designed to catch out anyone tailing off the subject.

A small ladies purse sized vanity mirror and a piece of blu-tac allowed the specialist to observe the Metropolitan Police Commissioner, it was pressed against the tiled wall where it reflected a view of the length of the platform as the specialist stood safely out of sight inside the platforms furthest exit.

Three trains came and went before Sir Richard stood and tucked his copy of The Time under one arm. The platform had three exits and his back was to the central one. Light appeared along the tunnel and the passengers stood watching the train approach. Behind the Commissioner the exit led to the Victoria Line platform, just forty feet away, and commuters needed to traverse that platform to exit the station or reach the northbound platform of the Northern Line. As the train entered the station and slid to a halt before Sir Richard, a Victoria Line train also halted at the platform behind him. The specialist watched in the mirror as the commissioner took a pace towards the Northern Line train and then turned swiftly, sprinting between the platforms and jumping aboard the Victoria Line train as the automatic doors slid shut behind him. Quite nimble and sprightly for a man of his age.

Having completed another anti-surveillance trick, apparently with success, the Commissioner was relaxed and safe in the assumption that he was tail free. The specialist was younger, faster, and did this sort of thing for a living so the move had been anticipated. Entering a carriage much further down the train it had however taken some effort to reach Sir Richards Tennant's carriage before it pulled in at Vauxhall.

Sir Richard did not depart the train at Vauxhall; he stayed on for several stops, rising to depart as Green Park approached. That was when the specialist made the mistake, gasping aloud in shock, as much as pain, when struck in the face by another commuters elbow. The sound drew the commissioner's gaze and his eyes widened slightly as he thought he saw someone he knew, but the specialist used the rising commuters as cover, moving out of view.

With the train stopped and doors open Sir Richard beheld the smiling face of Svetlana waiting for him on the platform. As he exited his head turned to look momentarily back towards the end of the carriage where the commotion had occurred, a slight frown furrowing his forehead but then a beautiful girl with come-hither green eyes and chestnut locks was grasping his arm affectionately and leaving lipstick on his cheek. He forgot all about what had just occurred except a reminder to himself to wipe away the lipstick before returning to the office.

The specialist watched from the safety of the crowd, allowing a safe distance to grow before following. The target had both her arms wrapped about the commissioner's right arm, clearly fond of him and chatting animatedly, just as vivacious and attractive as she had been reported to be, the heels of her stiletto shoes clicking on the flag stones. Sir Richard was clearly enjoying the moment, and the envious looks he was receiving from strangers.

The pair had lunch in a café and the specialist visited a sandwich shop across the road, keeping them in sight through the window. They parted after lunch, going their separate ways, and the target led the specialist north to the fringes of Hampstead Heath, to a grand Victorian era house with an indoor pool and glass ceiling.

Gaining access to a suitable surveillance pitch proved much easier than the specialist had feared it would be. The target was living rent free, house-sitting for the wealthy owners who had gone abroad for the duration of the war. The same held true for the adjoining property, but no house-sitters were in residence to ensure its safety, just an expensive burglar alarm that was not worth what the owners had paid for it. A trapdoor allowed access to the roof and from there the specialist settled down to observe, removing from the backpack a camera with video features and a paparazzi quality zoom lens.

The pool room was not unoccupied, the figure of another person reclined on a sun lounger, reading a novel. When the target appeared she did so shedding her clothing with the skill of an exotic dancer, dropping the items as she slowly approached the recliner at the far end until at last she was nude but for the heels.

Switching to 'Record' the specialist had first focussed on the dogs paw tattoo which was only just visible beneath the long mane of chestnut curls that bounced fetching off those delightfully wiggling buttocks. With the identifying feature established the view was zoomed out again.

Setting up a small pocket sized camera clamp stand the specialist carefully aimed the camera down through the glass ceiling before taking out the sandwiches and enjoying the view across the Heath as they were unhurriedly consumed. The specialist washed down the sandwiches with bottled water before replaying the recording. After editing a five minute highlight a mobile phone was plugged into the camera and the video file sent as an attachment to a cell number written on a slip of paper.

It took a surprisingly short time before a reply was received and the specialist read it with a slight feeling of regret. Perhaps the person on the other end had expected the target to be having rather vocal sex with a man, not another woman? The two word text messaged reply remained on the screen of the phone until the erase button was pressed and 'DESTROY HER' vanished.

Hampstead, twelve hours later.

Caroline peered out from a gap in the sheets and blankets that had gathered around her in a pile during the night. The light peeping through the cracks in the curtains did not bode well for the previous night's weather girl's promise that today would be one of fine sunny periods. It had sickly yellow hues rather than the intensity that comes from rays born of clear blue skies.

Her nose twitched as she tested the air, there was a scent in the air of toast but it was not recent, not fresh, and she contemplated remaining in the bed for another hour before accepting that to do so would be to put off the discomfort.

She bit her lip and groaned aloud as she rolled over on to the edge of the mattress and swung her feet to the floor, using her left hand to prop herself upright. The pain took her breath away and she sat there for a second before standing and tottering naked to the bathroom. Having accommodated the morning's first call of nature she stood and in doing so caught sight of herself in the full-length mirror that was fixed to one wall.

Cradling the plaster cast encased right arm with her left USAFs most newly promoted lieutenant colonel wondered ruefully how much that men's magazine would offer now, had they been present. The bruising down her left side was changing from black and blue to blue and yellow but the doctor had warned that the discoloration would be gone weeks before the bone of the ribs that lay below the bruising had finished knitting together.

She faced the other way and turned her head awkwardly, noting that the tread of the soldiers boot was still discernable between her shoulder blades. The sight brought back the awful memories of the gang rape that had almost taken place and she shuddered, taking a towelling robe from a hook behind the door and slipping it on before heading to the small kitchenette.

Only the smell of toast and the last vestiges of warmth in the kettle remained of her lover's breakfast. Svetlana had washed and dried after herself before leaving for the temporary job the Commissioner had offered her the day before as a translator in New Scotland Yard, an event celebrated by some amazing fun the day before, even if she had been more recipient than participant.

The tears for the loss of Patricia, Constantine, Scott and the two policemen Ben Stokes and Malcolm Pell had come after returning to the UK and learning what had happened shortly after their departure for Russia, months before. The debriefing that followed did not engender any satisfaction in a job well done after that news.

Sir Richard had packed them off to the countryside to a kind of health farm for policemen but the scheduled two week rest cure and physiotherapy had been curtailed suddenly. Now they were the bored caretakers of someone else's home, or at least she was, as of today.

She heard the letter box and frowned at the time, it was altogether too early for the postman and the owners had cancelled the papers. The threat against Svetlana meant they could not put their names to anything, even as trivial as a newspaper delivery. They were not to travel to previously frequented areas or contact friends and relatives, but Caroline was a stranger to London and no one knew she and the Russian girl were an item so the pilot felt quite secure.

A plain brown envelope sat on the mat with just a small HMSO, Her Majesty's Stationary Office, the printers for the British Government, and a stock number were printed on one corner. It bore just a handwritten letter 'S'. She opened it anyway and there was a clear plastic bag, a police exhibits bag with serial number and heat sealed ends, a biro signature was scrawled across the seals to prevent tampering. A single door key sat within, another tag tied to it, a classic court exhibit label as seen in countless movies. Svetlana's old cover name, Christina Carlisle, and the address of her flat in Kensington were printed upon it. Only Sir Richard Tennant knew they were here and Caroline was about sick of bumming around this house, so she decided there and then to learn something more about Svetlana. She would see for herself what music she liked, what art she had on the wall and to run her fingers over the Russian's pretty things.

The taxi dropped her at the other side of a small park from the address and after paying off the cabbie she walked painfully through, smiling and mouthing an apology at an elderly old ladies frown for disturbing the pigeons she was feeding.

The apartment block was something built with style in the 1920s and the Art Nuevo décor remained. Stained glass and burnished brass, plus the scent of wood polish greeted you at the street entrance. The small lift, or elevator as the English called it, bore a note of apology from the management as well as a health and safety compliant 'Out of Order' sign so she took the wide staircase instead.

She liked this building and its warm homeliness, its atmosphere of friendly welcome was quite palpable and she paused on the landing to savour it, her aching ribs were forgotten for now. It was as if the building *liked* you, she thought with a smile. She could quite understand how being unable to resume her residence here had upset Svetlana.

Not being ambidextrous she fumbled with the key before getting it lined up and into the lock, and then the door swung open to reveal the home Svetlana missed so much.

It smelled musty from the long absence of its owner and from where Caroline was stood just beyond the threshold she could see the resulting mess from where it had been searched for clues as to where the Russian girl had vanished. It was a rude change to the mood that the apartment block had engendered until moments before.

The coat rack lay on the hallway carpet were it had fallen during the struggle months ago, and a sprinkling of plaster dust lay like dandruff upon a dark jacket that had been hanging from it at the time. Caroline was glad that Svetlana was not here to witness this, and she hoped she could find some undamaged items to bring back, to cheer her friend and underline that she cared a whole lot for her, and with that thought Caroline stepped over the threshold.

As one, the pigeons took to the air in startled flight and the old lady in the park feeding them cringed involuntarily. The thunderclap of sound reverberated off the walls of the surrounding buildings and the anti-theft alarms of two dozen cars parked in the street outside the apartment block wailed and warbled. The buildings old but functional fire alarm bell sounded its strident tattoo, almost drowning the sound of glass that had once been window panes now shattering into smaller shards upon striking the ground below Svetlana's apartment.

Like an evil halo, a smoke ring that held the black signature of high explosive residue hung above the Kensington street before the breeze dispersed it.

New South Wales: 2 miles east of the Macquarie Pass.

Heat, tropical humidity, ants and the eye stinging sweat that trickled down his forehead were forgotten as the sound of a high velocity round signalled a veritable fusillade in reply, tearing into the tree canopies and undergrowth with indiscriminate fury.

Their victim tumbled from the mid reaches of an ivy smothered Eucalyptus tree, hanging by a safety line that vibrated as each round struck the body of the sniper. He was one of their own, sent to counter the British snipers who were having such a detrimental effect upon the morale of the Chinese troops facing them. The body in a ghillie suit was indiscernible in appearance to that of the enemy's snipers but he was 'in play' as far as the Chinese marines were concerned, and they vented their anger upon it.

Big Stef fired again, and a second Chinese sniper, the mate of the first one, tumbled into view down a slope where it received the same treatment from the trenches. They would not use this position again and edged away with painfully slow movements.

Two hours later they were hauled up the escarpment by rope and underwent a debriefing before finding food and a place to sleep.

"Two shots, two snipers, both from the Chinese 1st Marines?" the intelligence officer asked.

"Well you know how it is sir; you shoot one and five minutes later you have to shoot another." Bill said with gallows humour. "I've no idea what unit they were, their gear was pretty standard."

Sgt Stephanski nodded in agreement.

"Okay guys, it seems that you got their attention down there and those two snipers won't be the only team they sent in. I think a change of venue is in order, to keep them reacting to us and to minimise the risks to you so that area needs to be left alone for a while. Someone else can receive your gentle attentions."

Port Kembla

Commander Hollis shuffled forwards with the remainder of the line, edging ever closer to the entrance to the kitchens with the ever hopeful few asking those emerging what the size of the helping was, and was there any meat today?

There never was, never had been and never would be any meat in their diet, just rancid rice with boiled vegetables, rancid rice and vegetable soup and rancid rice and vegetable stew. It wasn't as if the guards were being unduly harsh, they were not exactly living high off the hog themselves, and had all lost some weight too, victims of the shipping attrition in the same way the POWs were.

The Australians companion nudged him, gesturing for him to make his move. The companion was the Russian Vice Admiral; they played chess almost constantly and had an old pocket size travelling set with three pieces missing from the original. The coloured stems of matchsticks now served as replacements for the lost, manufactured items, and they played for money, keeping tally as they went along. Reg owed the Russian a considerable amount of theoretical cash but his game was improving. If the war continued for another two years they should be quits. The prisoner in front of Reg hailed the next to emerge, asking him the same question and looked crestfallen at the reply until the next man emerged with a battered mess tin and the look of hope returned; and so it went on.

The prisoners had gravitated into small groups of friends, usually but not exclusively the same nationality. They tended to look out for each other and the small group of Taiwanese prisoners who had fled from Taiwan, to continue the resistance before being shot down and captured had already outed two spies the guards had tried to infiltrate into the camp. Having the Peoples Republic as an enemy gave all the nations present a common foe, so there was no need for internal rivalry. All that being said though it had taken just a week behind the wire for Reg to see the behaviour of some prisoner deteriorate as the lack of food took its toll. A group of twenty or so prisoners from the same container took on gang status until Vice Admiral Putchev had taken swift action. Several prisoners were beaten and robbed of their rations and one of the female prisoners was raped, but one evening the gang had received a visit from other prisoners who did not try to argue or reason with them, they did not call on them to do any honourable things, they simply took the three ring leaders, the biggest and the strongest, and the rapists, and they hung them. Next morning the Chinese had discovered the bodies, and ignoring the other injuries they bore, they had willing accepted the account of the Russian officer that the group had committed suicide. It was less mouths to feed and discipline was restored. It was the Russian way of dealing with a mafia, Putchev had explained.

The majority of the prisoners were Russian navy, but the numbers of allied prisoners began to swell slowly. Captured army personnel appeared from the skirmishes and patrol actions. US 10th Mountain men, Royal New Zealand Infantry, more Australians of course, with British infantrymen and a smattering of aircrew from all the nations. The survivors from the naval battle were few and far between given the weaponry used. Putting a lot of people in a metal vessel and then blowing it up does not make for a survival friendly situation.

In Reg Hollis's group were Phil Daly, Sgt Rangi Hoana, a heavily muscled Maori, from the 1st Royal New Zealanders, Pte Mal Chaplin of the 5th/7th and C/Sgt Colley Brackling from the Royal Australian Regiment.

Stephanie Priestly had been part of the group but she had eventually been segregated despite the two Australian men's best efforts to keep her where they could protect her. As more captured servicewomen arrived a second, smaller camp was constructed. There were only twenty in that camp but Reg eventually accepted that the women were safer where they were and the guards did at least treat them with a level of respect.

The group shuffled forwards another few steps and another prisoner was asked what the contents of his mess tin were. This proved an enquiry too far for Rangi Hoana who left his place in the queue to tap the constant enquirer on the shoulder.

"Listen, cannibalism was once an accepted part of my culture, and every time you whine I get hungrier, do you get it?"

It brought the group a little welcome silence.

Twice a day the prisoners were required to parade on a large area that was at times a dust bowl or a mud hole, depending on the weather. This was to check no one had escaped. In the morning, before breakfast, and at the hour before dusk the prisoners would be summoned to fall in for the head count. On occasion this assembly would be called at random times, normally for some announcement the Chinese believed to be of importance. The Chinese captors called these parades Accountings, or Kuàijì, (Hy-je) which the Australian prisoners quickly latched onto owing to how the pronunciation sounded to Western ears, and it was a dig at the poor diet the PRC served its captives. They also renamed the parade ground accordingly. When their guards summoned them to parade they shouted *"Kuàijì! Kuàijì!"* it was taken up by Australians calling "High Tea! High Tea! Darjeeling and fairy cakes are being served in the Tea Gardens!"

The other prisoners adopted the micky-take, to the bemusement of the guards.

Their group was now just a matter of a couple of steps from the entrance to the kitchens when the guards slammed the doors closed.

"Kuàijì! Kuàijì!"

It was greeted with catcall and whistles but it was obvious no one was going to eat who hadn't already, until they assembled on the Tea Gardens.

Not without grumbling the prisoners shuffled into lines for the accounting. This however was not to be a boring rant by the camp commandant.

The prisoners stood waiting, bored and hungry, but when the commandant came through the gates he was accompanied by the political officer, a platoon of armed guards with bayonets fixed, and others who dragging a naked and bloody Caucasian male through the gates and onto the Tea Garden.

He wasn't an escapee, it was early days yet and whereas an escape committee existed, their shopping list of necessary items would be a difficult one to fill. Tunnelling was the obvious route out but it was not practical without a source of wood to act as pit props.

The prisoner's ankles and the bones in his feet had been broken, he bore a swollen and gangrenous gunshot wound to the right thigh, the apparent cause of his capture in the mountains the previous week, and as all the fingers in his hands had been broken he could not hold the large sign that said 'War Criminal'. The prisoner was tied upright to a post and the sign was hung around his neck before the camp political officer screamed out the offences the prisoner had committed. Mass murder was mention several times, the slaughter of innocent civilians on mainland China, the unwarranted killing of men, women and children.

Whoever the prisoner was he was unrecognisable, his face swollen black and blue, teeth, finger and toenails removed with pliers. But he raised his head, unable to see properly through blackened and swollen eyes, shaking with fever from the terribly infected wound but looking straight ahead in proud defiance, unbowed and uncowed. Despite the torture he had received once the Chinese had discovered his part in the war, the only names he revealed, of the other troops involved, were those he knew to be already dead.

In shock that quickly turned to outrage the camps occupants now shouted their protests, drowning out the political officers words. At the political officers orders the guards cocked their weapons and stepped forward into the en-guard. The threat was implicit and the shouts died away, although not the seething anger.

Once all was quiet the political officer quickly turned, drawing a knife as he did so and cut the prisoners throat.

The absolute shock at what they had just witnessed lasted for a heartbeat, and then they surged forwards en-masse despite the guards, and both commandant and political officer drew their side arms. They worriedly backed away towards the gate as the guards gave ground, holding the furious prisoners at bay behind levelled bayonets until they too cleared the gateway and it was firmly shut.

Commander Hollis, Vice Admiral Putchev and a ships surgeon, a member of the Royal New Zealand Navy, ran to the figure tied to the post but it was too late, Major Richard Dewar, Royal Marines, had climbed his last mountain.

New Scotland Yard, Broadway, London SW1.

The Commissioner listened carefully to the initial forensic report on the crime scene in Kensington. The explosive used had been Semtex H and a fingertip search by members of the Specialist Counter Terrorist Search Team had discovered fragments of the device and that of the trigger in particular, a pressure pad beneath the mat inside the doorway to Svetlana's flat. Identifying the victim would have been difficult given the massive tissue damage, but Lt Col Nunro wore her identity tags from habit.

"The blast was directional, the shrapnel that was employed has been confirmed as being 3" nails and broken glass, and the quantity of explosives used was excessive, given the purpose and location." explained the scientific officer from the laboratories in Lambeth.

"Amateurs will tend to show themselves up for what they are when their inexperience leads to a level of overkill in their devices." said DAC Jennings of Special Branch who had control of the investigation. "What are your feelings so far, or do you need more time?"

"I am confident that the evidence will continue to point to a professional assassin, one from the Eastern Bloc and that person was, or is, Spetsnaz or at least received their training from them?"

"How so?"

"The pressure pad was home-made but constructed exactly as taught by those people, down to the dimensions of the apertures in the plastic foam keeping the firing circuit open until the victim, Lt Col Nunro in this case, trod on the welcome mat inside the door."

"Alright then, just to recap, the explosive alone was sufficient to guarantee the death of the victim?" asked the Commissioner.

"And then some."

"But the bomber was not some amateur wacko building it from instructions on the internet?"

"Definitely not." the science offer said.

"So why the shrapnel?"

"Commissioner, you are the policeman and I am but a humble scientist whose work touches on the genius, but I would say that there was possibly an element of the personal about this, the damage inflicted to the victim was huge."

"Thank you and we will not detain you any longer. Any signature twisting of wires etc., and DNA or fingerprints at this juncture would be gratefully received, I assure you."

With the science officer departed the commissioner and DAC Jennings moved to another issue, the assumed real target of the bombing.

"Svetlana disappeared from this building after seeing the newsflash about the incident on the BBC. I was on my way down at that moment to break the news about her flat but she was already gone when I arrived at the office she was using." explained the commissioner.

"She didn't know the American was the victim, surely?"

"No one did at that time, just that at least one person had been killed."

"Well I am sorry to say that she has simply vanished, dropped completely off the radar and that is despite an 'all-ports' with photographs within the hour of her leaving the office." said the DAC. "It's not as if she doesn't stand out from the crowd either." he added with some exasperation.

"You've seen her file, she is a resourceful young woman and taking her at face value would be a serious error."

"But one that she successfully exploits quite often." DAC Jennings stated. "However, running requires money, and you have to be visible while you earn it, so we will track her down before long." He sounded confident as that had been his experience in a long career as a detective.

"I hate to rain on your parade on that one, but I kinda suspect she may have been running on near empty on Day One, although that may not be the case now."

Art Petrucci, CIA Chief of Station, London, was another man who had mastered the trick of remaining inconspicuous at all times, he had sat through the meeting between introductions at the beginning and that point without making any previous comment.

"Go on?" prompted Sir Richard.

"We gave the young lady access to quite considerable funds when we sent her off into harm's way in Russia. Granted, and all, that she had not been entirely truthful about her relationship with the now, new Russian Premier, she needed that money by way of a persuader to turn Torneski."

"You turned the head of the KGB! *She* turned Elena Torneski?" blurted out the commissioner in surprise.

"We persuaded Torneski to help us kill a whole bunch of people so we could win this war, yes Dick." Art said. "We didn't exactly offer her a contract, pension and dental benefits."

"How much money are we talking about?" DAC Jennings enquired.

Art told them.

"Wow!"

"Half down, half when the world is again at peace so long as we won."

"You are now going to reveal how Svetlana's considerable ability and intellect has dropped a spanner in the payment works?" the commissioner asked with an expectant smile.

"The best looking god damn forger and con artist I never met, yes Commissioner."

Art went on to explain how the entire advance payment had disappeared from Torneski's secret account in Lucerne, and the second half of the payment from just one street away at another bank, the one that the US treasury had been holding it in on deposit. The security cameras showed the perpetrator of the thefts at each of the two banks, and also walking with a large blue-rinsed poodle trotting beside her from the first bank to the second. At the first bank, completely aware that she was under security surveillance, an unmistakeable Svetlana Vorsoff had even removed her Audrey Hepburn style dark glasses to look directly at a discretely sited camera and wink.

The signatures had been perfect; she held all the correct documents and had all the correct identifications and passwords which she had apparently memorised, including two, twenty six digit pass codes. Described by staff at both banks as elegant, chic, a very well-spoken young English woman, she was dressed in the most expensive fashion and had referred to the giant poodle as 'Sir Dickie'.

Sir Richard Tennant's laugh was more guffaw than anything and he slapped the top of his desk repeatedly as he did so.

"This is hardly a laughing matter, sir." DAC Jenner said reproachfully.

"That bit is." replied the commissioner, drying his eyes with a handkerchief.

"You realise of course that Torneski will also know who stole her money and her reaction will be the opposite of yours, boss?" the DAC stated. "But how the hell did she get original documents?"

"I think that was probably the point." Art said in reply to the first question. "That was the 'why' but as to the 'where', well I'd guess they came from Torneski's safe." Art opined. "She has a dacha in the woods where she plays with her girls in private. It is in the pre-op briefing you can both read in twenty five years' time." He smiled as he reminded them of the Official Secrets Act time limit.

"The post-op briefing states she met Torneski there to put the Presidents offer to her. So at some time before or afterwards she cracked the safe and pulled a switch on the Premier. I guess the documents must have been hidden in the hooker boots lining."

"Pardon?"

"She wasn't wearing anything else, the report is quite a kinky read...you can see that in twenty five years too."

Sir Richard made a show of working out on his fingers how old he would be when that date came around.

"I suspect I won't care, by then." he concluded sadly.

"So did the assassin miss? And will he try again?"

"I don't see Elena Torneski letting her get away with the money unpunished, but it is a moot point as I think she would keep sending people to try and kill the fair Svetlana, regardless." Art said with absolute certainty. "Sad to say her days are numbered, Svetlana is a dead-girl-walking."

"You say that with some conviction, Mr Petrucci, is there something else I have to wait a quarter century to read?"

"No Commissioner, some things just have to stay secret forever."

North of Bateman's Bay, NSW.

It was another humid and physically unpleasant day, and no matter what part of this country you worked, those damned ants always got you. Perhaps these nasty little bastards, fire ants, had followed them here from the forests near the Macquarie Pass, where they had previously worked.

It was a challenging ground to operate in. Large areas were basically charcoal, burnt out by the fires, so five cam changes were necessary, woodland, burnt timber and woodland once more when they got to where the enemy were, and burnt timber and woodland going back.

The targets were to be different this time to, veteran units had savvy leaders because the un-savvy were dead, so it was time to send the smart ones to join the dullards.

One at a time, the snipers removed the natural camouflage before stripping off their ghillie suits and turning them inside out. Old brown sack cloth, hessian, had been sown on in preparation; the strips doubled the garments weight so they prayed for dry weather and moved out. They went slowly, aware that dust would accompany any movement. If necessary they would have to use their water in the Camelbak each wore, spraying a little ahead of them to kill the dust at spots that had O.Ps covering them.

It was going to be a long day.

Sergeant Baz Cotter was chosen to lead a recce patrol by the company 2 i/c, which was a welcome relief for him to get out from under the serious hard work 2nd Lt Pottinger was proving to be. For the members of the patrol it was a welcome reprieve as the platoon commander had been slated to lead it.

Something was in the wind as the two armies had come to a kind of stalemate, fighting patrols going out to make the other sides nights ones that were sleepless, and ambush patrols to counter those fighting patrols. Now, those on-high in the ivory tower wanted a prisoner, and for this it followed that a recce for a suitable spot to carry out a snatch would have in it those who would carry out the actual task later. Baz went for his O Group with the 2 i/c and the platoon commander tagged along. Baz had no problem with this because Mr P lacked experience. The O Group itself was nothing special to Baz's mind but the platoon commanders ears twitched and he sat up straighter when the 2 i/c did the end of orders spiel. "Of great importance blah blah...a feather in the cap blah blah..." which Baz had learned to tune out of the process after about a week of real war fighting back in Germany. Second Lieutenant Pottinger though, Baz later concluded, still took all that shit seriously.

By tradition as much as practicality the patrol commander gets some say, if not all, in whom he wants with him.

"Any thoughts on who you'll take, Sergeant?" the 2 i/c had asked.

"Four One Bravo." Baz said automatically, choosing Dopey Hemp's section simply because it was their turn. He felt the platoon commander stiffen up beside him at the words but he did not think anything of it. He went to the Q Stores for specialist kit and Mr P stayed behind.

In Baz's absence his boss had tried to sell the captain on its being a bad idea following his platoon sergeant's choice of man power. Captains, or even lieutenants for that matter, do not take seriously the opinions of 'subbies'. The 2 i/c was aware of the rotation of patrolling tasks that Sgt Cotter employed and it was a good one. Mr Pottinger left in a huff, storming off in search of his platoon sergeant and determined that if any of the sections were praised for a job well done, its wasn't going to be 2 Section.

Baz was weighed down with kit as he worked his way along the track plan to Dopey's trench with the items to be doled out.

They had O.Ps out to give warning of an enemy approaching but still, he was not happy stood above ground next to the FEBA, forward edge of the battle area, arguing with his boss.

"Sir, with due respect, you will be leading the actual fighting patrol whenever it happens and not me, plus it will be a platoon effort. So who gives a rat's arse who lays hands on the prisoner?"

"Sergeant Cotter, I am beginning to think you are in cahoots with Hemp." He pointed at Dopey down in his trench, watching the argument but without a clue as to what had sparked off the latest lot of fireworks.

"Sir, again, it is my decision, and my decision was based on whose turn it is next."

"And I am the platoon commander, and I am telling you to change it."

The crack of the shot followed just a second after Mr Pottinger had pointed at his epaulet, and before the arrival of the thump of that shot being fired, Baz was already in Dopey's trench, below ground and shouting stand-to!

"Looks like you're leading the fighting patrol too Sarge." Spider remarked, on seeing the back of the platoon commander's head pebbledash the trunk of the tree beside his own firing bay.

They lay absolutely still for an hour before edging back from the firing position, by which time fewer pairs of eyes were watching intently for them.

On reaching the burnt out area they again removed the natural cam and reversed their ghillie suits for the long crawl back to their own   lines.

CHAPTER 4

Vũng Tàu airbase, Vietnam

It was unbearably hot in the hangar, the parachutes sat in rows upon its floor, the men removed combat smocks dark with sweat following another mission 'hold', and they waited, trying not to let the nerves show.

Word came to en-plane and the men kitted up again and stood in ranks where they received their 'Green Light Warning' delivered by an RAF 'Loadie', Air Load Master.

"You are about to carry out a parachute descent. Failure to jump when the green light is displayed constitutes disobeying a direct order and disciplinary action will be taken against you. In the event of a green light failure the number one will be despatched by the Air Load Master and the rest of the stick will carry out the descent in normal order. Failure to jump constitutes disobeying a direct order and disciplinary action will be taken against you."

No sooner had that taken place when they were again stood down, and removed their kit once more.

Most slept, they had been paraded at 0200hrs for a 0330hrs take-off that never happened. Dawn had now come and gone, cloudless blue skies were overhead, so how could a bit of weather be the holdup?

1,144 miles to the east the target was obscured by cloud as 'a bit of weather' became Tropical Storm 'Hola' and then mutated into Typhoon 'Hola'. High winds and parachuting do not mix well, especially when deep water is in close proximity.

A further complication was that of the *Mao* and *Kuznetsov* carrier combat groups and the accompanying ships carrying China's 3rd Army's 3 Corps to Australia. The 1st and 2nd Corps had taken ship on the southern military island of Hainan but 3rd Corps was required to take part in a propaganda show in Beijing, 1400 miles away as the crow flies, in eastern China. Using modern, state of the art equipment borrowed from the garrison, 3rd Corps paraded through the streets to raise the flagging morale of the populace before departing to take Australia by storm (unquote). Having reluctantly returned their borrowed rides the 3rd Corps moved to the nearby port of Tianjín, boarding and sailing over the Yellow Sea and East China Sea. It was expected to head south east from there, into the broad Philippine Sea but metrology showed the building storm and predicted it would skirt the east of the islands along the Philippine Sea. The Chinese fleet turned south west instead, which was a problem because the US 3rd Marine Expeditionary Force with the USS *John C Stennis* and the USS *Constellation* battle groups in the Philippines Sea heading north, expecting the Chinese to sail later in the week. The US ships altered course only to find the Chinese seemingly to matching the move. The US force altered course again but the Typhoon proved unpredictable and instead of running north it turned north west across the Philippine archipelago and the Chinese fleet swung back into the Philippine Sea, the two fleets were head to head, 700 miles apart.

Given that *Evensong* was showing the Chinese that the US carriers were apparently returning to Hawaii after Sydney was destroyed, did this manoeuvring mean that China knew the US fleet was 5000 miles closer now?

The US ships left the Philippines Sea once more, sailing into Leyte Gulf and navigating the narrow Surigao Strait under the cover of night to enter the Bohol Sea. It was familiar territory for one ship of the fleet that had already fired its guns in anger once before in those waters, pennant number BB-61, the elderly but reactivated battleship USS *Iowa,* which would provide gunfire support for the marines landing at Toledo.

The Gods love to play tricks and toy with the machinations of mortal men; at least that was how Admiral Jackson aboard the USS *John C Stennis* saw things because the Chinese turned back to the west, heading into the path of the storm, matching their move once again. However, it was not that the Chinese could now see his ships.

Malaysia had made her play at dawn, declaring war on China and bombarding the Chinese paratroopers holding the Spratly islands in preparation for amphibious landings, beating Brunei and Vietnam to the punch.

The 82nd Airborne Divisions 1st Brigade and the combined British and French airborne brigade were at Vũng Tàu on the coast of Vietnam, whilst the 82nd's 2nd Brigade were waiting at Phanrang 150 miles further east, 8000 men, the maximum that could be carried to the target in a single lift, given the available aircraft. Stood just inside the hangar, carefully in the shade were Lt Col's Jim Popham of the US 111th Airborne Infantry, Ben McWilliams of Britain's '3 Para' and Anton Meudon of the French Foreign Legion's 2 REP, all recent veterans of the war in Europe. They chatted quietly about their experiences as they waited for the order to don their parachutes and board the aircraft.

Morning became afternoon but by the time the temperature eased off the shadows had stretched far. The tropics do not have long, gradual evenings, they have an off-button not a dimmer switch, and as the night replaced day the troops headed back to their billets. Perhaps tomorrow would be the day?

PLAN *Zheng*, Visayan Sea, north of Panay Island, Philippines. Same time.

Refuelled and running on the surface, in trail a mile behind a replacement support vessel, the light tanker *Sentinel Sea*, Aiguo Li's new orders seemed to him to be keeping him where he could be shot at without any opportunity to rack up a tonnage score as other skippers were doing .

The loss of the borrowed North Korean covert submarine support vessel *Jeonseung* had been more of a blow to operations in Australian waters than the sinking of *Zheng's* sister ship, *Zing Shènglì*. Consequently Li was now ordered to play bodyguard to the *Sentinel Sea*.

The tanker contained a hold for diverse use in plying its trade around the Pacific Rim, carrying cargo as well as fuel. It had been in Hong King when the war started and being New Zealand flagged she was impounded. Modern communications, and navigational equipment, plus an upgrade in her derrick were all that had been required to fit her out for a new line of work.

There was a sea running, the wind whipping the white capped wave tops into a haze of water particles and the rain hammered down until caught near the surface by the wind produced by Typhoon *Hola* and bent horizontal. It stung the face of the captain and the lookouts that had a week before been happy to make it from Western Australia to the Java Sea, over an area that was proving to be a graveyard for Chinese shipping and warships. Now that they were returning there were fewer smiles. The war was not going well for China.

The wind increased in fury and drowned out the sound of the diesels growling as they charged the submarines batteries. More than a few glances were cast the captain's way, willing him to submerge the *Zheng* and continue charging the batteries using the snorkel, but Aiguo was in a masochistic mood and preferred his misery to be total.

South of the *Zheng* and *Sentinel Sea*, Admiral Jackson was at last certain that the Chinese aircraft carriers and troop ships had been diverted away from Australia and were heading west, to reinforce the Spratly Islands, and so the US Fleet in the Bohol Sea turned north. USS *John C Stennis* now had the wind at her stern, as did the USS *Essex* and the amphibious assault ships bound for Cebu, but no longer having the wind on their beam was little comfort for the troops of the US 3rd Marine Expeditionary Force, those who weren't already dry retching would puke up the last of their supper long before midnight.

Admiral Jackson was not a member of that small group known as *'The Choir'*, he knew nothing of a secret project called *'Church'* and *Evensong*, *Vespers* and *Matins* were prayer times for nuns and the clergy, weren't they? He was however not one to look a gift horse in the mouth when he was suddenly presented with the position, course and speed of all enemy vessels in the region, including a small tanker and submarine heading for the north end of the Tañon Strait.

Day 1: Operation *Vespers* (Airborne element) 0500hrs the following morning.

A soldier opposite Lt Col Popham vomited, decorating Jim's jump boots but after wiping the back of his mouth with his sleeve the pale and wan paratrooper mouthed an apology to his commanding officer, and promptly threw up again. The typhoon had passed through the islands during the night but the airborne stream had entered its wake, the storms unsettled residue. Already full 'Hurlers' the waxed air sickness bags were in plentiful evidence and the air stank with the perfume of digestive juices and semi-digested food, that as ever included tomato skins and carrots even if the sufferer did not recall eating any.

The airlift of the brigades was a complicated ballet as the transports carrying the men to war were not all the same type of aircraft.

Lockheed C-130 Hercules and Transall C-160s carrying the Anglo/French brigade were the first to depart from Vietnam, and an hour later the big Boeing C-17 Globemasters of the USAF Military Airlift Command took off in a stepped operation that was designed to deliver the last aircraft first, overhauling the turboprop powered transports and drop the US 1st and 2nd Brigades simultaneously, the 1st on the airfield and the 2nd north of the connecting bridges, preventing any interference by the Cebu garrison while the British and French took the airfield and held it.

Months before, the allied planners had considered airfield denial strikes and bombing raids of the supply depots and warehouses, but with so many Filipino's at hand to repair and rebuild at gunpoint it would requires constant return visits. The shallow waters of the islands would favour the defender and a smart enemy would turn them into a trap for submarines and carriers. Then of course the later work on the airfield, the runway extension and addition of the two shorter runways presented itself as a possible base of operations against mainland China. Operation *Dragon Lady* was the first effort that was penned. A colossal operation and one that was also involving most of the allied strength in the Pacific region. When first presented to Henry Shaw he had read only the first page of the proposal before taking out a ballpoint pen and adding some artwork, a stick character in ragged shorts sat on a raft built of driftwood that flew a tattered Stars & Stripes from a broomstick mast under the shadow of a mushroom cloud. A prominent letter 'F' was circled with a 'Must do better' in red ink before he handed it back.

On this day however things were going wrong despite their best efforts but the fleet could not remain undetected for long. A planned dawn airdrop from the east, when the sun would be in the defender eyes, was not going to happen. The storm had taken too long to vacate the area so they would not loop south of Bohol to make that easterly approach. This of course meant that the sun would be in their eyes, the attackers, but it would have risen too high above the horizon to be too much of an impediment to marksmanship as the sun would rise as they were still crossing the South China Sea.

The first aircraft to take off though did not do so from Vietnam but at 0100hrs from RAAF Tindall, a bare bones aerodrome 175 miles SE of Darwin. RAAF Darwin had been the original choice, but it had come under both surface to surface missile attack and naval gunfire on several occasions. The main runway had been severely damaged in the last attack and was no longer viable. With a far lighter fuel load the Globemasters could have used the second, shorter runway, and tanked immediately after taking off but it was simpler to use RAAF Tindall's single 2,500 metres runway instead.

The C-17s of 99 Squadron RAF could also have made that long haul without refuelling had they been carrying just paratroopers, but their payloads demanded that they have a long drink from the tankers of 33 Squadron, Royal Australian Air Force, in order to return the same way.

Flights of C-130s arrived from several RAF squadrons, No's 24, 30, 47 and 70 Squadron to carry 3 Para, 23 Engineer Regiment, the 105mm light guns of 7 Parachute Regiment, Royal Horse Artillery along with food and ammunition. The lead aircraft of No. 47 Squadron was captained by Squadron Leader Braithwaite on her first sortie after being promoted. Wing Commander Stewart Dunn was also flying the formations lead aircraft on his first sortie after promotion.

The Anglo/French formation flew low and in complete communications silence. It crossed the coast of Palawan without incident and without sighting any of the warring factions around the Spratlys. A fortunate happenstance as the USS *Constellation's* air wing which was to meet and escort the transport stream did not arrive on time. The carrier was over forty years of age, an old lady, and her steam catapult's failed. USS *John C Stennis's* air wing was CAP for the fleet and about to launch Wild Weasel flak suppression sorties on the target. It was impractical for the two carriers to switch roles. The USS *Constellation* repaired the catapults but she launched her wing very late.

With full knowledge that the Chinese fleet was to the north of the Spratly Islands the airborne transport stream followed a slightly more southerly course, keeping below the islands, although due to the 2nd Brigade taking off from Phanrang to the east, they were being carried on a slightly more northerly line, slowly converging with the Vũng Tàu stream.

Reports had reached the Chinese flagship *Mao* that the Royal Brunei Navy had sailed, bound for the southern Spratly Islands and the commander decided to deal with the smaller of the opposition's ships earlier rather than later. *Mao* launched an anti-shipping strike even though the range was extreme. *Mao's* strike aircraft carried mainly anti-ship and anti-radiation missiles with only a pair of Aphids for self-defence along with 150 rounds for the Su-30s 30mm cannons. They narrowly missed the Transall and Hercules carrying the Anglo/French airborne brigade and did not find any trace at all of the Royal Brunei Navy, but on turning back for their carrier they caught the big C-17s carrying the US 2nd Brigade without a CAP and the slaughter commenced.

Colonel Neil Hughes Brown, 97th Airlift Squadron out of Lewis/McChord AFB near the Rockies, put the nose of his aircraft, 'Pride of Seattle', down towards the South China Sea and made it there by luck as much as skill and judgement. The early morning sea fog and drab grey colour scheme was not a perfect patch by any means, but there were plenty of other targets that were easier to see. Eventually near the coast of Palawan the aircraft emerged from the fog bank. There were no other targets to distract the Chinese aviators and he had two Su-30s closing on his tail. He could not outrun or outmanoeuvre them, the Chinese carrier aircraft were shy of air-to-air missiles now but not cannon ammunition. He had two choices really, stay low and ditch in the sea near the shore or turn over the island and gain enough height for the mass of troops in the aircrafts belly to exit the aircraft by parachute. The first option gave him a better chance of surviving than the second, but men would drown, trapped inside the aircraft. He gave his orders and let the two Sukhois closed to gun range just off the shore before dropping the gear and flaps. The drastic loss of speed caught both the Sukhoi pilots by surprise and they overshot. Colonel Brown raised the gear and shoved the throttles through the gate, juggling the controls and avoiding a stall, just barely, as he strove for speed and height. The red light came on in the hold and the jump masters got the troops on their feet and hooked up. They had been lucky the first time and the same trick would not work again, or would it? As the first tracer round flashed by from behind Colonel Hughes banked hard right instead of going into a diving turn, as they enemy pilots expected, suddenly the target was looming large before them, the 169 foot wingspan and broad fuselage like an aerial wall and again they broke to avoid a collision, but not before Neil felt cannon round strikes reverberate through the airframe. The master fire warning sounded as debris, smoke and flame streamed from the port outer engine. There were twenty dead and wounded in the hold and the flight engineer shut down the port outer engine, activating the fire extinguisher.

The nose came down below the horizon and as the wings came level again the line of flight was bisecting the length of the island of Palawan. The jump doors opened, and the green light came on.

The large cargo ramp was of no use in any way, the static lines were hooked up for exits through the side jump doors in the fuselage.

The jumpmasters now had the task of cutting the static lines of the dead, and those they judged too badly wounded to jump unaided and they shouted and gestured for the sticks to exit.

When the aircraft attacked next it was not from the stern it was from head-on.

Smoke and flame belched from the shutdown engine but it was not of danger to the paratroopers boiling out of the side doors as rapidly as possible. Excluding the dead and wounded, only ten, plus the jumpmasters, still remained inside the aircraft when the cockpit exploded under the impacts of 30mm cannon rounds.

The 'Pride of Seattle' rolled inverted and dived into a mountain called Cleopatra's Needle, exploding on impact.

Both Sukhoi's turned for home but their wing members were shouting on the radio that they were being engaged by carrier aircraft, F-14 Tomcats.

Low on fuel and short on ammunition, the Chinese aviators got a taste of the helplessness the C-17 crews and their sticks of paratroopers may have felt.

The Tomcats were themselves a little on the light side where ordnance was concerned when they eventually took station protecting the transports, but *Mao* was now short a bunch of aircraft too.

China had a problem; their aircraft had been engaged by carrier aircraft far from any carrier they knew of.

It took an hour, an hour of technical debate at the various scientific levels and shouted accusations and denouncements at political ones.

Someone took the decision and pulled the plug on the photo reconnaissance and RORSAT satellites, and the People's Republic of China was suddenly back at her 1950s stage of satellite intelligence.

Arbuckle Mountains, Oklahoma.

"Oh my good God." The President said, stricken. "All those men?"

"*Church* is dead, long live *Church*." Joseph Levi stated with a tinge of sadness as he entered the briefing room.

The president went tight lipped and glared furiously at his chief scientific adviser, but Joseph had only just entered having been told that the grand ruse was over. He did not know the details of what had just transpired over the South China Sea.

The various advisers seemed to feel the need to voice their opinions unbidden, which is not how it was meant to work.

"Can we cancel the operation?"

"No, we have to see it through, Mr President."

"Mr President, it's over a third of the airborne force, simply gone before they could even arrived at the target."

"The mission called for ten thousand men, not five, we have to abort sir!"

"Three thousand men, artillery and ammunition....."

"If we try again in two days..."

His hand slapped down hard on the top of his desk, causing his water to dance in its glass.

"Be quiet, all of you!" the President 'did a Henry' silencing the room so he could take a deep breath, a step back and switched off his emotions for a moment as he looked dispassionately at the problem.

"If the Malay's hadn't tried for the Spratly's the Chinese fleet *could* have bumped into ours. If they hadn't then we *could* have two corps to fight in Australia instead of one...if that typhoon hadn't shown up...if, if, if... 'IF' is for losers." He glared at them. "We are fully committed now and with a little luck the enemy will assume that the aircraft and paratroopers were all part of the situation in the Spratly Islands." he glared at those who had so quickly been ready to fold.

"We play the hand we've got."

Mactan

The resistance movement on Cebu had infiltrated the work crews to get access to the island of Mactan which was to become fortified if the Chinese got their way. The plans for bunkers, those completed, those underway and those still on the drawing board had all found their way to the tropical forested hills that were the guerrilla's stamping ground.

The number and type of mobile anti-aircraft systems was known, including the position of camouflaged hides and firing positions on both Mactan and in and around Cebu City and neighbouring Mandaue City where the northern end of the bridges sat. The positions GPS coordinates, as well as a general description.

The airborne tanker fleet that were so vital to air operations between mainland China and Australia were to have massive hardened shelters but currently they were making do in camouflaged 'soft' dispersals, and the positions of all of these irreplaceable assets were marked for destruction by the planners.

Because of the absolute secrecy involved Garfield Brooks was unaware of the intended landings until a few hours before. He was further south at Barili, up in the hills west of Carcar dealing with the training of local fighters. It was an area the Chinese 6th Army's 86th Mechanised Brigade feared to tread so although it was not completely safe it did have more security than the hills to the north where Colonel Villiarin preferred to be. The Chinese stuck to the coastal roads and the main highways that crossed the mountain spine. The 86th were not bad troops but they were out of their comfort zone. They were well trained and equipped to fight a highly mobile mechanised armour war, one fought on the wide open reaches of the Siberian Plateau, against similarly equipped troops from Russia. The Chinese High Command had stripped two of the infantry brigades of their IFVs in order to get them out patrolling on foot.

Garfield quickly summoned his men and gathered those Filipinos he had already trained, before setting off north to set vehicle ambushes on those roads the garrison was so attached to.

Day 1: Operation *Vespers* (Airborne element) 0600hrs.

Once the dawn arrived, so too did the US air strikes, coming from low to the east had first removed the KJ-2000 AWAC and the CAP with AIM-54 Phoenix missile shots. Filipinos awoke to the sound of warfare on their doorsteps, peering curiously across the channel at the source of the explosions and machine gun fire.

A 'Wild Weasel' preceded the airborne stream by twenty minutes, picking off the radars or forcing them to shut down, tempting air defence sites to engage and malleting them if they did. The F-14 Tomcats and F/A-18E Super Hornets moved on to defensive strongpoints and bunkers. Two aircraft, with very brave crew, attempted to save their aircraft from destruction on the ground and to combat the attackers. They tore along the new 1,400m runway on afterburner but neither made it, one pass with two bursts from a Vulcan cannon put paid to the attempt. One pilot managed a ground ejected but his wingman did not.

AV-8Bs from USS Boxer and USS Essex would provide further CAS, close air support, but only for a limited period as they would also support the US Marines amphibious landing at Toledo and needed to refuel and rearm before that time.

Sukhoi-30s, a second KJ-2000, Antonov transports and assorted helicopters burned in their dispersals.

Despite the interception of the transports from Phanrang the surprise had been nearly total.

With the cessation of the air raid and departure of the aircraft back to the USS John C Stennis, a kind of shocked silence fell across the small island and the city just across the narrow channel. Residents looked across the water towards the destruction that had been meted out on Mactan, and then a droning sound from the south west became noticeable. More aircraft were approaching although these were not jet engines they heard but Rolls Royce Tyne and Allison T-56 turboprops.

In contrast to the swiftly diving and darting strike aircraft that had just raided Mactan and air defence sites on the main island, the newcomers were flying fairly low and slow, three abreast in a long column of twenty seven transport aircraft, the C-130 Hercules of Great Britain's Royal Air Force and the C-160 Transalls of the French, 61 Escadre de Transport.

From where they were heading, smoke arose from numerous fires, marring an otherwise blue sky as the stream of turbo prop transports lined up, using the smoke to judge wind direction and speed.

Beside the island, in the Mactan Channel was moored the damaged and fire scarred Russian Krivak class frigate *Samara*. She carried the same small tow crew as at the time she had been boarded and seized, after a fight during which her engine controls were smashed by the Russians when the frigate approached the Philippines. Unaware that Russia and China were no longer allied they had allowed a Chinese destroyer alongside. After the Russians had been subdued they had been locked below deck and a small tow party managed the ship as she was towed the rest of the way.

The Russian crew of the *Samara* and the rescued men of the *Syktyvkar* had been marched off to a POW camp and just the tow party remained aboard now. The frigate had no electrical power for her radars or fire control centre but she did not need power for all of the ships weaponry.

During the air strikes, the US aircraft saw only a badly damaged warship without power and no discernible threat at that point. The operations briefing had included all the relevant intelligence gathered by the Philippine resistance, and it had stated the vessel was non-operational and awaiting repair. They had better things upon which to expend their ordnance loads.

Chinese ratings now manned the two starboard and two port side 20mm mountings, carrying heavy boxes of ammunition up from the magazine.

Wing Commander Dunn was unaware of the disaster over the South China Sea, communications silence had been maintained until now, at least as regards the Anglo/French aircraft and only one code word had been received *'Dasher'*, which meant they were to get there as fast as possible and drop their sticks of paratroopers. Something had changed from the original plan, and it could as likely be good news as bad.

"Where are the rest?" a voice said on the intercom. "Where are the Mandaue and Lapu Lapu DZ forces?"

'Drop Zone Mandaue' was where the US 2nd Brigade was to land, near the bridge approaches on the main island of Cebu.

'Drop Zone Lapu Lapu' was the US 1st Brigades target, the Mactan side of the bridges, and the Anglo/French airborne brigade were bound for 'Drop Zone Zero Four' either side of the longest runway, runway 04, when approached from the west.

The 1st Brigade had in fact received warning of enemy aircraft in the area following the destruction of the transport aircraft carrying 2nd Brigade, and it had diverted to an even more southerly route but they were hustling to catch up, and were minutes behind but the transports had to slow before commencing a drop.

A pre-drop checklist was completed and this was then followed by a second, for the slowdown. The completion of the second checklist was marked by the flick of a switch.

'Red On'.

They were now some 40 minutes from the DZ and the men strapped their equipment container to a leg and stood. The container held the man's personal weapon in a sleeve along with his bergan and webbing. Some of the containers bore luminous white stickers and these were 'Must Go' loads that held radios, mortar, machine gun, anti-tank or medical equipment. In the event of the bearer being killed or wounded he would be divested of the container by whoever was passing for it to be deposited with company headquarters at the rally point.

The air load masters got the men on their feet and hooked up their 'Strops', the static lines. To the relief of all concerned the side doors on the left and right of the fuselage were opened, venting the accumulated perfume of vomit and high octane aviation fuel, the *Eau de Pegasus*.

"45 OK!...44 OK!...43 OK!..." A buddy-buddy check of the man in front by the paratrooper behind was carried out, starting with the last man in each stick and working forwards of course.

With nothing more to do except to continue standing with backs bent under the weight of their loads and wait for the green light. The howl of the wind through the open doors brought with it the scent of warfare, high explosive and burning petrochemicals.

130mph and at 800 feet the C-130s of No. 24 Squadron RAF led the Anglo/French stream.

There was some ground fire, small arms and light machine gun fire from the defending Chinese troops in their trenches on the beaches, a side window shattered as a few rounds scored, but nothing more serious occurred as they passed over the western shore of Mactan and were finally above the DZ.

Wing Commander Dunn reached forwards to activate the green light for the Loadies to begin despatching the sticks of paratroopers but his hand was suddenly not there anymore, just a bloody stump and cannon shells were exploding in the cockpit, destroying the instrument panel, and killing the co-pilot and flight engineer in a welter of blood, shattered glass and debris. Cannon shells struck all down the left side of the fuselage causing carnage amongst the closely packed men. Three engines were on fire and he could barely see for glass splinters in his eyes, a gale was tearing through the cockpit and he had a hard time keeping the aircraft steady with one hand, but there was no pain, not yet.

"GET THEM OUT!" he was able to shout over the intercom to the Loadies. "GET THEM OUT! GET THEM OUT!"

Most of the paratroopers from B Company, 3 Para, in the stick on the left side were dead or wounded, and the RAF crew were urging out those on the right side as fast as they could, they were still doing so when the aircraft bellied into the ground beside the end of the runway and somersaulted into the sea beyond.

Aboard the *Samara,* the sustained fire of her 20mm cannons hammered at the Hercules transports, flying slowly and from their right to left without jinking, committed to the low altitude and slow speed necessary to deliver paratroopers and pallets to the DZ. The morning sun caught the shiny brass of the empty casings as they were ejected, at a cyclic rate of 500 rounds a minute the empty shell casings struck the metal deck and bounced with a metallic ring, the spent cases rattling and multiplying. The loaders had hands pressed to their ears such was the noise. A blue grey haze of cordite hung over the mountings as they tracked the aircraft, ignoring the paratroopers that were exiting and instead seeking to destroy the transports, before swinging back for a fresh target.

No. 47 Squadron followed, a slightly longer interval between the squadron formations and both guns picked up Michelle Braithwaite's aircraft, tracking it for a moment before opening fire.

Fragments flew off the C-130's nose, the cockpit windows shattered and both the port outer and inner Allison turboprops first streamed black smoke before bursting into flame.

The Chinese gunners and their loaders manning the frigates 20mm mountings on the starboard side vanished in a mist of red. Pulverised tissue and the fragments of exploding 25mm cannon shells resulted from a pair of US Marine Corps AV-8B Harrier's strafing runs over the moored warship. They raked its gun mountings, the AV-8Bs Gatling-type Equaliser cannon expending ammunition at a phenomenal cyclic rate of 2000 rounds per minute. Just two of the briefest of touches on the gun button ended the fire from the frigates starboard side. The cannons were damaged by the high explosive rounds and the gunners and loaders dead, but the surviving ratings were already unshipping the port side 20mm auto cannons.

The piles of bloodied empty casings rattled under foot and the dead were dragged away to make room. The damaged guns splashed into the muddy water of the channel as the ratings set-to in mounting the replacements. The enemy is the enemy, but that does not make him any less brave or determined than those he is fighting.

Passing over the frigate the USMC Harriers stayed at just 200 feet and banked right to egress the area, flying low over Cebu City, avoiding a sky suddenly full of paratroopers from 3rd Battalion Parachute Regiment, and pallet loads, the 105mm light guns of 7 Parachute Regiment, Royal Horse Artillery, and ammunition. There was more on the way with the USAF C-17s approaching in the wake of the British and French drops.

Sandy Cummings, RN, flew the lead AV-8B, flying over the city beyond the channel before bending back around until again flying above the waters of the Mactan Channel, re-attacking the Krivak. His wingman sheered away, targeting an armed barge that was engaging the Harriers with 7.62 machine guns. The barge disappeared in a welter of spray and splintered wood as the Marine Corps aviator walked his rounds across it.

Selecting two Mk-82 250lb retarded bombs Sandy pickled them off, the weapons ballutes deploying behind them, slowing the weapons plunge and allowing the low flying Harrier to attack and egress safely. Both weapons penetrated the frigates superstructure and completed the destruction of the *Samara* that the Pearce Wing had begun weeks before in the Indian Ocean.

Squadron Leader Braithwaite held the aircraft steady for the paratroopers to exit. Her co-pilot feathered the damaged engines and pulled the fire handles on the port side engines, shutting off the fuel flow and returning his hands to lightly hold the controls, ready to take control if the aircraft captain were to be killed or injured. Flames from both damaged engines flickered and died. Thick black smoke pillared aloft from a crashed and burning RAF Hercules that lay on the eastern shore of the island. The tail plane of another protruded from the waters offshore, bodies floating face down beside it. The departing aircraft from No. 24 Squadron included damaged aircraft with wounded aboard. They had dropped their loads and now began the long flight back to Vietnam. Michelle did not follow; her aeroplane was not going to make it. She called up the next senior in No. 47 Squadron and relinquished control. Her flight engineer was seriously wounded and screaming in pain but they were now over water again and could not put down. Opening the throttles of the starboard engines she applied pressure on the rudder to compensate for the yaw caused by the lop-sided power source before adjusting the rudder trim wheel. She turned towards the main island, intending to gain height for the Loadies to bail out before she made an emergency landing. No one answered on the intercom and there seemed to be no open area she could use for this. She was struggling to regain altitude lost in the turn and advanced the throttles on the starboard engines some more, adjusting the trim wheel further still. The mass eviction of Mactan's residents by the Chinese troops had swollen the already significant shanty towns of squatters, there was nowhere close by so she headed over the city. Her side windows had been shattered by the ground fire but the screen held, cracked but still there.

"Check Barnet." she shouted to her co-pilot over the winds noise. Flying Officer Greg Barnet, the flight engineer, had fallen silent, the screaming tailing off suddenly.

Tracer flicked by and through the large rent in the side of the cockpit she caught a glimpse of a narrow road with open topped military trucks full of Chinese troops and a tank with a crewman firing on them with a heavy machine gun, although with more vigour than accuracy.

A dirty tail of smoke followed the aircraft from its slowly wind milling port engines, rents in the wings and fuselage from the cannon shell strikes were clearly visible to the faces turned upwards to watch the damaged transport as it flew low overhead, women crossed themselves and a priest in the street produced his crucifix and offering a blessing for those the machine contained, making the sign of the cross as it headed south west, parallel to the shore.

"Greg's dead, probably blood loss...I'll check the back." the co-pilot informed Michelle.

When he returned he had a shock for her.

"We've still got a full load. The port side loadmaster and the first five of the stick are dead so that side couldn't jump in time, and a cannon shell severed the starboard strop cable so they couldn't jump either." The main parachutes the men wore required a rigid anchor to clip on their static lines to. As the jumper goes out of the door the canopy is pulled out of the parachute pack on his or her back.

"The paras want us to go back so they can all go out the port side door instead."

They didn't have the altitude for them to jump now; turning back for Mactan would be disastrous.

"Get them unhooked, toss the parachutes out the doors to save weight, and get them strapped back in the jump seats." she ordered. "I'm looking for a place to put down so tell the Loadies to get it sorted and then get back here."

The Hercules continued, passing beyond the city limits, heading down the coast but those fields they now began to encounter were bordered by tall trees, mahogany and coconut palms.

They sank lower and lower until she was despairing of finding any suitable place. Visions of coming down on a crowded barangay flashed before her eyes but at last she saw a large open area directly ahead, rice paddies judging by the glister of water on its surface. They could not turn and bank so they could go around again. It was a straight in approach for a wheels up landing and hope they could clear the line of palms along its eastern border. This was it, their one chance and she ordered the rear cargo ramp to be lowered, to assist a quick exit.

"Flaps 50."

Carcar with its quaint old rotonda and bandstand was over her right shoulder and farm workers in the fields were turning and gawping at the sight of the crippled air force transport at little more than tree top height.

"Flaps 100...BRACE! BRACE! BRACE!"

She unconsciously sucked in her stomach as they reach the line of coconut palms, the belly of the aircraft brushed the tree tops, carrying off palm fronds and she cut the throttles and fuel to the engines, spinning the rudder trim wheel back again as the starboard engines thrust dropped off. The nose began to drop and a left bank threatened but both pilots heaved back on the controls and stamped hard on the left rudder pedal, forcing the failing machine to flare with wings level instead of nosing in or digging in a wingtip and flipping over. Bricks have glided better, was her final thought before they hit hard, slamming both pilots forwards against their harnesses. The Hercules sent water and mud sluicing outwards as it struck and slid along, a brown bow wave bending up and over the high wings. The wet surface was not slowing them that quickly and the far edge of the field, marked by a high earth bank and yet more trees, was looming up fast.

The nose of the aircraft, already damaged by the frigates 20mm cannon fire, crumpled as it struck the bank, flinging Squadron Leader Braithwaite against her straps a second time.

In the hold of the aircraft a loadmaster pointed at the open cargo ramp and shouted a command at the paratroopers.

"Get out, now!"

No one moved, not until a 3 Para sergeant translated the Loady's words into a command that paratroopers could understand.

"GO!" and they went.

It took a few minutes to remove the dead crew and troops and when Michelle emerged the paratroopers were nowhere to be seen, and she assumed they were in cover.

The C-130 was readied for destruction and a curious crowd of locals began to gather. Filipinos seem to have cornered the market on ignoring what is on the TV to rubberneck at anything out of the ordinary. Only a local boxing hero could keep a crowd in front of the goggle box despite a nearby fender-bender or vocal dispute between neighbours.

The first sound of gunfire occurred and Squadron Leader Braithwaite looked around for the paras. The Filipinos faded swiftly away.

"They've gone already, ma'am." a Loadie told her. "They were a bit pissed off and said something about picking a fight."

"It seems they have found one."

The roar of small arms fire and the detonation of mortar rounds and grenades sounded across the waters of the channel to the Filipino audience on Cebu. The British and French paratroopers had landed under fire from the airfield defenders. Nothing was exactly as planned; it never was except on exercise. B Company, 3 Para, was short a platoon, D Company was shy half of its strength, but at least they knew theirs was in Carcar, down the coast.

The companies had rallied and quickly rehashed who was assaulting what.

2 REP had lost men who had parachuted into a mine field and others who had been carried beyond the shore by the wind and drowned, burdened beneath equipment in the waters of the Cebu Straits, but both units reorganised, set up mortar lines and moved out into the assault.

The last parachute delivered an inanimate figure to the centre of the runway, shot by the defenders after departing the final French Air Force C-160 Transall, the 2 REP Legionnaire joined other figures that were being tugged unfeeling along the ground by canopies that had not collapsed. Some bodies lay attached to parachutes that had not fully deployed, the Hercules of No. 47 Squadron had lost three of their number over the drop zone, No. 24 Squadron had lost four and not all of their loads had made it out safely.

All the hardened positions had been attacked by the carrier aircraft from USS *John C Stennis* prior to the arrival of the airborne forces although not all were completely destroyed. Once these and the defenders foxholes were taken the assaults axis shifted to the buildings. Those who surrendered were blind folded and corralled before being sent to the rear holding area, those who didn't were killed in place as the paras and legionnaires reached them, moving from room to room, building to building without pause.

At last the final resistance was snuffed out and the NATO troops reorganised, breathing heavily, sweat soaked, carrying injuries and wounds they chose to ignore, and all suffering from a desperate thirst. House clearing, FIBUA, uses up men, ammunition and the contents of water bottles at a ferocious rate.

Beyond the airfields boundary lay the remains of the town of Lapu Lapu, and there the Chinese troops filled rifle magazines, checked their arcs of fire and waited.

Silence fell over the airfield, but only briefly. No rest for the wicked, with the exception of the half strength D Company, 3 Para which got the cushy job of manning the perimeter. Shouted commands took the place of gunfire, and the hurried unloading of the equipment began. The men converged on them, the pallets of ammunition and equipment that sat beneath large collapsed cargo parachutes. The gunners of 7 Parachute Regiment RHA ran to their guns, unstrapping them from their pallets before manhandling them into a gun line.

The arrival of the C-17s of the US 1st Brigade brought more ground fire from defenders north of the airfield in the partially demolished town of Lapu Lapu.

As the USAF Globemasters approached two abreast from the west at 800ft, the RAF Globemasters approached in single file from the east at 50ft, looking for all the world as if about to make wheels up landings. Rear cargo ramps opened and the lead aircraft descended further, to just twelve feet above the tarmac and flying almost the entire length of the extended main runway before a drogue 'chute pulled a pallet from its belly. A second pallet sat inside its cargo hold but the shedding of so much weight would cause the aircraft to 'bounce' up beyond safe delivery height. Having despatched half their loads the No. 99 Squadron C-17s flew around to make a second delivery. Only one aircraft despatched parachutists at a more sedate altitude. On landing these men ran to the runway and likewise collected the pallets contents.

Despite being 'on the same side' there were no waves, no cheers and no sign of any 'hail fellow, well met' from the men of 3 Para. The newcomers mounted their vehicles, started up and moved off, the lead Scimitars commander first unfurling a large standard and attaching it to his armoured vehicles antennae. Grinning vehicle commanders raised two fingers at the airborne brethren as the squadron of vehicles followed the flapping emblem of the Guards Division.

"Well." said 3 Paras CO. "At least they made the effort to actually arrive this time."

Lt Col Jim Popham, 111th Airborne Infantry Regiment, 82nd Airborne Division, was number '1', the lead man of the first stick in the leading pair of aircraft. With his left hand he supported his equipment container which rested on his left foot. His right hand 'guarded' the D Ring of his reserve parachute, preventing its accidental snagging. Activating a parachute within an aircraft tended to have fatal consequences for the wearer and catastrophic ones for the aeroplane when the jumper was dragged out and took a section of fuselage with him. He used his left foot to help him heave the equipment container forwards as he took his place just a step from the open jump door. Above the door the red light glowed, the glass of its neighbour a dull and unlit green. He wondered, not for the first time, why no one had written a comedy sketch about a brothel in the clouds. His left hand gripped the containers handle and the right hand now supporting him against the doorway. He remained there, the toe of his right boot forward of the left where it would add purchase when the moment came. The boot was the only part of him not in shadow; bright sunlight illuminated it and his neighbours now drying vomit that decorated it. Ignoring the pain in his back from bearing so much heavy equipment, and straps almost tight enough to cut off circulation, he waited calmly, setting an example. There was some graffiti beside the door, a 'Chad', its big nose and eyes protruding over a brick wall *"Chad Says Mind the First Step...It's a Doozy!"* Looking out he saw it was a beautiful morning, blue skies and a blue sea. He was at the starboard door so his view was of the Cebu Strait and the island of Bohol. It was quite a sight, calm and idyllic, he was enjoying the view when the dull green glass became shiny emerald.

"GO!"

He heaved the container forwards over the sill and followed it out. As always he forgot to close his mouth, so he was still none the wiser as to whether that simple act prevented the sensation of falling, or rather plummeting. Never a keen enthusiast of parachuting, Jim had applied for the airborne because his best friend had also. The friend flunked the course and masculine pride had not allowed Jim to back out. He now endured the three seconds of very unpleasant near-panic until the canopy opened, ready to pull the reserve 'chute D Ring, grasp the folds within and fling from him in the hopes the two devices would not become entangled. However, looking up he saw the main parachute was a nice big circle of inflated fabric. He had a twist in his lines and kicked out violently; rolling his shoulders as he did so to rotate his body and clear it. He was now facing towards the Mactan Channel and he could not help but notice an absence of parachutes floating down on its far side.

Where the hell was 2nd Brigade?

First things first, he unstrapped his container and unclipped it from his harness, letting it fall the fifteen feet of its retaining rope to hang below him. To land with the heavy container still attached to his body was to court broken legs, pelvis and shattered knees.

Jim could feel the breeze on his neck and pulled down hard on his left riser to spill air from under the right side of the canopy, turning him until he felt it against the front of his right ear. He drifted backwards at an angle, feet together, knees bent, chin on his chest and with elbows trying to touch but never succeeding. Jim kept his feet together but turned them to point half right. He saw the illusion of stasis turn to the reality of ground rush and braced to impact that ground and roll, but instead he plunged through the glass roof of an abandoned paint factory.

When he arrived at the O Group following his units rallying he drew snorts of laughter from the other battalion commanders.

"This week" said the CO of 3 Para in a yokel accent. "Oi will mainly be sporting the national colours of Spain."

Jim had come through the roof and his collapsing canopy had snagged a girder, just saving the Popham family jewels but he had ended up astraddle two of the giant containers of the factory's product, with one leg in a vat of yellow paint and the other in red.

The fighting in the ruins of Lapu Lapu was fierce, and bloody. Marines of the People's Liberation Army Navy in barracks near the docks had deployed following the arrival of the British and French, and were about to launch a counter attack on the airfield when the US 82nd's parachutes appeared above their heads. Men were shot in their parachutes, helpless to fight back, and those who landed amongst the Chinese Marines were butchered. The still standing walls and telegraph poles were snares for the parachute canopies and those who were snagged and left dangling were shot without mercy.

The American paratroopers rallied and set about cleaning house with the same level of accord for their enemy as had been afforded to them. An empty barbed wire enclosure in the 3rd Army's stores area had been adopted as a POW compound for the captive soldiers and airmen resulting from the Anglo/French assault, but only a smattering of Chinese marines were added to their number.

Day 1: Operation *Vespers* (Amphibious element) 0530hrs that morning.

USS *Constellation* launched its CAP fully an hour and seventeen minutes late. All the tanker support in the world was not going to make up for that.

The fleet cruised north, entering the Tañon Strait at its narrowest point with Admiral Jackson stood with his hands behind his back and both fingers crossed. Seven thousand, eight hundred yards, plus change, which was the distance from Negros to Cebu at the southern entrance to the straits.

He had received intelligence on the Caltrop Mine from the Cebu resistance fighters via Major Garfield Brooks' small Green Beret detachment. A naval officer involved in the minelaying operation had been waylaid whilst visiting a brothel and persuaded to tell all he knew. The mines batteries of four high speed torpedoes that produced an ultra-sonic wave before them, loosening water molecules to permit their quite scary acceleration, nought to ninety knots in three seconds. The range was only five hundred metres and the warhead was small, but all the same, it was an area denial weapon to be reckoned with. As to the mechanics and technical side, the captive either did not know or he expired rather than reveal those details. No-one one on the allied side knew how it detected approaching vessels, how it differentiated between friend and foe or how to detect the mines. Garfield had lost one of his men, a diver, in trying to learn more. Currently the biggest minesweeper on the planet was leading the formation. The USS *Iowa* with her thick armoured hull, laid down in 1940, was performing the role of the idiot mine detector, fingers in ears, eyes closed and stamping on the ground almost. Her armour should save her as she cleared a channel that at least was the theory.

With some relief he watched the small Lilo-An ferry terminal draw level, the where the channel bends sharply through forty five degrees to the northeast and begins to widen. The fleet, in single file, a sixty year old battleship at its head and aircraft carriers, cruisers, destroyers, frigates and amphibious assault ships could pick up the pace in order to recover the aircraft engaged on the Mactan strike. It was now just 76 miles along the strait to Toledo.

Zheng was still on the surface but with fully charged batteries, and still following *Sentinel Sea* on a bearing of 255° along the Tañon Strait with Toledo on her port quarter. They would at least not have to call in at the big construction site that Mactan had become but the detour to avoid the minefields along the eastern passages of the island of Cebu was time consuming.

Captain Li had been sleeping for a few hours before returning to the conning tower. They did of course have lookouts as even though they were in relatively friendly waters the possibility of collision at any time was very real, in peace or war. There was more space to move in the Kilo's conning tower than there had been in the old Juliett, not much, but enough to seem roomy to him.

Radio silence was a matter of course, and as they had signalling lamps they could still communicate with the *Sentinel Sea*. The captured tankers commercial band navigation and weather radars were being used instead of the Kilo's powerful search radar.

Li was peering up at the sky and enjoying the blue and cloudless expanse when he was returned to the business in hand.

"Captain, the *Sentinel Sea* is signalling."

The flashing signal lamp on the tankers starboard bridge wing was easy for Li to read but he let the crewmen do their jobs. Morse had been abandoned for a while for most people but it was an effective means of transmission of short messages.

"Message reads 'Radar contact...'"

The sound akin to a freight train gave the rating pause and then the USS *Iowa's* 16" shells landing astern of the *Zheng*, and those straddling the *Sentinel Sea* made the remainder of the messages translation unnecessary.

"...LARGE SHIP!" the lookout shouted, completing it anyway, as sea water drenched them.

"Starboard 30...give me revolutions for twenty knots!"

The tanker had been momentarily blocked from their view by the water spouts but she emerged from the spray with her hull and superstructure glistering wetly in the early morning sun and unscathed. She apparently had her helm hard over now but with only 7000 yards of sea room either side it was a manoeuvre that Li would have tried only slowly and with care, but the bow wave seemed to be increasing.

"Not a good idea." Li said aloud, and as thick black smoke belched from the ships single funnel he shook his head critically.

"As if that is going to help against radar assisted gunnery."

"Captain?" the lookout asked, as if he had trouble with the captain's last statement.

"Well they aren't using Ouija board fire directors, now are they?" he laughed. "Sound the diving alarm; clear the bridge, lookouts below!"

The next salvo directed at the *Zheng* landed where they would have been if they had maintained their previous course and heading.

"Good shooting." Li observed. "Submerge the boat...forty feet."

Water spouts again straddled the slower moving tanker and a large angry orange and red fireball arose as a shell scored a direct hit.

Li pulled the hatch closed above him and secured it before sliding the rest of the way down the ladder gripping the outside.

Either someone knew all about them or someone didn't care and was shooting at anything that moved.

"Sonar...what is happening with *Sentinel Sea*, is she stopped?"

"Yes Captain, I can hear breaking up sounds, she's still on the surface but going down." he was told. "It won't be long."

"Take us over there and keep this depth for the time being." Li studied the chart for a moment.

"Okay, there will be ASW helicopters overhead shortly and we have nowhere to run to so I want us as close to her as you can get once she goes down. Something like this worked for me before."

Li of course knew nothing of *Church* but its existence had become a distinct possibility owing to events 600 miles away. *Zheng* and the *Sentinel Sea*, their position and their mission were known to NATO until a few moments after the submarine submerged and the politburo killed the downlink from their satellites, denying *Church* access.

All the Chinese assets vanished from the screen at Project Church, so the fleet would have to find her the old fashioned way.

An hour after engaging the two surface contacts in the straits the battleship USS *Iowa* forged past a dipping ASW helicopter at 30 knots, throwing up a huge bow wave in the narrow confines of the straits to the delight of the naked and cheering Filipino kids splashing in the shallows. The ships 16" turrets were swung out to starboard, the muzzles of her main armament now blacked as she bombarded known enemy positions. The Chinese invaders were getting a kicking and the kids cheered each shot as much as they welcomed the man-made rollers the warships wash created. Water spouts appeared to the stern of the vessel, 155mm rounds fired from two batteries in the mountains. The Iowa was saved by her speed and the incoming rounds were back-tracked on radar. Had the protagonists been two miles closer the Chinese PLZ-05 guns would have scored with every round, but 'The Big Stick', as *Iowa* was nicknamed, was just beyond range of the laser guided rounds the guns had available. USS *Iowa* increased speed, straining her old engines and managing 32 knots, almost her best. Her three main turrets tracked around, the muzzles of all nine guns elevated and she fired a broadside.

The arrival of the sixteen inch shells had a devastating effect on the gun batteries and a second salvo arrived for good measure.

Aboard the *USS John C Stennis*, a vessel also making quite a splash on the shores either side, the first strikes were launching against positions around Toledo but there was of course the loss of the US 82nd's 2nd Brigade to cope with. Major General 'Snowy' Hills was on the secure line from Mactan where an ad hoc attempt to force both bridges had met defeat. There were pillboxes, four of them on each bridge and all were protected from missile attack by rocket and mortar netting. Artillery would be counterproductive but a counter-attack by the Chinese was just a matter of time. They could not wait for nightfall but he had another plan. The reserves would take the bridges and hold until the US Marines crossed from Toledo and relieved the airborne force. It robbed the airborne of any flexibility but they had no option. 3 Para would attack the newer, most easterly 'Marcelo Fernan' Bridge, and the Foreign Legionnaires of 2 REP would take the western 'Osmena Bridge'.

Elsewhere, the Filipinos were doing their best to delay Chinese forces that were heading to the city. 86th Mech was scattered about the island on garrison duties but if it reformed they would be hard pressed to contain it. 3rd Marines helicopter fleet was going to be busy elsewhere for a while but they had airpower on their side and USS *Iowa* for gunfire support to clear away opposition in the mountains.

The deck lurched violently beneath Admiral Jackson's feet and the lights went out in the USS *John C Stennis*' CIC, to be replaced by emergency lighting.

On shore the kids stopped dancing and waving.

Captain Li's wish to do what submariners were supposed to do had finally come true as *Zheng's* 3M-54E 'Sizzler' anti-ship missiles scored on both carriers and her 533mm torpedoes struck the *Iowa's* stern.

Day 1: Operation *Vespers* (Airborne element) 0713hrs.

Much of the town of Lapu Lapu, named after the warrior who had slain Ferdinand Magellan, had been demolished to make way for barracks and more warehouses. Not all the buildings had been earmarked for destruction though and the 82nd Airborne's 1st Brigade had just finished clearing an office building near the shore, between the two bridges. Major General Hills, Brigadier Francis Burton of the US 1st Brigade and Brigadier Ripley Hartiss of the Anglo/French airborne brigade entered the building's rooftop machine room. The bare concrete walls were pitted with shrapnel scars and its panoramic windows blown out. Their boots sent spent cartridge cases rolling noisily across the cement floor as they found themselves a position to discretely view both bridges without attracting attention to themselves. A dead Chinese sniper lying against one wall was ignored, but the residue from hand grenades lingering, the stink of burnt almonds causing Snowy to sneeze.

Behind them on the airfield the Royal Engineers were clearing the runway surfaces of anything that could be sucked into an engine intake or burst a tyre in readiness to receive aircraft twenty four hours earlier than scheduled. Even from their vantage a dirty haze could be seen from beyond the mountains. USS *Constellation* was on fire, dead in the water in the Tañon Strait where the crew were now abandoning her. USS *John C Stennis* was damaged but capable of air operations and USS *Iowa* was under tow and working to patch a rent in her hull and pump out the flooded engine room. Without electrical power her 16" guns would remain silent.

Major General 'Snowy' Hills and his brigade commanders had their own battles to fight and if the navy sorted out their problems and were able to lend a hand as originally planned then fine and dandy, but the airborne were used to adapting and making do, of pulling the fat from the fire despite the odds.

They were too far from either bridge to see the bodies of the American dead from the first attempt to take them. Smoke marred the paintwork of the bridges, the result of strikes by javelin missiles on the protective mesh of presteel bars and chicken wire in front of the block houses. The bars were welded together to defend against RPGs and anti-tank missiles, and the airborne force lacked the large stock of the missiles that would be required to reduce that barrier. The block houses only mounted light machine guns apparently, but they had proved sufficient. The US paratroopers had tried to use smoke for cover, fired from 81mm mortars, but the effectiveness was negligible as the few rounds that landed on the bridge, and not in the water, had produced a short lasting screen, rapidly dispersed by the breeze blowing along the waterway.

GPMGs in the sustained fire role were going to provide cover, albeit of mainly psychological nuisance value for this next attempt, a simultaneous attack on both bridges with the Scimitar armoured reconnaissance vehicle of the Blues & Royals squadron.

Snowy Hills glanced at his watch.

"About now I think."

Right on cue there appeared three of the light armoured vehicles on the approach ramps of each of the bridges, coming out of side turnings and accelerating hard to 50mph, their Rarden cannons firing mixed high explosive and armour piercing rounds in bursts of three. Sparks appeared where a round struck a steel rod but the rocket fences were ineffective against the 30mm cannon fire. Tracer arced over from the GPMGs but only a fluke ricochet had any hope of entering a gun port and doing any damage

Chinese snipers and riflemen on the bridges added their fire to that of the blockhouses but it was having no effect on the buttoned up armoured reconnaissance vehicles. An RPG round left a trail of dirty exhaust in its wake as it narrowly missed one of the speeding Scimitars and the GPMGs fire shifted, seeking to suppress any more of the anti-tank fire.

The remaining troops of Scimitars followed at a far more sedate speed, that of a rapid walk, providing physical protection from small arms fire to the men behind.

With typical national rivalry the French Foreign Legionnaires of 1er CIE, 2e Régiment étranger de parachutists, and A Company, 3rd Battalion, Parachute Regiment were looking over their shoulders at each other across the intervening 1,400 metres between the bridges and shouting to the vehicle commanders to speed up. The Legionnaires began a slow jog as 'their' Blues and Royals crews acquiesced. Moments later the British Paratroopers began to draw ahead. It was as well that both units were superbly fit as the men ignored the incoming small arms fire bouncing off the protective Scimitars and were soon sprinting behind them, urging the vehicles to even greater speed.

The distance between the foot of the ramps and the defensive block houses at the two bridges was at a variance and the fast moving troop on the eastern bridge were therefore warned just in time that automatic weapons were not the only weaponry the blockhouses had. The troop commander's vehicle on the western bridge was engulfed in fire as flame throwers sent streams of burning fuel a hundred metres.The crew of the stricken vehicle bailed out only to have the streams of flame played over them. In mortal agony they leapt from the bridge, falling to their deaths in the water far below.

The remaining Blues and Royals Scimitars of those lead troops braked hard and pounded the structures with armour piercing fire, first one and then the other. A hand appeared from a gun port, waving a piece of white cloth but it went unseen or ignored, the 30mm cannons continued until satisfied that all resistance was ended. The Rarden cannons were then levelled at the second pair of blockhouses further along each bridge.

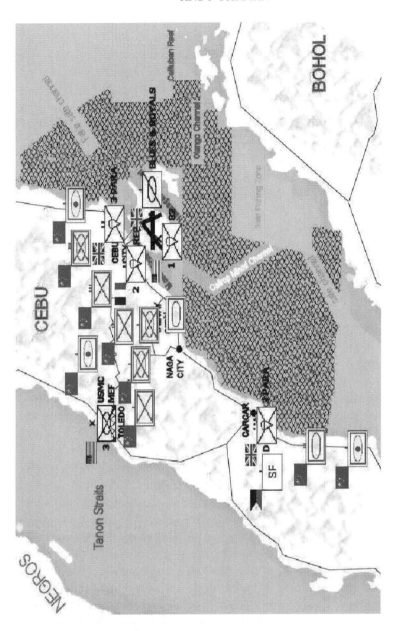

Operation '*Vespers*'

Snowy and his brigade commanders watched the paratroopers on both bridges leave the cover of the vehicles and employ fire and maneouvre to hunt down the snipers and Chinese infantry.

The remainder of the Anglo/French airborne brigade flooded across the bridges and began digging in on the far side.

"Too close to call." he said. "But those guys are going to be arguing for the next hundred years about who reached the far bank first."

The burning Scimitar began to blow itself apart as the flames reached the ammunition but thanks to the Blues and Royals the bridges had been taken in less than fifteen minutes.

In Toledo the marines of 3rd Expeditionary Force were ashore and moving inland, the point section of an armoured reconnaissance platoon had forged ahead to reach the foot of the mountain road and encountered Chinese heavy armour in well concealed and sited positions.

As a garrison guarding against, and combating, guerrilla forces, the 86th Mechanised Brigade of the Chinese 6th Army were mediocre, but engaging in conventional warfare against regular forces they were back in their comfort zone and very good indeed. The US Marine Corps had come to Cebu looking for a fight and it had found one.

An air battle ensued north of Cebu between land based fighters from Chinese bases on Luzon and the CAP from USS *John C Stennis*; consequently a Sea Stallion off USS *Boxer* took the lengthy roundabout route from Toledo to Mactan skimming the waves of the Tañon Strait. As it rounded the southern tip it spotted tanks and IFVs being ferried across the strait from Negros. An AV-8B sank the ferry and its sisters at the Sibulan ferry dock but an unknown number of reinforcements were heading up the coast road. Garfield Brooks small group of Green Berets and resistance fighters had ambushed one armoured column at a choke point along the road, in the narrow streets of Carcar, and were already calling for help in light of the resulting street fighting. He had acquired some members of 3 Para from a shot down British C-130 and their professional help was a bonus, but Garfield's force was seriously outnumbered.

The marines were fully engaged and that left Major General Hills with the decision to either send some of his already depleted force or advice Garfield to return to the mountains and preserve what he still had.

The Sea Stallion landed and unloaded thirty two bound and hooded prisoners, the survivors of the submarine *Zheng*, plucked from the waters of Tañon Strait after their vessel had been forced to the surface by depth charges and then sunk by gunfire. Not all the crew had made it out before it made its final dive; her captain was not among them.

At lunchtime the first artillery rounds began to land on Mactan, targeting two buildings at first, pounding first one and then the other.

In the newly set up field hospital in the basement beneath the old airport Departure Lounge the lights went out and darkness fell before the field generators kicked over noisily and gave the surgeons light to see again. Ten minutes later the water stopped running as the desalinization and pumping plant were destroyed.

The first organised attacks came an hour later after the artillery switched to the 2 REP positions in the grounds of the University of Cebu, next to the bridge. Mortar fire joined in and did not lift until the Chinese infantry, supported by tanks, were themselves taking casualties. 'The REP' admired the training, courage and discipline of these troops but they killed them all the same.

After a pause it was the turn of 3 Para, and the results were the same.

The city garrison fell back and reorganised. The costly reconnaissance in force of both units positions now gave the Chinese a clearer picture of what they faced. Reinforcements from other islands began to arrival in the early evening and the shelling began of both positions.

Politburo, War Bunker 21, Nanking Province.

Marshal Chang, Defence Minister Pong were the only two remaining in the chamber after Chairman Chan ordered the rest to depart.

The Chairman had been trying to cut down but he was now chain smoking.

"Why have the Americans led us to believe that troops from Europe were coming through the Suez Canal?"

"To make us reinforce Singapore?"

Marshal Chang wondered if the West was also cursed with politicians, the holders of dumbed down degrees, who somehow felt they were some kind of ruling elite by right of birth?

Minister Pong's answer was studiously ignored by the Chairman.

"A distraction, or a deception plan of some kind, Mr Chairman." Marshal Chang replied.

"You know this for a fact Marshal?" the Chairman asked. "I don't, and I am not afraid to admit that I don't know that Europe's veteran armies are coming via Suez, or if they ever left Calais for that matter?"

The Chairman glared at them before going on.

"We are losing submarines in the north Indian Ocean to those curry eating bastards next door, and all because you, the experts, did not recognise the signs." His fist hit the surface of the desk. "Where are the European armies?"

"I don't know, Mr Chairman"

"Does anyone?"

Day 2: Operation *Vespers* Arbuckle Mountains, Oklahoma.

It was the final *Choir Practice*, the last time the entire *Choir* would be gathered together and dealing with *Church* business.

"So when will they be able to see us?" asked Terry Jones. "Can they see *Evensong* for the hoax that it was, in a week's time or a month?"

"*Church* is no longer of any use to us but they cannot see our ships either, not yet anyway." Sally Peters assured him. "They have one great big nightmare ahead of them debugging their system before they see anything that they can trust."

"Excuse me for one moment while I remind you all of three things." Terry said. "Never assume an opponent is *less* smart than you are, never assume an opponent is *not* smarter than you are, and of course never assume he will tackle a problem from the same direction that you would."

"It is inconceivable that they can have debugged the system in a day." Sally protested. "No matter how smart they are."

"Is our system secure, Sally?" the President asked.

"Yes sir." She replied emphatically.

"Then they would need to get their intelligence from someone else as a stop gap measure." Terry stated. "It is what I would do."

"I don't think that they have any friends left, and we would know pretty damn quickly if anyone started moving their stuff into orbit above the region."

"What about Russia?"

"They don't have enough left to risk losing more and as agreed they are informing us of any changes in orbit."

"Nothing coming south, no geocentric RORSATs to tip the Chinese as to where our ships are?"

"No Mr President, just their Kondor-138, a photo recon bird, and they tell us it is going to be repositioned and shifted down to low orbit to watch the Spratly Islands."

"Seems reasonable, so let us move on."

The Indian and Pakistani navies had been having some success in locating and sinking Chinese submarines waiting in ambush for the convoys carrying the European armies to emerge from the Suez Canal.

"If they have not worked it out yet, they will soon, but we won't know when that is, not anymore." Joseph said with regret. "They will be poring over these satellite images of Ms O'Connor's."

"The days of *'Church'* were numbered once we elected to use it for *Evensong*, but it served its purpose well. Their 3rd Army was already having a lean time of it in Australia with our own submarines putting on the squeeze to its supply line, and now we put a hitch knot in it." The general said. "*Matins* can proceed as planned, as it is too late for them to intercept the convoys now. The best they can do is to collect their 2 Corps, which was defending Singapore from our digitised phantom convoy borne army, and either reinforces Cebu or their 1st Corps in Australia"

"*Vespers* is looking desperate though, particularly on Mactan. The attacks of last night were reportedly pretty much Korean War era human waves, for God's sake" The President was looking at the casualty lists. "Those boys are surrounded by a sea full of mines on three sides and the Chinese on the other.

"Don't worry about the paratroopers; they are in airborne hog heaven, Mr President." Carmine stated. "If they weren't surrounded they'd have nothing to brag about and blame the other services for, between this war and the next."

Day 4: Operation *Vespers* (Airborne element)
1119hrs.

Several attacks during the night had managed to get quite close to 3 Para's positions, right up to the thickly strung coils of concertina wire, all of which had come from the Chinese own defence stores that had been earmarked for Australia. The M18 Claymore mines that had been placed in front of the wire were supplemented by Chinese Type 66 mines from the PLA 3rd Army's supplies, and these differed from the M18 only in the idiots guide on the back being in Chinese script.

The night attacks had been determined affairs which had exhausted the emplaced Claymores and their copies but the attacks kept on until dawn, when the snipers took control of movement in the British and French lines. There had been no opportunity to replace the Claymores so work parties were already been warned for the task after last light, this coming evening.

The Chinese dead were starting to smell rather ripe very rapidly in the hot sun, which was another unpleasant facet of fighting here, as opposed to their last battlefield, Germany.

The sun was already high in the sky, and that sky was a deep cloudless blue, just as it had been for the previous three days. The destruction of the desalinisation plant was now the cause of the men's greatest discomfort and water was rationed to a half pint a day. If the 3rd Marines did not arrive today though, the ration would be reduced to a quarter of a pint.

"Anyone got any buckshee water?" a voice asked from one of 3 Platoon, A Company's trenches, the occupant wisely not sticking his head up to make the enquiry. The Chinese had some very good snipers out there somewhere.

"Sorry mate." A voice answered.

"Nope."

"I'm in a tropical paradise praying for rain, how sad is that?" said the parched enquirer.

"A guy in C Company got shot in the arse last night while doing a rain dance on the edge of his trench." another said conversationally, somewhere over in 2 Section.

"It wasn't a rain dance; it was just the Dance of the Flaming Arseholes with different words he made up." A Welsh voice said from the platoon's gun pit, and it sang a few lines.

"The tosser got what he asked for then." someone else offered up harshly. "That was bloody awful."

"It took his balls off, I heard?"

"Well that's just nature's way of ensuring that come World War 4 the gene pool will be rid of wankers doing the wrong pagan themed dance at inappropriate moments, isn't it like?" offered the gentleman from Llanfairfechan in final judgement. There was little sympathy for the would-be Shaman from C Company but a lot of sniggers.

"A guy in the Assault Pioneer Platoon made a piss still." another trench added. "He's selling it for twenty fags."

"The still or the end product?"

There was a moment's silence.

"I didn't think to ask."

"Well you should've." said the gun pit. "It's likely to leave a bad taste if you were wrong, boyo."

"How do you make a piss-still anyway?"

"A long trouser leg and loads of soil. The soil filters it."

"Anyone got a spare pair?"

"Nah."

"Well" called gun pit. "There's a guy on the wire who don't need his no more."

'Really?"

"He's only a five foot Cantonese Commando like, so you'd have to filter it through twice."

The crack of a high velocity round brought a second of silence from the men as they listened to the sound of someone's helmet bouncing away down the slope to the waterway behind them.

"You okay?" gun pit asked. "You didn't stick yer head up for a look did you?"

"Aye." the, now, sheepish voice replied.

"Well there's a silly sod of an Englishman for you, isn't it!"

"I made a start on the piss-still though..."

In his hide, the sniper wondered what all the laughter was about.

Jim Popham wore a dead man's camouflage trousers but his jump boots still bore a little colour here and there. He left the two riflemen who had accompanied him in cover as he himself crawled through the rubble, staying low and slow so as to avoid raising any dust. He did not go all the way to the forward O.P though, staying in cover to call out softly.

The O.P near the north west of the island doubled as a listening post at night and had heard noises coming across the water all through the previous night following a mass attack that had forced the Legionnaires across the channel to give more ground. 2 REP's perimeter was shrinking as attrition began to bite.

Jim had come out to listen when it had first been called in around midnight.

"It sounds like dem guys is doin' stone masonry over there, sir." Sergeant Tony Beckett had told him at the time.

'Over There' was a bricks and mortar factory on Cebu's shore, with wharfs along its western side. The south side which faced them was just sun-bleached brickwork. It was the closest point to one of the few spots on Mactan's northern shore that was not locked in by concrete docks or sea walls.

Beckett had rejoined what had remained of the battalion in the UK during the formation of 111th. The President had delayed Beckett's return to Germany after the delivery of Colonel General Serge Alontov and the disc that became known as 'Church' until the final battle had been decided. Beckett had been with 4 Company in the old Coldstream/82nd lash up, and the President's action had probably kept the young man alive, although Tony was having guilt trips. All his squad had been amongst the dead on Vormundberg's muddy hillside.

"Sergeant Beckett?" Jim now called out.

"Just listen quiet like, sir." Beckett's voice answered.

Listening was the problem though as the marines had fought their across the mountains and were now noisily stopped by another obstacle, a solidly built former US Officers Club that had been built by the same engineer who constructed the first airbase on Mactan, back in the late '40s. Funny how these things can bite you in the ass a generation or two later.

The former officers club the US Marines were loudly attacking was now an exclusive restaurant and hotel, or rather it had been until it became the residence of the commanding general of the garrison, and fortified accordingly. It had an amazing view out across the city, Mactan, the Cebu Straits and to Bohol, and the tenure upon Mactan's airfield by the stricken USS *Constellation's* air wing had been curtailed by artillery observers on its terraced garden. Visiting aircraft now made pallet drops of water and medical supplies without landing.

The single road from Toledo had proved a serious impediment to the US Marines who had lost men and vehicles to mining that had dropped stretched of the road down the steep hillsides and ravines into the valleys below, and those sections required bridging by the engineers before they could continue with the advance.

Jem Stanford of the US Marines and Snowy Hills had already surmised that the Chinese were probably looking to force the bridges, retake the island fortress and pull up the drawbridge behind them, as in blowing the bridges. They would then tough it out until the Chinese fleet and their 3rd Army's 3 Corps secured the Spratly Islands and came to the rescue.

The US's own naval units had withdrawn beyond the range of land based aircraft to lick their wounds and repair the damaged vessels. The Tañon Strait was now blocked to anything drawing more in draft than a tramp coaster as the USS *Constellation* had gone down with her bows toward Cebu and her stern pointing at the Negros coast, blocking the deep water channel.

The US Marines held Toledo and most of the mountain road now, aided by the fact that the PLA's 86th Mechanised and those reinforcement from neighbouring islands were in and around Cebu and Mandaue.

Serious damage had been both given and received by the resistance forces and their regular troops from the Green Berets and 3 Para at Carcar. The residents evacuated the town before two companies of Type 98 main battle tanks from the PLA 70th Mechanised Brigade that was garrisoning Negros had arrived. With diminished stocks of all types of ammunition, and in particular anti-tank weapons, Major Brooks had planned to try the old fashioned tactic of Molotov cocktails from the rooftops onto the armour passing through Carcar's narrow streets. but the Chinese infantry burned the town that first night, and had motored through the charred ruins with machine guns blazing at dawn the next day. There was nothing that the small force could do except withdraw back into the hills with those who had survived.

"There, hear that?"

"Armor." Jim said. "Not much it can do over there, except to the REP guys."

The wall of the factory fell outwards with a massive splash into the shallows. Dust billowed outwards too but from it emerged that venerable favourite for amphibious assaults the Type 63 light tank. The Chinese had chiselled away the cement between the bricks during the night, leaving enough of the brickwork to act as pillars and prevent the roof from landing on their heads. They had next moved the tanks inside the factory, as close as possible to the exit point out of the channel that the O.P currently occupied.

A pretty good plan for a surprise night attack so why throw away that element of surprise now, in daylight? The US Marines must be close to breaking through, Jim surmised.

"I thought all the waterways were mined?"

"Apparently not everywhere...Beckett, leave the O.P and follow me!"

There was no argument coming from that quarter, Tony and his trio grabbed their equipment and ran up the back after Jim. Jim Popham's men were covering them all as they ran back into cover, and Lt Col Popham was calling for the reserve troop of Scimitars. The first rounds of Chinese artillery rounds began to fall and the sound of the 'incoming' sent everyone diving for shelter.

The banks of the waterway had been recognised by the *Vespers* planners as a weak spot and likely approach for an enemy. It had been heavily mined with China's own Type 72 anti-tank weapons from the stores on the island.

The artillery rounds first fell in the Mactan Channel whereupon the enemy observers began 'walking' the barrage up the beach. The unpleasant work of half a night by Jim's men was slowly but methodically undone as the shells worked the beach over.

Six-wheeler Type 92 IFVs were next entering the water in the tanks wake, literally.

The US 111th Airborne Infantry were dug-in back from the shoreline or had built rubble sangars. Jim and the four men made it back to their lines.

The defenders obvious move was the wait for the armour to crawl out of the water and hit them with all the AT weaponry they possessed. They had far more RPG-26s than they had water, so it should not be a problem. The artillery observers on the mountainside who had evicted the Navy air wing now set about preventing the 82nd men from doing just that.

"Bugles and whistles?" the voice from 3 Platoon's 2 Section shouted. "My granddad told me about them in Korea, they aren't still using those are they?" The noise had come from the north east, a direction they had not been attacked from before on account of the ground being, basically, a bog. It was distracting though.

Another Chinese tactic in Korea had been to arm half a regiment with swords, axes and broom handles, and the other half with rifles and machines guns. They sent the first half off with its medieval level of weaponry and the second half following close behind. The UN forces expended much of their ammunition on the first wave.

Quantity versus quality, and all that stuff.

"Holy...STAND TO!"

Not all of the dead from the final battalion strength night attack had in fact been *hors d combat;* over two hundred had endured the heat and stench throughout the morning.

IFVs, tanks and a thousand infantry on foot were emerging from cover over half a kilometre away to the north, but two companies worth were sprinting forwards less than a hundred metres from the wire.

The leading men threw themselves on the coils for their comrades to use as thoroughfares into the 3 Para positions. The expended Claymores had not been replaced from the previous night and A Company were immediately engaged in close quarters combat.

Major General Snowy Hills watched quietly, a centre of calm amidst the hubbub in his divisions operations centre. Jem Stanford's 3rd Marines were breaking through on the mountain so it was all or nothing down on the plain.

2 REP and 3 Para were receiving human wave attacks, an amphibious assault was coming ashore on Mactan and the Chinese seemed to be happy to expend their remaining artillery ammunition in a frenzy. The safest place was apparently on the bridges themselves.

The divisions own artillery was sat in deep recesses hand-dug by the gunners and covered by camouflage nets where they fired continuously. The 105mm guns of the US, British and French were creating hills of empty shell cases behind the positions, tossed there by gunners stripped down to the waist, shiny with sweat and moving like automatons as they served the guns.

General Hills only reserve were the lightly armoured Scimitars of the Blues and Royals, and those vehicle's best defence were their rapid acceleration and speed. The 30mm AP rounds were proving effective against the Chinese 6 wheeler IFVs, particularly at the sides. However, only seven of the vehicles remained now, three were burning on the edge of the airfield where they were supporting a 111th that was in danger of being overrun. If that happened then the artillery gun lines would be the Chinese armours next victim.

A Javelin missile struck one of the big Type 98 tanks just short of the wire, killing it with a single hit but it was the Chinese-made RPGs that the paratroopers were favouring. The FGM-148 Javelin missile took its own sweet time with each missile that was connected to the CLU, and as a result the captured weapons were more popular even if several were required to make a kill.

The stink, like a Parisian public convenience in mid-summer, hung over all the gun pits of the Para's and French Foreign Legionnaire's. GPMG barrels, glowing red hot were dropped into old shermouli cans filled with the crews urine and those barrels still hot replacements were swiftly connected to the weapons bodies with barely a pause in the firing.

The Chinese infantry came on, and on, seemingly never ending and the dusty floors of the gun pits were becoming paved in spent 7.62mm brass casings and black metal links.

Bodies lay thickly about the positions, Chinese mainly, but paratroopers and legionnaires were evident in the mix, the result of the hand-to-hand fighting after the surprise rush into their lines. Once again, entrenching tools had proved their worth in dual usage.

On the small island Jim took twenty men, each with as many RPGs and Javelins as they could manage and led them to the right flank of Charlie Company and behind the Scimitar tank troop that was there. Only two of the vehicles, as the third was shaking with the force of internal explosions two hundred yards away, and the large Guards Division flag on its antennae was crisping in the flames.

They had to plug the flow of amphibious armour crossing the channel, and looping around the side of the enemy penetration was the way he planned on doing it.

His companies were fully engaged so his battalion headquarters were providing this effort and James Artemus Aluicious Popham, Lt Col, was not going to send men to do what he would not.

They used smoke for cover from view, and the vehicles themselves as protections from small arms fire as they crossed a shell pitted taxiway and entered the ruins of the town.

The sounds of all-out battle from across the water in the direction of 2 REP echoed off the walls that still stood in the dead town as they neared the waterway and changed direction, jogging behind the vehicles and knowing that time was critical.

The dirty exhaust fumes of swimming vehicles hung like a haze in the still air above the water as the US paratroopers got into cover and made ready their weapons.

Climbing up the side of a Scimitar Jim shouted to its commander, a Corporal-of Horse, pointing across the channel to where the armour was still appearing.

"Hit those, the pillars, not the armour."

His men began firing on the tanks and IFVs in the water, and the Scimitars turrets rotated, steadied and the cannons began firing three round bursts, the 30mm shells visible as they arced over the intervening space to impact on the brickwork.

It was working, the combined fire chewed away the brick of a pillar before moving to the next until the remaining ones were no longer capable of holding up the steel girders of the building and it started to sag, slowly at first and then with then as momentum took over the remaining pillars collapsed and a great pall of dust hung over the ruin.

The Corporal-of- Horse laughed aloud but then someone gave the world a shake, some giant shook the earth so that the ground and the sky rotated before Jim's eyes, and when it stopped someone was screaming in agony. Blood caught the light as it fountained upwards, bright red arterial crimson, and with something of a shock Lt Col Popham realised that both the screams and the blood were his.

Kondor-138. 18° North of the Equator in low orbit.

It took some time and considerable expense to realign the 'smart' photo reconnaissance satellite. Its memory had several thousand shapes programed into it which, if seen, would trigger an automatic response. It was merely facial recognition software that included those things a human photo recce analyst spends hours looking for. From faces to firearms, tattoos to tanks and car number plates to carrier combat groups; it watched for them all as it orbited the planet because Kondor-138 would not 'sleep' between passes over the contested Spratly Islands. Wide awake, it remained alert for chance encounters.

CHAPTER 5

Brisbane, Queensland: Saturday 15th December, 0214hrs.

The long voyage to Australia, and Operation *Matins,* ended as the first Ro-Ro entered Moreton Bay and discharged its vehicles at the docks. Having arrived via the longer, more scenic, route, and thereby avoiding the prying eyes of Chinese intelligence, the convoys had crossed from the Atlantic to the Pacific during a night passage through the sparsely populated lands bisected by the Beagle Channel at South America's tip.

Tank transporters and heavy plant low loaders supplemented the railways in transporting the European forces and equipment into New South Wales, the final 350 miles of a 14000 mile journey from one battlefield to another.

Far south of the discharging convoys a tricky military maneouvre was being carried out by several units. A relief in place is an ideal moment for an enemy to catch two units while neither is fully deployed for defence. Deception plans and artillery barrages are tested methods of keeping the enemy too busy to cotton on to what is occurring under his nose. This night however it was being done stealthily and if the PLAN 1st Marines twigged what was going on they may well assume it was a rotation of companies, a frequent occurrence on the defence line in NSW.

Brigadier General Patrick Reed, 1st Guards Infantry Brigade, shook hands with Humphrey McGregor, commanding The Highland Brigade, and relinquished the Guards positions. Humphrey, his staff and the COs of the Cameron Highlanders, Argylls, London Scottish and Royal Scots Greys had arrived three days before to see the ground, touch base with the other elements and thereby ensure a smooth transition.

The Guardsmen, the Blackhorse and the small Queen Elizabeth's Combat Team moved back to just east of Bowral, to a location at the foot of Mt Gibraltar, a large rock which may possibly bear a resemblance to 'The Rock' ten thousand miles away but no one knows for sure, owing to the many thousands of trees that bedeck it, unlike its namesake of course. On arrival, a parting of the ways took place with the M1A1's of the Blackhorse Cavalry, RTR and RGJ returning to their parent units.

Further south, 8th Infantry Brigade moved to a staging area near the town of Nelligan beside the Clyde where the CO of the Wessex summoned Sgt Baz Cotter and a number of other men to the cluster of 9x9s that made up battalion headquarters. The CO pinned an MM on his Baz's chest, awarded for his part commanding the defence of the autobahn junction at Brunswick, and hand him the symbols of his new status, second lieutenants pips.

"Oddly enough." the CO stated conversationally. "The convoys sailed with everything to fight a war but nothing to denote rank so I hope you don't mind these being second-hand."

Baz accepted the low profile fabric tab.

"Could I ask whose they were before, sir?"

"Your predecessor." the CO said. "But don't worry; they seem to have washed out well."

Open-Season on second lieutenants only ended when they became first lieutenants.

The CO was still smiling evilly at the expression on the face of the newest member of the officer's mess as he moved on to the next soldier receiving an award.

The centre of Bowral had an old world feel about it, in Australian terms. Most of the shop facades seemed to visitors to be suffering a crisis of identity as some buildings seemed typically English, whilst the remainder would not have gone amiss in some Wild West boom town, with the exception that they were built of brick, and the bricklaying had a distinctly English style. Modern Australia is unique unto itself, but the Empire Theatre in Bong Bong Street was of the same design and appearance of many 1920's or 30's built cinemas in rural English towns. The café next door was pure Dodge City however.

With the Australian 1st MP Battalion providing the security around the theatre the army borrowed it for the day, but despite the posters and advertising hoardings it was Pat Reed who was appearing in Cinema 1, not 'Finding Nemo'.

"ROOM!"

Being 'The Guards,' rank was no barrier to being called to their feet or to sit to attention just as they had done as Sandhurst cadets on Day 1, or as a common 'Crow' at the Guards Depot, Pirbright, as was the case with the Welsh Guards CO who had played a bugle and side drum, with less than average skill, in the 1WG Corps of Drums before realising that obtaining a Queens Commission beat working for a living.

Pat Reed strode to the front of the theatre and nodded to the Brigade Major.

"Carry on, please."

"SIT...easy!"

All the battalions COs and there Ops Officers were present, likewise the Life Guards, Hussars, Royal Signals, RA, REME, RE, RAF rep, AAC, Royal Loggies and the liaison officers from their hosts and from the 5th US Mechanised Division. The RTR Troop and Lt McMarn's platoon of Royal Green Jackets had rejoined their regimental formations, which were attached to the Australian Army along with the rest of the UK's 8th Infantry Brigade.

"Gents, with the arrival of our vehicles we are now once more 1st Guards Mechanised Brigade of 1st Guards Mechanised Division. 2nd Guards Mechanised, the Scots with the Grenadiers 1st and 2nd battalions in their FV-432 upgrades, are across the way at Burradoo. As the Guardsmen here are all aware, it has been a very long time since so many units of the Household Division have fought together." He smiled at his audience. "A word of warning though for any that do not know me well, do not get too comfy with the 'mechanised' title, you are likely to have more blisters on your feet than your arse."

The tankers of the Kings Royal Hussars and the Life Guards looked quite smug at their infantry cousins discomfort.

"And now as time is short, I will not hang about." Pat addressed the assembly with those preparatory words.

"Pens at the ready, fingers on buzzers...here we go"

Upon the cinema screen was projected a map of the PTO, pacific theatre of operations.

"As of 0900hrs this morning the Philippine islands of Cebu and Mactan were officially liberated following the surrender of the Chinese 86th Mechanised and its attached odds and sods. So it is exceedingly difficult for the PRC to reinforce their 1st Army Corps here by air or sea. I have seen the necessary tanker plan that would be required to bring a single enemy fighter to Australia, and it is reassuring, to us, that it is unlikely to happen. The air assets they have here will not be reinforced" He looked at all the faces and saw at least one furrowed brow.

"Any questions before I move on to the meat and veg of the orders?"

"Why are we moving into the assault now? Why not spare the guys and gals any more casualties and starve them out?" The RAF representative had a valid point. The war had inflicted heavy losses on all the armed services.

"A good point and a reasonable one. The answer is that civilians in the occupied areas, and our own comrades in barbed wire stockades, are facing the prospect of starvation, and as the purpose of an army in a democracy is to protect the people, that is what we are doing."

There were no more questions.

"Ground." The map that now appeared had the Fleet Air Arm Base, HMAS Albatross, at the lower left corner and the coastal town of Gerringong at the top right. Since its capture by the Chinese the airfield had been a major thorn in the side of the NATO forces in the mountains, forests and hills.

Pat described the area the brigade would be operating in, in generalised form, and the objective in greater detail.

"Any questions so far?"

There were none.

"Situation; enemy forces...since the enemy first landed their 9th Tank Regiment and 14th Infantry have been digging in and firming up around the town of Nowra, which the gentlemen from the Irish Guards will be well familiar with as I having been tasking them with recceing the approaches for the last fortnight."

An overlay showed the results of the reconnaissance patrols with enemy positions, strengths, weapons and field defences such as minefields and wire. The fighting patrols that had also been recently sent to snatch prisoners had added to their knowledge of what they were facing.

"This is everything, is it Liam?"

"Yes sir, down to the last tin can strung on their wire...as of 0500hrs yesterday." The Irish Guards CO stated with absolute certainty.

"Sure about that?"

"Yes sir." Lt Col Faloon nodded emphatically.

"Good, because in thirty six hours' time when the brigade attacks, it will be one up, two back, and the Irish Guards are the up."

"I am overwhelmed at your generosity, and I am certain that your name will on the very lips of my men as they cross the FEBA, although not necessarily in flattering terms, sir."

Pat let the laughter fade.

"The good news is that there are no chemical or biological weapons available to the Chinese 3rd Army and this has been confirmed by two sources, the prisoners of war providing the enemy with their forced labour, and SASR CTRs. The only reason the magazines weren't blown by the SASR operatives was the proximity of POWs and civilians." Pat looked them all in the eye. "We thought the same was true of the Red Army at the Vormundberg though, and look how that turned out. So the boys and girls continue to carry the necessary at all times, regardless of the intelligence to the contrary." Pointing to the sea Pat Reed added a rider. "The navy claims that there are no, repeat no, operational submarines still operating in these waters. It is too far from home and the support vessels are allegedly on the bottom, so they say there is no chance of further missile attacks."

They were all watching him and waiting for the 'But'.

"Better safe than sorry, so pass the word that section commanders are to inspect their men and enforce the carrying of full NBC...okay? Any questions?"

He moved on to the next item.

"Situation; friendly forces, the 2nd Guards Mech' will be on our tail until we have taken our objective, and will pass through with a change of axis to the east, collecting half the Life Guards armoured reconnaissance squadrons and Dougal Willis's Hussars, and they will advance to contact the eight miles to Shoalhaven on the coast, with the river on their right." Pat tapped the airfield to the south of the town. "The Aussie and Kiwi SAS squadrons have been working out of the forests of the Yawal valley to the west, and in best Long Range Desert Group fashion they will raid the airfield and attempt to destroy all the aircraft there before withdrawing back into the forest." Pat waved for the next screen which had the town of Gloucester to the north and the Bega Valley to the south. Virtually all of the occupied coastal plain that was currently in Chinese hands.

"While we are engaged with our own bit of business the ANZACs will be showing us whinging Poms how it is done when they take Bega, the southern extent of Chinese occupation, and begin to drive north, with the help of other whinging Poms of 8th(UK) Infantry Brigade and the Royal Tank Regiment of course." He next pointed to the top of the map.

"Meanwhile, the US 5th Corps consisting the 5th Mechanised Division, 10th Mountain Division and the ladies and gentlemen of the

2nd Marine Expeditionary Force, will attack south east out of the Hunter Valley and take the city of Newcastle before turning south."

Pat returned to their own area of responsibility.

"We are cutting the Chinese 1st Corps up into edible pieces, and we, the Guards, will dig in and act as the anvil to the ANZACs hammer before we drive north, collecting the Highland Division on the way, but the ultimate goal is to squeeze the Chinese 3rd Army until the only place they have left to go to is Sydney, or surrender."

It took a further hour to provide the COs' with the details they required for their own units before Pat closed the proceedings.

"Gentlemen, we went to war with just the bare essentials and we carry the scars to prove it. It has been a long road but the end is in sight, and as we now have the kit to finish the job and go home, let us do just that, and let us do it well."

Wessex Regiment: Bega Valley, NSW. Monday 17th October, 0400hrs.

The long and seemingly never ending journey in pitch darkness, the bumpy road and the tedious, constant stopping and starting, all without any explanation as to the cause, was now over. The Unimogs pulled into trees beside the colourfully name Jews Creek and the troops dismounted quietly. The infantry barely had time to stretch out the knots and massage away buttocks numbed by purely functional seating before they were hustled away to the start line by guides equipped with PNGs.

Inevitably Baz had men who had managed to get lost in the relatively short distance from the vehicles to the invisible line the guides indicated was the FEBA, the forward edge of the battle area. No one was ready as the time of departure approached and from the CO on downwards the good leaders exuded calm as they sorted things out, whilst the bad ones assumed that the harder they kicked something the quicker it would fix itself.

They were on radio silence, the sets switched on but they kept a listening watch only, unless in contact of course. The order to move was conveyed by runner and it got a little lost. D Company's OC realised A Company were no long in front of them, so it was a little like starting a twenty year old Ford Escort on a cold morning, they got moving but not without pushing, shoving and a few muffled curses. Bergans made all the more heavy with the addition of 81mm mortar rounds and a thousand rounds of mixed link brought groans as the men used their personal weapons as props to assist themselves off their knees and into the advance to contact with China's best.

A Company of The Wessex Regiment was the spearhead with B and C to the left and right, the tip of an infantry arrow advancing with the Princes Highway as the axis of advance. D Company was in reserve, to the rear but following A Company so that the view of the four rifle companies from above was one of a diamond shape. Behind D came battalion headquarters and Support Company, its machine gun and mortar platoons in two halves that leapfrogged one another, setting up gimpy and mortar lines to provide supporting fire if called upon to do so, before packing up and hurrying forwards to deploy once again. 3RGJ was to the left rear of the Wessex and the Light Infantry to its right. Behind 8 (UK) Infantry Brigade came the ANZACs of the RAR, Royal New South Wales Regiment and the Royal New Zealand Infantry Regiment. The infantry moved in almost complete silence but on the flanks were the Leopard 1s and newer M1A1 replacements of the Australian 1st Armoured Regiment, and the UK's Challenger 2s of the Royal Tank Regiment. To the front of this slowly perambulating triangle ranged the ASLAVs of the Light Horse, and a flight of Apaches from 3 Regiment, Army Air Corps.

The sun had risen and the straps of 2Lt Cotters Bergan were digging into his shoulders when contact was first made. Men gripped their weapons a little more firmly at the sound of combat to their front.

"Baz...er sorry... Mr Cotter sir?" a voice called in a failed stage whisper. "What's going on?"

"Price, do I look like the bleeding oracle? Well do I?" Baz fixed the rifleman with a look. "Rumour has it, it's the Third World War, or hadn't you noticed?" Baz then shook his head wearily "Now shut up and watch your front."

The firing tailed off and twenty minutes later they drew level with one of the Australian ASLAVs sat at a drunken angle, half in and half out of a ditch beside the road. It was still burning and its crew were a little distance away, covered by their ground sheets and awaiting collection by the graves registration detachment. Four hundred yards further on another vehicle, a Type 98 tank, was also consuming itself with the resulting thick black smoke marring an otherwise blue sky. Several Chinese infantrymen lay equally dead, killed by the same Apache gunship that had avenged the Aussie armoured recce troops of the Light Horse.

A mile from Bega the sound of modern warfare returned, initially just with an exchange of small arms fire between the point section and the occupants of a trench, but it grew and grew in intensity until the mortars and the GPMG SFs of the machine gun platoon were in constant action, soon to be joined by 105mm and 155mm artillery rounds.

B and C Companies moved up beside A Company but D halted and began to dig shell scrapes. Behind them to the left and right the Green Jackets and Light infantry were doing the same. 1RAR and the New Zealand infantry, however, could be seen hurrying forward on either flank and Baz could no longer see the tanks comforting presence.

Baz had just finished his shell scrape and got himself comfortably ensconced, with his bergan below ground too, when the order was passed back verbally to move forward, as is ever the way.

The Chinese knew they were there now so there was no mileage in maintaining radio silence for all but those who were up to their waists in muck and bullets, although it did seem to have taken two contacts for that to have occurred to the senior management.

"Hello all stations Four, this Four Nine, nobody told you to move!"

To Baz's left Dopey Hemp's camouflaged face turned towards him.

"Send three and four pence, we're going to a dance!"

The dedicated smokers' relit cigarettes stubbed out moments before and Baz removed the heavy bergan and settled himself back into the shell scrape.

There was a loud whistle from forward and Baz saw CSM French pointing at him and miming the winding motion of turning a car engine with a starter handle.

Out-*bloody*-standing!

"Twelve Platoon, prepare to move!"

The CSM did have some good hand signals for them though, pointing at the mortar line and GPMG SFs. Baz knelt so that a No.3 on the guns could open his bergan's top flap and remove the single, long, thousand round belt, and a hundred yards later he was relieved of his two 81mm mortar rounds also.

Ah joy!

Feeling almost bionic 12 Platoon now hustled forwards with Baz receiving a quick set of radio orders. Removing his bayonet he banged the blade loudly against his own helmet to get everyone's attention and held it aloft for all to see before attaching it. They all followed suit, snapping the steel into place and giving the bayonets a twist to ensure the retaining lug had been locked.

They were striding out now, butts of weapons firmly in the shoulder.

Passing through a gap in a hedge he encountered the first Wessex dead, lying unmoving under the bluest sky Baz could ever remember, and he took a moment to look at it in case he too would never see another of its like ever again.

1 Section was 'up' with 2 on the left and 3 on the right. They crossed between enemy fighting positions, trenches and more dead, their own and the Chinese.

The end of the captured position was marked by A Company who were occupying the rear trenches and now facing towards Bega.

Words of encouragement, warnings, and gallows humour were shouted their way from A Company.

"Good luck boys."

"Watch yer selves, they're hard buggers."

"Don't get shot Steve...you still owe me a tenner!"

"Pete...if you get topped can I shag yer wife?"

"You may as well, I already shagged yours!"

The smell of cordite, gun smoke, and the burnt almonds scent of high explosive was tinged with that particular smell that results in a dying man releasing his bowels.

To the left and right the Aussies and Kiwis, as well as the Wessex B and C Companies, all remained down in the prone position. They had taken an infantry battalion's position after a hard and vicious fight but now the advance to contact was resumed.

12 Platoon were now the point section, stepping short as the ground began to slope away before them. The quiet was restored with only the sound of their boots moved through foot high grass for ten minutes. The green grass and fragrant wild flowers, a pastoral setting Baz Cotter would have liked to have enjoyed over a picnic. A perfect vista, a perfect warm summer's day to enjoy with the family. Only a skylark's song was absent.

Private McKenzie and L/Cpl Silva, the 1 Section gun group, abruptly dropped down among the wild flowers. The crack of high velocity rounds only registering on his consciousness like an afterthought.

"COVER!"

Dash, down, roll, sights, observe...

...nothing.

A butterfly landed upon Shaun Silva's neck, its gossamer touch should have tickled and elicited a reaction but Shaun was beyond ever doing that again.

"Anybody see anything?"

"Hello Four One this is Four Nine, do you have a sitrep for me, over?"

"Four One, Four One Alpha has two down, no shooter seen...wait out."

They could not stay here all day waiting for the enemy to get bored and go home, although on a purely personal level that thought had merit.

"Dopey...send someone on a dummy run."

Cpl Hemp picked Spider as he was closest to another piece of cover. Webber rolled onto his side, keeping out of sight as he undid his bergan's straps, and after a moment to prepare he launched himself off the ground and towards a fold eight feet away. Turf ripped up about him and Spider went down screaming.

"Section...three hundred...eleven o'clock...water trough in field...two o'clock from trough...two clicks...enemy gun group!" Dopey Hemp had seen the muzzle flash and 2 Section engaged it while Baz sent the OC his sitrep and requested a mortar fire mission, which was refused as they weren't going to expend hard to replace mortar rounds on a single gun trench.

First thing first was to win the fire fight, show them who the boss was and keep their heads down. Once that was achieve the rate of fire was reined to preserve ammunition, fire control being exerted by the section commanders.

1 Section was down over half its fire power without the gun group, ergo they were too under-gunned to leave behind as a point of fire so Baz looked for cover that would allow the platoon to get closer without being seen. There was none.

Baz pressed the quick release clips on his bergan's straps before he made the rolling motion with both hands, to signal they were going to do it the hard way, skirmishing forwards.

The art of skirmishing is to judge how long it takes an enemy to see you, aim at you and fire at you. If you are up on your feet longer than three seconds you are living on borrowed time.

Jez Hancock had come to him from B Company on promotion to sergeant and Baz pointed to himself, meaning Jez would give covering fire as Baz moved first. The sections had all been numbered off and those numbers were etched on their brains, they moved by half sections, by even and odd numbers.

In case someone had spotted him he rolled before getting up and dodged to the side, a little zigzag, and then he was down, rolling, setting his sights and firing an aimed shot at the Chinese gun group.

It was tiring, very tiring, but as they closed with the Chinese machine gun the enemy tried to bug out.

No way.

The GPMG does not have a single shot facility; it is automatic repetitive fire or nothing. 2 Section's gun was keeping the Chinese gun group pinned with accurate but short bursts, double-tapping the trigger to expend two rounds at a time, although a really good gunner could single tap.

With the rest of the platoon getting dangerously close to the line of fire the 2 Section gun 'switched', it picked a point an enemy doing a runner from the trench would head for, and by switching they denied them that option.

As the gun switched 1 Section closed on the enemy, careful not to bunch up on the position and it was Cpl Dave Whyte who grenaded them in their hole before he followed through with the bayonet for good measure.

The platoon moved beyond the trench and went to ground in all round defence with Baz signalling Dopey to come up with his section.

With a very hot barrel to contend with the gunner made-safe, gripped the gimpy by its butt and put it over his shoulder, finding the point of balance and high tailing it over to rejoin the platoon.

Dopey left just one of their number to care for Spider who had been shot through the shins.

They stayed there in the fragrant wild flowers, under a perfect blue sky, as the rest of the company caught up and 13 Platoon took over as point.

Two miles north of Nowra, New South Wales. Monday 17th December, 0700hrs

"Fortune Cloverleaf, *Smackdown* is flight of two Foxtrot One Fours, eleven hundred pounds of fuel internal for thirty minutes on station, loadout is CBU, Mk-77 and 250 pound retarded."

"Roger Smackdown, a very good morning to you, we will have trade for you in a jiffy, please wait out." The Irish Guard's FAC's voice

was a calm and pleasant Irish lilt at complete odds to the cacophony going on in the background. The British had not expected an easy time of it and the Chinese 9th Tank Regiment was not disappointing them. Snatches of a fiercely fought ground war arrived in stereo to Lt Comdr. Pelham with each transmission from the forward air controller.

As promised, they soon had their first tasking of the day and turned east towards the battlefield.

Pillars of smoke, the funeral pyres of men and vehicles, were visible from the moment the F-14s descended through thick cloud on clearing the high ground of Morton National Park. The Chinese may have been on short rations but they had all kinds of ordnance to spare. The Guards Mechanised Division had been spotted by a forward O.P whilst still traversing the Kangeroo Valley, beyond Cambewarra Mountain. It was unfortunate but an armoured unit on the move tends to be a little low on stealth. As they had emerged from the woods at the base of the mountain the enemy had been ready for them. The leading unit, the Irish Guards, had been shaking out into a more extended formation on countryside not unlike the North German Plains from the mountains to the sea. Nice for long range tank gunnery and the Chinese had some good ones.

To the west of the F-14s, roughly centred over the Ettrema Gorge, the 'orphans' cab rank , the surviving aircraft from USS *Nimitz* and USS *Constellation*, orbited and awaited the FACs call.

"I don't see them...anybody have eyeball on the target?" The sun was still fairly low in the sky, shining in their eyes and making observation difficult. The Chinese were very good indeed at avoiding the attentions of NATO close air support by hunkering down when aircraft where about. The target indication described the enemy as a tank in a small copse, fifty metres west of a farmhouse with a red roof. She eventually saw the farmhouse, and the copse, but no tank.

"Zero One this is Zero Two, I have a visual on a small structure at the corner of a field just east of the copse with exhaust fumes visible."

The 'structure' was a vehicle of some description with rust streaked corrugated sheets laid over it and around its sides. The early morning chill had revealed the ruse.

"Zero One, roger...any evidence of SAMs that you can see?" Her ECM was silent, showing no radar activity that suggested the presence nearby of AAA.

"Zero Two, negative, just the fake hen house."

"Zero One, okay, take it."

"Roger...Fortune Cloverleaf this is Smackdown Zero Two coming in hot with two 250 pounders from the southwest."

"Roger."

Nikki watched her wing man descend and begin his ordnance run, coming across the British armoured vehicles from their rear.

Aboard Smackdown Zero One her ECM detected a SAM radar had come up and the 'hen house' suffered a structural defect as the vehicle rotated its turret towards the approaching F-14 Tomcat. It was no tank; it had two barrels, not one.

The Type 59 SPAAG locked up the low flying F-14 and fired a long stream of shells from its auto flak cannons, both airburst and armour piercing rounds.

Nikki saw the puffs of smoke from flak all around the other aircraft and the bright flash of striking rounds hitting its port wing. The wing and the fuselage parted company with the crew ejecting but the Tomcat had already begun a sharp roll to the right. Both seats, with their occupants still attached, hit the ground and bounced, spinning dizzily before crashing down into the field in a welter of flung earth.

Zero Two's killer reversed, ejecting smoke grenades to cover its retreat, magnesium and phosphorus providing a hot, IR defeating screen for a limited period. It encountered the cow field's wooden fence and ground it beneath the steel caterpillar treads.

Nikki rolled inverted and dived, selecting a 250lb retard bomb and calling in her intentions to the Irish Guards FAC.

Having reversed behind the copse the Type 59 spun on its tracks and headed east. Its radar detected the diving F-14 and its turret rotated with remarkable speed, its twin 59mm cannons elevating but the US Navy aircraft was punching out chaff as well as flares, reducing its targeting options to that of 'best guess'. Tracer rose to meet them, some exploded in their path and others, the armour piercing rounds, tore past like meteors.

Candice let out a startled yelp as they were hit by shrapnel from the flak but she was pretty much the solid veteran now, forty sorties had taken place since that first mad scramble to get airborne at RAAF Pearce.

They released their bombs but they were stick heavy as Nikki recovered, and the ground uncomfortably close.

The FAC confirmed destruction of the self-propelled anti-aircraft vehicle but Smackdown Zero Two was visible to the right, burning at the edge of the field. One for one was a bad trade off; it was not a good start.

Two miles north of Nowra, New South Wales. Same day, 0730hrs

The abandoned township Cambewarra Village had been occupied and hurriedly fortified, stopping the Irish Guards again soon after they had overcome the first line of resistance. A further tank, a Hussars Mk 10 Chieftain, and three Warriors had been lost.

2CG had hooked right, its vehicles threading their way through trees and on to Tannery Lane, chancing to luck and driving fast along a road straight enough to seem Roman in origin. Passing scattered dairy farms until reaching dead ground to the north of the Cambewarra hardpoint.

1 Company's Warriors crossed a small ford before crashing through fences and hedges into field to the right. 2 (Support) Company entered the stream and used its banks for cover. The Mortar Platoons FV432s halted in line, opened their top lids and pivoted the 81mm barrels to point in the direction of the Chinese position. They were close in and the elevation of the tubes was steep, pointing at the cloudless blue of the sky.

1 Company were already reaching the edge of the village as 4 Company arrived and followed on in its wake. 1 Company may have been the old sweats, the veterans of the European unpleasantness with 1CG, but the weeks spent holding the Macquarie Pass had seasoned the remainder. Momentum can save lives when exploited at the right moment and no one dilly dallied.

1 Company's Warriors arrived in the residential streets, crashing through garden walls at the edge of the village where the guardsmen debussed and began the energy sapping job of FIBUA, fighting in built up areas, clearing it, house by house.

3 Company flanked the village and the IFVs went into cover where they could put down fire on anyone leave its southern or eastern extremes.

The fire into 1IG's right flank was curtailed but they needed a breather so 'The Micks' went firm and 1 Welsh Guards passed through them and immediately into the assault.

Tanks were burning, blown up or simply motionless with just a small penetrating hole in the armour plate. The enemy tanks had sallied forth to meet the approaching Warriors of the Welsh Guardsmen. Two companies worth of Type 98 tanks intended to slug it out with their opposite numbers but the air assets on call and the longer range of the British tanks 120mm rifled guns destroyed them. The day that had started badly was now improving.

The Irish Guards first opponents had been the anti-tank platoon and a company of the 14th Infantry supported by a company of their 9th Tank. Having fought their way forward and defeated those enemy a second infantry company had ambushed the Irish Guards right flank from Cambewarra Village. 2CG were going to be digging the second company out of the village for another hour or two at least, after which they too would also need to reorganise.

The Taff's rifle companies were still fairly fresh, which was as well because a company of infantry and another of tanks remained defending Nowra.

The 1st Guards Mechanised Brigade was just a half mile from its objective and 2nd Guards Mechanised Brigade now emerged onto the plain.

Four hundred metres from the edge of Nowra Mark Venables Challenger was struck by a HESH round that failed to penetrate and Tango One One's driver jerked the vehicle sharply right, and then back again to throw off the unseen shooters aim.

Before them sat the outskirts, single storey residences set among the trees. Mark Venables spotted the movement first, a Pampas grass plant that rotated? It had lost some of its camouflage when it had first fired and it lost most of the remainder now as it fired a second time. The Challengers armour saved them again but One One shuddered to a halt, its engine stalled, leaving vulnerable and out in the open.

Mark grabbed the override and slewed the turret around.

"FIRING!"

The Challenger rocked back on its sprockets as it fired, sending a tungsten steel sabot screeching across the intervening space. The last of the long grass stalks took flight and the hatches flew open. The crew began emerging as the first flicker of flame became visible and Mark switched to the 7.62 coaxial chain gun, the Chinese tank commander tumbled down the side of the turret and the gunner dropped down through the hatch, back into the flames. He lowered his aim but the driver had not been hanging about, he was off the vehicle and out of sight before the flames reached the ammunition and the tank blew up.

One One's own driver was trying to coax the big Perkins engine back into life without flooding it, and the rest of the crew felt the hairs on the back of their necks rise. Targets like they were presenting were just too good to pass up.

The engine caught, roared, and they jerked forward again, heading for some cover.

"Thank Christ for that boss." his gunner stated with feeling. "I was..."

A hammer blow struck the Challenger and flames engulfed the turrets interior.

The Coldstreamers were still engaged in clearing Cambewarra and the sound of fighting from there was audible from where Pat Reed summoned the COs of 1IG and 1WG. A quick O Group and a quick reorganisation followed.

The infantry who were cammed-up now divested themselves of flora and fauna, and hessian strips that broke up the shape of equipment. Fire was a very real by-product of house-to-house fighting so all unnecessary, flammable, items were removed. Oddly enough the section commanders sent out foragers to find thin, strong branches that were also straight and these were snapped into roughly 3' lengths and brought along. Gaffer tape, PE4 or the nitro headache inducing PE808, guncotton charges, detonators, fuse cord and of course storm matches. The safest doorway into a defended building is one you make yourself, so the sections of branches and the gaffer tape create the 'X' frame on which a small charge of PE is likewise secured with gaffer tape to the tips of the upper arms. Placed against a wall and the fuse lit before retiring to a safe(ish) distance the charges blow 'mouse holes' big enough to allow the assault team, the Entrymen, to enter once designated 'grenadiers' lob grenades inside. If those preparing the mousehole charges had PE808 to work with they wore gloves as they moulded the charges into shape. Nitro-glycerine from '808' is absorbed through the pores and the immediate effects of the poisoning are the mother of all headaches.

Grenades, rope, water and stones. A stone thrown into a room sounds the same as a grenade being thrown in and makes defenders take cover.

The Irish Guards cordoned the north of Nowra as the south of the river received mortar and artillery fire to prevent reinforcement or retreat. With no further ado the Welsh Guards began the process of house clearing, FIBUA, fighting in built up areas.

2nd Guards Mechanised Brigade moved past, heading east with A and C Squadron of the Hussars detaching themselves from Pat Reed's brigade, along with a squadron of Scimitars from the Life Guards.

The bridge across the wide Broughton Creek remained intact but the wooded Back Forest hill beside it was an obvious defensive position. It commanded both the bridge and the road to their objective, Shoalhaven on the coast. The Scimitars gave it some clog, intending to go firm once across the bridge but the defenders let the leading troop cross, waiting for the following troop's commanders vehicle to reach the centre of the bridge before they blew it.

In one fell swoop the Life Guards lost five vehicles. The troops which had crossed was hunted down by infantry with RPGs, and the second troop lost an additional vehicle on the bridge which did not reverse quickly enough to get out of range.

It was five miles to the next crossing and that too was likely to be a trap.

'Terry' Thomas, commanding the 2nd Guards brigade, was calling forwards the Royal Engineers to survey the blown bridge, and banks, for the suitability of bridging units when a SASR patrol arrived with a solution. They had constructed a sunken bridge months before in order to move about unchallenged. It sat two feet below the surface and remained a secret from the enemy. It was a mile up river at a spot where dairy cattle had watered, before the Chinese had eaten them all of course. The only problem was a weight issue as only the Household Cavalry Scimitars were sufficiently light to cross without destroying the submerged structure. The 432s were twice the weight of the SASR six wheel LRPVs and of course the MBTs were obvious no-no's.

So, the Grenadiers and Sappers put on a convincing act of preparing to throw a bridging unit over the demolished section under fire, and the mortars put down smoke and HE to enforce that illusion. That smoke screen also covered the Scots Guards as they waded across undetected, followed by the Life Guards Scimitars.

2CG completed the clearing of Cambewarra and rejoined the their brigade in time to hear the sound of bagpipes, the strains of Highland

Laddie wafting on the wind. The Scots Guards had taken Back Forest Hill and the road to the sea was open.

Puckapunyal Army Base, Victoria: Same day 0800hrs

Turning onto finals and descending towards runway 03 of 'Pucka's' short tarmac strip, Nikki noticed that the tentage was thinning out rapidly in expectation of moving to HMAAS Albatross once it was recaptured by the British Guards Division.

The Pearce Wing had been revitalised by the arrival of USS *Constellation's* air wing and the army training establishment was one of three fields they were using.

The wheels screeched briefly and having only 700m to play with she braked firmly. Having completed the roll out she followed black-washed arrows on the grass to a dispersal, flanked as ever by earth filled cargo containers that acted as blast walls.

Gerry was there waiting and she saw his expression when he sighted the damage, a flicker off fear before the façade of rugged humour dropped back into place.

"Steve and Monica?" he asked after she had shut down and exited.

She answered with a brief shake of the head and added a few words.

"Fifty nine milly ess pee."

"The same one that did that?" he nodded toward the starboard vertical stabiliser which looked like a giants sawn-off had been used on it at close range.

"Yup."

The crew chief came over, clucking his lips and shaking his head.

"Patching it will take an hour but the avionics took a hit and you have lost a hardpoint somewhere."

The armourers were removing the unused ordnance and she now saw a cannon round had amputated the rearmost portside ordnance hardpoint. The 500lb JDAM that had been there was now obviously sat in a field somewhere with UXB status. A matter of inches had been the difference between breathing and instant oblivion.

"That could have made your eyes water a bit" Gerry observed.

Nikki looked around for her RIO but Candice was in the shady side of the dispersal, flight helmet under one arm, batting her eyelashes at her latest target, an F-18 driver with Gerry's new squadron.

185

Nikki was hungry and she and Gerry left Candy and headed to the RAAF Mess tent which was also under deconstruction but had pre-prepared sandwiches, coffee, tea and rocket fuel, an orange flavoured cold drink that was high in electrolytes but removed your teeth enamel, or so it was rumoured.

They sat outside on a fallen tree trunk, away from the labouring cooks folding away the canvas and trying to jam the end results back into bags they had slid out of with far greater ease a week before.

"Any news on how it is all going so far?"

Gerry's squadron was supporting the ANZAC advance back to the coast across the Bega Valley.

"We lost Danny Bigsopp covering the Pom Tornados going in over Merimbula Lake, the Tornados took out the runway okay but Danny ditched in the sea a hundred yards or so off the beach, and those mongrels machine gunned his life raft from the shore."

"You get them?"

"Oh, yeah." That was it, just two words. When Gerry was reticent it meant a lot had gone unsaid. Nothing to describe the flak, the AAA or the ground fire from defences now fully alert as he had settled accounts.

"You Yanks are doing well, I hear. They are already in Newcastle's suburbs." he added and turned to peer off at the horizon, raising a hand to shade his eyes as he tried to make out what type the aircraft were that he had just heard.

"The Brits have a tough nut to crack but they are making progress." Nikki said, but Gerry did not answer, frowning at something in the distance before a look of alarm crossed his features and he shouted whilst dragging Nikki backwards off the tree trunk, flopping back to lie protectively on top of her.

"AIR RED!...AIR RED!"

The scream of multiple jet engines passing low overhead was painful on the ears, as was the cannon fire that tore into the tented area and those working there. A series of massive explosions made the ground leap beneath her and then the raiders were gone. Only now did the air raid siren begin.

Gerry rolled off her but she remained laying there, her hands covering her head as rubble and debris fell back to earth, the result of the 500lb and cluster bomb units the attackers had dropped in the hit and run raid.

Jumping over the log Nikki ran back towards the dispersal. There had been one canvas wall still standing in the mess tent and that was now peppered, ripped and ragged by shrapnel and the cooks lay still and bloody. Only a middle aged reservist in a white apron that had turned bright crimson was sat upright, deathly pale and muttering to himself reassuringly.

"It'll be al'right; the doc will fix this easy, just a stitch or two." He was clutching his belly, trying to prevent any more of the shiny entrails from pouring out.

"MEDIC!" Nikki shouted but did not stop until she could see the rest of the way to where her F-14 had been. One of the hefty earth filled containers was lying some twenty feet from a crater and the burning wreckage of what had once been an aircraft. The Tomcat, ground crew, armourers and Candice LaRue were all gone. She turned to speak to Greg, to voice her horror but he was not beside her. Only now did she feel the wet stickiness of blood on her neck and it wasn't hers. The wounded cook was where he had been, still sat upright but silent now, and with eyes glazing over. She ignored him and ran on to the tree trunk, to where Gerry was lying unmoving.

"MEDIC!"

C Troop, D Squadron, 1st (AU) Armoured Regiment: Rose Valley, NSW. 19 miles south of Port Kembla. 0242hrs Sunday 23th December.

The Princes Highway was still the axis of advance, a whole week and one hundred and sixty nine miles later, as the crow flies.

The 1st Corps of the Chinese 3rd Army was drawing in on itself, not running away, so 'Tango Four Three Alpha' was not on the highway but to its left, using the elevated roadway as cover from suspected enemy positions near the sea.

This was an area of New South Wales that actually looked a lot like the old South Wales, just north of Llanelli, not that any of the crew could vouch for that.

The long highway from Bega was littered in places with burnt out vehicles, the victims of strikes by the NATO air forces, artillery and nuisance raids by Australian SASR and New Zealand NZSAS Patrols in six wheeled LRPVs.

A narrow strip now known as The Devils Highway to the south of them. A 666 metre wide strip of land between Burrill Lake and the ocean was where a Chinese logistic regiment had been caught out in the open by the air force. Forty seven fuel tankers and trucks carrying stores, ammunition and the like. The lead vehicles were taken out and then the rear, trapping those in between. Of course those remaining tried to either get past the burning vehicles at the front. It had been a log jam and the men below were helpless but it was a high value target. Enough fuel and ammunition to draw out the fighting ever longer. When D Squadron arrived the vehicles were still there, charcoaled along with the occupants. The combat engineers attached to the pommy Guards had created a detour and thrown a pontoon bridge across the inlet at its narrowest point, but the breeze had been from the west, blowing over the fire blackened causeway and Chuck Waldek, in the loaders hatch next to 2Lt Burley, had up-chucked, no pun intended, down the hatch and down Che Tan's neck, the smell had been that bad. The inside of the turret of their second hand M1A1 was a small space in which to perform the pugilistic arts but they had nonetheless managed to do each other some damage.

'Tango Four Three Charlie', their venerable old Leopard 1, had been hit during one of the attempts by the Chinese 14th Tank Regiment to clear the way to Canberra. The round had caused damage not repairable within three days and so it was replaced. Their new ride had seen action in Germany and had itself been damaged at some point before being purchased, or donated, to the Australian Armoured Corps. Whoever had taken the time to respray the interior in bright white fire retardant paint had not swept up. Che had found a small section of fire-charred jaw bone wedged beneath the gunners seat.

The regiment had seen changes, the addition of another squadron and the creation of a second battalion, equipped with all used but good condition Abrams. The regimental commander been killed in an air strike and everyone moved up one. Lt Jenkins went from Troop Commander, to Squadron Adjutant, to Squadron Commander in the space of a fortnight, all thanks to air strikes. HMAAS Albatross and Merimbula had been the bases of operations where all the sorties against the defenders had originated in the ANZAC and Pom sectors.

When they had taken Bega, Pambula Beach and Kalaru the long drive north had begun, leading them past the Fleet Air Arm base. On the first day of the campaign Albatross had been raided by special forces to curtail those air raids, it was back in friendly hands, but driving past it the wrecked Chinese aircraft were still where they had been when destroyed by the SASR.

"Whinging Pom Monkey at One O'clock, boss." Che informed Gary. A British RMP corporal with filtered torch was indicating they go left. Gary checked the map and saw they were now close to their harbour area where they would ready for the final push to evict the Chinese 3rd Army from Port Kembla, and shove them north into ruined and irradiated Sydney.

From 'owning' ten thousand square miles of Australia the Chinese now held an area twenty five miles long and ten miles deep. No one held the ground north of them, no sane person would want to. The US 2nd Marines, 10th Mountain and 5th Mechanised Division had cleared Newcastle and then moved to the north west of Kembla, giving Sydney a wide berth. The Jocks, The Highland Brigade, were to the west and the ANZACS, with their tame Poms on attachment, had locked down the south along with the Guards Division.

It was dark in the harbour area, too dark to carry out maintenance on the vehicle without breaking black-out discipline, so they ate cold rations and slept.

USNS *Mercy*: Bass Strait, 100 miles SE of Melbourne. 1135hrs, Sunday 23rd December.

Jim Popham lay pale and wan, attached to tubes and drips. He looked curiously shrunken when Pat entered the ward, his eyes dark hollows. Pat had spent the last couple of hours visiting the wounded from his so he had the whole poker face thing mastered. Visiting Mark Venables had been particularly difficult as the Hussar had been badly burned.

"No grapes?" Jim managed a painful smile at Pat not bearing gifts.

"Sorry, the greengrocer and florists were closing early for Christmas."

Pat Reed took a seat beside the paratrooper's bed and looked around the ward. It was pretty full.

The *Mercy* was a converted supertanker and a pretty impressive vessel. Along with her sister ship, *Comfort*, they were taking the burden off hospitals on shore.

"What's their story?" Pat asked, nodding to the bed opposite.

"Soon to be weds, apparently." Jim said.

Nikki Pelham had her hand gripping that of the patient in the bed opposite, and the two of them seemed oblivious to everyone else around.

"They didn't think he was going to make it for a day or two."

"So what is your prognosis then?"

"Apparently the surgeon worked wonders and I can still play the saxophone, which is also slightly miraculous as I couldn't play one before I got hit."

An artillery round had hit the Scimitar that Jim had been stood upon.

"So how is it going then Pat, are they going to fold do you think?"

"In a word, no."

No one knew what was motivating the Chinese politburo, but it certainly did not seem to be common sense.

"General?"

A navy nurse had her professional smile in place and he looked at his watch. It was time to go.

"Take care Jim, I will look in on you again."

"Don't forget to duck, Pat."

A Chinook took the visitors back to shore. Pat looked down at the big white hospital ship, its red crosses emblazoned along the sides and wondered how many new visits he would be making after the next attack.

Port Kembla. Monday 24th December.

0400hrs and a ground mist covered the coast to the south of the port of Kembla. The full moon in a cloudless night sky illuminated it, and those preparing for battle viewed it with either wonder or dread.

At Albatross the crews had been roused for the first sorties of the day and Nikki looked at her coffee and decided on water instead. Across the mess hall table her new RIO almost had a permanent startled look about him, and she wondered if he had even started shaving yet.

Her RIO looked at her with trepidation. This was his first operational sortie and the driver was a legend, Commander Nikki Pelham.

Absolutely no pressure at all, hey?

"Er, Ma'am...the flight surgeon was looking for you?"

She had felt pretty dreadful these last few days since the air raid, but with her promotion had come the position of XO, and XOs didn't wuss out. Maybe someone told the flight surgeon she was out of sorts? Post-traumatic stress disorder after surviving two vaporised carriers and nine months almost constant combat. The only other possibility was the mandatory drink and drugs tests, and she did little of the first and none of the second.

"I'll catch him later," she said dismissively "Come on, it is time for the mission briefing."

He had no idea what today would entail.

"What are we doing, CAP?"

"CAS for the Brits."

"Is CAS more difficult than CAP?"

"It's just a walk in the park, Kozanski"

"Johnson Ma'am, my name is Johnson."

"Yup, that fits."

Thirty miles north at that same moment in time the most important meal of the day was being eaten cold out of a can of compo and very little time was spent over the washing-up before moving off to the FUPs.

"Company Sarn't Major Osgood?"

"Sir?"

"You are a tad over-dressed aren't you?" RSM Tessler stated critically. Oz was cammed up and ready to go, stood beside one of the company headquarters FV-432s and about to seat himself with the FAC.

Oz had been in the thick of it in the very first battle of the war but had been put in the back seat, as it were, for a rest in Germany. He was now equipped more like a buckshee rifleman in one of the sections instead of someone with a job at the back of the fight.

There was no one else in earshot.

"Take care of yourself out there mate," Ray offered him his hand.

"You too, and now I'd best get aboard before the grown-ups notice."

The battalion mounted up and moved out, heading for the forming up point and thence to the start line.

At 0500hrs the artillery opened fire, targeting the Chinese forward positions and at 0530hrs the combined NATO divisions stepped off.

At Albatross Nikki performed the pre-flight inspection on her aircraft as it sat like a brooding bird of prey in its cage of blast walls. It was a D Model, a rare breed these days, and the only one with 'The

Orphans', the survivors of the *Nimitz* and *Constellation*. Nikki was also of course the last survivor of the *John F Kennedy*, and the last time she had flown an F-14D had been off its deck. This aircraft sported a brand new red star, her twentieth confirmed kill, which made her the navies top serving scorer with a four victories lead on the next nearest contender. Aces of course will still carry out a thorough pre-flight unless scrambled, checking surface condition, panels and fasteners, looking for leaks and misplaced screw drivers, and FOD hazards a tired mechanic could have overlooked. Twenty three headings on the checklist, with sub headings in between, before she signed for it.

Out in the darkness the airfield was very much alive despite the blackout.

British Tornados and Jaguars, Australian and US F/A-18s, and of course the Tomcats. The odd menagerie that had been The Pearce Wing was gone now, and so to had many of its colourful members. Even a skilled pilot is on borrowed time flying elderly F-5s and Hawk trainers against the Sukhois of the Chinese and Russian naval air wings who were their opponents. The half strength wings had been reinforced by new aircraft from China, via Mactan and the tankers based there. That of course had ended with the capture of the airfield and base there.

Over three thousand miles away to the north west the Italian, German and French air forces were operating out of Mactan and Mindanao, where Christians and Muslims had put aside their differences for the time being and ended Chinese occupation with the help of French and British marines. The writing was on the wall for the People's Republic but saving face seemed more important than suing for peace.

The enemy naval air wings in Australia were the first item of business today for the RAF. The Tornados were bombed up with JP233 runway denial weapons and the Jaguars were the Wild Weasel flak suppressors paying an early morning visit to Illawarra airfield, on the edge of the lake by the same name. It was the last operational airbase in Australia that the Chinese had.

The remainder of 'The Pearce Wing', the Orphans and the Aussies, were providing close air support for the ANZACs and British Army ground units along with USAF A-10s out of Jervis Bay, with USAF F-15s and 16s flying CAP out of Canberra International, as were the tankers, AWACS and JSTARS. It was set to be a busy day and a crowded sky.

"Elephant Walk in ten, Commander." She was hailed by a ground marshal.

"What's an Elephant Walk, Ma'am?" queried her new RIO.

Nikki couldn't help it, and smiled as she spoke, despite thinking sadly of the last person to ask that of her.

"About fifty miles a day, lieutenant."

Rangi Hoana was the first to notice.

Sat on a thunder box he saw that there was no-one in the nearest watchtower. The dim electric lighting was still present along the fence top but the sentries were absent. Weak from dysentery, as was everyone in the camp, he finished his business and hobbled to the end of the line of portaloos to look along the fence and then he hurried, as best he could to the Russians container waking Karl Putchev with the news that the gates were still firmly barred but that the guards had disappeared.

"Do you think they shipped out?" Reg Hollis asked.

"Hardly likely, everything is pretty well blockaded, from what we've heard..." the sound of the opening barrage began as a distant rumble, like thunder in the mountains.

"No, I think they have gone off to fight." Karl Putchev stated. "A maximum effort."

"Where are the work party from yesterday, did they come back last night? Perhaps they heard something?"

Two hundred prisoners had been loaded up and taken away the day before and a check revealed they had not returned. It wasn't unusual for them to use the prisoners for work details, even in sensitive areas where the men had returned with titbits' of information Karl Putchev somehow seemed to be able to pass on.

They waited for an hour, to be completely certain that the guards were not coming back from some urgent task, before forcing the gate to the women's compound and checking they were still safe and well. Finally they forced open the main gate, and took tentative steps beyond it, wary of a trap. It would be a shame to get shot when liberation was just a few miles distant.

The barracks and administration blocks were empty, as was the food store of course.

"I think we should make a run for it." Someone said.

"Run where, and why?"

They stayed put, within the confines of their stockade, voluntarily this time, and waited.

The engine start up went without a hitch and they sat there for several minutes waiting for the marshals to light their wands and guide them forwards.

Nikki applied the right brake when the marshal pointed to their starboard gear, turning onto the taxiway.

Her RIO was twisting about in his seat, no doubt gawping at the sudden appearance of so many aircraft in close proximity to one another and all plodding along. Not quite nose to tail, but pretty close. Two replacements, both F-14As, were assigned to *'Smackdown'* flight and they followed the leader.

Royal Air Force Jaguars of No. 54 Squadron took off first, followed by the flight of three Tornado GR4s from 31 Squadron who were carrying out the runway attack. That was all the Tornados that were left, aside from two damaged aircraft being cannibalised for parts to keep the trio flying. The RAAF F/A-18s followed them, and finally The Orphans.

Climbing to 12,000ft they tanked over the sea with warships of the allied sat below on its mirror-like calm, waiting to be called upon to lend gunfire support also. It was crystal clear with visibility good enough to watch the specks engaged over the airfield. The Jaguars attacked and the first Tornado went in but sheared off without releasing the ordnance.

"Abort, abort...friendlies...." A bright flash cut off the rest of the transmission as the aircraft was brought down by ground fire.

A Jaguar finished the transmission. The two runways, north/south and east/west, had POWs penned near to the runways in concertina wire enclosures. The 30 detonating submunitions would undoubtedly cause fatalities among the prisoners and the British pilot did not find that acceptable.

Illawarra was still operational and the Sukhois were now coming up to meet them.

Baz Cotter and 12 Platoon walked slowly north as the darkness gave way to the first rays of daylight, and as that light increased he beheld with some awe the colossal allied effort, with men and machines moving at a walking pace, as far as the eye could see.

8 Infantry Brigade were in reserve, dogging the steps of the ANZACS. It was never going to end any other way, the Australians were going to be the ones to end the invaders. Everyone else was

welcome to come along and watch, but this, today, was their fight, it was personal.

Ahead, the artillery landing on the first positions lifted, shifting to the rear and the men from the 'Shires waited for the sound of small arms, and tank guns, but there was nothing. They did not stop, they carried on advancing until they reached the positions and found them abandoned.

Where the hell was the Chinese 3rd Army?

Pat Reed and Major General Norris Monroe, commanding the ANZACs, were parroting the words of many, *"Where had the enemy gone?"* The outer defence line had been abandoned.

"I am guessing that if the Chinks still have a nuke we will find out about it the hard way." Norris said.

"Is there another explanation?" an aide queried. The shortage of fuel and food caused by the blockade could be a factor, but it wasn't like the Chinese to dodge a fight. They were the enemy, but they had guts.

The Highland Brigade to the west and the US troops to the north were not advancing, they were to ensure the Chinese went into the sea or into the nuclear wasteland of their own making, but their O.Ps and patrols reported the same thing, the Chinese had apparently withdrawn back into Woolongong or Port Kembla, but no one was certain of that.

Only at the airfield at Illawarra did everything seem to be business-as-usual. A raid had failed and the enemy had scrambled, going for the heavily burdened fighter bombers, but F-15s and 16s blocked the way and an air battle was being fought.

The advance continued unopposed.

1 Company, 2CG, had driven onto their first objective and debussed, looking for a fight and finding none.

As per the battalions plan, 3 Company passed through 1 Company and continued the advance to the next known positions with 1 Company remaining on foot, shaking out into arrowhead with the Warriors and 432s following.

For whatever reason, and probably overconfidence was probably in there somewhere, 3 Company drew further ahead than the tactical bound which had been decreed.

The Life Guards were ordered ahead and they reported abandoned positions right up until the airfield where they found the enemy were alert, and far from pulling out. The sound of small arms, Rarden cannons and mortars carried back to the advancing infantry. The Scimitars pulled back, breaking contact and finding an over watch position.

2CG was the right flank of the Guards Divisions advance; to their right, was the Royal New Zealand Infantry Regiment, the ANZACs left flank. To the ANZACs right was the ocean, and to the front, in the path of this critical boundary, was a wooded feature called with some grandeur, Pudding Mountain. Pudding was a hill, a medium sized and tree covered hill. In front of its base were the next known defensive positions, with another a little way up, and both appeared as abandoned as the first.

3 Company's OC ordered 9 Platoon to dismount and go up the Pudding through the woods on foot, while the remainder slowly motored along the hills western side.

Oz had heard the Jocks bagpipes played when they took a hill near Shellhaven, so when he heard a bugle he assumed that it was 9 Platoon doing likewise, playing copycat, but more bugles sounded, tuneless, just a lot of noise to induce confusion and panic.

"Three this Three Two...Contact! Contact!...!"

Oz worked it out.

"One Company, standstills...FIX BAYONETS, and take cover!" CSM Osgood's voice carried over to the New Zealanders who looked amused rather than alarmed.

Major Llewellyn, the 1 Company OC, had also worked it out and he was calling the CO and informing him that they were under heavy infantry attack and asking for the rest of the battalion to come up on the hurry-up. Lt Col Innes-Wyse looked through his binoculars and could see nothing of the sort though. The remainder of 2CG continued at a walking pace.

As clearly and calmly as if he was running a range day back at the School of Infantry, Brecon, Oz shouted commands to the 1 Company men.

"Three hundred... targets to your front...Watch and shoot!...Watch and shoot!"

The platoon commanders sent men to collect Claymores from the vehicles stores but they had time to place only three of the directional mines and return, unfurling the firing cables as they went.

There was some ragged small arms from up in the woods, audibly recognised as the SA80, and a whole lot of AK fire followed by grenades.

No further transmissions were received from 9 Platoon and the bugles got closer.

Captain Regitt, the 1 Company 2 i/c, sent a fire mission request for the wood line at the base of the hill, but it was dismissed out of hand owing to the last known location of 9 Platoon and the proximity of the remainder of 3 Company, albeit they were outside the danger area.

Accurate salvoes of RPG-26 from the west side of the hill now began impacting the Warriors of 3 Company from the flank.

The CO now realised that there was something extraordinary happening and ordered 4 Company and 5 Company, the last being the battalions wartime establishment of a fourth rifle company, to move forward to where they could engage whatever was being hidden by the trees as it came down the hill.

The Rarden cannons of 1 Company's Warriors, their GPMGs and those of the rifles sections opened fire first, and finally the riflemen.

Four thousand men of the People's Liberation 3rd Army's 2nd Infantry Brigade had lain packed together on the Pudding all night, silently waiting for the Allies. The tactic they used was one that had been tried and tested, it had almost bought victory in Korea when unleashed on 25th October 1950. From Jamberoo, four and a half miles inland and picturesque Kiama Heights on the sea shore, the Chinese, also in brigade strength, attacked the left flank of the Guards, with the Irish Guards as their target, and the ANZACS 1st Battalion, Royal Australian Regiment, astride the coastal Princess Highway.

B Company, 1st Battalion, Royal New Zealand Infantry Regiment and 3 Company, 2nd Battalion Coldstream Guards were completely overwhelmed by human waves.

To the north, the 5th US Mechanised Brigade's 'Duke' Thackery was one of the few who had faced such attacks before, as a fresh faced young lieutenant in the Ia Drang Valley.

Northwest of Woolongong the US Corps was already dug in, which was not the case for the ANZACs and the British of course.

"Smackdown Zero One this is Red Plume One One, check in?" The 2CG FAC was a Geordie sergeant and although he was filtering out the regional inflections, his voice was raised to the level of shouting

in order to be heard over the close quarters combat. Someone was sure as hell in trouble, she thought.

"Zero One, *Smackdown* is a flight of three times Foxtrot One Fours with fourteen hundred pounds of fuel internal, max of forty five minutes availability, loadout is CBU, Mk-77, 250 pound retarded and a K of twenty mike mike...wotcha got for us Plume?"

"Red Plume One One, IP is at junction of head of Crooked River and railway line...track from IP to target is Two One degrees... distance Four decimal Three miles... elevation Two One Two feet...large number of infantry in the open at 34°42'9.84"S... 150°48'54.30"E...friendlies are danger-close, I say again danger close, at Two One decimal Three degrees, also Four decimal Three miles from IP, and will use smoke to mark friendly, I say again friendly position...drop NORTH of the smoke...egress to the south east...as quick as you can please."

"Zero One roger, three minutes with Mk 77s...you sound close-in Plume?"

"Red Plume One One, many thanks...close enough for a high five on the pass."

"Zero One roger, hang in there...*Smackdown* flight echelon left...now!"

They let down to two thousand feet and on crossing the IP stayed left of track in order to attack west to east. They could see black smoke from mortar and artillery rounds that was drifting away, the shellfire and mortar fire pausing to allow the US Navy aircraft to carry out their ordnance runs.

"Zero One, Plume, pop that smoke.....I see yellow."

"Plume confirms yellow!"

Nikki felt a jaw dropping moment as they now approached close enough to make out more detail. Looking half right out of the canopy and noting that the typical British knack of understatement was alive and well and embodied in the Coldstream Guards FAC. It was almost medieval, the 'large numbers' were a sea of humanity breaking upon an area marked with yellow signal smoke. The Chinese numbered in the thousands and the friendlies were a hundred, if that, and the FAC was down there where the fighting was hand to hand.

Banking hard right the F-14s came down to just a hundred feet above the ground.

Zero Two and Zero Three released the moment that they saw her Mk 77s drop away. There were enemy still pouring down the hillside beyond the embattled Geordies and after egressing to the west the F-

14s circled to come back around. There were far more targets than the flights ordnance load though.

The air had suddenly a very busy place with the Pearce Wing aircraft and the A-10s active in the five mile stretch from the shore to the township of Jamberoo. Fifteen thousand Chinese infantry in a colossal human wave launched against nine thousand Australian, New Zealand and British in tactical formation, advancing in the open.

'Zulu' is a prefix at the beginning of a callsign to denote an empty vehicle. Zulu One One Alpha was only technically empty, 1 Section of 1 Platoon were busily engaged twenty five metres from the vehicle but had sent Guardsman Blackley back to fetch more ammunition, as much as he could carry. The driver and gunner were in the Warrior, the vehicles GPMG and 30mm Rarden firing into the approaching masses when it was hit, and hit again repeatedly by RPG-26 projectiles. The vehicle, its additional firepower, ammunition reserves for the section, and the three men were lost. The remaining IFV's gunners prayed that the temperamental 30mm cannons would stay stoppage free and that the stored HE cannon rounds would miraculously multiply in number.

4 and 5 Company stopped before reaching the besieged 1 Company, debussing a hundred metres short as the Chinese had already closed with the Vormundberg veterans. Their fire was preventing 1 Company from being enveloped though as the enemy infantry began to lap around the flanks.

Captain Regitt concentrated on the mortar and artillery fire missions while Sgt Chamberlain, the 1 Company FAC, got some 'air on the go' and threw a marker smoke grenade.

From left the right the three F-14s screamed over the enemy's heads in a staggered line, but in contrast to the fast moving aircraft the ordnance they released seemingly fell in slow motion.

The three Claymores had already been expended before the air strike arrived. The frighteningly determined enemy mass absorbed the first mines blast, and the second, and then the third with barely a pause. Firing on the move, but with only the lead troops able to put rounds down on the British, the inaccurate fire was offset by the sheer weight of the charge.

Six Mk 77 canisters struck the ground and burst open, the white phosphorous igniter lighting off the 75 gallons of kerosene and benzene each one contained. It differed from Napalm B as the

Polystyrene had been removed and kerosene replaced the petrol filler. Less hazardous to store, the immediate effects were identical.

Lying prone and working methodically, Bill Gaddom was working the bolt, aiming, firing and working the bolt again. More used to engaging single targets at ten times the current range, he was fast running out of ammunition. Sgt Stephanski was on Bill's right, already 'out' and the slide locked to the rear of his Glock 17. Big Stef's face was pale with shock; his last round had taken an attacker in the face but not before a bayonet had been driven home. The sniper section sergeant was attempting to stem the arterial bleeding from the neck wound.

Oz felt the heat on his face and then the fierce gust of wind on his neck, the result of the vacuum created by four hundred and fifty gallons of fuel igniting explosively. The flames created a wall between them and the hill, but those enemies to their immediate front came on regardless. CSM Osgood rose up and in one flowing motion, parried aside a bayonet tipped AK and butt stroked the wielder, driving the toe of the SLR's butt into his temple, returning at once to the en garde before thrusting his bayonet into a throat, twisting and recovering once more, parrying, thrusting, and defiant, like a bear cornered by dogs.

"Get forward, The Wessex!"

Baz looked at the lone Australian in the turret of the IFV who had just shouted, leaning over the side of a Light Horse armoured reconnaissance ASLAV as it sped past, with two M113s following as best they could.

"That geezer, the vehicle commander, had white hair," someone observed.

"Well they haven't had a proper barney with anyone since Vietnam, so promotion must be dead men's shoes or summat?" another said.

General Norris Monroe, commanding the ANZACs, was the man in question. He had ordered the vehicle's driver to move as far forward as the battalion headquarters of the 1st Battalion Royal New Zealand Infantry. As the dust cloud that the vehicles had raised hid their departure into dead ground, the Wessex CO was ordered to get forward to the top of that same slope and dig in, fast. If anyone had claymores they needed to be sited immediately upon arrival. The Kiwis would fall back to them and together they were to prepare to defend against a massed infantry assault. The battalion, spread out as per normal for an advance to contact on foot, behind the ANZACs, was loaded down with full bergens, but it did its best, doubling the five hundred metres, breathing heavily on arrival but got busy straight away.

To the left of the Wessex, the Grenadiers were also hurriedly digging in, and to their right the Royal Green Jackets, and beyond them the LI. To the LI's right was the sea.

The New Zealand infantry battalion never did appear out of the dust, but the Chinese 54th Infantry Brigade did. The Kiwis last stand had been heroic, defiant to the very end, and General Norris Monroe had been the most senior allied soldier to fall that day.

The fine product from Accuracy International was a thoroughbred, but its current task was akin to hitching a Derby winner to a plough. The barrel of the L96 was the hottest it had ever been, hot enough to raise blisters if touched, although it was not glowing red, as the barrel of the GPMG to the snipers immediate left was doing. He had already tossed his water to the gun group to cool the barrel, and so had Sgt Stephanski. The GPMG was misfiring, the rounds being set off by the heat before being fully seated in the breech. Big Stef was down and now lying motionless on Bill's right but the sniper was unable to aid his friend.

From habit, Bill carried two full magazines of 7.62mm ammunition for the weapon, and a box of twenty, for a rainy day. Today was that day.

The Ghillie suited snipers had hitched a ride with 1 Platoon, and were now on the company's right flank.

He aimed, fired, worked the bolt to eject the empty case and slid a single round into the chamber, closed the bolt, fired and repeated the movement. There was no time to recharge the ten round magazines and on firing the fortieth round he removed the rifles bolt and flung it as far away as he was able before rising to one knee. Bill drew one of his back-ups, a 9mm Glock 17, and began double tapping. Two magazine changes went smoothly before he dropped the Glock and drew his second, and last, back-up, a Model 36 Smith & Wesson revolver that was older than he was. Bill continued firing aimed shots at the endless mass of bayonet wielding Chinese infantry, but the revolver had but five chambers. A careful and thoughtful marksman, he had never failed to count his rounds and accordingly he had never suffered the embarrassment of having a hammer fall on an empty chamber. This morning however, he very deliberately allowed that to happen. The dead-man's-click seemed somehow appropriate under the circumstances.

A second ordnance run was initially intended to deliver the CBUs to the still plentiful targets between the hill and the line of burning jellied kerosene, but the aviators switched to guns instead, strafing the Chinese infantry who had now reached the company of guardsmen, walking the rounds in as close as they dared, so close that empty 20mm cannon cases fell among attackers and defenders alike.

The third ordnance run was carried out by just two of Smackdown flight. They had all taken hits from ground fire but Zero Three waved off with an engine shut-down, turning back towards Albatross trailing smoke. CBUs had been dropped north of the fire line on the third run and now the 250lb retard bombs were delivered to the wooded hillside. There were still plenty of enemy down there, the enemy having swept over the right flank platoon in a killing frenzy of rising and falling bayonets, the morning sun reflecting off the steel. The F-14s last strafing run had broken the back of the attack on the remainder of 1 Company. Three of its IFVs were now burning but the rest of the battalion had come up, and the shell fire from warships off the coast was being added to that of the artillery and mortars.

The Tomcats, now with empty weapons stations, had remained until they had expended all of their cannon ammunition, and turned back to HMAAS Albatross.

Nikki's taxiing exceeded the speed restrictions posted on the airbase and she did not shut down, opening the canopy and remaining strapped in as a hot rearm and refuelling took place. The infantry attack was losing steam and the last of the enemy aviators was floating down under canvas, but apparently the Chinese tanks were coming out to play. The battle still had a ways to go.

Reloading the Vulcan 20mm rotary cannon was the last task completed, and the ground marshal at first waved her forward, but abruptly ordered a halt on receipt of some message on his headset. With engines back at idle and the brakes set, the ground crew placed the ladder beside her aircraft and the crew of Zero Three, accompanied by the flight surgeon appeared.

Nikki was kind of testy as she watched 'her' Cat taxi away without her. Whatever was going on here had better have a damn good explanation. She rounded on the Flight Surgeon.

"Sir?"

"Not everyone in that aircraft is qualified to be there, Commander."

"What?" she turned to look suspiciously at Johnson.

The flight surgeon smiled, which was something he had not managed to do for a while.

"Congratulations, your last toxicology test shows you to be one sober, pregnant, aviator."

The fighting ended at last on the battlefield south of Pudding Mountain, but beyond it a tank battle raged. The Australian 1st and 2nd Armoured Regiments, 1 Royal Tank Regiment and the Kings Royal Hussars were outnumbered on the ground but not outmatched. To the chagrin of the Aussies equipped with recently delivered M1A1s, the aging Aussie Leopard 1's rifled 105mm gun outranged them, and what was even worse the bloody pommy Challenger and Chieftain 120mm rifled guns were the kings of the battlefield.

With the A-10s now refueled and rearmed at Jervis after providing CAS over the infantry fight, they began fulfilling their original purpose by killing tanks too.

The Pearce Wing pounded Pudding Mountain's wooded slopes, and other likely places a few thousand of the enemy could be waiting in ambush. Dropping high explosive and incendiaries until the woods burned.

As the killing of machines by machines grew more distant, the infantry gazed in shocked awe at that which had occurred closer to home, and far less impersonal. Not all the enemy infantry had perished, several thousand were surrendering and many more were wounded, but ten thousand lay dead.

Baz Cotter was one of those numbed by the noise of bugles, the masses of bayonets, and the hatred behind them. The slope before them was thick with the enemy dead and the crest held three and sometimes four deep.

His bergen sat behind the shallow shell scrape he had managed to dig with an entrenching tool now bloodied at its edges, and hair adhered to that. The bergen was open, its content spilling out from where spare ammunition, grenades and a special forces version of the Claymore had been retrieved hurriedly. The SF mine had been smaller and lighter than standard, and acquired by illegal means, the rare item being won in a card game weeks before. As for the unpoliced bergan, well that would have earned him a few dozen push-ups at the top of Church Hill, the steep road with false summits that leads to the Sennybridge training area at Brecon, Powys.

Dopey came over and sat down heavily next to him, handing ID tags over.

The 2 i/c of his section, L/Cpl Roger Goldsmith, and the 'old man' of the platoon, Pte 'Juanita' Thomas, Spider Webbers replacement, and the only non ex C (Royal Berks) member of the section. Baz remembered running across a bridge in Germany with Pte Thomas, but it seemed a hundred years ago now.

"I never asked," Dopey said to Baz "but why was his nickname 'Juanita'?"

"He only had one tooth, one eater." Baz replied. "He kept his false teeth in his pocket for safe keeping when we were out on the beer. Scared away all the crumpet too...silly old bastard." He added both sadly and affectionately.

They sat for a while in silence before Dopey voiced an opinion.

"Thank fuck for Claymores."

"And A-10's."

"And the matelots on HMS *Whateveritscalled*, which was bunging over shells like there was no tomorrow."

"This incline, too."

"And training, don't forget the training."

Major Llewellyn and Oz took it in turns to play medic, tending to each other's wounds. The ex-coal miner had a deep wound in the fleshy part of the thigh that neither man had a dressing big enough for so the OC took Captain Regitt's as he had no further use for it.

They had lost 1 Platoon and half of 2 and 3. Guardsman Stevenson, the company clerk, and Sgt Chamberlain were the only survivors of company headquarters, along with OZ and the OC.

Lt Col Innes-Wyse was joined by Pat Reed, the CO looking rather ashen at having lost the best part of half of the battalion. Pat knew how that felt and after a few minutes helping him dust himself off, figuratively speaking, he went over to where what remained of the men he had commanded in Germany, were doing the same.

On arrival there he found OZ propping himself up by leaning against one of the Warriors, geeing on the crew to find more ammunition for the 30mm. All the IFVs had expended their entire stock of HE before also going through APSE, armour piercing special effects, the special effects being white phosphorous.

"Company Sarn't Major Osgood?"

"Yes sir?"

"You are making the place look untidy, so be a good Coldstreamer and lie to attention on a stretcher somewhere until a proper medic deals with those wounds."

It was saddening for Pat to see how few remained now, but he spoke to those familiar faces that could still answer and went to see for himself those who no longer could. Bill and Big Stef, their faces camouflaged more thoroughly than the riflemens, looked as though they were merely sleeping. He said a silent prayer for them all and moved on to the job he was paid for, running the brigade.

The Irish and Welsh Guards were also reorganising, but the 1st Guards Mechanised Brigade was no longer going to be spearheading the division, the Scots Guards and both battalions of the Grenadier Guards were passing through them to resume the advance to contact with whatever else the PLA's 3rd Army's 1st Corps had in store.

The ANZACs had also taken losses, although no one yet realised their commander was among the New Zealanders dead.

The ANZACs would not permit the British 8 Infantry Brigade to liberate the last occupied piece of Australia, not while they could still muster a single rifle section.

From the ANZAC ranks, four New Zealand and three Australian infantry companies had been overrun; the remainder sent the wounded to the rear, recharged their magazines, replaced the smoke and fragmentation grenades and wiped the gore off their bayonets before stepping off again, shaking out into spearhead formation once more.

"Target IFV."

Che Tran peered through the sight, using the IR facility despite bright sunshine.

"Another cold one." The Chinese fighting vehicle was yet another vehicle out of gas and abandoned in the streets of Port Kembla. The crews of these fighting vehicles had doubtless joined the ranks of the infantry for the last suicidal attack on the allies. Thousands had died in order for the PRC's leadership to save face, to show the rest of the world it was still to be feared and respected. The prisoners the allies were now taking tended to be rear echelon types, but the Australian tanks and infantry moved tactically despite the evidence before their eyes.

SASR were carrying out a heliborne assault of 3rd Army's 1st Corps HQ, fast roping onto the roof of the Woolongong City Council building, but they found only pen pushers and bean counters, all of whom were happy to surrender.

The Chinese armour that had attacked was now burning to the south of them and naval gunfire had malleted the last of the enemy artillery.

"Boss...skinny sailors at twelve o'clock!"

C Troop had arrived at a vast barbed wire enclosure where both Reg Hollis and Admiral Putchev came out to meet them, making the liberation of the town complete.

Australian National Flags began to appear on the roofs of buildings in Woolongong and Kembla, and hung from windows as it became clear that New South Wales was back in the hands of Australians.

Several hours later, as the operations officers for all the units in Australia began working on plans for the liberation of Singapore, Taiwan, Japan and the remainder of the Philippines, the Politburo finally bowed to the inevitable, replacing Premier Chan and calling for a ceasefire.

President Kirkland ended the call and looked up at the clock on the wall of the conference room and wondered if this was in fact the first time a war really had been 'All over by Christmas.' The time was 2359hrs.

CHAPTER 6

Jamaica: Tuesday, 18th January.

Private yachts were not an unusual sight in the bay and the latest arrival was not even close to being as ostentatious as some of the vessels. They also had beautiful bikinied young things sunning themselves on their decks, but aboard the *Krasivaya Dama* the beautiful girl strolling naked about the decks wearing mirrored aviator's sunglasses and a captain's uniform cap was the owner and not the owners 'niece'. She stayed beneath the sun awnings generally, but when she sunbathed she did so at specific times, retreating back to the shade at the gentle chimes of a small travelling alarm clock, almost as if she were hiding from something aloft.

She dined alone in the best restaurants, lovely, although aloof from the other diners.

Her picking up a local boy of enviable physique and a packed lunch box in his speedos, and taking him back to her yacht for the night was matched by the seduction of a blonde French scuba instructress for a one night stand. These were the acts of someone scratching an itch rather than reaching out for companionship.

Despite these flings she remained rather lonely, and one evening she accepted an invitation to a rather notorious regular weekend pool party at a shore side villa. She partied hard and fell asleep, sated and naked, on a sun lounger beside its pool.

She was awoken next morning by a maid who was worried that the sun, already well above the horizon, would inflict a bad sun burn on the girls back, but 99 miles above their heads Kondor-138 had already passed by twice in an orbit that also included the Spratly Islands. Its recognition software was working as advertised.

Still in London, in the low rent bedsit, the specialist received a text message and immediately departed, returning the key to the landlady and took a cab ride to Bond Street. A gold credit card bought a first class seat on a flight to Kingston, Jamaica, new luggage and a new wardrobe.

USS John C Stennis: The Tasman Sea, 50 miles south east of

Sydney, Australia. Wednesday, 19ᵗʰ January, 2359hrs.

Pennant number CVN-74, The USS *John C Stennis*, still marked with the scars of war was a fitting gathering place for the memorial service, held three months exactly from the moment the city had been destroyed. The President of the United States and the Australian Prime Minister cast wreaths upon the waters. The tide would carry the items the remaining way to shore, to the ruins of the city and the final resting place of so many.

General Henry Shaw attended, standing as close to the spot where his eldest children had last lived and breathed, as close as the experts would allow.

Once the midnight memorial service had ended the President was preparing to depart with Prime Minister Perry Letteridge, when he saw the lonely figure still stood at the edge of the flight deck staring into the night, towards the horizon.

The President and the Chairman of the Joint Chiefs had not spoken in three months, not since the night Sydney had died, with Matthew and Natalie Shaw aboard their ships in the harbour. Henry had made no move to alter that situation even now, and as rumour had it that he was about to resign from the service, Theodore Kirkland crossed the flight deck.

"Henry?"

General Shaw turned and the President could not but help notice the change in his top soldier in just three months.

"Mister President, sir?"

"I was sorry to hear of Jacqueline's passing."

He meant it genuinely, but it was as if there was now a wall between the President and his once closest advisor.

"We received the flowers, thank you sir."

He caught the whiff of the peppermints Henry used constantly to cover the smell of bourbon, and the eyes confirmed it, and those eyes also held no spark of the amity they had once held.

"Is it true that you are leaving the service, General?"

Instead of answering, Henry asked a question of his own.

"Is it true that you are planning to bankrupt the UK and the other European countries that kicked the politicians out?"

The general may have been absent from the President's side but he was well informed nonetheless.

"That is not technically correct, no." But he knew that Henry saw it for the lie it was.

"And you are backing the Vietnamese in their claim on the Spratly Islands, instead of the Philippines, Mister President?"

He was indeed very well informed indeed, the President concluded.

One of the terms of the ceasefire was the withdrawal from the islands and relinquishment of any future claims upon it by the People's Republic of China. Vietnam had occupied them upon the departure of the Chinese troops.

Various US oil companies had already brokered a deal with the Vietnamese.

"That is not yet something we have released to the public, but yes."

"Why?"

"Because they have them, and possession is nine tenths of the law."

"They didn't fight Mister President, they waited until others had weakened China and then they sneaked in the back door. The Filipinos didn't stop fighting, not even after they had been occupied."

"It's politics."

"It's disloyal, it is cowardly, it is dishonourable and as such it is unbefitting of the office...sir!"

The President looked at Henry, feeling his temper rise.

"I believe we had a similar discussion once, and as you couldn't even grasp the realities back when you were sober, I see no point in continuing this any further."

Mike and another agent had been stood a discrete distance from their principle, but they had taken two steps closer as the voices were raised.

"I wish you well with your retirement General."

The President turned on his heel, and snapped an order at the Chairman of the Joint Chiefs without deigning to look at him.

"Be sure that you make it happen, and soon!"

Theodore departed, boarding Marine One without another word or glance.

As the sound of the helicopters rotors faded Henry was still looking toward the horizon. He put a hand inside his uniform jacket and withdrew a slim hip flask, but his fingers had snagged another object along with it, a faded beer mat. Henry could not read the faint writing in the darkness but on replacing it inside his jacket he tossed the hipflask into the sea.

Montego Bay, Jamaica: 0900hrs, Monday 24th January.

The legal system in the former colony remains essentially British, and as such the young constable who had first boarded the *Krasivaya Dama* off South Negril Point presented himself at the mortuary in order to provide continuity of evidence, in other words, he was to confirm that the body upon the slab and the body he had accompanied from the yacht's main cabin to the mortuary two days before were one and the same. Constable McKenzie's Inspector had added a requirement of his own to that of the young officer's duties to the coroner. It was a matter of pride, his Inspector had explained.

Constable McKenzie was not from Kingston or any of the more 'lively' areas of the island; he had been raised in a small inland village and had seen a grand total of two dead bodies in his twenty years. The first had been his next door neighbour's granny when McKenzie had been five. She had been laid out in her best Sunday dress and the blocks of ice placed around the bed had slowed what his father had termed 'the ripening'. The Granny hadn't looked dead, she had just looked asleep. The most memorable part of the whole occasion had been young McKenzie having his hands slapped for trying to lift the pennies off the old ladies eyes, to see if she was in fact awake.

The second body had been the chestnut haired young woman on the boat. She had also been on a bed, and she hadn't looked dead either, at least not at first. He had felt embarrassed at intruding on a scene of obviously quite recent intimacy. She had been lying naked upon the rumpled sheets; face down on the red satin covers and with those glorious locks spread out like a chestnut veil and the tattoo of dogs paw marks on her right cheek. Blood splatter on the mirrored headboard was the first clue that she was not in fact sleeping. The colour of the sheets had hidden the large amount of blood actually present.

His sergeant drove him to the mortuary and pulled the car up outside the front entrance.

"Are you ready boy, got your notebook and a pen?"

McKenzie held up the notebook, it was opened to the page where he had recorded the delivery of the body the previous Saturday morning and he fumbled in a pocket before producing a biro, much chewed upon at one end.

"Yes, Sarge."

"Does it work?"

The young officer ran the nib back and forth on one corner of an inside cover of his notebook, making rapid zig zag motions before looking at his sergeant apologetically.

The thirty-year veteran rolled his eyes upwards before handing over his own.

"I want it back or you will be walking the beat all next month."

McKenzie exited the car, carefully closing the door behind him.

"And remember what the Inspector said?"

McKenzie bent to look back into the car.

"Yes Sergeant, I shouldn't faint or throw up."

The sergeant studied him for a moment before putting the car into first gear.

"Away with you now before you're late boy," his 'skipper' growled. "I'll be back in an hour to pick you up."

The car started to move off and McKenzie braced himself to enter the building.

"And if you've puked up over yourself you'll be walking behind the car!"

He raised a hand to acknowledge he understood as the car drove away.

He entered the mortuary, stepping out of the heat of a fine Caribbean morning into the air-conditioned reception area. He wasn't sure if the cool breeze that wafted over him was for the benefit of the living, or just a higher tech method of ensuring the residents did not ripen.

After signing himself in the young constable was shown along a corridor and upon opening the double doors at the end he had his first experience of an entirely different atmosphere.

It is a strange smell, a unique mix of sterilising fluid, formaldehyde, antiseptic, uncooked meat, gastric juices and last meals at every single possible stage of digestion.

A pair of mortuary technicians noticed the young officer enter and his naturally dark complexion became edged with grey as he sampled the smell for the first time. They looked at each other and winked. A probationary constable, quite obviously, so there would be some sport this fine morning.

Constable McKenzie swallowed the bile that had risen, and surveyed the white tiled room. There were only two other people in the room; living that is, and both wore disposable plastic aprons over their white coats, and those aprons were already blood splattered.

"Are you the forensic examiners?" He did not actually know what the proper title would be, but it sounded right.

"No officer, we just prepare them for the pathologist, and he will be here at any time now so why don't you find the body you are here for and he can start with that one."

Neither of the men made a move to assist him and McKenzie took in the white tiled room with a dozen stainless steel 'slabs' that had supine shapes resting upon them. A sheet covered each shape with just bare feet protruding from under one end. He saw that tags were tied to toes, just like in the movies, but he had no desire to lift any of the sheets.

"Er, she would be the white woman with the very long and curly, reddish hair, brought in last Friday."

One of the mortuary workers approached the nearest sheet adorned corpse.

"Well that's a problem then." He gestured to the young officer to come closer and the folded back the top of the sheet.

Constable McKenzie stared wide at the thing on the slab.

"You see we shave them in order to cut off the top of the skulls with a circular saw." A flap of skin remained at the back of the head allowing the top of the skull to hang open like a lid. The brain had been removed and was sat in a steel dish beside the head in readiness for a proper examination.

"It's to save time, we prepare the bodies and the pathologist just goes from one to the other, digs around a bit, prods here and there, writes his notes and moves onto the next one." The mortuary technician gripped the skin that had slipped down from the forehead when the cut had been made, making the face unrecognisable. Taking a firm grip he pulled the skin upwards, drawing back the folds from where they had sunk towards the chin.

"Is this her?...ah no, it's a man, well let's try another..."

Constable McKenzie had become very pale indeed but the appearance of the pathologist spared him further unnecessary torment by the technicians.

There had only been the one murder victim brought in over the weekend and this was his priority of the morning, a plainclothes detective accompanied him into the room and the demeanour of the technicians altered slightly.

"We will start with the woman from the boat....Constable can you confirm that this is the same body?"

The same technician took McKenzie by the arm and immediately led him to the end of the line to where the technicians had known the woman to be all along. He then grasped the sheet and uncovered the corpse with a flourish.

The breakfast Constable McKenzie had been trying to keep in place now started to rise. As well as removing the top of the head the technicians had already opened the chest cavity and the officer looked again at the ruined face, wrecked by the .45 calibre round that had entered through the back of her head.

"Yes sir that is the woman I found in the yacht's cabin....."

"Duly noted," said the pathologist, addressing the back of the hurriedly departing young officer.

The examination of the body took half an hour, during which it was discovered that a stainless steel crown had replaced a molar at the back of the lower jaw, a practice only carried out within the borders of the old Soviet Union.

A motive for the killing had yet to be established although robbery may well have taken place. A safe had been found open but empty.

The pathologist answered the detective's queries during the course of his examination of what had once been a very beautiful young woman.

No, there was no trace of semen in the vagina, anus or gullet, however there was evidence that sexual activity had been occurring either at the time of death or very shortly before. The killer had been a lover, quite possibly, and had probably slain her during the act, or alternatively whilst she had been astride another, as yet unknown lover, whilst her back was to the killer. The heavy .45 calibre round fired at close range into the back of the young woman's head would have proved instantly fatal.

No, there were no ligature marks on wrists and ankles, no defence wounds and no sign of injury aside from that fatal wound.

The toxicology report proved negative for illegal substances and as only a small amount of alcohol had been in the victims system at the time of death, the sexual activity had probably been of a consensual nature.

At last the doctor had removed his latex gloves and turned to the detective.

"I don't suppose you know who she was?"

The detective shook his head.

"The safe had been opened and there were no documents to be found on board, no passports or even any photographs." He consulted his own notebook.

"The yacht was purchased with cash in Columbia and renamed; and there are no details as to the purchaser."

"Drug related?" the pathologist queried.

The detective answered with a shrug, meaning it was not going to be a great shock if it was found to be cartel related. There may have been a war going on but that had not stopping drug smuggling, if anything it had increased.

"How about fingerprints and DNA?"

"Ah yes, they were taken as a matter of course but we drew a blank on our records here, so we sent them off to London and to the FBI."

"Perhaps I can help with that?" a voice stated from behind them, and the doctor and detective turned to face a large man who had plainly not spent long in the sun. The off-the-rail suit he wore was probably adequate for a summer wedding in England but it was sweat stained from the Caribbean heat and rumpled from the flight in an economy class seat.

"Broadhead, Foreign and Commonwealth Office," the stranger identified himself, handing across his government identity card before removing from a thin attaché case a sheet of paper bearing the set of fingerprints and an orange coloured folder bearing the printed title 'National Identification Bureau'.

"We were quite excited when we received your set of dabs," he explained. "You see we have been looking for this woman for some time now, so my department chief had me on the next flight out here."

The detective, who after many years cultivating a cynical outlook on life and therefore thought himself never to be surprised again, now found himself to be just that. He handed the Englishman back his I.D after looking at it closely, and nodded to the pathologist that he was satisfied with the bona fides.

Broadhead of the FCO opened the folder and extracted a colour photograph, which he handed to the detective.

"We knew her as Christina Carlisle, but her real name was Svetlana Vorsoff, a Russian national."

The detective looked at the photograph of a beautiful young woman and then handed it to the doctor. He looked at the thing upon the slab and shook his head sadly.

"What was she known for, Mister Broadhead?"

"Well, it seems she was KGB and she was involved in espionage before the war," he stated with a degree of relish. "She...*ahem*, shall we say that she specialised in 'pillow talk', if you get where I am coming from?"

The man from London claimed back the photograph, replacing it in the file and handed over to the policeman a copy of a National Identification Bureau record with its own photographs attached with paperclips.

"I'd like to sound mysterious and say that I cannot tell you any more than that, but I really don't actually know anything further, however I hope I have at least helped you in some small way?"

The detective thanked him but when Mister Broadhead enquired as to how the investigation was going, he stated rather formerly that it was proceeding and arrests would follow before long.

The man from the Foreign and Commonwealth Office received a copy of the pathologists report before leaving the mortuary, pausing on the steps to gaze at the bustle of life going on around him.

Inside the mortuary the detective was so pleased at the news that he could give his boss that it never occurred to him that the bureaucrat, a pen pusher from London, had been unaffected by either the smell, or even by the sight of the sliced open cadavers.

'Mister Broadhead' took a handkerchief from a pocket to mop his brow before continuing down the steps where he encountered the pale and dejected form of Constable McKenzie sat on the bottom step. He patted him on the shoulder in passing.

"Chin up son, it's a part of the job we all get used to eventually."

McKenzie looked up and nodded his thanks for the kind words, but the man in the crumpled suit was not dallying for a chat, he was hailing a cab.

The patois of the taxi driver brought a smile to his face as he lounged back in the rear seat, admiring the views being pointed out by the owner of some seriously long dreadlocks. Instead of turning right for the airport the cab turned west, and travelled along the edge of Montego Bay. On Southern Cross Boulevard his driver took both hands off the steering wheel and both eyes off the road in order to point out the Bob Marley Performance Centre and enthuse at the talent of a dead musical genius, which was particularly worrying as he could see the drivers of cabs driving in the opposite direction were engaging with their passengers in the same manner. No head on collisions or dreadful pile ups resulted though, and shortly after turning onto Sunset Drive he was delivered safely to the door of the yacht club.

After paying the cab fare he entered the building and made his way to the bar, where after purchasing a long cool cola with lime and crushed ice he stepped out onto a terrace that overlooked the sea.

The lunchtime business rush was still well over an hour away and as such the terrace held only one other person, but after casting his eye around at all the vacant tables the man from the FCO approached the table occupied by a lone female, elegantly dressed in light, fashionable designs that were ideal for the climes, and sporting close cropped, platinum blonde hair.

"May I?"

The woman, the possessor of a great tan and photographic models physique looked up from the broadsheet crossword she had apparently been struggling with.

"Please do, I was about to leave anyway."

With a smile, 'Mister Broadhead' sat opposite, placing the attaché case on the table between them.

He did not seem to take offence at the familiarity in which she drew the case to herself.

She opened the attaché case and withdrew the orange folder, the contents of which she studied earnestly.

He looked over at the newspaper and saw that the crossword she had apparently been battling with was in fact complete, and probably had been in around ten minutes flat.

Eventually she closed the folder and returned it.

"So I'm dead then?" she queried, a flash of amusement on her face.

"Your fingerprints and DNA records have been exchanged, and eventually the Jamaica Constabulary will conclude that Svetlana Vorsoff was the victim of a robbery that went wrong, slain by persons unknown."

He placed a hand inside his jacket, delving into the pocket there and took out an envelope which he handed across.

"As requested."

The blonde examined the British passport that the envelope contained, and she knew without asking that it was the real article, not some clever forgery.

"Who was she and what happened on the yacht that night?" he asked.

She returned the file and closed the attaché case.

"KGB, and a rather close friend of Elena, one would suppose." replied Svetlana. "As to the 'what', well I hardly think your blood pressure would stand it." The flash of Vorsoff gaiety and mischief that had been absent since London made a brief reappearance in the hoot of laughter that his expression caused, but it faded as quickly as smoke on the breeze.

"She went by a rather pretentious codename, and it was she who killed Caroline."

Broadhead considered that for a moment, recalling an incident on a tube train.

"I think I saw her, and if that is true then I am deeply sorry as I it means I may have led her to you in London."

"Elena would have found us one way or another, so you must not beat yourself up over this, and it was not I who was the target in London, but Caroline."

Svetlana withdrew a pair of sunglasses and placed them atop the silvery buzz cut before finishing her drink.

"Elena relishes inflicting emotional pain on others, and quite perversely upon herself also, or why else would she have sent her latest girlfriend to inveigle her way into ones affections in order to Shanghai me back to Russia?"

"You knew this?"

"Her obsession?" Svetlana rolled her eyes. "Well of course I did." Svetlana appeared a little disappointed in him. "There is more to this whore sat before you than you apparently realise."

The offhand use of that vulgar word made him wonder if she accepted that as her lot in life. The intelligence, the intellect locked away inside her, was therefore just so much lost potential and even a hardened copper, such as he was, saw the tragedy in that.

"Well, at the very least I hope that the new identity will allow you to stay clear of her from now on," he stated apologetically.

Svetlana paused and looked him in the eyes, holding his gaze for a moment as she weighed her words, before tapping the envelope with a white painted fingernail.

"Dear Sir Dickie, what on earth leads you to believe that I made my request in order to run away, hmm?"

In those green orbs the eye candy façade was lowered for a fleeting heartbeat, and he felt a chill.

"Yet another of her lovers running for the border, but this time with all the blood money? Well that is a short lived fiction indeed, and one that Elena will see through before very long so I had better make use of the advantage whilst I still have it."

She stood.

"There are some envelopes in the centre of the newspaper, and I would be grateful if you could ensure their delivery?"

He stood, and quite formerly he gave a little bow.

"Of course."

"Thank you." She leaned across as if to peck him on the cheek but instead kissed him fleetingly on the lips.

"This is probably goodbye."

"I know, so you take good care of yourself, Miss."

He watched her depart before flicking through the pages of the newspaper until he found seven envelopes; three were addressed to the wives of the Pell, Stokes and Scott Tafler, whilst three had postal addresses for Constantine's mother, Caroline's and Patricia's parents, and the elderly occupants of a farm outside Moscow.

He gathered up the envelopes and placed them into the inside pocket of his jacket but paused as an article in The Times caught his eye on the very page where the envelopes had rested. The first summit of world leaders since the war was due to be held at an exclusive ski resort in the Swiss Alps. A byline added that Russia's glamorous Premier would be taking advantage of the slopes during the breaks, having tirelessly worked towards peace and rebuilding ties with the worlds community etc etc.

Sir Richard looked thoughtfully in the direction Svetlana had taken before checking his watch. He had enough time before his flight back to London to enjoy the warmth and blue skies a while longer, so with a happy sigh Sir Richard Tennant, senior policeman for the Metropolis of London, relaxed and finished his drink.

Annapolis, Maryland, USA: 0845hrs, 9th February.

The term 'chapel' hardly did justice in describing the beautiful structure that served the spiritual needs of those he lived and worked at the United States Naval Academy, thought the President. He had spent long minutes in silent prayer, alone inside the building having used his position to ensure that for a short time he would be the only worshiper there.

A muffled cough reminded him that he was not entirely alone, and never could be whilst in office and he stood slowly, reluctant to leave the peace and wished for solitude that this place held.

His posse of Secret Service agents had at least given him space, positioning themselves at intervals along the walls at ground level and in the gallery. He nodded to Mike and saw the man's lips move, murmuring into a discrete radio microphone to inform the rest of the detail that 'Knight' was moving.

An agent opened the door for him and he emerged into the sunlight of a pleasant February morning, and decided to walk to Farragut Field, ignoring the cars waiting outside Buchanan House, the one-time home of the Superintendent of the Academy, and now temporary residence of the President of the United States of America.

The President glanced up at the room the First Lady occupied but she was not stood at the window watching her husband go, and he doubted that she would ever again play the dutiful wife, no matter how public the occasion.

He felt the loneliness keenly, the need for companionship, and had to force himself not to walk stoop shouldered as he strolled along Chapel Walk towards the Severn River.

The academy was quiet, it lacked the hubbub of a training facility in full flow and there were fewer than fifty Midshipmen here. Those who had been in training at the start of the war had largely been siphoned off, depending on their level of training into vacant berths as the casualties had mounted.

He paused when he drew level with the bronze statue of an Indian brave...*Native American*, he corrected himself. The statue appeared to have been defaced, painted somewhat less than artistically from the shoulders down and he read the name of whom it represented. *Tecumseh*, the kindly man who had befriended the pilgrims, and saved them from starvation.

He did not know what the daubing with paint was all about, but Henry would have done. Henry knew the history behind countless military traditions whereas the president had held the military in contempt for many years, and had no interest in such things, at least until relatively recently.

He missed Henry and he deeply regretted the harsh words spoken.

The last time he had seen Henry had been aboard the USS *John C Stennis*, staring into the night, his back turned as Marine One departed.

Henry had disappeared after arriving back from Australia. Using up his outstanding leave he had dropped out of sight by losing himself amongst the displaced masses and neither the CIA nor any other intelligence services had been able to track him down.

A few young faces watched from the windows of Bancroft Hall as their commander-in-chief passed by, his circle of agents on the alert despite the location watched those faces, ready to call out targets to the riflemen on every rooftop.

The President turned right and his walk took him past Santee Basin and along the top of Farragut Field to stand and look along to Chesapeake Bay.

It occurred to him that he was stood between two worlds, behind him stood the foremast of the battleship USS *Maine*, sometimes called the longest ship in the US Navy because the mainmast stood in the grounds of Arlington cemetery, on the far side of Washington DC to where he was now standing.

Washington DC, the irradiated city was abandoned now and the state capitol of Maryland was to be the site of the new White House, while the city of Baltimore had become the new capital city of the United States of America.

It lacked the ring to it that Washington DC had but the President, along with a sizeable portion of the population of Maryland, was opposed to the renaming of Baltimore to that of New Washington.

Work was already underway to build the new residence at the edge of the Naval Academy on the corner of College Avenue and King George Street. It would be a virtual replica of the White House and the President felt that that should be a statement that it was business as usual.

Much of the world resembled the post war Europe of sixty years before but this time there was no Marshal Plan to aid the rebuilding. America demanded a return to the old way of doing things.

Today he would begin to address the problem of Great Britain and the other European military governments. His administration was under pressure from those who held the big purse strings, who had tried and failed to resume business, to their satisfaction, with those countries because the military men who were in charge now would not bend the rules or take bribes to grease the way for them either.

The beating blades announced the approach of Marine One, an aircraft less pleasing to the eye than its predecessor, but the rugged looking CH-53E Sea Stallion and its back-up aircraft projected a no nonsense aspect of the presidential office.

The President gestured to an aide who handed across an attaché case before standing back, watching the large helicopters settle onto the grass of Farragut Field

The President Theodore Kirkland did not hurry aboard; he

rehearsed in his head the speech he would make in a few minutes time from the saluting dais in Baltimore. The world would see the might of America displayed at the victory parade to salute the fighting men who had now all returned from foreign shores. The world would hear his words and the underlying threat aimed at those who had overthrown their democratically elected governments. America was the land of the free and her military did the bidding of her government, not the other way around.

There would be no copycat military coups in the USA because the people were satisfied with the way their civilian government worked, and his administration was determined that like governments should also stand in Europe.

The parade was not the big event of the day though, a meeting with the oil companies and industrialists was scheduled for an hour later, and there the fall of the European military governments would be planned.

The side door of Marine One opened and two crewmen placed steps for their commander-in-chief to mount, he walked confidently forward and boarded, seating himself alone in the belly of the Sea Stallion.

The aircraft differed from the troop carrying version, sound proofing would allow the VIPs who may be aboard to hold a normal conversation and a bank of TV monitors showed the president six different channels, five of which were now displaying news programs whilst the sixth was set to the stock market. He lifted a telephone style receiver from its mounting beside his head and wished the pilot a good morning before turning down the volume on the monitors.

He opened the attaché case and removed a file from within, but there were no neatly typed pages inside, and the file bore the printed title 'Operation Armageddon's Song', a name he vaguely recalled from somewhere. Some small objects tumbled out into his lap. He stared for a moment, muttering to himself how his aide was about to find himself in the unpleasant position of being on the job market during a recession.

He picked the flimsy items up with the intention of tossing them away, but instead took a second to look at the cheap pieces of coloured cardboard. They were stained, aged, and the dyes had long begun to fade. On one side was borne an advertisement for a bar in Borneo whilst the reverse carried the logo of a well-known Far Eastern brewery, but there could also be discerned some handwriting in the margins.

Too many of the words had faded away with time to be read with the naked eye but it appeared to be some kind of declaration and the president was now more curious than he was annoyed. He extracted his spectacles to better read the spidery writing in the light of a sun that streamed through the left side window.

"Well I'll be damned.......!" he breathed, as he deciphered the signatures at the end of the beer mat constitution.

Movement on the TV monitors caught his eye because all six stations were now showing exactly the same image, depicting a live feed of the crowd's rapturous applause in downtown Baltimore. This was not supposed to be happening. He had been briefed that only CNN would broadcast the event live, the others channels would show the edited highlights at normal news times.

His eyes dropped from the monitors to the beer mats in his hands, and then to a sun shining through the wrong window if they were supposedly flying north, before returning to the screens showing the Joint Chiefs of Staff had taken the dais without him, and standing at their fore was Henry Shaw, General, USMC.

ENDEX

Aftermath

Colonel James Popham US Army – G5 (Plans) 82nd Airborne Division.
Major Garfield Brooks US Army – Instructor: Mountain & Arctic Warfare skills.
RSM Arnie Moore (Rtd) - Chief Technical advisor for the movie 'Vormundberg'.
Captain Nikki Rich (nee Pelham) – CAG: USS *Winston Churchill*- San Diego
Gerry Rich (Former Flt Lt RAAF) – House husband. San Diego.
Mike Arndeker (Former Lt Col. USAF) – PTSD Counselor.
Tony Loude (Former UK PM) – 5yrs: Treason. 15yrs: Attempted murder.
Marjorie Willet-Haugh (Former SIS chief) - 5yrs: Treason. 15yrs: Attempted murder.
Victor Compton-Bent (Former UK PM) – 2yrs: Expenses fraud. 2yrs: Tax Evasion.
Lt Col Rapagnetta – Vice Chairman: Italian Military Government
Colonel Leo Lužar – Chairman: Hungarian Military Government.
General Patrick Reed – Chief of the UK General Staff.
Major Mark Venables – Succumbed to burns.
Don Caldew – Chief pilot for the aerial cinematic unit, on the movie 'Vormundberg'
WO1 Colin Probert – RSM 1CG.
WO1 Ray Tessler – RSM 2CG.
WO2 'Ozzie' Osgood – Tactics Wing, School of Infantry, Brecon.
2Lt Dougal Ferguson, Nova Scotia Highlanders - Missing believed KIA.
Sgt Russell Blackmore, Nova Scotia Highlanders - Missing believed KIA.
Danyella Foxten-Billings – 10yrs: Attempting to pervert the course of justice.
Simon Manson – Cashiered. Co-Defendant with Foxten-Billings. Suicide, pre-trial.
Sir Richard Tennant (Rtd) – CEO Tennant Private Investigations PLC.
Lt Col Hector Sinclair Obediah Wantage-Ferdoux – CO 1RTR
Rebecca Hemmings (Former REME) – Owner: Hemmings Heavy Maintenance PLC.
Guy Thomson ex G Sqdn SAS – Author 'How I won the war, and everyone else was a xxxx'
Sqdn Ldr Michelle Braithwaite – CO No. 47 Squadron RAF.
Nancy McGonnigle (nee Palo. Former Sgt USAF) – Married Liam McGonnigle of Galway.
Lt Barry 'Baz' Cotter – Regular Commission 1RGJ and author 'Bugles, Bayonets and Hate'.
C/Sgt Dopey Hemp – CQMS C (Royal Berks) Company, 2 Wessex, and still a barman.
General Pierre Allain (Rtd) – Author 'The Honorable Mutineers'
Lt Cmdr Sandy Cummings RN – Joint Harrier Force.
Elena Torneski (Russian Premier) – Skiing accident, deceased.

Trivia

Volume Three and Four sidetracked me with the details of commercial and military satellite operation. There are a fair few dead satellites up there but as it would cost more to refuel them than to replace them. Their technology has been superseded anyway and therefore there are two disposal options, up or down. Down requires vastly more fuel to accomplish safely than boosting to a higher orbit but there are two places that spacecraft go to die. A graveyard orbit of about 403km above the Earth and a cemetery, of sorts, 3900 km South-East of Wellington, New Zealand at the following coordinates 43°34'48"S 142°43'12"W. Even if you could dive that deep it would not be advisable to visit. Aside from the exposed nuclear reactors of military satellites that were guided to splashdowns there, it is a toxic dumpsite for chemical weapons and old Soviet nuclear reactors.

I found the potential for new stories lying about everywhere I happened to research. For instance, there was a tiny coral atoll in the Pacific, six hundred miles from anywhere, but a hundred feet deep in inedible crabs, bad tempered sea birds and nitrogen rich Guano. (Bird poo.)

That atoll became at various times, a pirate base, a significant fertilizer resource, a retreat, a military base, the scene of several shipwrecks, and also of serial rape and murder.

The atoll's sole financial asset is long gone, but the crabs remain. (Isn't that just like life?)

Île de la Passion

French Guiana was a place I knew virtually nothing of until an attack upon the ESA facility by either China or Russia seemed to be a necessity. It is a place that was much fought over by the old European empires.

When Wolfe brought an end to the French rule in North America, France was in a quandary as to where to relocate those colonists who wanted to leave. Return to France was not an option for a bunch of losers, but they were good Catholics in the clutches of the heathen Protestant British, they had to have their souls protected if nothing else. French Guiana was the eventual site for those who had lost 'New France' to end their days.

Has anyone seen 'Papillon'?

Henri Charrière, 'Papillon', was a prisoner in the colony but not on Devils Island, that was a fabrication. Only people convicted of treason went to Devils Island.(Good movie though!)

There are whole websites dedicated to fans of Henri Charrière, and discussion groups debating the type of crimes the fans would consider committing in order for them to be incarcerated and live out their fantasy of being a Henri Charrière, and escaping from somewhere on coconuts. Suggestions that, *1/* The book was intended as a novel, and not a memoir, *2/* That Henri is dead (Born in 1904 so he'd be pushing 110 at the time of writing), or *3/* That he really was a murderer and deserved to be a convict, can lead to expulsion from the various groups.

Papillon makes life imprisonment *Cool!*

The odd case of the destroyed tooling.

The F14 Tomcat was without doubt a phenomenal war bird and one that arguably still had a decade or so left of useful life. Aircraft, like champion boxers, one day meet the young hungry wannabe who hands them their ass. No one stays at the top indefinitely. The mystery is however, why did Dick Cheyney order the F14D production halted when it was still on top of its game, and why was it so important to have the tooling destroyed so none could ever be built again, without a huge cost implication?

The ignominious end of the Aussie 'Pig'.

The F111D of the Royal Australian Air Force was quite iconic but getting a little long in the tooth. Of the forty three aircraft in the fleet, eight have crashed since 1973, twelve have been sold to museums or put on static display, but twenty three were chopped up and buried.

Now that wasn't very polite!

(Since the publication of edition 1 I have since learned that the original purchase agreement specifically prohibited resale of the aircraft by Australia and consequently the sale of the aircraft to a major arms dealer was cancelled after the US Government intervened. Apparently the aircraft could only be returned to the USA or rendered permanently unusable. Those they could not give away to museums and airbases as gate features were stripped and buried.)

Characters (In no particular order...)

I was asked whom the characters in Armageddon's Song were based upon, and to be honest there are a few who are amalgams of people I have met throughout my life.

'The President' is an easy one as I tend to picture a situation and hear dialogue form before I write. I found that the 'ideal' of a President was not a real person but rather one created by Aaron Sorkin. At least so far as speech and mannerisms, in my mind's eye anyway, President Josiah Bartlet, as portrayed by that brilliant American actor Martin Sheen, pretty closely fits the bill. Mine of course is a little more complex as will be discovered. A good person by nature who may have trouble sleeping some nights, owing to his being forced to work in dirty political waters.

'Regimental Sergeant Major Barry Stone, 1st Battalion Coldstream Guards' is a combination of three terrifying individuals (to be a young soldier in the British Army in the early 1970's)
RSM Torrance, Scots Guards, who reigned over the Infantry Junior Leaders Battalion at Park Hall, Oswestry in Shropshire.
Garrison Sergeant Major 'Black Alec' Dumon, The Guards Depot, Pirbright, Surrey and later Garrison Sergeant Major London District. And finally Regimental Sergeant Major Barry Smith, 2nd Battalion Coldstream Guards.
Sergeant Major Torrance was outwardly fierce but inwardly fair, and an ideal individual to be dealing with a couple of thousand 15 years old schoolboys who had to be turned into the next NCO Corps of the British infantry.
'Black Alec' is of course a legend. Those dark, sunken eyes and unblinking, cold stare. 'Captain Black & The Mysterons' except for that voice, the gruff Yorkshire accent that barked a command out on one side of a parade square and flowers in their beds outside Battalion Headquarters a quarter mile away would wilt and die.

RSM Smith was a pretty decent actor I think. The act was to make everyone, including young subalterns, believe he was perpetually angry and a heartbeat removed from downright furious.
I was on barrack guard one night when one of the old soldiers, an 'old sweat' with a few campaigns under his belt, and as it turned out at least one demon, went berserk. He had a rifle and bayonet attached to it in a barrack room he was trashing. The Picquet Officer voiced the possibility of arming the Picquet Sergeant, with obvious

consequences, should the soldier in question make a fight of it, which he would have. The RSM intervened, whatever past trauma was troubling the soldier, he knew about it. He sent everyone away except for a couple of us and he waited out the storm. The RSM entered on his own an hour later, and spoke in a normal voice for long minutes before exiting and handing me the rifle before leading the soldier to the medical centre, speaking quietly to him all the time. Next day, RSM Smith was of course once more a heartbeat removed from outright furious.

General Henry Shaw USMC, another easy one, but also oddly out of time. It was back in 2004 when I added General Henry Shaw, and in my mind Henry is Tom Selleck as 'Frank Reagan' except that 'Blue Bloods' was not yet screened. Possibly Mr Selleck played another role around that time which was solid, professional and reliable-to-the-end in character. If I say so myself I do like General Henry Shaw, I could serve under a leader like that.

Sir James Tennant, the Commissioner of the Metropolitan Police is to me 'Foyle's War' Michael Kitchen an exceptionally talented British actor of the finest type.

WO2 Colin Probert, Coldstream Guards.

When we first encounter Colin he is out in the 'Oulu' shadowing a patrol on Sennybridge training area. He is a bit senior to be 'Dee Essing' as a man of his rank should be running the office, keeping on top of the admin and as the company level disciplinarian; he should be ensuring no one is slacking off. Officers are not going to do that. However, Colin is a soldier, not an administrator and not a 'Drill Pig', so getting out with the students is something he would contrive somehow.

Colin is a Geordie from Newcastle who did not fancy shipbuilding, when there were still ships to be built of course, and made his way to the Army Recruiting Office armed with his O level certificates.

Brookwood station is where he arrived at 'The Depot' he may even have visited the gents before the 4 Tonner arrived, and seen

'Flush twice...it's a long way to the cookhouse!' graffiti on the wall of trap one.

'Cat Company' aka Caterham Company, is where Colin would have been introduced to the first mysteries of the British Army in general, and The Guards specifically.

A Platoon Sergeant and a buckshee Guardsman/Household Cavalry Trooper (the B.R.I, Barrack Room Instructor) would teach them how to iron, polish, bumper and buff, plus who and who not to salute.

I can see him sat on the end of his bed, sporting the haircut to end all haircuts as he polishes his boots for the first time, wondering what the hell he has let himself in for.

Colin is 6' 2"tall, so initially he would have been posted to 4 Company on arrival at Victoria Barracks, Windsor.

Selection takes place on height alone when you are a lowly and buckshee Guardsman. The tallest go into 1 Company; the next go to 4 Company. The short arses, 5'10" dwarves in comparison, find themselves in 3 Company. 2 (Support) was a mixed bag which could reduce a Drill Pig to drink as they were the specialists, the Mortarmen, Recce Platoon, Anti-Tanks and Assault Pioneers. They came in all shapes and sizes.

With promotion and courses such as Section Commanders, Platoon Commanders, and the All Arms Drill Wing, Guardsman Probert has become a Warrant Officer.

Sergeant Osgood.

Nobody knows his first name, and even Mrs Osgood calls him 'Oz', but he joined the army from the coal mines, tired of strike pay and bleak prospects.

Oz is already married when he joined the army, and Sarah had a baby on the way back then.

The Osgood's and Colin will have quickly to become friends. When Janet and Colin eventually marry, Sarah would take the newly wed under her wing and show her the ropes, guiding her away from pitfalls such as those purveyors' of innuendo, and assassins of character, the pad-hags.

With Colin and OZ away on exercise or deployed on operations the wives support each other.

Christina Carlisle/Svetlana Vorsoff.

I recall once seeing Anna Chapman, before she was notorious, and being struck by the way she stood out in a room, at complete odds with spooks such as Terry Jones in the book, but I fancy Svetlana would have that same effect.

At 5'10" tall, with curly chestnut hair to the backs of her legs and a dancers physique, Christina/Svetlana, is too strikingly beautiful to be a spy.

Having been robbed of a normal life and set to bedding whichever men and women the state required Caroline/Svetlana still had greater expectations. She does not object to the bedroom gymnastics it is just that it is not on her terms.

The Seventh Chief Directorate, into which she had been recruited, dealt with visiting foreign diplomats, politicians and businessmen. Her mind and high IQ are of little importance to her employer, it is her talent as a seductress and her talents between the sheets that are the only assets they value.

Somehow, Christina/Svetlana winds up in London with a flat in Knightsbridge and a legitimate six figure salary job at a leading merchant bank in the City.

She is living the life, or is she?

Major Constantine Bedonavich.

Constantine was an able and courageous pilot. He drove the SU27 Flanker until younger pilots were on the verge of making the old man of the regiment look precisely that.

His wife, Yulia, until recently the Prima Ballerina at the Moscow State Ballet, had friends in high places and instead of Constantine leaving the service he instead moved to London to take up the post of Deputy Military Attaché at the embassy of the Russian Federation. The good major did of course need to undertake a course in fieldcraft and trade craft for 'new agent and asset handlers' at the embassies.

Yulia's involvement with a billionaire entrepreneur and the divorce which followed, served to drive Constantine into his work rather than into a bottle, and the major developed into a highly capable spy handler.

Sir Richard Tennant.

Sir Richard wears two royal jubilee medals, his 'undetected crimes' medal aka Long Service and Good Conduct medal, along with the Queens Police Medal, but two other ribbons occupy the first two spaces. The General Service Medal with Northern Ireland clasp, and the South Atlantic medal. The Commissioner had not always been a copper; he had spent six years in the Blues and Royals, serving in the Falklands War as well as a couple of tours in Ulster.

Rather than sign on for another three years Corporal of Horse Tennant became Constable Tennant and attended the Metropolitan Police Training School at Hendon.

Theodore Kirkland (The President).

I have not given Mr Kirkland a political party affiliation. It does not really have any bearing on the story whether he is a Republican or a Democrat, he represents America in this story.

At the start of the tale the President has no affection, nor enmity either, for the military as he is just an academic who found himself in politics without actually encountering the military along the way.

I have left him as a good man but with a few flaws, because he is only human, and one who happens to be in the chair when a war starts.

Vadim Letacev (The Russian Premier).

My apology for coming up with a wholly unoriginal villain. He is Charles Dance (with his bad head on) and Vlad the Impalers more sadistic brother.

A man with no redeeming features, megalomania, a serious case of psychosis and probably halitosis too!

Lieutenant of Paratroops, Nikoli Bordenko.

"Ey, kak dela?" ("How are *you* doin'?")
I had a platoon commander once who was pretty much the suave and dashing Nikoli. The Joey Tribbiani of British Airborne Forces, until injury forced a change of pace, and he came to us. I was never quite sure whether the injury was caused by landing badly after jumping out of an aircraft, or a bedroom window?

Good officer and a good soldier.

CAST

The Americans

Theodore Kirkland	The President
Gen Henry Shaw USMC	Chairman of the Joint Chiefs
Terry Jones	Director CIA
Joseph Levi	CSA, Chief Science Advisor
Art Petrucci	CIA Chief of Station, London
Max Reynolds	CIA Langley
Scott Tafler	CIA Langley
Alicia O'Connor	Computer game programmer
Ben Dupre	Director FBI
Dr David Bowman	USS *Commanche*
Admiral C Dalton	USS *John F Kennedy*
Admiral Conrad Mann	USS *Gerald Ford*
Admiral Lucas Bagshaw	USS *Nimitz*
Captain Joe Hart	USS *Commanche*
Captain Rick Pitt	USS *Twin Towers*
Commander Kenny Willis	USS *Nimitz*
Lt Cmdr. Natalie Shaw	USS *Orange County*
Lt Col Matthew Shaw	USS *Bonhomme Richard*
Lt Nikki Pelham USN	USS *John F Kennedy* & USS *Nimitz*
Lt (jg) Candice LaRue	USS *Nimitz*
Col Omar Chandler	USAF
Major Caroline Nunro	USAF

Captain Patricia Dudley	USAF
Major Glenn Morton	USAF
Lt Col 'Jaz' Redruff	USAF, AC Air Force One
Major Sara Pebanet	USAF, Co-pilot Air Force One
Sgt Nancy Palo	USAF Air Force One
Major Jim Popham	82nd Airborne
Lt Col Arndeker	USAF
Captain Garfield Brooks	Green Berets
Senator Walt Rickham	US Senate
General 'Duke' Thackery	5th US Mechanised Bde
RSM Arnie Moore	82nd Airborne
Captain Daniel King	Black Horse Cavalry
Master Sergeant Bart Kopak	Black Horse Cavalry

The French

Admiral Maurice Bernard	*Charles De Gaulle*
Admiral Albert Venesioux	*Jeanne d'Arc*, ASW Group
Lt Arnoud Bertille	21e Régiment d'Infanterie de Marine

The Filipinos

Colonel Villiarin	Cebu guerrilla forces
Sergeant 'Bat' Ramos	Philippines National Police

The Russians

Vadim Letacev	Premier
Admiral Pyotr Petorim	Red Fleet
Marshal Gorgy Ortan	Army Group West

General of Aviation Arkity Sudukov	Air Force
General Tomokovsky	Army Group West
Svetlana Vorsoff	KGB 'Sleeper'
Anatoly Peridenko	1st Chairmen of reformed KGB
Elena Torneski	2nd Chairman of KGB
Alexandra Berria	KGB stringer
Col Gen Serge Alontov	6th Guards Airborne
Lt Nikoli Bordenko	6th Guards Airborne
Major Constantine Bedonavich	Deputy Military Attaché, London
Vice Admiral Karl Putchev	*Mao*

The Australians

Perry Letteridge	Prime Minister
Gen Norris Monroe	1st Brigade
Cmdr. Reg Hollis	HMAS *Hooper*
LS Craig Devonshire	HMAS *Hooper*
AB Philip Daly	HMAS *Hooper*
AB Stephanie Priestly	HMAS *Hooper*
Flt Lt Gerry Rich	15 Squadron RAAF
Flt Lt Ian 'Macca' McKerrow	15 Squadron RAAF
Sergeant Gary Burley	1st Armoured Regiment
Tpr Che Tan	1st Armoured Regiment
Tpr Chuck Waldek	1st Armoured Regiment
Tpr 'Bingo' McCoy	1st Armoured Regiment

The New Zealanders

Barry Forsyth	Prime Minister
Sergeant Rangi Hoana	1st Bn Royal New Zealand Infantry Regiment

The Chinese

Guozhi Chan	Chairman
Tenh Pong	Defence Minister
Marshal Lo Chang	Peoples Liberation Army
Admiral Li	PLAN *Mao* Task Force
Captain Hong Li	PLAN *Mao*
Captain Jie Huaiqing	PLAN Special Forces
Captain Aiguo Li	PLAN *Dai*

The Brits (Second to None and therefore on the right of the line!)	
The Rt Hon Tony Loude MP	PM
The Rt Hon Peter Dawnosh MP	PM
The Rt Hon Victor Compton-Bent MP	PM
The Rt Hon Matthew St Reevers	Defence Minister
The Rt Hon Danyella Foxten-Billings	Defence Minister
Marjorie Willet-Haugh	'M' Head of SIS
Sir Richard Tennant Commissioner	Metropolitan Police Commissioner
Lt Col Hupperd-Lowe	1CG
Lt Col Pat Reed	1CG
Major Simon Manson	1CG& 2CG (pre Australia)
Captain Timothy Gilchrist	1CG
RSM Barry Stone	1CG
CSM Ray Tessler	1CG & 2CG (pre Australia)
WO2 Colin Probert	1CG
Sgt 'Oz' Osgood	1CG
Guardsman Paul Aldridge	1CG
Guardsman Larry Robertson	1CG
L/Cpl Steve Veneer	1CG AA Section
Guardsman Andy Troper	1CG AA Section
Guardsman Stephanski 'Big Stef'	1CG Sniper Section
L/Sgt 'Freddie' Laker	1CG Sniper Section
S/Sgt Bill Gaddom	RMP attached to 1CG Sniper Section

Major Stuart Darcy	Kings Royal Hussars
Major Mark Venables	Kings Royal Hussars
2Lt Julian Reed	Royal Artillery
Sergeant Rebecca Hemmings	REME LAD attached to 1RTR
Major Richard Dewar	Royal Marines, Mountain & Arctic Warfare Cadre (M&AWC)
Corporal Rory Alladay	Royal Marines M&AWC
Lance Corporal Micky Field	Royal Marines M&AWC
Sergeant Bob McCormack	Royal Marines M&AWC
Sergeant Chris Ramsey	Royal Marines, SBS
Major Guy Thompson	G Squadron 22 SAS
Guardsman Dick French	G Squadron 22 SAS
L/Sgt Pete 'Sav' Savage	G Squadron 22 SAS
Lt Shippey-Romhead	Mountain Troop 22 SAS
Flt Lt Michelle Braithwaite	47 Squadron, RAF
Sqdn Ldr Stewart Dunn	47 Squadron, RAF
Rr Admiral Sidney Brewer	HMS *Ark Royal* ASW Group
Rr Admiral Hugo Wright	HMS *Illustrious* ASW Group
Captain Roger Morrisey	HMS *Hood*
Sub Lt Sandy Cummings	HMS *Prince of Wales*, Fleet Air Arm
Lt 'Donny' Osmond	HMS *Prince of Wales*, Fleet Air Arm
Lt Tony McMarn	3RGJ
Captain Hector Sinclair Obediah Wantage-Ferdoux	1RTR
Anthony Carmichael	KGB 'Stringer'

Janet Probert	Army wife
Annabelle Reed	Army wife
Sarah Osgood	Army wife
June Stone	Army wife
Jubi Asejoke	South London teenage criminal
Paul Fitzhugh	IRA 'Safe House' provider
PS Alan Harrison	Metropolitan Police
PC Dave Carter	Metropolitan Police
PC Sarah Hughes	Metropolitan Police
PC John Wainwright	Metropolitan Police
PC Phil McEllroy	Metropolitan Police
PC Tony Stammer	Metropolitan Police SFO SCO19
PC Annabel Perry	Metropolitan Police SFO SCO19
Cpl 'Baz' Cotter	Wessex Regiment 'Four One Bravo'
L/Cpl 'Dopey' Hemp	Wessex Regiment 'Four One Bravo'
Pte 'Spider' Webber	Wessex Regiment 'Four One Bravo'
Pte Adrian Mackenzie	Wessex Regiment 'Four One Bravo'
Pte 'Juanita' Thomas	Wessex Regiment 'Four One Bravo'
Pte George Noble	Wessex Regiment 'Four One Bravo'
Pte Mark Barnes	Wessex Regiment 'Four One Bravo'
Pte Shaun Silva	Wessex Regiment 'Four One Bravo'

Terminology & Acronyms

Terminology &	Acronyms
Numeric	
1CG:	First Battalion Coldstream Guards
1RTR:	First Royal Tank Regiment
2CG:	Second Battalion Coldstream Guards
2LI:	Second Battalion the Light Infantry
3RGJ:	Third Battalion Royal Green Jackets
'5':	Slang term for MI5
'6':	USN carrier borne strike aircraft (Intruder)
'A'	
A-6:	USN carrier borne strike aircraft (Intruder)
A-10:	US built single seat, close air support, tank killing aircraft (Warthog)
A-50:	Russian built AWAC version of the heavy Il-76 transport aircraft (Mainstay)
AA:	Air-to-Air
AAA:	Anti-Aircraft Artillery
AAC:	British Army's Army Air Corps
AEW:	Airborne Early Warning
AFB:	Air Force Base
AFV:	Armoured Fighting Vehicle
AGM:	Air-to-ground missile
AIM:	Aerial Intercept Missile
AK-47:	Updated derivative of the Kalashnikov assault rifle
AKM-74:	Romanian derivative of the AK-74
ALASAT:	Air Launched Anti Satellite missile
AMIP:	Area Major Inquiry Pool (Metropolitan Police)
AMRAAM:	Advanced Medium Range Air to Air Missile (Slammer)
AN-72:	Russian built transport
Apache:	US built helicopter gunship in service with US and Allied forces
APC:	Armoured Personnel Carrier
Army:	3 x Corps + combat and logistical support
Army Group:	3 x Armies
AP:	Anti-Personnel
ASW:	Anti-Submarine Warfare
AT:	Anti-Tank
ATC:	Air Traffic Control
ATF:	Bureau of Alcohol, Tobacco, Firearms
ATO:	Ammunition Technical Officer (Military bomb disposal officer)
AV-8B:	US developed version of the Harrier II.
AWACS:	Airborne Warning And Control System
AWE:	Atomic Weapons Agency (Aldermaston)
'B'	
B1-B:	US built supersonic swing wing early stealth bomber (Lancer)
B-2:	US built stealth bomber (Spirit)
B-52:	Heavy USAF bomber (The Buff aka Big Ugly F***er)

Backfire:	Russian built supersonic swing wing bomber (TU-22M)
BAOR:	British Army Of the Rhine
Battalion:	3-4 Rifle Coy's + combat and logistical support (Bn)
BBC:	British Broadcasting Corporation
Bde:	Brigade (3 Bn's + combat and logistical support)
Binos:	Binoculars
Blackjack:	Russian built supersonic swing wing bomber (TU-160)
Blinder:	Russian built supersonic bomber (TU-22)
BMP:	Tracked AFV
Bn:	3-4 Rifle Coy's + combat and logistical support (Battalion)
Boomer:	Ballistic Missile Submarine (SSBN)
Box:	Slang term for MI5 (Post Office Box 500)
Bradley:	US AFV
BRDM:	Russian built four wheeled Reconnaissance vehicle
Brew:	Tea
BTR:	Russian built eight wheeled APC
Buckshee:	Free item
Buckshee:	New and inexperienced
Buff:	B-52 Heavy USAF bomber (Buff aka Big Ugly F***er)

'C'

CAD:	Computer Aided Dispatch
CAG:	Commander Air Group
CAP:	Combat Air Patrol
Carl Gustav:	84mm medium anti-tank weapon
CBU:	Cluster Bomb Unit
CCCIR:	Police Information Room Senior Controller
CCCP:	Cyrillic alphabet for 'Union of Soviet Socialist Republics'
CG:	Coldstream Guards
Challenger:	Current series of British MBTs
Charlie Gee:	84mm medium anti-tank weapon
CHARM:	120mm self stabilising main tank gun with rifled barrel
Chieftain:	Former series of British MBTs
CIA:	Central Intelligence Agency
CIC:	Combat Information Centre
CIC:	Commander In Chief
Civvy:	Civilian
CNN:	Cable News Network
CO:	Commanding Officer
CO:	The Commissioner's Office (NSY: New Scotland Yard)
Colly:	Her Majesty's Military Correction and Training Centre (HMCC)
Company:	3 x Pl's + logistical support (Coy)
COMSUBPAC:	Commander Submarines Pacific
Corps:	3 x Div's + combat and logistical support
Coy:	3 x Pl's + logistical support (Company)
CP:	Command Post
Cpl:	Corporal
CQMS:	Company Quarter Master Sergeant (Colour

	Sergeant rank)
CSA:	Chief Scientific Advisor
CSM:	Company Sergeant Major (WO2 rank)
CTR:	Close Target Reconnaissance
CVR(T):	Combat Vehicle Reconnaissance (Tracked)
CVR(W):	Combat Vehicle Reconnaissance (Wheeled)

'D'

DEEP STRIKE:	Air and SF attacks on logistical targets 100k + behind the lines
DefCon5:	Peacetime
DefCon4:	Peacetime; Increased intelligence; Strengthened security
DefCon3:	Increased force readiness
DefCon2:	Increased force readiness – Less than maximum
DefCon1:	Maximum force readiness
DF:	Defensive Fire
DF:	Direction Find
Div:	3 x Bde's + combat and logistical support (Division)
DPM:	Disruptive Pattern Material (Camouflage)
DZ:	Drop Zone

'E'

E-2C:	US built Carrier borne early warning aircraft (Hawkeye)
E-3:	US built AWACS based on Boeing 707 (Sentry)
Eagle:	USAF swing wing, twin engine, single seat, all weather, fighter (F-15)
ECM:	Electronic Counter Measure
ELINT:	Electronically gathered Intelligence
EMCON:	Electronic Emission Control (Radio and Radar silence)
EMP:	Electro Magnet Pulse
ESM:	Electronic Surveillance Measures
Expo:	Explosives Officer (Police bomb disposal officer)
Extender:	Aerial Tanker derived from Boeing 707 (KC-135)

'F'

F-14:	USN swing wing, twin engine, two seat, strike fighter (Tomcat)
F-15:	USAF swing wing, twin engine, single seat, tactical fighter (Eagle)
F-15E:	USAF swing wing, twin engine, single seat, all weather, strike fighter (Strike Eagle)
F-16:	US built multi-role fighter (Falcon)
F-117A:	USAF stealth fighter bomber (Nighthawk)
F-117X:	Northrop experimental stealth fighter bomber testbed in service with USAF
FAC:	Forward Air Controller
Falcon:	US built multi-role fighter (F-16)
FAO:	Forward Artillery Observer
FBI:	Federal Bureau of Investigation
FEBA:	Forward Edge of the Battle Area
Fencer:	Russian built two seat interdiction and attack aircraft (SU-24)
Flanker:	Russian built single seat, twin engined fighter (SU-27)
FLIR:	Forward Looking Infra-Red
Flogger:	Russian built single seat, single engine fighter

	(MIG-23)
FLOT:	Forward Line Of Troops
Fox One:	Radio call from a pilot announcing his firing an AIM-9M Sidewinder missile
Foxbat:	Russian built high speed interceptor (MIG-25)
Foxhound:	Russian built high speed interceptor (MIG-31)
Foxhound:	Infantryman
FPF:	Final Protective Fire
Frogfoot:	Russian built close air support, ground attack aircraft (SU-25)
FRV:	Final Rendezvous Point
Fulcrum:	Russian built single seat, twin engined fighter (MIG-29)
Fullback:	Russian built advanced two seat fighter bomber (SU-32)
FUP:	Forming Up Point

'G'

Gdsm:	Guardsman
Gimpy:	General Purpose Machine Gun
GPMG:	General Purpose Machine Gun
GPS:	Global Positioning System
Green Beret:	US Army special forces unit
Green Maggot:	Sleeping bag
GRI:	General Research Institute (Chinese espionage service)
Grumble:	Russian built anti-aircraft missile system

'H'

HARM:	High speed anti-radiation missile
Harpoon:	Anti-shipping missile
Harrier:	British designed VTOL Strike fighter
Hawkeye:	US built Carrier borne early warning aircraft (E-2C)
HE:	High Explosive
HESH:	High Explosive Squash Head (shaped charge warhead)
Hind-D:	Heavily armoured helicopter gunship
Hornet:	US built all weather strike fighter (F/A-18)
HUD:	Heads Up Display
HUMINT:	Intelligence gathered by humans

'I'

ICBM:	Inter-Continental Ballistic Missile
IFF:	Identification Friend or Foe
IL-76:	Russian built heavy transport aircraft
Intruder:	USN carrier borne strike aircraft (A-6)
IR:	Information Room (Metropolitan Police)
IR:	Infra-Red
IRST:	Infra-Red Search and Tracking

'J'

Jaguar:	British/French ground attack aircraft
JNAIRT	Joint Nuclear Accident and Incident Response Team
JSTARS:	Joint Surveillance and Target Attack Radar System (air to ground surveillance)

'K'

KC-135:	Aerial Tanker derived from Boeing 707 (Extender)
Kevlar:	Carbon fibre armour
Klick:	Kilometre / a thousand metres

'L'

L/Cpl:	Lance Corporal
L/Sgt:	Lance Sergeant
Lancer:	US built supersonic swing wing early stealth bomber (B1-B)
LAW:	Light Anti-Tank Weapon
LSW:	Light Support Weapon
Lynx:	British, fast, tank hunting helicopter
LZ:	Landing Zone

'M'

M&AWC:	Mountain & Arctic Warfare Cadre (RM Specialists)
MAC:	Military Airlift Command
Mach:	Speed of sound (at sea level = 1,225 KPH / 761.2 MPH)
Maggot:	Sleeping bag
Mainstay:	Russian built AWAC version of the heavy Il-76 transport aircraft (A-50)
MAW:	Medium Anti-Tank Weapon
MBT:	Main Battle Tank
Mess:	Sleeping quarters/Dining area/Bar/social organisation
Met:	Metropolitan Police
MFC:	Mortar Fire Controller
MIG-23:	Russian built single seat, single engine fighter (Flogger)
MIG-25:	Russian built high speed interceptor (Foxbat)
MIG-29:	Russian built single seat, twin engined fighter (Fulcrum)
MIG-31:	Russian built high speed interceptor (Foxhound)
Mirage:	French air superiority fighter
MLRS:	Multi Launch Rocket System
MP:	Member of Parliament
MP:	Military Police
MP5:	Heckler & Koch MP5 9mm SMG and carbine
MRCA:	Multi Role Combat Vehicle
MRR:	Motor Rifle Regiment
MSTAR:	Battlefield radar system

'N'

NAAFI:	Navy Army Air Force Institute (shop and bar facilities for British forces)
NAS:	Naval Air Station
NATO:	North Atlantic Treaty Organisation
NAVSAT:	Navigation Satellite
NBC:	Nuclear Biological Chemical
NBC:	National Broadcasting Company
NCIS:	National Crime Intelligence Service
NCO:	Non Commissioned Officer
Nighthawk:	USAF stealth fighter bomber (F-117A)
NSA:	National Security Agency
NSY:	New Scotland Yard
NVG	Night Vision Goggles

'O'

O Group:	Orders Group (Briefing)
OP:	Observation Post
Oppo:	Buddy
Oulou	In the countryside. In the middle of nowhere.

'P'

PC:	Police Constable
Peewits:	Possession With Intent to Supply (The Misuse of Drugs Act 1971. S 5 (3)
Pickle:	Release bombs
Pl:	Platoon: (3 x Sections)
PLA:	Peoples Liberation Army
PLAAF:	Peoples Liberation Army Air Force
PLAN:	Peoples Liberation Army Navy
Platoon:	3 x Sections (Pl)
PLCE:	Personal Load Carrying Equipment (Webbing)
PM:	Prime Minister
PNG:	Passive Night Goggle
PRC:	Peoples Republic of China
PS:	Police Sergeant
Ptarmigan:	British, secure battlefield communications system
Pte:	Private

'Q'

Q Bloke:	Quartermaster
QM (T):	Quartermaster (Technical) - (WO1 rank)
QRF:	Quick Reaction Force
QRH:	Queens Royal Hussars

'R'

RA:	Royal Artillery
RAC:	Royal Armoured Corps
RAF:	Royal Air Force
Rapier:	British AAA missile system
RE:	Royal Engineers
REME:	Royal Electrical and Mechanical Engineers
Replen:	Replenish
Rfn:	Rifleman
RIO:	Radar Intercept Officer
RM:	Royal Marines
RMP:	Royal Military Police
RN:	Royal Navy
ROC:	Republic Of China (Taiwan)
ROC:	Generic term for the Taiwanese military
ROE:	Rules Of Engagement
RORSAT:	Radar Ocean Reconnaissance Satellite
RQMS:	Regimental Quarter Master Sergeant (WO1 rank)
RSM:	Regimental Sergeant Major (WO1 rank)
RV:	Rendezvous Point
RVP:	Rendezvous Point

'S'

SA:	Surface-to-Air
SA80:	British 5.56mm calibre individual weapon
Sabre:	British tracked reconnaissance vehicle
SACEUR:	Supreme Allied Commander Europe
SAM:	Surface to Air Missile
Samaritan:	British tracked armoured ambulance
Samson:	British tracked armoured recovery vehicle
SAR:	Search-And-Rescue
SAR:	Synthetic Aperture Radar
SARH:	Surface to Air Radar Homing
SAS:	Special Air Service (recruits from British Army)
SASR:	Special Air Service Regiment (recruits from Australian Army)
Saxon:	British, wheeled APC

SBS:	Special Boat Service (recruits from Royal Marines)
Scimitar:	British tracked reconnaissance vehicle
Sea Harrier:	RN V/STOL Fleet defense aircraft
Sentry:	US built AWACS based on Boeing 707 (E-3)
SFO:	Specialist Firearms Officer (Police)
SIS:	Secret Intelligence Service
Sitrep:	Situation report
Six:	Directly behind (Six o'clock position)
SLBM:	Nuclear powered ballistic missile submarine
SLR:	Self-Loading Rifle
SMG:	Sub Machine Gun
SO12:	Special Branch (Metropolitan Police)
SO13:	Anti-Terrorist Squad (Metropolitan Police)
SO14:	Royalty Protection (Metropolitan Police)
SO16:	Diplomatic Protection Group (Metropolitan Police)
SCO19:	Specialist Firearms Unit (Metropolitan Police)
Spartan:	British tracked vehicle for AAA, MFC, Engineer or Recce
SP HVM:	Self-Propelled High Velocity Missile
Spearfish:	British advanced, high speed, wire guided torpedo
Spirit:	US built stealth bomber (B-2)
SRAM:	Short Range Attack Missile
SS:	Surface to Surface
SSBN:	Ballistic Missile Submarine (Boomer)
SSG:	Diesel powered guided missile submarine
SSGN:	Nuclear powered guided missile submarine
SSK:	Diesel powered attack submarine
SSN:	Nuclear powered attack submarine
Starstreak:	British advanced, high speed anti-aircraft missile
Striker:	British tracked AT vehicle
STOL:	Short Take Off and Landing
SU-24:	Russian built two seat interdiction and attack aircraft (Fencer)
SU-25:	Russian built close air support, ground attack aircraft (Frogfoot)
SU-27:	Russian built single seat, twin engined fighter (Flanker)
SU-32:	Russian built advanced two seat fighter bomber (Fullback)
Sultan:	British tracked, armoured command vehicle
SWAT:	Special Weapons and Tactics

'T'

T-64:	Russian designed MBT
T-72:	Russian designed MBT
T-80:	Russian designed MBT
T-90:	Russian designed MBT
TAO:	Tactical Action Officer
TAVR:	Territorial Army Volunteer Reserve
TEL:	Transporter Erector Launcher
Thunderbolt:	US built single seat, close air support, tank killing aircraft (A10 / Warthog)
Tomcat:	USN swing wing, twin engine, two seat, strike fighter (F-14)
Tornado F3:	British/German twin seat, swing wing fighter
Tornado GR:	British/German ground attack aircraft
Tpr:	Trooper

Triple A:	AAA (Anti-Aircraft Artillery)
TU-22:	Russian built supersonic swing wing bomber (Blinder)
TU-22M:	Russian built supersonic swing wing bomber (Backfire)
TU-160:	Russian built supersonic swing wing bomber (Blackjack)

'U'-'V'-'W'-'Z'

UGM:	Un-Guided Missile
USAF:	United States Air Force
USMC:	United States Marine Corps
USN:	United States Navy
USSR:	Union of Soviet Socialist Republics
VTOL:	Vertical Take Off and Landing
Warrior:	British AFV
Warthog:	A-10: US built single seat, close air support, tank killing aircraft
Wild Weasel:	Dedicated, specialized, AAA suppression mission
Willy Pete:	WP: White Phosphorus
WO:	Warrant Officer
WP:	White Phosphorus
ZSU:	Russian designed series of Self –Propelled AAA vehicles

ABOUT THE AUTHOR

Andy Farman was born in Cheshire, England in 1956 into a close family of servicemen and servicewomen who at that time were serving or who had served in the Royal Air Force, Royal Navy and British Army.

As a 'Pad brat' he was brought up on whichever RAF base to which his Father had been posted until he joined the British Army as an Infantry Junior Leader in 1972, at the tender age of 15.

Andy served in the Coldstream Guards on ceremonial duties at the Royal Palaces, flying the flag in Africa and on operational tours in Ulster, and on the UK mainland during Op Trustee.

In 1981, Andy swapped his green suit for a blue one with the Metropolitan Police but continued an active volunteer reserve role in both the Wessex Regiment and 253 Provost Company, Royal Military Police (V).

After twenty four years in front line policing, both in uniform and plain clothes he finally moved to a desk job for six years at an inner city borough, wearing two hats, those of an operation planner, and liaison officer with the television and film industry.

His first literary work to be published was that of a poem about life as a soldier in Ulster, which was sold with all rights to a now defunct writers monthly in Dublin for the princely sum of £ 11 (less the price of the stamp on the envelope that the cheque arrived in.) The 'Armageddon's Song' series began as a mental exercise to pass the mornings whilst engaged on a surveillance operation on a drug dealer who never got out of bed until the mid-afternoon. On retirement he emigrated to the Philippines with his wife Jessica where he took up scuba diving and is a member of the famous IGAT running club.

LT HENRY SHAW USMC

OUT IN DECEMBER 2014

Printed in Great Britain
by Amazon.co.uk, Ltd.,
Marston Gate.